THE FIERY WOMEN OF ANGELS FOUR

THE FIERY WOMEN OF ANGELS FOUR

And The Women Who Dared To Make Their Dreams Come True

A Novel by J.W. Perry

Forward by
Mr. Richard Poad, MBE, MA
Chairman, Maidenhead Heritage Centre

Library and Archives, catalogued in Publications.

ISBN 978-0-9914218-2-4
8 6 4 2 0 9 7 5 3 1

Revised 2020 H/VI, Printed and Bound in the United States
Cover by Judy Bullard

DEDICATION

This story is dedicated to the gritty women of World War II who either suffered on the battlefield or by proxy; the wives, mothers, and sisters who peeked through their draped kitchen windows to see the somber uniforms walking up the walkway to the front door preparing the hand of anxiety to become the fist of grief. The humpback olive drab sedans with the large white star on the side that crept through streets searching for a particular address terrified every woman praying it wasn't their house or apartment. Women and grandmothers fed hungry kids with limited rations of every food, except pickles, and they were rarely on grocer's shelves. Gas for the car and oil for heating or lamps was rationed to less than half the usual need. On the battlefield, in an airplane, driving trucks and jeeps, with a socket wrench under a new tank, or tugging giant barrage balloons to needed airfields, women served and sacrificed.

The women of the British Air Transport Auxiliary and American WASPS of WWII were particularly exceptional, using talents usually granted men, abilities that saved the lives of untold soldiers while setting a precedent for the benefit of future wars. We will not likely see fearlessness and determination of that magnitude ever again.

FOREWORD

James Perry's immensely readable novel of World War II romance has a broad sweep, taking the reader from the war in the Pacific to Great Britain, Germany, France, and even North Africa. The tale of love and betrayal is set against a well-researched historical background of courage, skill, and sacrifice, especially on the part of the women who flew scores of different airplanes for the Air Transport Auxiliary. The women formed a very special sisterhood and *The Fiery Women of Angels Four* is a worthy tribute to them all.

Richard Poad, MBE, MA
Chairman
Maidenhead Heritage Centre
Berkshire, UK

INTRODUCTION

During the summer of 1943, a unique event for allied combat aviation unfolded. A small squadron of hand-picked American and conscript women ATA ferry pilots began intensive training to fly as exclusive escorts, piloting armed *Spitfire* fighters. It was only for the protection of intra-island air taxis of VIP and other sensitive cargoes such as critical medicines and top-secret documents. The stealthy squadron was to be supported exclusively by women, from mechanics to medical staff, armament crew, fuel gangs, and cooks; women all, except for its two highly decorated veteran RAF Flight Instructors.

The sprawling Martlesham Heath Airfield, just ten miles from the North Sea, was just one of England's 600 RAF Airfields. It was an unlikely but perfect home base for this risky experiment. The location was determined in part by the planned transition of RAF Martlesham Heath being turned over to the United States Army's Eighth Air Force. The handful of women pilots and support personnel would usually be billeted in residential housing where the American pilots were also housed. As the last of the RAF personnel vacated the airfield late in the summer, rather than move to the barracks on the airfield, the Americans opted to stay in their cushy British billet homes. This allowed the small squadron of elite women to slip into the unused RAF pilot's married men's quarters on the remote north end of the field, quite unnoticed.

World War II was naughty in many ways, not the least of which was the rostrum for romance, as relationships bloomed as yeast in a warm oven. They were usually oddly formed and often failed, yet most of the unwavering women that emerged from those misguided relationships engineered some of the most daring and gutsy feats of aviation, all driven by a steely range of motives from emotional to cerebral. Secrets were born, lived, and destroyed in a matter of months, leaving behind legacies chronicled for generations. All this was forged by the amalgamation of the volunteer Sisterhood of Angels Four, all dedicated to doing their part in the extermination of the murderous Third Reich.

PREFACE

Maria Fuentes sat uneasy in the British made *Supermarine Spitfire*, racing through the bumpy English air at 4,000 feet. The angels four altitude assigned for the *Anson* escort that early morning in October 1943, was an ill advised altitude, tempting the Luftwaffe's hunter *Messerschmitts* to drop down from the sun and do corporal harm to unsuspecting RAF fighters or small transports. Maria, and her wingman Alex, strained their eyes trying to negotiate the sun's glare fearing for trouble from the east. It was no use, as the bright rays bleached their eyesight creating a white sheet of nothingness. Aside from the immediate dangers in the air, Maria allowed her mind to massage her pestering conscience aroused from a prickly spat with her partner the day before. The whole thing was a mess. She felt guilty having been seduced in the first place, and more so after breaking it off. She was usually focused and completely in command of her feelings. Having made the dangerous sea voyage to Liverpool and negotiating blusterous male instructors, here she was, the most talented *Spitfire* pilot in the air, man or woman. Today she was unsettled. She squirmed in her seat, twisting in her body-hugging harness while tormented by her mangled biorhythms.

Normally, Maria was comfortably at home behind the robust Merlin engine of the *Spitfire*. She embraced the smells, sounds, and G-forces of the fighter. This morning she was abnormally anxious. For the first time she was aware of the cold hard steel of her pilot's seat while feeling an unusually tight harness and flying helmet. She struggled to create space and find a direction to look that would avoid the rays of the intense early morning sun. The brightness pierced through the cockpit manufacturing beads of sweat above Maria's lip. She wanted this hop to be over and be safely back in her flat at the airfield. She had reason to be restless as she still worried about the safety of her brother who had tangled with the Japanese in the Pacific near Midway. Then there was that magnet drawing her into the company of the RAF Flying Officer who caused the nasty conflict with her ex. Today was just different.

The escort for the *Anson* was uneventful, but then to climb up another two thousand feet to return to Heath made no sense. After another ten minutes, still at 6,000 feet, Maria's sight off her right wing shook her to the core. When she came to her senses, she pushed the R/T radio switch to call her wingman. Then all hell broke loose.

. . . . . .

Luftwaffe ace, Otto Kelter, retracted his landing gear on the *Messerschmitt 109* leaving the small airfield in Norway off his left shoulder. It felt so comfortable to be back in German air after his extended medical convalescence. His old squadron commander in Africa, Werner Schröer, now commander of Luftwaffe II Squadron 27 back in Wiesbaden-Erbenheim, was true to his promise after Otto's dust-up in Sicily. With 29 victories, Kelter was on his way for one last easy mission set up by local German intelligence inside the Air Transport group in Maidenhead. After anticipating receipt of Germany's Knight's Iron Cross Medal, today's mission would give him his needed 30 aerial victories. Then he could return to his old job of training new fighter pilots desperately needed by Göering's Luftwaffe.

With the sun warming his back, the crisp morning air gave way for the menacing *ME-109* as it climbed to 8,000 feet. The German felt nostalgic, reminiscing back to his Bavarian glider flight experiences and his naïve meeting with Luftwaffe leaders to beg his way into flight school. He wondered about his priest at the Church where he grew up, himself a veteran of WW I. He missed his younger brother working at Willie Messerschmitt's factory in Augsburg, a juicy target of the RAF with its bombing of Germany's manufacturing capabilities now a high priority. He thought of his father and was troubled for his safety because of his unclear politics, making him physically at risk to the Gestapo who was intensifying its reach more and more deeply into civilians not fanatically behind Hitler. It didn't matter that his son was an Ace with the Luftwaffe.

The German fighter pilot was also battle drained. He cut his combat fangs in the Spanish Civil war, then plastered Russian bombers on the ground and air in Operation Barbarossa early in the war. Then Kelter suffered that blast furnace in North Africa that nearly killed him, in operations supporting Field General Rommel. He was just tired. He knew the Americans were near completion of a fighter that would have long-range escort capabilities that could ultimately swing the air war heavily to the Allies. The German turkey shoot of American and British bombers was all but over. He had done his part. Now he just needed to complete this mission, collect his Knight's Cross, then fade into the history books of Germany's best combat pilots.

Just ahead was his target, the black-tailed *Spitfire* of the two-man flight, totally unaware of his presence. Between the sun at Kelter's back and a handful of hunter assignments into England over the past few weeks, he was not expected. He settled in abreast the right wing of the two, then curled up and over while pressing his cannon switch unleashing cigar sized bullets into the British fighter with evil results. Death was in the air that morning, more numbers to add to the masses already buried, creating more business for the weary burial details and weary notification specialists.

CHAPTER ONE

Time to Disrobe

In 1919, only a year after the end of World War I, Deborah Elizabeth Rosen entered the free but broken world, the daughter of proud, Harold and Phoebe Rosen, and a particularly proud two-year-old brother, Edward. Her childhood was in and around Lancaster, 80 miles west of Philadelphia.

Lancaster was dubbed the All-American City that featured rich farmland and thriving businesses with Anchor Hocking and Hamilton Watch Company. The 'Rose City' prized Washington Boro tomatoes with rich soil and ideal sun, thrived in nearby farms.

She grew up in lockstep with Edward, as their father enjoyed success as the area's commercial real estate broker, while her mom stayed busy as a popular piano teacher. They made innocent fun of the few thousand bearded and long dressed Amish, who settled into that area in the early 18th century. Their horse and buggies clopping along their dirt roads, secret ways, and rumors of incest, made them easy targets of ridicule from racist adults and bullying kids. Phoebe was hopeful Maria's education would be more than just "intellectual freedom and critical learning" offered at Lancaster's Franklin & Marshall College. However, it suited Deborah just fine as the cost was affordable and it would serve as a 'good start.'

As youngsters, Deborah and Ed grew very close, simultaneously seduced by the sounds and smells of the barnstorming airplanes of the 1930's, mostly near the brand spanking new Lancaster Airport. The new aerodrome attracted bi-planes with swollen tires that routinely kissed the alfalfa and sorghum in nearby fields as they took eager riders into the world of the aeroplane by the pioneers of Barnstorming. On a day that would change their lives and lives of many they would touch, they watched with awe as the pilot gently bounced to a stop just yards from where the eager Rosen youngsters were watching with wide eyed awe. An elderly passenger gingerly eased to the ground with a grin as wide as the grain, corn, and soybean fields. He had just enjoyed rubbernecking from half a mile over the hills of Eastern Pennsylvania.

As the curious youngsters neared the grasshopper-smeared airplane, the line of probable passengers seemed to meander and stretch forever, at least from their small perspectives. The pilot would load a passenger and fly off, weaving and yawing around and into the friendly puffy cumulous clouds. Darting in and out simulating a fighter pilot playing hide and seek with the enemy, the airplane would sometimes roar just a few feet off the ground, the ecstatic passenger waving with a painted smile hinting fright on the inside.

When the slippery bi-winged wonder taxied to a halt, the pilot heaved around and swung out of the airplane in one smooth motion. He eyed the sun kissing the horizon and made the disappointing announcement that there would be no more flights that day. Interrupting the harmonic moan, he veered on to announce, if at least twenty would commit for the next day, he would spend the night under the wing of the *Jenny*, and fly one day more. He counted eighteen, then repeated his count. Tucked behind the line of adults, two tiny hands peeked out. "What do we have here? Hmm. How old are you guys, I mean kids?" In near unison, "eleven; nine and a half."

"That's a might young, don't you think?" The eighteen hopefuls began to push in, listening to the smiling Ed Pangborn talk to the smallest of the lot. The smiling pilot would love to oblige, but they were so little. "I'll tell you what, if you bring me a signed note from both your parents, I'll let you go. How about it?" He could scarcely hear the affirmative replies as the two spun around and raced as fast as they could in the direction of their dad who just might appreciate the chance for his special children.

As the warm sun settled below the corn fuzz and slipped beneath the horizon, Pangborn tucked himself into the down-filled sleeping bag with his flight pillow and thought back to his youth. With the wing of the airplane his roof, he dozed off from the quiet shuffle and sniffing of neighboring cows to dreams of his own eagerness to fly. He thought quietly to himself, '*I really hope those kids can come.*'

The next morning, the eighteen, with another half dozen new hopefuls, greeted the sunrise with a thermos of coffee and other breakfast goodies for the grateful Pangborn. One husband and wife had presented a basket of freshly baked biscuits and homemade marmalade. He ate more than his fill, then excused himself to suit up for the short walk to a neighborly barn for his morning privy and spit bath.

When he returned, his eager customers stood in a meandering but orderly line. The brother and sister were nowhere to be seen. As Pangborn began adjusting his thin leather gloves, he could see in the distance a tall man with a kid in each hand. They were half walking and half running, a gait slower than if each kid had influence on the vote of pace.

"Well, well, who do we have here?" The

stranger held out his hand and introduced himself. Before he got out only the first syllable of his name, Pangborn, said, "I think I know you?" The father looked curiously at the pilot, searching his own memory. "I'll be a son-of-a-gun! Is that you Lieutenant Pangborn? You were my instructor in Houston, at flight school!" Then they embraced as brothers, as they were in a sense.

"My Heavens, we have a lot of catching up to do, but for now, do I have your permission to take these splendid looking young aviators with me for a spin." "Indeed you do." He turned to the small, bewildered enthusiasts and asked if was okay for them to go first, to which they kindly agreed. "Okay up you both go. I have only one canvas flight cap, so who gets it?" They both raised their hands, just as their dad pulled one from his belt. "Here's one Lieutenant. An old relic I dug up from years ago." Debbie already had Pangborn's cap snuggled over her fluffy locks, so the father flipped his leather cap to his son. "Off you go now, and you kids be careful."

At first, the two excited kids were squeezed together like the meat of a pecan. Within minutes Pangborn could see them waving and laughing. They were filled with a level of joy only a handful could appreciate. The 25 minutes flew by too quickly for the energized brother and sister, as it did for most of the other vicarious aviation enthusiasts. When the day grew late and the crowd reduced to curious bystanders, Clyde Pangborn walked slowly to the three. "Harold Rosen, how the devil have you been? S'cuse my French, kids," looking down at the two bobbing like carnival apples. The boy extended his hand, "my name is Edward, but you can call me Ed, and this is my little sister Deborah. We call her

Debbie." With a smile wide as the Mississippi River curving through New Orleans, he managed, "so you are, and I am pleased to meet you. I like your name, Ed, which happens to be my middle name. Can I visit with your dad a few minutes?" While the two men stood close and were struggling for words, Harold offered the only sensible thing. "Why don't you come with us to supper?" With the miniature fliers jumping up and down with approval, Pangborn accepted; actually looking forward to learning about the aviation experience of his best student.

With Phoebe's roast beef stew, cornbread and stewed tomatoes, washed down with local dairy fresh sweet milk, she and the glowing new aviators cleared the table while the two men began to remember the past. "Call me Clyde. By the way, what did the Air Service do with you after you left me in Houston?" "Well, Clyde, thankfully I didn't last very long. I was sent to England in April of '18 to fly for the RAF, then transferred to Beauvais to join 79 Squadron. I flew 42 missions before being shot down near Sailly sur la Lys just south of Dunkirk in August. I flew the *Sopwith Dolphin* with four confirmed kills. I had four others, all balloons, but couldn't confirm without a witness. On what was to be my last hop, I was flying wingman for Ed Taylor, a friend of mine from Rhode Island, who had just shot down his fifth, a balloon. That made him an ace. I was the witness for him, then I shot down my fifth, a *Fokker D VII*. Unfortunately, Ed, my only witness, was shot down and mortally wounded only a few minutes later. The same antiaircraft ground fire that shot him down was my curse too, some shrapnel having destroyed my engine, and another piece slammed into my left thigh.

"The bone was damaged just enough for the

RAF to send me home. We were losing so many pilots over there; time seemed to be against us all. The French took most of the casualties, as well as the Russians. I consider myself lucky, as I now enjoy a fine business, a great wife, and two kids ... and well, you can tell how proud I am of them both. What about you?"

"Before I talk about me, I have to admit, Harold, I am really impressed with your story and family, but as you suggest, if I had been sent to The Front, odds are that I wouldn't be here enjoying this great meal and agreeable visit with you. But, all that said, I think I made a decent contribution to the war. You are one admirable example, and who knows, your legacy may yet unfold with either or both of your children. I sense a sparkle in those two; sparks that could easily develop into first class firecrackers.

"Anyway, during my instructing days and especially later when barnstorming really took off, I found a way to get comfortable flying upside down and teaching the students the same techniques. I heard for a fact that several students later used that maneuver to survive dogfights or guide crippled birds safely back to the base. Maybe indirectly, at least, I was responsible for a few damaged or better, a few downed German *Fokkers*." "I would bet on it, Clyde!"

As the two were absorbed in their world of aviation, with hand gestures waving like drifting birds, little Edward and Deborah wouldn't fathom that special day with Pangborn sealing their lot as future aviators. Whatever anxieties the Rosen couple had for the safety of their two precious children, they understood the drive and responsibility to answer their call to soar, whether in peacetime or wartime. The two young Rosens were smarter, more able, confident, and resourceful than any of the other kids their age. They had a gritty sense of place, permitting them to answer any call to arms, which they would. Deborah's father's successes gave her and her brother the privilege of flying lessons, first at ground school where they learned navigation, weather, and the communication disciplines required by the FAA. Ed was first to solo in the workhorse of civilian flying, the reliable *Piper Cub*.

Deborah watched from a nearby hangar at the airport, as 19-year-old Edward and the instructor took off for several practice touch-and-go landings on the northwest and southeast runway. At the end of the second landing, the airplane taxied back to the warm-up area of the runway. She wondered, '*What is going on? Why are they just sitting there? Is Ed in trouble?*' Debbie just couldn't contain herself. Her heart was pounding as if she were in the airplane. Abruptly, the upper and lower doors on the copilot side opened as the portly instructor dropped to the ground. He turned and gave a short salute and wide smile to Edward then walked a few feet away.

The engine of the *Piper* revved additional RPM, as the airplane held short of the runway, causing the instructor to hold on to his hat lest it imitate a tumbleweed and scramble away. She could imagine Ed checking his oil pressure and temperature, his radio settings and preparation to call the tower. She could almost recite what his words would be. After clearing his throat, "Lancaster Tower, *Piper* Two Six Tango ready for takeoff, runway three one." In a few seconds the *Piper* wobbled to the end of the runway as Edward increased the throttle to it's most forward position to move the airplane down the runway. As the airplane gained speed, it fishtailed slightly, then began to rise and create a streamlined figure. As Deborah's heart regained own footing, the little *Piper Cub* lifted smoothly off the ground. Just as expected, the airplane slowly gained altitude, and two miles away and 1,000 feet above the earth, the airplane leveled off and began its slow turn back to the airport. Deborah could hardly breathe. She would be doing the same maneuver in only a few weeks and didn't realize whether her feelings were the thrill of seeing her brother in the air, or of being scared of her own solo experience yet to come.

Ed slowly turned downwind and started a descending turn perpendicular to the imaginary extension of the runway. He eased the throttle back as he made his final turn to the runway. "*Piper* Two Six Tango, cleared to land." Ed steadied the nose of the airplane down the middle of the runway. He concentrated on his airspeed so as not to stall, a habit pounded into him as if a tent stake. The airspeed indicator was pegged at 45 MPH, safely above the 36 MPH stall speed. As he neared the ground, Edward eased the throttle back and let the airplane settle to the runway. He had done it, while his 17-year-old sister was jumping like a jack-in-the-box in the nearby hangar. After two more successful but bouncy landings, Ed was greeted by his grinning instructor, abruptly cutting Ed's necktie in half, the ritual of one's first solo. Then Ed grabbed Deborah and hugged her into the air and whispered, "You're next!"

A few months later, they traded places, as Edward nervously watched from the same hangar while his sister repeated the solo. He watched her repeat the unique entry-routine for the Piper, putting her left foot on the step, then leaning forward over the front seat. After all that, she put her left foot past the stick, brought the right foot in, and lowered her small body backwards. '*Calm as a cucumber*, he thought. *She's a natural*', and that frightened him a bit.

After the short flawless flight and landing, she half tumbled and jumped to the ground and rushed headlong to Edward. "I did it, Eddie, I did it!" "Of course you did, Sis, and better than me." She didn't own a necktie to cut, so she brought one of her dad's, to be just like her brother. They were brother and sister pilots, destined to make a difference in a war that loomed ever so real as the 1930's came to an end.

That decade had shaped their lives so profoundly that it would drive them into the 1940's on the wings of others before them. The romance of flying during those formative years had really bitten young women. By the hundreds, from runways carved from the evergreens in Maine to dirt fields in Texas and hilly Appalachia, teenage girls became lured into the achievements of high fliers Amelia Earhart, Jackie Cochran and Nancy Love. The list and influence was international with fliers such as France's Hélène Boucher, Englishwoman Amy Johnson, Aussie Jean Batten, and English born and South Africa's adopted daughter, Beryl Markham.

In 1938, at the beginning of Deborah's junior year at Franklin & Marshall, she learned that FDR had approved a program that would train civilian pilots. Soon, the grist of the rumor mill began to float, chiefly at the popular and active Mainline Airport in nearby Paoli. The rumors became a reality when the Civilian Pilot Training Program started for real in April, offering a 72-hour ground school course followed by 35 to 50 hours of flight instruction. This was just perfect, as Paoli was only a few miles east along U.S. Highway 30 from Lancaster. Deborah and her family had remembered vividly the publicity the airfield had gotten during the summer of 1934 when renowned black pilot, Charles Anderson, had given a joy ride to a young black brother and sister, Matthew and Viola Corbin. As a teen, Deborah logically thought that if blacks can fly, women surely could.

In December, Deborah almost knocked her father out of his favorite chair exclaiming, "Dad, President Roosevelt has announced that he is approving a proposal to train 20,000 new pilots, through civilian airfields by civilians, with a few of the graduates to be accepted into the Army Air Force. The advanced pilot training school is an answer to my prayers! It is starting at Villanova University and West Chester State and should find its way here to Paoli. I am sure of it. Our Government is paying for nearly all of the fees for the training. Perfect for us, and great for the airport. They will be flying the *Piper J-3* made right here near Lock Haven."

He just smiled and nodded, then resumed reading his newspaper. He knew his son and daughter would not be denied these new programs, having studied the details beforehand. Better to help than to hinder, as he would want the same opportunity if it were he at that age. Still ....

"Edward, could Phoebe and I have a minute with your sister? We won't be long." Ed was agreeable, needing to study new Air Charts he had just received. "What's up Dad? Where's Ed? We were supposed to be at the airport in just a little while." "Deborah, your mom and I have discussed your desire to apply for the new pilot's training program. We have some concerns." "Oh, why? You do know I'm a safe pilot and would do great." Phoebe spoke just above a whisper. "Honey, we are aware of all that. There is a strong possibility that this country will be at war in the near future." "Why us? From what I hear there might be trouble in Europe, but the people over here are tired of war. Roosevelt even mentioned it only a few months age. Eleanor, too." Harold spoke softly to maintain the somber subject matter.

"Baby, I have few government contracts that are leasing large tracts of land just north of us. They are maintaining collection warehouses for airplane parts and other wartime supplies. Our government is in the process of making formal agreements with England, France and other European countries to authorize these shipments. In return, if we were pulled into war those countries would lease us land for our armed forces. This process might take another year or so to be ratified. Deborah, we would not be doing all this maneuvering if we were not expecting war." Phoebe piled on. "Sweetheart, your brother will likely be a part of the war, and your father would be too if younger. Thing is, you are our precious daughter who has a lifetime of flying to enjoy. There is love, babies, and no telling what other pleasure awaits you. We can't bear the thought of losing either of you, but losing you both would crush us to death. See the mother's view."

Deborah, with glistening eyes, asked to give it some thought. She was trying to think it through. '*This just isn't fair*'" she thought. *'it's just pilot training, not enlisting in the Army. I have to make them understand.'*

Later that same day, the 19-year-old daughter spoke to her mom and dad. "I thought this through and will make you a deal. Let me do just this training. It is free and there is no obligation for governmental service. If there is ever a war, I will not get involved without your permission." Now it was Deborah's parents who asked for time to discuss the proposal.

"What do you think Honey? She does have a point." "Truthfully, I will have to agree with her. We recognize how talented she is with an airplane and we know her character. She is honest to a fault and is clearer headed than of any I know her age. She is devout in her faith and the most popular student at Yeshiva. She observes Shabbat even more faithfully than the two of us. Her heart is so genuine; we now have to trust her. Also, she might not even be accepted." They both agreed. Now it was their eyes moistening as the anxious parents told Deborah they would accept their daughter's proposal.

Of the two, Harold was more enthusiastic. In late 1940, through his influence as a WWI veteran, the Mainline Airfield was able to confiscate a new *Waco* bi-plane, with a powerful 220 HP Continental radial engine, built in nearby Troy, Ohio, for the use of trainees and instructors. Women were not normally accepted at these schools because the government expected the graduates to be available for military service since the schooling was basically free.

Once more, Mr. Rosen prevailed with his help in the acquisition of the newer more powerful *Waco* trainer, making it easier for Deborah to quietly enroll into the program. The next year, Deborah was in the air every day possible, mostly weekends, the only time she could take time from her job at the college.

When the 21-year-old wasn't grading papers at Villanova or honing her skills with a newfound passion, French and Spanish, she was piling up flight hours in the *Waco*. She found time to scour the University Library for news articles of RAF exploits in England, especially about the Battle of Britain. She devoured story after story of determination and heroics of the small nation's pilots in repelling the Nazi air invasion from July 1940 until the end of October, finally getting the upper hand against the arrogant Luftwaffe. How the British civilians endured all that day and night reprisal bombing of London was just beyond her imagination.

Just two months later, she was thrilled to learn the famous British Aviator Pauline Gower had selected eight elite women to fly for the ATA along side the men, ferrying military airplanes from the factories to the many RAF squadrons scattered all over Great Britain. The declaration of war also became the declaration of women actively flying warplanes in support of the brave RAF and allied pilots to come.

As the smoke was clearing from the cowardly attack on American soil at Pearl Harbor by the Japanese in December of 1941, Deborah became restless to get in on this daring opportunity for women pilots. Ed was already in Grand Prairie, Texas, in his third month of training to become a pilot for the Marine Corps. She had heard about the famous Jackie Cochran's invitations to skilled women pilots for service in England. *'I've got enough hours, what about me?'*

Deborah marched back to the negotiation table with her parents. "It is just ferrying airplanes from the factories to the maintenance units or squadrons. Mostly it is just flying the mail or supplies around. The leader of the women pilots is a famous woman herself whose father is a Member of Parliament. It is first class all the way and pays handsomely too! It is safe and does not involve combat. What do you say?" Harold and Phoebe couldn't say no this time. Their

Debbie was now a young woman with talents beyond her years; a very special soul worth trusting.

When their phone rang in late January, it would be the late Christmas present she wanted, her destiny was gaining focus. She had been invited to travel to New York, and if accepted, on to Montreal's Dorval Airfield to tryout and hopefully train for the celebrated Jackie Cochran, America's distinguished woman aviation pioneer. Deborah would gather with 75 other assembled hopefuls to meet Cochran in England to join the British Air Transport Auxiliary to ferry combat airplanes. A team led by American General Robert Olds, the new commander of the Ferry Command, had singled out Deborah as one of the 75 candidates that had the required 300 pilot hours needed, narrowing the field of fliers considerably. Her nightmares that would lurk in the shadows disguised as dreams would soon be coming true.

In early February, Deborah packed her bags for the 163-mile train ride to New York City. She got in late and stayed the night at the Savoy Hotel, then was directed to Mrs. Cochran's cosmetics business office on Fifth Avenue for the interview. After Cochran was satisfied that Deborah easily had the qualification for screening in Montreal, she was invited with three other candidates to a cocktail party at her River House Flat. Cochran's aviation awards and celebrity collections were encased along an entire wall that included her favorite bobble, a jeweled cigarette case with the stop-and-go red rubies and green emeralds. The trophies seemed endless. The party was a blur, with the tinkling of champagne glasses and fizz of elixirs and alcoholic potions that she avoided. As tired as she felt, a little alcohol would not be wise.

She hoped she made a positive impression, then made a polite early exit. Jackie was impressed and made a mental note to forward the professional bearing of Miss Rosen to Pauline Gower in the morning. The impression must have been acceptable, as she was asked to fill out a formal application, then told she would be notified in a few weeks for further instructions. Deborah was bummed that she was chosen to make the trip in the late spring or early summer; she found the train ride back to Lancaster a long one. *'Why wait? " Nirvana is expecting me.'*

Her parents, feigning disappointment, were privately jumping up and down inside. They would have her for a few more months. Their daughter was special to them, especially to her father. Deborah had grown up into a beautiful auburn haired young woman. She was accomplished, kind, and attractive from the inside as well as the outside. Her nose was altered by a non-elective rhinoplasty when she was 16 to correct developing respiratory deficiencies. She had naturally Ava Gardner lips with her cupid's brow curves framing perfect teeth. Her scattered freckles on her cheeks and shoulders were the subject of many fireside theories. In particular, about whose side of the family might have sailed into the enchanting Irish seas for the taste of persuasive men or charming 'Mollys' or 'Bettys.' Deborah's smile was her own and genuine, disguising a most extraordinary steadiness in her determination to fly. Her family and friends all agreed that she was their well-rounded daughter with talents yet to be revealed.

After what felt like years instead of months, Deborah finally got her notice on the last day of May. She left a few days early to go back through New York to get her final instructions from Mrs.

Cochran's secretary, Mary Nicholson Webb, who was also selected to go to Montreal. Cochran would have Nicholson bring up the rear guard in the last group of pilots sailing by ship to England.

In Cochran's office on Fifth Avenue, Miss Rosen received paperwork and instructions on how to meet up with Mrs. Cochran in Liverpool, customs details, and entry visa papers, etc. She was given a copy of the confidential telegram (that she never received), describing the British Women's role in the ATA and the reason for the handful of American women joining them, outlining the salary, travel expenses, rank system, uniform requisitions, and general information about Dorval Airfield and accommodations in Montreal. She was also assured that there would be no combat involvement, although there might be a few flying assignments across the English Channel into Europe, depending on how the war progressed.

She was teased with the possibility of flying the British *Hurricane* Fighter and support aircraft similar to the *Miles Master* and *Avro Anson*, the reliable light duty twin-engine utility bomber and air taxi. The same telegram would be sent by post to her parents to help answer the many questions they would certainly have, and instructions regarding mailing addresses in Montreal and England. After one day of reviewing her instructions and other miscellaneous forms, she spent the next day touring the bustling magical borough of Manhattan in New York. As she took in the sights, she was mindful that she first had to satisfy her instructors in Montreal with her flying ability to get a final go-ahead for the risky transatlantic sailing to England.

After returning home on June 1, Deborah, the

aviatrix to be, hugged her tearful parents and promised to write often. Her own warm tears trickled down her young cheeks falling softly on her mother's braided rug. No turning back now, she thought, but it hurt inside to see her parents so grieved. She never really thought of it, but here it was, back to Grand Central Station, to Montreal, and finally through customs and on to join the other women in her group, the fifth of six groups. They would be screened over the next few weeks, to make the handful from the original 39 that would make the trip to England.

• • • • • •

Deborah found her lodging, the Mt. Royal Hotel in Montreal, and unpacked for the stay. She had been told to bring her flying helmet and goggles to the Dorval airfield just 12 miles from the hotel. Her challenge was to impress the instructors during her six hours of flying in the powerful *Harvard* trainer.

With little fanfare, the eager young woman from Lancaster and the other six were given a flight physical and at long last taken to their flying instructors. They were introduced to the *Harvard*, which sported sophisticated instrumentation and greater engine power than the airplanes than most flew. The summer meant they would they miss the foggy Montreal weather that mimicked English weather, the earlier groups had to negotiate. They would meet the English maritime weather in due time.

The first time Deborah crawled into the low winged advanced trainer, she greeted the 600-HP two-ton beast with a '*how do you do*'? The tandem seat airplane was noisy and leaked its share of oil, but did the trick. It was described as a cross between an over built 5,000-pound tail dragger with a temper like an irritated Brahma Bull with enflamed privates. Deborah, fighting a cold for the first week, sniffled her way through a thorough familiarization of the airplane from the nose of the propeller spinner to the taillight at the bottom of the rudder. The unfamiliar instrument panel revealed new systems she never imagined. The landing gear, power knob, flaps, pitch lever, carburetor heat control, and stall warning horn was just the start. There were flaps, pitch lever, inertia starter, the manual fuel boost pump called the 'wobble pump', and more. She almost swallowed her Juicy Fruit when she heard Wobble Pump, learning a valuable lesson on why not to chew gum in the cockpit.

After a limited familiarization, she was in the air. Between the loud engine and array of new instruments, she began with a shaky level of confidence. She learned the Touch-and-Go practice landings were now termed 'Circuits-and-Bumps.' With their French accents, her instructors pronounced them Seercuts and Bemps, while proceeding to shred every other aviation phrase she needed to learn. Because of the Canadian's brogue, Deborah's learning curve tended to be steeper than she had imagined, as lucky Nancy Miller drew American instructor Harry Smith.

Deborah was only a few days from finishing her training in the Harvard. The morning flight included controlled spins, this time without the instructor. Weather was overcast, 1,000 feet with ceilings at a modest 4,000 feet. After rumbling down the runway, she retracted the gear and flaps on her way through the clouds to the sunny skies above. Climbing to

6,000 feet, she throttled to maneuvering speed and dropped the nose while shoving the stick into her left leg. She observed two then three rotations back to 4,000 feet, leveling off just above the clouds. '*What a kick,* she thought. *Let's try the other way. Back to 6,000 feet and then an opposite spin.*' Just as she throttled back and before she could move the stick, there was a sinister silence. The noisy 600 horse powered engine was quiet and the propeller motionless. 'O*kay, let's not panic.*' Deborah tried restarting the engine, now motionless and unresponsive. '*Darn!*' Calculating her estimated distance and bearing from the airfield, she radioed Dorval her location to be 6,000 feet and 10 miles northeast of the field. Coaxing her 5,000-pound glider into a gentle turn, she eased the nose to the southwest and tried the restart procedures again.

After setting her transponder to the emergency frequency 7700, she waited to hear from Dorval. "*Harvard* Three One Six, fly heading two four zero degrees and descend to 900 feet just below the cloud cover. We show you nine point five miles. Tower instructions to follow when you are closer to the field."

Deborah gingerly moved the needle on her gyrocompass to 240 degrees. She trimmed the airplane to slow from 145 mph to just above the 100 mph glide speed recommended in the pilot's handbook, then acknowledged Dorval's transmission.

She was in the soup flying slowly and carefully on the assigned heading, when the radio blurted. "*Harvard* One Six, we have you at five miles and 3,100 feet. When you break through, fly runway heading two four zero degrees, cleared to land runway 24. She replied, "Dorval wait one, Three One Six." She knew there was no room for error, remembering that runway 24 had a marsh bog with basketball sized boulders on the front of the threshold. "Dorval, negative on 24. Please vector me to runway 28."

"*Harvard* One Six, we can do that, but you may be short." "Roger Dorval, One Six out." "*Harvard* One Six, make one half standard turn to heading one nine zero for right base to runway 28. You should break out just about two miles east of the airport. Report situation when clear of clouds, over." "Roger, Dorval, *Harvard* One Six, out."

By now Deborah was feeling the sweat from head to toes. Deborah glanced at her near empty fuel gauge. Her stomach relaxed a bit, keenly aware the lighter Harvard's glide speed could be extended a little. She trimmed the nose up slightly, easing to 90 mph. She could still not see anything but grey outside, then a break, with the airport straight ahead to her right. '*This is going to be really close.*'

"Dorval, *Harvard* One Six field in sight at 800 feet. I may be short so have the emergency crew ready, out." At 70 mph now, the stall warning horn began intermittent annoying beeps. With delicate nose adjustments, she teetered on the edge of stalling by milking every foot of extra distance the airplane could give her. As she made the slight right turn to the heading for runway 28, she knew she was going to be short. Pleased of her runway choice giving her hard pack dirt a few yards in front of the runway's threshold. She dropped the landing gear, tightened her harness, and cracked open the canopy to greet the crisp Canadian air. The controllers in the tower held their breath, watching the 4,000-pound aircraft level off from the turn toward the runway, then touch down just short onto the hard pack. The tower breathed a sigh of relief when the unforgiving *Harvard* heaved to stop only inches from the asphalt runway, tamed by a diminutive warrior woman. She rode back to the aerodrome office in the first fire truck exchanging smiles with the two relieved fire rescue-men. All she remembered from them was repeated, "wows!" The young lady just earned a pedigree that could only grow as she tamed the deceitful beast of outward charm.

Deborah's training came to a close after three annoying flights negotiating Dorval's pesky crosswinds. Deborah passed with flying colors, her flying skills punching her travel ticket to Halifax for the trip to England as one of the six Americans to make the voyage. Deborah's pride and confidence swelled as she had learned that Cochran reviewed women's aviation records all over the country, with only 39 selected for screening in Montreal. She was one of the elite 25 who earned the voyage to England.

The personnel documents Dorval officials gave Deborah seemed uncommonly thin, not to mention them misplacing her Flight Logs. Nevertheless, she was given a voucher securing her passage to Liverpool. They assured her that it would all sort out sooner or later, with the remaining missing files and logbook eventually getting to England. She was reassured they would for sure be forwarded. The positive news was that the next day she would receive her packet with travel vouchers and instructions for lodging in Liverpool and Maidenhead check in.

Most women were proud of their achievements at Dorval, but Deborah was in a personal funk, 500 miles from home and family. So far so good, but still.. She was anxious if she could meet the challenges of military airplanes and the danger they promised. Did she pack enough, too much, or all the wrong stuff? Can she make her parents and Edward proud?

The small envelope she had been waiting for came as promised with her instructions and travel voucher, but missing her logbooks. She was directed to the passenger steamer *Winnipeg II,* scheduled to depart on July 11, for the dicey ride to England. The 25-year-old passenger ship was a better draw than what some of the other groups would encounter; a transatlantic voyage on mostly especially old rusty merchant ships.

The massive steam whistle of the 440-foot ship boomed, signaling the foggy beginning of the three-week trip from the first leg to Halifax then on to Liverpool. Three of her group had been sent home for illness or "unsuitability", so it was just her, quiet Nancy Miller, Opal Anderson, tall as a cornstalk, an irascible Chicagoan with a personal trunk of swear words that would shock even the saltiest Yukon lumberjack.

The Captain briefed the women on the dangerous roaming tentacles of the German Submarine U-Boat network. The subs patrolled the shores of Western Europe to the Caribbean, all the way up the coast of the U.S. from the Carolinas to New York and Canada, including the St. Lawrence Gulf where they were headed. The risk was authentic with *U-boat 553* having sunk two freighters earlier that May. The women were thinking that the risk of crossing the Atlantic might be greater than ferrying airplanes. They were right.

Deborah's sea journey finally began for real on the *Winnipeg II*, neatly tucked in the corner of the pier on the St. Lawrence River. Despite the smells of smoke, fuel oil, fish, human body odor, and tiny cabins, her boat chugged along revealing charming villages and stunning landscapes. As the cargo ship wormed its way through the Thousand Island Archipelago, Deborah leaned on the sticky handrails thinking about home and the decision to leave. The myriad of lighthouses and peaceful bays sliding by eased the burdens of her imagination gouged by the briefing of possible German submarine activity.

The *Winnipeg II* stopped at the ports of Sorel, Three Rivers, Baie St. Paul, and St. Eloi, gathering food stuffs, wheat, ammunition, lumber, steel, and a variety of other essentials for the war needs in Europe. As the ship rounded the turn on the east end of the Gaspé Peninsula to make the southerly course change to Halifax, they slowed to make an unscheduled stop at the small village of Percé City, guided by the nearby 290 foot high pierced rock the French called Roche-Percé. Deborah wanted to stretch her legs one last time before getting to Halifax on the journey to Liverpool. As the town center was a short walk from the freighter, she quickly spotted the quaint Café Champêtre with two small outdoor tables for morning sunrise watchers. She ordered a cup of strong coffee and a croissant and let the rays of the morning sun smear her face with vitamin D. Settling in with the coffee, she saw a rumpled newspaper on the unoccupied table nearby. She rearranged the small tabloid to get the front page where it belonged. After getting the somewhat soggy paper organized, she was startled by the coffee smeared headline of the *Halifax Chronicle.*

U-boat sinks two freighters, killing 18.
Survivors picked up at Fame Point
Lighthouse and Gaspé

At approximately 05:50 just before dawn, on Tuesday May 12, a German submarine just south of Anticosti Island torpedoed the British Freighter Nicoya with 88 passengers and crew. Twenty minutes later another torpedo was loosed, which destroyed the ship. The 62 crew, one gunner, and ten passengers were helped ashore at Fame Point Lighthouse later in the day. The presumed dead included one gunner and five crewmen. The ship was reported to have carried general cargo and some aircraft parts from Montreal, according to sources.

Twenty minutes later at about 06:10, another single torpedo from the same U-boat, presumably, sank the Dutch Leto, hitting squarely in the engine room. The 4,700-ton freighter chartered by the British War Ministry was lost eight miles north of Cap de la Madeléine. The cargo reportedly was only grain. Our sources report the First Engineer and ten crewmen were killed, while the forty-one survivors were helped ashore at Gaspé.

Editor's Note: "This newspaper has been deluged by the citizens of our St. Lawrence estuary with complaints of poor support from the Canadian Royal Navy to protect river traffic from Montreal to Halifax. It seems as though the German Wolfpack submarines prowl the waterways at will, with little regard for our

Corvette Class destroyers, knowing they are too small, too slow, and just no match for the U-Boats. With America's entry into the war, the Canadian War Department should have known more and more supplies would be needed in England, creating predictable attractive targets for the Subs. Our sources report the St. Lawrence is guarded by only one Bangor-class minesweeper, two Fairmiles-class motor launches, and one armed yacht. How long do we have to wait until we get the protection our civilian boat masters and crew deserve? Please write to your Senate and House of Commons Representatives and demand their attention to the matter as quickly as possible. How many dead does it take to get some action?" The Editor

Deborah's coffee grew unfriendly as her anxiety smoldered. She knew there was danger, as the little town of Gaspé lay just a few miles from where she sat. Her Californian shipmate Miller had alerted Deborah about the dangers, but the naïve Rosen wasn't too concerned, until *now*. Miller was so right, even though they hadn't even started across the Atlantic. She and Nancy both wondered how Cochran could put her women in so much danger. Why couldn't there be airfields for testing in the states, since leaving from Boston or New York harbors made more sense and were less risky? She just shook her head, tucked the paper under her arm, and paid the bill. She nodded toward the apron bound gent sweeping the sidewalk, and shuffled back to the *Winnipeg II*.

As they got underway and resumed sailing, the steamer finished easing around the northern New Brunswick peninsula, then powered southeast toward the northern tip of Nova Scotia in the threatening waters of the vast St. Lawrence Gulf. After seven long days filled with more frequent stops than the Seventh Avenue Local from the Bronx to South Brooklyn, the boat neared Halifax Harbor with Fort George as its welcoming landmark.

The three Americans took the opportunity to use their free time with a visit to the Fairview Lawn Cemetery. This was the final resting place of many of the RMS *Titanic* victims recovered by cable laying ships from the Halifax area. Miller found the grounds keeper and inquired, "Sir, why weren't the bodies returned to their homes." "Cause White Star Line wouldn't pay for it," he then shrugged and walked away. A bit sobered, the women finished their walks at the beautiful Halifax Public Gardens, first opened in 1867. The eclectic gardens still had its Victorian charm of expansive lawns and majestic trees 75 years later.

On July 9' after taking on more cargo and food, the *Winnipeg II* set sail once again, this time as part of a large convoy for the longer leg of the journey across the Atlantic to Liverpool. Nancy, Opal, and Deborah leaned on the ship's railing as the *Winnipeg II* tooted its deep-throated funnel horn, while the women listened to the echo off the hillsides around the lush countryside of Halifax.

Opal looked at Nancy and asked, "I wonder how those giant horns work?" Nancy looked at Deborah, who just shrugged. "Opal, I really don't have a clue, and truthfully, that doesn't concern me. What does interest me, is how many ships are in this convoy, and how long is this bloody trip going to take. Right now I am going to find the ship's bar. Maybe the bartender will know about the horn. Wanna come?" Without a word, the three scuttled below and didn't find that bar, merely a sweat stained crewman who introduced himself as Third Mate Benjamin.

The amused Benjamin wasn't much help on the bar or horn question. Terms like compressed air and steam escaped the women's notice, but 'no bar' they understood. At least he offered insight about the *Winnipeg II* and her mission. While the young women nursed their disappointment of no brew or gin, he explained to the three, "Travelling in convoys lessen the odds of the U-boats spotting us, since a cluster of twenty or more ships looked the same on radar from thirty miles as a single ship. Ships are normally five across and six deep like we are doing now, each traveling from nine to thirteen knots. We have to huff and puff at thirteen, as our top speed is only fourteen knots. When possible, two or maybe three combat ships would be part of our group, but not the case for *this* convoy." The three Americans were glued to his every word. "With calm seas and no mechanical difficulties, we should reach Liverpool in twelve days which will seem like twelve years as long as German subs keep lurking. Has anyone mentioned Liverpool's situation? Their puzzled expressions were the answer. He knew to make it short, skimming over the dates and bombings suffered from August 1940 until May of 1941. He knew they would learn the rest in just a few days.

Opal, satisfied on about the horn question and his summary of Liverpool, tendered her thanks, promptly leading Miller and Rosen to their rooms where she planned to share her prized bottle of

Sherry. There they toasted Benjamin and a safe journey for all.

After what seemed like months at sea, the three finally arrived after 23 and a half days. Liverpool was a shock. "Third Mate Benjamin left out some details, ladies," Miller spat. The dock smelled of fish, spoiled vegetables, and garbage smoke. Even though protected on the eastern coast of the Irish Sea, it unashamedly displayed ugly scars of German bombs.

The three women held hands as they made their way from the pier. "Look, Nancy, at the rubble left by the ammo ship Malakand that exploded last year. It's still a mess." "It is for sure, Deborah, it is more than a mess. It is so frenzied I don't see how they get anything done. I guess wartime isn't a neat and tidy enterprise. Let's get out of here and to the hotel." They wondered when the next attack would come, day or night? Bombers or attack Junkers? Laughter was rare and hard to find, day or night.

At the pier, barrage balloons from 500 to 1500 feet drifted back and forth, tethered to the mooring lines designed to give German fighter/bombers second thoughts of any low attacks. During the taxi ride to town, the solemn women saw countless bomb craters. Several blocks were completely flattened with foundations sticking up like homemade grave markers. Buildings, which had been disemboweled, were just rusty skeletons, inviting rats and other scavengers. Chimneys were still pointing to the sky, but jagged and smokeless. St. Luke's 130 old Anglican Church was just a façade, gutted by a lucky German bomb.

Probably because there were only the three, Jackie Cochran wasn't at the pier to welcome them as she had for the earlier groups. She did, however, leave instructions with an aide and driver regarding the arrangements for overnight stay at the Adelphi Hotel, as well as the next day's transportation to London and the Savoy Hotel where they caught up with Cochran. Deborah had another nagging cold and was more bone-tired than ill. She excused herself early and slept the night soundly, totally unaware of the sirens and night bombings. Miller spent the night hidden under her bed huddled next to Anderson. Neither got much sleep as both looked exhausted at breakfast the next morning.

Still, a bit refreshed and fed, the three women took the train to Maidenhead and RAF's White Waltham Airfield in Berkshire. Upon reporting in, Deborah was told of some confusion on her paperwork. It didn't seem to matter to the admissions people since she was sent on to the physical exam process without her file and log books. She was told she would be directed to Director Gower's office to sort it out. Opal was in the same boat, so Deborah didn't fuss.

Deborah was caught off guard and protested when asked to disrobe by the ATA medical examiner. "Doctor Reginald Barbour's orders," they said. Just as she was about to remove her blouse, she was startled by a commotion in the adjoining room. It sounded like Mrs. Cochran, but she couldn't be sure. Rosen and the others in line were asked to wait for a bit until 'a certain matter' was handled. After about five minutes it got quiet, and the door opened. The nurse told Deborah and the others they didn't have to disrobe after all. The Chief Medical Officer Archibald Barbour had withdrawn the order. Policy had been changed. An investigation, much to Gower's embarrassment for her friend, revealed the adult 8mm movies in Barbour's office wouldn't have been in the mainstream of moral standards. It took a call from Cochran to d'Erlanger to reverse the useless policy, winning the first of several disputes with the Brits.

CHAPTER TWO

Sawdust and Privilege

Tabloid anointed Jacqueline Cochran, 'Queen of the Skies,' exceeded her ambitious dream to 'travel with the wind and stars.' She was president of the Jackie Cochran Admiration Society with a trophy case to support the hubris. She was a close friend with the more publicized Amelia Earhart, but Cochran's swagger reflected a dissimilar flair. The public took to the more publicized lanky Earhart, with her boyish hair, leather jacket, and riding pants. She *looked* like a rough and ready aviator, while a journalist described the nine year younger Cochran in 1938, as the prettiest woman she had seen. She described Cochran's soft brown eyes, shimmering golden hair, and lovely clear skin, the touch of Aphrodite. At the end of her flying career, Cochran held more speed, altitude, and racing records than anyone, male or female. At Earhart's funeral in 1937, it was Cochran who struggled through Earhart's eulogy, having listened to Earhart share misgivings about her globe circling flight with her just weeks before at Cochran's Indio desert home in California.

She was tumbled into a sparkling jewel by the coarse grit of poverty and hard living. Born in 1906 to poor mill workers in northwest Florida, Jackie, née Bessie Lee Pittman, had to fight from her corner at a very early age. Her heritage may not have been royalty, but she felt otherwise, as she rose from the sawdust and lint of swampy Florida Panhandle sawmills and child labor hungry Georgia weaving factories. She had only two years of formal schooling, but was intuitively smart. She was a man's man but still feminine, sometimes to the extreme, and one occasion she was seen to check her makeup before climbing from her burning airplane after crash landing.

The feisty Cochran always pushed to the head of the line beginning at the young age of seven, when she supervised 15 other young girls, then learned how to clean and adjust the complicated weaving looms. She did not seek altercations, but wasn't afraid to hit an older church gent who got a little too friendly.

Cochran was different from birth. Her parents knew so, but couldn't explain it to themselves, much less to their energetic and enigmatic daughter. As a mere teenager, she married Jessie Hydle, a young aircraft mechanic from the nearby naval base at Pensacola. She became Jacqueline Cochran after moving to California a few years later, finding the name in a phone book (some say). Her poverty in the Florida Panhandle was such a searing humiliation, she did everything to distance herself from the misery she suffered. It was also the engine that drove her to success in every enterprise she attempted. Her poverty and lack of education didn't slow her, just the contrary. She transformed from being a barefoot girl who stole chickens to help feed her family to a decorated pilot who dined with royalty and business potentates.

Young Cochran tried nursing for three years, but it didn't suit her. Her first real job was sweeping the floor and being a 'shampoo girl' in a beauty parlor. The word 'can't' was not in her vocabulary, as she eventually owned a multi-million dollar cosmetics business. She made better than average money and rose well above her early circumstances. She loved the sight of an airplane and believed that one day she would fly.

She read, she listened, she asked questions, and never took 'no' for an answer. She believed in hard work, persistence and God, not necessarily in that order. She made her first flight in 1932, having convinced the instructor to let her take the written test verbally, her only recourse as she still suffered from lack of a formal education. She could not read.

The next year, Jackie moved to the San Diego area where she mastered the art of flying. In 1936, 30-year-old Cochran married 44-year-old financier Floyd Odlum, her 'special friend' since 1932. He gave her the financial support needed to pursue her passion in the air and on the ground. From their first meeting in Miami, Floyd was her advocate and cheerleader, urging her further into the world of aviation. He saw in her a special light and knew she was among those who collected every drop of spray from the wave of optimism.

In 1935, with best friend and race competitor Amelia Earhart, she entered her first prestigious transcontinental Bendix Air Race. She set three major flying records in 1937 and was the first woman to win the Bendix Race the following year, presented by Eleanor Roosevelt. She and the First Lady were a 'Mutual Admiration Society', both stumping for women's rights to work and to succeed shoulder-to-shoulder regardless of race, sex, or social status.

Cochran wasn't timid in using her early friendship with the First Lady, and now it was imperative to get her support and counsel. As much as Eleanor Roosevelt had a special adoration for Amelia Earhart, she had a special respect for Cochran, the brasher of the two fliers. They became fast friends, often celebrating Jackie's air race victories.

Jackie always felt welcome to reach out to the

First Lady, doing so just days after Germany invaded Poland. She felt a need to solicit Mrs. Roosevelt's support for woman aviators, should the U.S. get sucked into war with Germany. She forecast a bottleneck of aviation preparedness with a lack of trained pilots, which could be mitigated by qualified women pilots. A mere three weeks later E. R. replied, agreeing in principal adding that the best channel for Jackie's idea would be through General Hap Arnold, the new Chief of the Army Air Corps. Eleanor joined others urging Jackie's patience and encouragement for her to assemble details regarding training and leadership of such an organization.

Jackie was a stranger to patience. She didn't take long to make contact with General Arnold. She knew she couldn't just pop in like before the war, as General Arnold was in one place only briefly; rarely in one place for a long time. Nonetheless, she intercepted him by phone two weeks later.

"Good morning, General, thanks for taking my call." "Skip the formalities Jackie, it is really nice to hear from you. I was expecting your call. Wouldn't have anything to do with women flying in the bloody war, now would it? I already have Nancy Love bugging me with the same notion." If Cochran's phone had been made of plastic, she would have squeezed it into pieces. She couldn't stand Love niggling around the military, fully aware that she was much more qualified to do the job, and Nancy Love Harkness knew it.

"General, I'm aware that some days earlier, Mrs. Love approached several in the government about a vague idea that might include women pilots, but I will get to the point about my proposal. It is comprehensive, but before laying it out, I need a few days to round up FAA pilot records and find out just how many women we are thinking about. We will need women with inclusive logbooks and fresh time in sophisticated airplanes." "Sounds like a plan, Jackie. I like your thinking. There is no fire, so take your time. Give me a jingle when you finish your research, then we'll talk further. It would be a logical idea to copy Colonel Olds on any paperwork you might send in advance of calling. In fact, send it to him, and copy me. That's even better. Hate to be short, but gotta run. Take care of yourself and thanks for calling. Bye now." Jackie mused, '*What have I got myself into now?*' Like a shot, Jackie' pulled together a findings team. After several weeks of hard labor by her team, the phone rang. "Ms. Cochran, Aynie Truesdale here." "What have you got for me?" "Ma'am, with Civilian Aviation, they found 2,733 licensed women with roughly 250 of them having between 150 and 300 logged solo hours." "Great job Aynie, and thanks!"

Jackie fired letters to all of those 250 women, seeking their interest, then sent her findings to Colonel Robert Olds, the creator and head of the Army Air Corps Ferry Command.

Olds knew women would come in handy to ferry airplanes from the factories to training airbases across the country, as well as both coastal ports for shipment to operational squadrons in Europe and Asia. Hap Arnold also knew Cochran could put it together but had to be patient as the politics of war had to roll out its own agendas. Late that year, Cochran posted her letter to Olds, detailing the number of qualified women available, along with a plan to build a coalition around the ferrying men, as well as an outline of the organization the women would require. She wasn't hopeful for a quick turnaround, thinking it would be some time before she would get a reply.

It would be a while before Jackie could do much more, only wait, not her strong suit. In the meantime, in late 1939 through all of 1940, as England struggled in the Battle of Britain, Cochran continued to fly. She broke both the national 100-kilometer and international 2,000-kilometer speed records. She continued to outclass herself by establishing a woman's national altitude record and broke the international open-class speed record for men and women.

True to Cochran's prophecy of the need for women pilots for the U.S. in her letter to Mrs. Roosevelt, it was revealing itself across the pond. Britain was really beginning to feel the manpower strain on their RAF pilot squadrons, as the war was now a reality. Watching the thinly veiled buildup of Hitler's armed forces since 1935, it was an undeniable war in the making. The government and military began to prepare, while most Europeans disregarded the inevitable until Poland was attacked on September 1, 1939. The war of all wars was on.

• • • • • •

Earlier that July of 1939, the Undersecretary of State for Air, Harold Balfour, was buzzed by his secretary to inform her 41-year-old boss that his 10:00 appointment with the Director of the BOAC was in the foyer. "Come; have a seat, Director." "Please, it's just Gerard." "Then it must be Harold." They shook hands enthusiastically, as they both had deep respect for the other. Both men with entirely different backgrounds were coming together to forge plans to protect their beloved England.

Balfour was a product of the military, having served with distinction in World War One. He earned two Military Cross awards for shooting down nine enemy aircraft making him an Ace. After the war he was elected to Parliament serving in the Air Ministry. He was plain in appearance with a receding hairline, giving him some distinction if not years.

While Harold Balfour oozed military, Gerard D'Erlanger radiated finance and management. With a movie star physique and face, D'Erlanger was himself an accomplished pilot and now a director of British Airways at the young age of 33.

"Gerard, Sir Francis Shelmerdine and I have both read with interest your opinion of us heading into war and the subsequent need to retool our thinking for civilian aviation. So we thought it might be worthwhile to hear you out." "Thank you Harold. You are right on both counts. We *are* headed for war and there *will* be a need to rearrange our aviation assets, both equipment and people. It is no secret that Hitler and Göering have thumbed their noses at the mandates of the Versailles Treaty, especially article 198 banning Germany from having an air force.

"We both know about their airline pilot schools that are brazenly training military pilots, even opening a public fighter airfield in Herzogenaurach. That airfield was to be an organizational and equipment facility, but what they are doing is first phase training for fighter pilots. If the Nazi's are defying the treaty with this type of activity, you know where we will be in a short while, maybe even months. We don't have the luxury to wait until they attack one of our Allied neighbors for us to develop a plan."

"It seems as though you have given our

situation a great deal of thought. Go on." D'Erlanger was prepared. "Harold, when the war does begin, we know our overseas routes for not only BOAC but all airlines will be severely restricted. Naturally we will have to impound all civilian airplanes, so airline pilots, other commercial pilots, and a great many private pilots scattered from Brighton to Glasgow, would have no airplanes to fly and nowhere to fly them even if they had them. These talented and experienced aviators will be essential in flying non-combat missions, most of them in their middle 30s like me, too old for the RAF." "Calling yourself talented, are you?" They both laughed at Balfour's shy humor. "I don't know how large a pool we can assemble, but there are many who are slightly too tall or short and some with hearing or vision impairments who would love to fly for our country and make a contribution to the war.

"These civilian pilots under the scrutiny of the RAF can provide air transportation to move dispatches, supplies, the wounded, and occasional VIPs. There will be a need to move airplanes from the factories to the maintenance units and often to the squadrons scattered from Brighton to Glasgow. All they have to do is get airplanes into the air and land safely, usually flights of less than an hour."

"Gerard, I do think you make logical arguments and a sensible solution to problems that war will create. I will make a recommendation to Shelly that you outline a detailed plan and make yourself its Director and Commodore. It might be wise to get specific with the number of pilots with Class A licenses that have more than just a few logged hours beyond their basic training. Details of structure, salaries, training, et cetera, would also be helpful. When war breaks out, at least we we'll have a plan."

In mid-August, D'Erlanger rang Balfour's office. "Good Morning, Gerard. How are you getting on with your new assignment?" "Rather agreeable, Harold, better if it wasn't for our dithering weather. After all that rain for the first three weeks, we are now suffering in 26 degrees so you can imagine the humidity. I can't wait until September. I wonder about the Scots? Just the opposite I imagine?" "Quite right old chap, quite right."

"I know you are curious, so here goes. My written report will be on your desk within the fortnight. I retrieved the Class A Pilot's report with names of gents with 250 plus hours and am nearing the end of the interview process. We have a modest number to get going, reasonably adequate for now, and have already commenced training. I am comfortable all will be qualified to transport personnel or other material needs. The men who came have been eager, over a hundred early on. I have received doctors, farmers, factory managers, barkeeps, and journalists. They arrived in every costume, size and shape; one eyed, one legged, one armed, legally deaf, fat, skinny, tall and short they came, and are still applying. I see the older and frightfully young, all with varying degrees of education. Most are eccentric to a man and nary a lazy man among them.

"Harold, we are starting them in the *Tiger Moth*, unless they have more than 500 hours. Remember, the planes we're flying have no radios and bare navigation systems with only a compass. The more experienced chaps we will put in the bigger

Harvards. We will pay them 40 pounds per annum and give them the rank of Third Officer.

"This program has been remarkable thus far and clearly rewarding. It would make a splendid cinema. Anyway, we are putting the lot in a dark blue uniform with the light blue shirts and forage caps, like the RAF. We top it off with a navy blue ascot and our new ATA insignia. You can't imagine how puffy they all feel, often being mistaken for the RAF. They are going to be contracted to me at British Airways with oversight by the RAF. It's a messy organizational chart, but while awkward to some, it works."

"Gerard, it sounds like a splendid start. Keep me posted so we can implement the program more extensively if circumstances demand."

The weather did cool off that September, but it was holding hands with the clouds of war when Germany invaded Poland on the very first day, creating those 'demanding circumstances'.

That very day, Balfour was on the phone with D'Erlanger, "It's come, Gerard, wartime's official; full on for sure! Put your people to work and get more aboard straight away. You were right in your comments a few months ago, the RAF is already short of manpower. We can't spare even one pilot for ferry duty. I'll leave it to you to figure the logistics, and don't hesitate to ring me if you need anything. God save the King."

The first months were very tiring for D'Erlanger. Although the ATA men were flying great ferry sorties, the tricky part was getting the scattered pilots gathered from all over England at the end of each day. D'Erlanger devised a plan of collecting most of the pilots with other ATA pilots in dedicated twin-engine *Ansons* for the return trip to their respective ferry pool airfields. Those who weren't recovered had to improvise to find rail, bus, or other means to get back to their bases. He knew they would encounter smoke stale railcars packed with eager soldiers, or have to hitchhike back.

Initially, the ATA leadership struggled to add more qualified pilots and trainable recruits, barely keeping pace with the ever-increasing aircraft production. Eventually their efforts prevailed beyond expectations.

In September of 1939, only a few days after war with Germany was declared and the men of the new ATA had just begun their training, Jackie Cochran's alter ego, Pauline Gower, was eagerly waiting for the chance to get women involved in aviation, just as Cochran had campaigned for a year earlier.

• • • • • •

Mary de Peauly Gower, born in July of 1910, was clearly fashioned from the same matter as Cochran, Earhart, Markham, Raiche, and the African American, Willa Brown. They all powered on beyond the thrills of flying to excel in every aspect of the airplane. They were interesting, inquisitive, intuitive, and untiring. Most were accomplished in other fields, like Brown who was an educator, activist, and businesswoman; Earhart an essayist, editor and author. Raiche was a markswoman, dentist, gynecologist, linguist and artist. As for Cochran, she owned her own successful cosmetics company and ran for Congress, while Beryl Markham found success as adventurer, horse trainer and author.

Gower was always fit, with brownish blond hair, vivid blue eyes, and a mouth that portrayed determination with its signature twist. She enjoyed the life of the privileged with her solicitor father a Member of Parliament and mayor of Turnbrige Wells. She enjoyed the social class of an insider as she would come and go at her leisure with England's decision makers. The versatile Pauline Gower not only owned her own joy riding and taxi flying service, she was an author and poet.

Sir Robert Gower provided the best education available to women for Pauline and her sister, which was an unusual aspiration for females in the 1920s and 30s. In those formative years, Gower learned to play several musical instruments and write, mostly poetry and short stories. Not a sedentary lady, she was the main standout at the Covenant of the Sacred Heart football team as well as a contributing member of the Tunbridge Wells Tennis Six. At sixteen she was given up for dead when an ear abscess became infected. The resilient Gower bounced back from her dangerous surgery, almost as good as new. The physical limitations on her pace and choice of play, however, would linger for years.

Pauline was enrolled in a finishing school in France, only to give that privilege away to pursue her passion for flying, an avocation she felt was the job of the future. She was fiercely determined to make a living at it, with or without her father's support. Her father did not approve of this folly, temporarily withholding his financial support. Pauline scrambled, giving lectures on flying and holding violin recitals to fund her flying. When her father finally conceded to her passion and bought her a used two-seat *Spartan* on her 21st birthday, she had already earned her Class B rating, qualifying her to carry passengers. She was the youngest of only three women in Great Britain to hold that rating. Eventually, Pauline and close friend Dorothy Spicer created 'Air Trips', a business of flying passengers for fun. The two also flew as part of aerial circuses to hone their skills, forgoing popular races due to the expense.

At the outbreak of the war, Pauline had earned her navigator and instrument ratings while active in the National League of Pilots. With those achievements, several thousand hours of flying under her sash, and freewheeling with the leadership of Parliament, it was no surprise and cleverly well-timed for her to show up at an October cocktail party as a guest of her father only days after England's declaration of war and formation of the ATA. It was easy to corner its new commander and old friend, Gerard d'Erlanger. After having no luck on women flying for the ATA with the Director-General of the Civil Aviation, Lt. Col. Sir Francis Shelmerdine, maybe her long time friend would help.

"Congratulations, Commodore. You now have the enviable pleasure of being able to crawl into one of those new *Spits*, or at least a *Hurricane*." D'Erlanger liked Gower. Although she was from political gentry and only five years his junior, she was like a kid sister. He especially liked her exhaustive energy and intuitive ability to lead. Even though he was a might envious of her flying exploits, he could nonetheless converse with her familiarly. "Pauline, what a lovely surprise to see you here! Are you with anyone?"

"Only Father, but I wouldn't be surprised if he

tries to sneak out early. My solicitor father has learned that someone is planning a surprise birthday party for him next month, so he is trying to lie low. You know how he hates birthdays. He is part of his own conspiracy to organize a foxhunt for November 10, that's on a Friday. What he doesn't know is that Mother knows his cloak-and-dagger ruse, and has the party scheduled for that evening. Most of the gang on the hunt is in on the double-cross. It should be fun, and will be the last social until this bloody war is over.

"Not to change the mood, but I have an idea. With the line of thinking you successfully presented to Shelmerdine and Balfour last month for the formation of a ferry service manned by civilians, how about including women? I know how to round up at least a hundred or so, more than capable of flying anything put in front of them, including *Spitfires* or *Ansons*. I know the RAF is thin and you need a boatload more pilots, so what do you think? Isn't the vast British sky large enough to embrace talented men and women."

D'Erlanger suppressed what might have been a twitch of a smile, halfway encouraging Gower to present her idea. He was a good-looking guy, even out of his ATA uniform, who enjoyed his pipe as well as his tonic and gin. He put down his drink on the three-legged round marble table and reached for his silver stemmed, walnut-bowl Half Bent Billiard. Watching Pauline as he squinted with one eye over the scooping of his tobacco and tamping it into the pipe's bowl, with the other on the quizzical Gower. She was watching intently his every move and every breath, trying to get a sense of his thinking. After a successful lighting, he asked. "Do you think we could get it past Shelmerdine or Balfour?"

"I don't think so, we *have* to. The ATA is your baby and the small numbers you have now aren't going to be enough. I know you will get additional pilots, but for now you could use the likes of our friend Amy Johnson, who can fly anything, she's an expert mechanic. There are many same as her. So why not?"

"Pauline, that is definitely a reasonable plan as we really need the addition to our men. I have a meeting with Shelly on Monday. Since I agreed to manage the ATA, he owes me a favor. Let me have a go at him." In another time and place, Pauline Gower would have embraced Gerard d'Erlanger, but the urge quickly passed; she had a lot of work to do. "Thank you, Gerry. You won't have any regrets and Britain will be stronger for it!" D'Erlanger warned, "Pauline, Shelly and Balfour shouldn't be a problem, but I still have to run this by the RAF, as they call the shots for what happens on the airfields. I will call you early next week and give you my findings. I don't expect smooth sailing, but I am optimistic we will get at least a reasonable start and make your vision, our reality."

D'Erlanger prevailed. On November 14, Pauline received a letter from Shelmerdine directing her to recruit eight women pilots to staff an all-woman pool at Hartford Aerodrome, effective December 1st. She was to recruit twelve to start, knowing a few would likely drop out. Gower and D'Erlanger got expected resistance from RAF leadership, even beyond what he had expected. With the directive from Shelmerdine, they at first agreed to twelve women for the first group, and then had to bend to the Air Ministry who wasn't keen to the idea, reluctantly approving eight women, the number mandated earlier from

Shelmerdine. It was a small concession for the intensely controlling Ministry and the higher ups of the RAF. The RAF also specified the women have 600 logged flight hours, many more than required of the RAF. The headwinds of resistance began to blow.

After a vetting of the final eight testing in small De Havilland *Tiger Moth* airplanes, from twelve that were chosen to try out, the press introduced the final eight announced in January 1940. It included a feisty but deeply capable 22-year-old Joan Hughes, five-foot-two licensed at fifteen, and flight instructor at age eighteen; Honorable Margaret Runciman Fairweather, daughter of Lord Runciman; Mona Friedlander, international women's ice hockey player; Rosemary (Rees) Lady du Cros, ballet dancer, and Margaret Cunnison, Chief Instructor from Perth in southeast Scotland.

They were installed as second officers and given a salary of 238 pounds sterling per annum inclusive of flight pay of 8 pounds sterling. This was thirty percent less than the men, creating a battle for Gower more than eager to fight for this equality. Their working uniform consisted of knee-length tube skirt or slacks, one-piece sidcot flying suit with a quilted liner, sheepskin leather Irvin flying jacket, blue service tunic with four pockets, a belt with a large brass buckle, greatcoat, and a forage cap. The women had to purchase their own blue shirts, black nylon stockings, black shoes, and black necktie.

The newspapers were 'Johnny on the Spot' to feature these women in newspapers and newsreels, which caught the attention of proud wives and truculent husbands all over Britain. They weren't rough and rural looking; they were graceful and fashionable with their flight gear and parachutes dangling over their shoulders. The next month, many came, and after that, even more with conscripts from remote as Holland, South Africa, and Argentina.

Resistance among the RAF testerone was disagreeable and mean spirited at first. As time wore on, the men realized these women really could fly and made a huge difference in RAF pilot manpower issues. The stubborn few who couldn't see the benefits of these ATA women were the anti-feminists who stewed in their own stinky juices.

. . . . . .

Back in the states in the early summer of '41, Cochran was keeping a watchful eye on the women of Gower's ATA, now pressed into service to ferry *Hurricanes*, *Spitfires* and even mid-range bombers from the factories to the fighter hungry RAF front line airfields. During a White House Luncheon as an Awards Committee member for the prestigious Collier Trophy for the greatest achievement in aviation, she resumed her chat with Hap Arnold.

"Good evening, General. It's a pleasure to find you here." "Likewise, Jackie. You seem to be quite the news today, winning races here and there. I'm quite proud of you. We need to visit about the matter between us, but let me first introduce you to a friend of mine, Clayton Knight." After the introduction, Knight elaborated to Jackie of his role directing the U.S. Ferry Command, an off the books group that shuttled back and forth across the Atlantic with expert air and ground support crews needed by the Brits. The conversation had Jackie highly convinced that women could and should be included whenever possible, but just weren't. She excused herself from Knight and caught up with Arnold again.

"Oh Jackie, I am glad you came back." What do you think of Clayton's arrangement?" "Well to be truthful, it is another example of what our women could be doing. Speaking of, did you get your copies of my workup I sent to Olds? It's all there, the list by name and experience of qualified women well over 150 strong." "I did Jackie, and meant to send a note. We are still a bit premature, but I do think sooner or later we will be doing what the Brits are doing now. Say, why don't you get together with Knight, let him grab you a plane and hop over to England and see how Gower is doing with her ATA women?" That was like asking a girl if she liked silk stockings.

It was a win-win idea. It would keep Cochran off his back and still provide a valuable service. Besides looking in on Gower's women, she could also check on the Knight's Wings for Britain program to see if Mr. Knight was doing the job he described. All the while Jackie Cochran is doing what she loves, flying heavy airplanes on long trips.

Cochran's husband Floyd Odlum leaned on his old British friend, Lord 1st Baron Max Beaverbrook, had just been appointed the Minister of Aircraft Production to make it happen and get his wife an airplane. Lord Beaverbrook, a bilious elf like character, (and Churchill's best mate) eagerly agreed, an excellent first test of his wily and self-confessed 'creative procurement talent.' After several twists and turns, they located Lockheed's passenger version of the *Hudson* bomber at Floyd Bennett Field in Long Island, the *Lodestar*, the same class as the bomber and perfect for pilot testing.

After several eight-hour days of grueling but

successful workouts in the *Lodestar*, she passed and was approved to fly the Lockheed *Hudson* bomber from Montreal to RAF Prestwick in Southern Scotland. On the morning of June 18, 1941, with the help of Captain Grafton Carlisle and a radioman, she became the first woman to fly a bomber across the German patrolled Atlantic. Twelve days later, she received a call from Hyde Park for her to join Eleanor and Franklin for lunch at their Hyde Park estate home in Crum Elbow. At the two-hour meeting, the President introduced Cochran to Robert Lovett, Assistant Secretary of War, who asked her to put together a proposal for the use of women. '*Again?*' She thought ill of government procrastination.

Housed at the Ferry Command HQ, she availed herself and her staff to the Civil Aeronautics Administration, correlating her previous research with that of the Civil Aeronautics Administration. Their findings agreed with the Civil Aeronautic Board's numbers. Screening nearly 3,000 women's pilot records, the number was the same, 150 to 200 with serious experience. Expediting her findings to Arnold at the end of July, he was still in a 'wait and see' mode. Wait and see ended on December 7th, 1941, when the Japanese bombed the United States into World War II. By the end of the month, Cochran was sending telegrams to invite nearly 150 women to travel to England and help the British ATA as well as set the tone for a similar program for the United States, soon to have its own need for ferry pilots. She received 75 responses that she paper-screened down to 45 who would get invitations to Dorval Airfield in Montreal for final flight-testing. The women selected would travel in small groups from Halifax to Liverpool on England's west coast.

CHAPTER THREE

The Dutch 'Uncle'

After nearly two years service with the Women's Auxiliary Air Force, Alexandra Gaestel was making her mark as one of the first of several foreign woman aviators to join the new ATA training facility, doing so on an RAF airfield 86 miles west of London. She grew up in the Netherland's province of Gelderland, in its capitol Arnhem, a stone's throw from the western border of Germany. Her Dutch mother, Suzie Wick Dekker, was an accomplished painter and small gallery owner, having commissioned portraits of government officials in Germany, the country of her husband, Siegfried. He, a small town politician whose allegiances blew as a warm summer breeze or an icy winter blizzard, the season determined by the most generous remuneration. Between her art and his city government ties, Mr. Gaestel became real chummy with the German politicians and grew even friendlier in the later 1930's as war appeared inevitable with Hitler's meteoric rise to power. Siegfried was a salty, briar smoking, self made man, with a puffed ego when rubbing elbows with members of the new National Socialist German Worker's Party; the party that swept into power in 1936 with unlikely WWI infantryman Corporal Adolf Hitler regrettably at the helm.

Around the Gaestel house, Alex's dad rarely demonstrated affection, an anomaly for a father who would influence Alex's sexual identity. His response to Alex's achievements in school or sports always implied her falling short of perfection. If she scored a

99, he faulted her for not making 100. If she did make a perfect score on an exam, he would respond that the teacher must be too easy. He raised the bar so high for Alex, she could never impress her father. Harsh discipline, endless disapproval, unbending, standards and general hardship became his coat of arms.

Siegfried came by his ruthless demeanor honestly, as a middle child between two bullying brothers and a father as rough as a sun-dried corncob. The engine of Alex's soul that drove her was ferocious, but around the house with her father, it was reduced to a quiet two-cycle engine. Suzie wasn't much help as the dutiful Dutch wife and mother, going about her business without any comment or activity that would rile the mister. Her forced ambivalence towards Alex and lack of motherly physical affection would spin Alex on her sexual axis to stop on parts unknown. The Gaestel parents were preoccupied to land on the right side of the geo-political majority; staying at arms length with the raucous élan from their next-door German citizens. The family remained content to let Alex find her way, doing her own thing, her way.

In early 1932, sixteen-year-old Alexandra begged her father to use his contacts for her to take flying lessons at a local flying Club in Cologne. Flying was a waste of time according to Siegfried, but it kept Alex out of his hair. The Netherlands had negligible interest or resources for pilot training, so Alex looked the German Air Sports Association for the prospect of getting that desired training. The GASA was formed by Hitler to encourage flying clubs all over Germany after the WWI Treaty of Versailles.

It wasn't hard fr Alex to get accepted, although Siegfried wanted Alex to think it was a big favor, when in reality it wasn't. Even though the Russians had women pilots, Germany was ambivalent to the notion. She applied and was accepted into the GASA. In the beginning, the Flying Association was a poorly disguised civilian enterprise, but in time, would be openly transformed into the German Luftwaffe. It was firmly guided by Field Marshall Herman Göring, a WWI fighter pilot Ace who found favor with Hitler. The thousands of members of the clubs and Lufthansa Aviation Schools were technically civilians flying airplanes and gliders for the presumed pleasure of its members, but motives were all military.

Alex was of strong Dutch stock with thick bones, large hands, and skin the shade of burnt umber. Contradicting her masculine hands and arms, her features were soft and not for lack of character and to most, quite eye-catching. This interesting woman was allowed to come and go as a male or female, learning all the Flying Association could teach. Alex was intuitively smart, inquisitive, and ambitious. In a short ten months, before the Germans rounded up all the Dutch-built *Fokkers* and sent them to Russia, she learned the basics of flying and even achieved several hours in the lone Dutch made *Fokker XIII* that somehow found its way to the Cologne Club. The *XIII*, an upgrade to the *Fokker II*, was a conventional single-bay bi-plane with staggered wings braced by wire struts. Alex sat in an open cockpit, with the undercarriage nothing more than a fixed tailskid. The wings were made of wood skinned with thin plywood and the fuselage of welded steel tubes with a fabric covering. As Alex became a complete master of the *Fokker*, she longed for larger and faster airplanes.

Alex's flying urges were kept alive and well by

reading exploits of English-born and Africa's 'naughty daughter', Beryl Clutterbuck Markham. Alex was impressed she had flown non-stop from Abingdon-on-Thames in the heart of England to Nova Scotia in 1936. Alex pored over Europe's newspapers that couldn't get enough of the Turkish woman, Sabiha Gökçen, who flew bombing missions in action against the Dersim Rebellion in 1937 in her oversized bi-winged *Breguet-19* bomber.

Alexandra had stacks of magazines filled with the feats of Amelia Earhart, heart struck by her short disheveled hairstyle, her lanky frame, and of her waving from the window of those really big airplanes. The image turned her on to both the pilot and the airplane. '*My, oh my*', she would say to herself. '*My, oh my! If only to be near her!*' Alex fantasized about being Earhart's lover and copilot, but would have been disappointed to know Earhart was attracted to men. On one occasion, however, it was rumored by the *Penny Dreadful* tabloid, she was a 'special' friend of George Putnam's wife Dorothy, before Earhart stole George away. It was by an improbable mutual agreement that Dorothy and George parted amicably so George and Amelia could be together. '*Whatever scent Earhart wore, it sure did the trick,*' Alex mused.

Alex continued to fly and fly frequently, fitting in four years of college at the State University of Ghent, founded by the Dutch in 1830. The Flemish center of extended learning had a worldwide reputation for free and higher thinking. Alex absorbed both the French and Flemish languages, with English a third language, all the while flying from the Ghent Airfields near the confluence of the Rivers Scheldt and Leie. She was close enough to make the Dunkirk to Dover a regular day trip to practice her English at a farmhouse above the cliffs where the curious farmers gladly shared a bite of food and sip of tea to marvel at her still warm bi-winged airplane. When she could find a taker to pay for the petrol, she would fly on into London for a night at the theater. *A 'bold one, that Dutch woman'*, muttered among those who knew her.

The Gaestel family's main source of income to help pay for Alex's hobby came from Mr. Gaestel's innovative capers from city offices to police commissioner to the mayor, as well as Suzie's art sales. In 1936, as the clouds of conflict billowed thick and dark, Siegfried called his daughter into his study and asked her to close the door. *' Uh oh, now what,'* she thought. Alex sat in the velvet tub chair across from her father's desk. The small fireplace crackled wistfully, as Siegfried twisted the cigarette into its four-inch holder. As the smoke from the freshly lit Ernte 23 swirled upward, Siegfried placed his pack of matches on the red and gold cigarette pack.

"Alexandra, over the years I may have given the impression that I did not care so much for you." He let the words hang and watched his daughter eye him like a cat, preparing to launch. When he smiled, she relaxed. "My dear daughter, I have been stern with you in matters of your maturity and activities, mostly flying. I had to push you into a hardened woman that you have become. I did so because I anticipate a wicked war between Germany and her enemies of the Great War. Today, I am convinced that will be the case. I had to shape you tough and smart to keep you alive and safe during this difficult time. The weak and unsure will be the largest casualties, and I can't bear to think of you as such. And for the record, I am proud of what you are and who you are. As proud as any father, anywhere in the world." Alex began to mist as her father motioned her to come to his side. Their hug was brief but long overdue. They both regretted that it had been so very long since their last. She sat on his lap and put her head between his shoulder and chest.

"My dear girl, as a precautionary move, I am moving you and your mother to the rural southern region of England near Taunton in Somerset. If it is war, no matter my fickle allegiances, war would be rough, even brutal, especially for women. I need to do this to take care of you and your mom, no matter what. So, let's hop up and see what is causing those delicious kitchen smells."

As Alex continued to grow into a young woman, she and her father seemed to have turned their adversarial connection into one quite conciliatory. Time and maturity seemed to have been just the tonic to turn father and daughter into a functioning alliance.

Alex settled into the rolling hills of England, lazing on the River Tone, matriculating to the ancient University of Bristol, a short distance to the north of Taunton for a second major. She was attracted to the school because one of their recent graduates shared the Nobel Prize in 1933 for his study of Atomic Theory and its applications. With Alex's determination to get graduate quickly, she studied through the summer quarter to earn her degree in engineering in 1939. She was an easy fit for their graduate school that September, where, for starters, she studied how aerial photography was used in map-making. It was the next best thing to aeronautics, and a study that would serve her well in a few short years. The relationship with her mother was a peaceful co-existence.

Between her flying and coursework, she lived in the library where she found her first intimate relationship with a very feminine fencing instructor, Madeleine DeBois. While Alex wasn't particularly looking to other women for companionship, she was drawn to 'Maddy' for her intellect, effervescence, and sense of humor, qualities the boyish men at the university didn't possess. Her smooth skin, tantalizing French scent, and playful sense of humor were like an industrial magnet with her hair floating around her shoulders in a silken curtain. Alex was hooked the moment Maddy stuck out her hand and declared, "Glad to do your acquaintance. My name's Madeleine." Her presence was one of all pleasure and invited no questions, agreeing with Alex's 22-year-old emergent hormones.

The daughter of a French chemist, she, like Alex, was spirited away to England as Hitler's sword rattling grew in ferocity by the month. Madeleine was French through and through. A Parisian, Madeleine knew the ways of the mind and pleasures of a liberated woman. When in Paris, Alex's new friend amused her libido with men and women, preferring women mostly, primarily because it drove her parents crazy. She felt women were quite easily maneuvered to accommodate her sexual preferences, some found in Hindu Kama Sutra illustrations.

Maddy's liaisons took place in the back corners of large poorly lit bookstores and occasional ladies' room stalls. Her mating skills were sharpened at Parisian nightclubs like the Chez Moune in the red light district on Pigalle. She was introduced to Edith Piaf, the twenty-three-year old crooner and frequent entertainer at Moune, one who was never shy about singing in the shadows of the larger venues.

Alex was a perfect fit for Madeleine; mature but

still somewhat naive, brusque, and curious to the bone. When Alex made strong eye contact, Maddy intuitively understood. She just smiled and tucked her slender hand under Alex's chin and lovingly murmured, "Alexandra, love never moved where it was told. Never has, never will. But I must warn you. You need to be extra careful as universal society will not fathom this unique friendship, as I do not fully."

Her words gave Alex less inclination of guilt when she enjoyed the company of her own gender rather than men who seemed preoccupied with their bloated opinions of themselves. She appreciated her mother's dual admonitions over the previous twenty years, despite activity not at all true to her behavioral norms.

Nonetheless, Madeleine kept Alexandra content long enough for her to be sucked into England's war labor pool. If Alex couldn't be an RAF pilot, she could at least be close to them. As Great Britain and Western Europe began bracing for Germany's inevitable attacks on their home soils, she quit graduate school after just two semesters at age 24, and answered the call to the war's needs in June of 1940.

Alex reported to the exam center in Cirencester, on the lower east edge of the Cotswolds, to be assessed and get four weeks of basic training for the Women's Auxiliary Air Force. With her background at Bristol, she easily passed the battery of written tests, and only a week later after a short train ride, she piled into a waiting lorry taking her from the train station to RAF Bridgnorth in Stanmore, Shropshire, 140 miles northwest of London. The assignment had a few surprises for the Arnhem native and her new pals.

The housing was a series of wooden huts, cold concrete showers, and a toilet with limited privacy. Alex rather liked looking over the various shapes of her recruit mates; slim, squatty, full bosomed, straight and curly hair; a veritable visual buffet for the Dutch WAAF recruit.

The beds were lined up in rows of 30, making changing into nightwear for bedtime another routine with no privacy. Some women were 'Ho hum', about the inconvenience; other shy ladies muttered, 'Oh dear.' The *'Oh dears'* managed to rustle like contortionists under the blankets on their cots to get into nightclothes, but after a while, they marched with the flow. Anything for the war! ..for most of the women, that is. The unpleasant 'flow' included what women humorously called the medical inspections that would follow them throughout their postings at the WAAF, the safeguard against scabies, babies, and rabies; the check for lice, pregnancies, and venereal diseases. The safeguards always seemed invasive, but necessary.

Alex's lectures droned on far too long, the last subject almost intolerable: hygiene and all matters sexual. Alex scanned the room to note any of the women who seemed relaxed about the subject. She would likely become friends, making the environment highly enjoyable, as a cat licking her paws.

The one pleasant matter that softened the tedium for Alex was the uniform, smart and even verged on stylish. Then there was the kit, likened to the American GIs' duffle bag. The clumsy kit, merely *on loan*, was handed out in a white tube shaped canvas bag about 12 inches across and four feet high. Unpacking was okay, but putting the personal items that covered her cot back into the tube, was like repacking a sausage. The kit included two pairs of shoes, eating utensils, bathroom personals, towels, and three shirts. Then add pants, foul weather coat, shoeshine kit, underclothes, jacket, tin hat, and a smattering of small miscellaneous items. Throw that over the shoulder and add the gas mask, and you have a bona fide WAAF. Over time the kit would grow with toothpaste, notepaper, face powder, lipstick, cream, smokes and chocolates. The women were obliged to buy those items with part of their meager pay of ten shillings per week.

Alex didn't know if she would be cooking or driving lorries, but didn't care really. The variety of jobs available seemed endless. There was parachute packing, lorry driving, catering, weather service, early warning radar, telephone service, codes and ciphers, photograph analyzing, intelligence, and plotters. Alex was aware of the new ATA that was formed to ferry military airplanes. She was keeping an eye on the progress of the women pilots, currently consigned to flying the tame *Tiger Moth* trainers. Maybe later she would test the waters and apply, particularly if they began flying the sexy fighters or lumbering bombers. 'The *Moth* would be so boring.'

For the time being, she concentrated her attention to recruit training at RAF Bridgnorth, the Training Command for the WAAF. After four weeks of marching and learning the basics of her role as a WAAF, in September 1940, Alex Gaestel was on the front line of her group's Passing Out Parade in her service of His Majesty the King. At the same time, the Battle of Britain raged on miles above the British skies, creating a tapestry of contrails that stretched to the horizon and beyond.

Her first assignment for balloon school was (conveniently) at nearby Stanmore Park on Old Church Lane near London, where the balloons were made. Alex was amused at how the caboose-sized, deformed, elephant-shaped curiosities and their cables deterred low-level strafing and bombing. That alone was herculean, as the deployment was changed daily to prevent the Germans from getting familiar with where the balloons would be. They were raised and lowered by cables on motorized winches from 1,000 to 5,000 feet in some cases.

Alex halfway enjoyed her ten weeks of training, learning the arts of repairing, and, in particular, the raising and lowering of the large canvas balloons. The oddly shaped hydrogen balloons were scattered all around in cities, beaches, and airfields; some positioned low and some high. She commanded the crew of the Fordson Sussex Balloon Winch Tender, a lorry that moved to various locations, as needed.

Accommodations for Alex and her balloon crew were a bit on the meager side, with mostly temporary buildings of 50 feet by 20 wide, equipped with double bunks or steel cots, shelves for clothes, a space heater, coal-box-stove for cooking, food storage shelves, food prep counter, two mess tables, a sink, dish storage area, and sanitary facilities. It was no surprise Alex's military aspirations were not satisfied at the primitive balloon camp. Her military skills needed a challenge.

As word got around of Alex's education and background, many instructors and especially students encouraged her to apply for Special Services, where members of the WAAF with higher-level skills were in strong demand. That encouragement lifted her confidence and seeded an interest that became an aspiration. With her education and knack for numbers and equations, after a formal application and subsequent testing, her service category would indeed change to 'Special Services,' a broad array of possibilities for men and women with specific skill levels and university backgrounds.

For starters, Alex was promised a radar station as soon as one became available, an assignment they assured her could be just a stepping-stone to more challenging work if she was exceptional. Until her orders were finalized, the many fine pubs in the Middlesex region surrounding London kept her busy if not content. The back street *Abercorn Arms* served a slap-up lunch, and *The Vine and The Hare* not far from the school were the party pubs. She became an expert on the relaxing elixir specialties like India Pale or Ole Bill.

Alex Gaestel finally received her orders a few days before Christmas, then made her way to radar training at Yatesbury for six weeks. In mid-February, she trained further at Southampton for refinement in the discernment of tracking and direction of images on the Cathode Ray Tube, a curriculum taking six months.

In July, Alex suffered a major interruption in her world of tadpoles and blips, as word spread that ATA woman, Winnie Crossley, ferried a *Hawker Hurricane* fighter and Margie Fairweather, a *Spitfire* on July 19th. Alex knew that would be just the beginning. *Now* she would send in her application. They would surely recognize her experience and rush her application to the head of the line. She would check her posts every day for several days, then weekly, then seldom. She had given up.

In late September of '41, the *Medina*, a 1931 vintage paddle steamer ferried her to the coastal town of Cowes on the Isle of Wight. The Red Funnel paddler wasn't famous for her beauty, but reliability was her reputation. The eleven-knot diesel engine trudged the 20 miles through the Solent Straits of the island in only two hours. It was relaxing to soak in the beauty of the coastal landscape and estuaries that trickled into the straits from the mainland. As Alex sucked in the cool saltwater mist, she pondered what the Radar Station outpost of Ventnor would be like.

It wasn't long before another woman who announced herself by spitting over the side of the *Medina*. She turned and held out her hand. "Hi, they call me Wendy. Sorry about the spit, but the wind was not to my favor on the other side." She looked Alex up and down and noticed the lightning symbol sewen on her sleeve, "Going to Ventnor?" Before she answered, Alex asked if she were Jewish. "That's an odd question." Well, I saw the spitting and all," like the father on his rebellious Mariam." The woman just laughed and shared that it was her last spit from her small wad of chewing tobacco.

"As to the Ventnor question, why do you ask?" "Just curious. That's where I'm headed." "Me too, we can travel in together." "Didn't see you at radar school." "Actually, I am being reposted. Was at Rye for a bit, but after a while they moved us again."

"Alex, Alexandra Gaestel, Aircraftwoman 2nd Class. Started in Balloons, which was a bit crazy, then radar school at Yatesbury on Salisbury Plain with 70 other women surrounded by 7,000 men. With a vow of secrecy, we learned about the marvel of radar. During training, we watched the blips of RAF and German fighter pilots really having a go at each other. We hardly slept."

"I know about that, Alex, as Rye was busier than a crumpet shop on a Sunday morning. September of last year was a really rough patch. I hope this slight lull will continue. What do you know about the bombing of Ventnor last August? Twice, no less."

"Well, as you know, the people at Radar are hush hush about everything. From what I can gather, on the first bombing, *Junkers* from a larger formation headed for the radar station. Spits intercepted them, but 15 managed to get through and hit the station. Some service buildings were destroyed, but only one soldier was hurt. I heard they had to move to Bembridge on the east coast for a while, and that's about all I know. As long as there is a hole to jump in, we should have no worries. It will be fun to see what's in store for us.

"Wendy, I may not be here long, as I have applied for the ATA." "Good luck with that. I hear the waiting queue is as long as your arm, probably longer. I hope you get a rabbit's foot for it though, and sooner than later." The paddler bumped the pier at Cowes on the very south point of Isle of Wight. The two radar specialists jumped ashore and headed for the Southern Victus bus station. They scrambled aboard the light blue and red bus with their trusty kits over their shoulders. Their transportation vouchers for the 22-mile ride were stamped as they took window seats to enjoy the scenery through Newport and Whitely to the Radar Station.

At the gate, the sentry looked at their paperwork and directed them to the nearby camp and headquarters. The Adjutant thumbed through their papers and looked at Alex. "Miss Gaestel, you have quite a background. Why aren't you with the ATA?" "Well sir, I just did apply, knowing women flying the fancy stuff now, you know. I'm not too hopeful as I hear the queue is a mile long, which is no surprise to me. So, it may be a while."

"At any rate, if you like what you do here and are splendid at it, ask about being a filterer. If you do that well, you can be an officer, which is higher pay and likely additional responsibility." Alex deposited that coin of wisdom into her crowded memory bank. "By the way, since you are the only two women here, it wouldn't be fair to the men here to give up the spacious bedding arrangement to suit your privacy, so we have ordered a billet for you in town at the Alexandra Gardens. It's rather large for two, but, having just had several soldiers there, you might expect company or perhaps be moved after a while. For the time being though, it will be a luxury for you."

Alex and Wendy tossed their gear into an empty front seat and scrambled into the back seat of the appointed jeep. It was a bit further up the hill, around the esplanade, east on Belgrave, and right on Hambrough Road, which gives way to Dudley Road. Within 100 yards of the road becoming Dudley, the jeep stopped. "Here you are, Ladies. I'll give you a hand with those bags." The young women had been assigned Villa Number Seven of eight villas, owned by Mrs. Olita Dashwood. The ground and first level front rooms loomed very large, with high ceilings, bay windows, and magnificent views. The rooms shouted lush with decorator appointments and expensive accessories in just the right places. The main reception rooms had polished marble flooring and oversized slate fireplaces. When built, they would have been among the finest houses in Ventnor.

Mrs. Dashwood was quick to the rules. "Breakfast is at 7:30 sharp because your ride down to the station picks up at eight. Dinner is at 6:30 and, if you are kept late, you will find several pubs nearby where you can eat." With their belongings stowed, the jeep returned them down the hill to let the women get acquainted with Ventnor Radar Station.

From the start, it was clear Aircraftwoman 2nd Class Gaestel was gifted. From their Chain Station radar towers on the flat plain above their underground bunker, she interpreted the blips and their meaning faster than any in her group. The timely information was forwarded to the filterer so it could be summarized and plotted with other reports from other spotters all along the coast, and ultimately reconciled with the known RAF aircraft in the air.

More importantly, Alex learned the chain of communication between the elements of radar from the chain stations around the coast and coastal observers with binoculars. Then all that chatter of information was assembled from filter stations to HQ Fighter Command filter, to the operation rooms, on to Group HQ, and finally to the appropriate sector control. Sector would then scramble fighters; all that in a matter of minutes to get the fighters in the air to intercept the incoming bombers and/or fighters.

With the new technology of identifying RAF airplanes with identification equipment, Alex could talk directly to Sector Control, who would in turn talk with the pilot and give him exact heading and altitude to the enemy. Knowing the direction to fly and altitude to be searching, the RAF had the clear advantage.

To Alex and the rest of the team, when the German blip disappeared, there was cheering. When an RAF blip disappeared, there was dismay. For the British pilots sitting in their *Hurricanes* or *Spitfires*, the information from the plotter to Sector meant they had two or three minutes to maneuver their backs to the sun or climb and gain an altitude advantage, all the while looking in the direction of the Luftwaffe adversary.

Because of this defensive curtain of eyes on the ground and Chain Radar Stations, RAF pilots wouldn't feel the pain of a 20 mm bullet blasting through his chest, creating a hole the size of his wife's fist and be aware for one, maybe two seconds, then go dark and die. Instead, he will have the upper hand, use it to live and tell the story of how he splayed the German like a gutted trout. Caught up in the insane rush of the event, he remembered twisting his neck and gritting his teeth, realizing that it was the moment of living longer or not, then the thumps of his cannons, spitting tracers into the enemy. He would remember the event until he was an old man returning to the timeworn overgrown airfields and museums where it would become clear, without the multiple levels of radar and intelligence available to him, he might have been fish food.

Rarely did those pilots know how to thank each link in the coastal chain of early warning. But it did matter, and the word frequently did get back from the RAF Squadrons to Sector Command and each radar station that called the plotting rooms.

As promised, Alex and girlfriend Wendy parted company just before Halloween after Alex received orders to the Government's Code and Cypher School at Bletchley Park. At Bletchley, Alex learned handling and forwarding information of the most sensitive nature; information to come in handy later in her service.

In April of that next year, in 1942, she became restless, and applied *again* to join the ATA that was finally getting to realize qualified women were needed to ferry the larger class military airplanes, even the four engine bombers. The women of the ATA had started their own pilot training program at RAF Thame, on the outskirts of Haddenham, for women with meager or no pilot experience.

Busy with codes and ciphers, while keeping one eye on her mailbox, she continued to wait and wait again, for what seemed like ages. When she received word she would be interviewed by the ATA, she was overjoyed and apprehensive at the same time. *' What if my flying skills are too rusty, then what; back to my old WAAF job? '* Only nine days later, after giving up hope that the invitation was frozen to death by a blizzard of red tape, she got the call she had been waiting for.

She waited nervously while Wallace Pond, the input processor at White Waltham Airfield flipped through her application and logbooks. The mousey man had small brown teeth and cauliflower ears with a chin that could crack walnuts. The unremarkable ATA officer asked, "With all of these hours, why are you just now applying?" Caught flat footed, she had to think a minute.

"You know, that is an excellent question, Sir. When the war first started, I wanted to help in any way I could, and actually liked my jobs with the WAAF. The responsibilities made me feel important, like I was really making a contribution. When I radioed contacts that Sector gave the RAF section leader or pilot of the location of enemy airplanes and we knocked one down, I was part of it all. To be honest, I hate to say it, but I have applied to the ATA twice since May of last year and received no answer. I had pretty much given up hope until I got the message to report to you. To be really truthful, when I learned Miss Gower was allowing women to fly the more serious airplanes, I knew that was my real destiny. I can and want to do it, and will train others."

"By the way, it's Senior Commander Gower,

Miss Gaestel. We need to get that clear. Now, why did you choose Germany the place to learn to fly?" Without hesitation, she smoothly remarked, "Because Holland didn't have any of the pilot schools in the eastern part of the country where we lived." "Was your father in favor of this?" "Yes, of course. He was very supportive and actually helped the flying club get the better airplanes for us to fly."

"I see. Moving right along. As we have been inundated with applications, it has resulted in scores of women that have been on the waiting list to be interviewed for service in the ATA. We simply haven't had the manpower to respond to everyone, so I hope you will accept our apology. Why we didn't get your first application is lost on me, so apologies for that, too. After reviewing your application and logbook, I am authorizing you to report to the ATA straight away to begin ground school training at Barton-in-the Clay just north of here."

That was that, and the not-so-little Dutch girl, Alexandra Gaestel, was now a genuine civilian pilot candidate for the British Air Ministry. As Alex literally skipped out of the administrator's office, Mr. Pond called in an aide from the nearby room. "Get Commander Gower on the phone for me, please." Gower worked on the second floor office of the small two-story brick building next to the Operations Department of the airfield. The ATA offices were conveniently perched behind de Havilland's hangars and workshops.

"Miss Gower, I have enrolled Alex Gaestel into the ATA training program as you requested. I would recommend your staff continue to monitor her 24 hours a day, as I share your uneasy feeling about her allegiance, and am especially wary of her father who I would not consider a friend even if we are favored to win this war. She learned to fly in Cologne, so we don't know how much of the Nazi propaganda she might have absorbed."

Gower swiveled left then right in her chair, and as she handed a sheaf of papers to her secretary, Mary Nicholson Webb, she covered the mouthpiece of the phone and whispered for her to remain in the office.

"I agree with you, Mr. Pond. We have been uneasy about her, even with her service in sensitive positions with the WAAF, but now every able experienced pilot is a critical need. It is better to have her out of those WAAF posts, because we need her flying ability in our ferry service. If she is indeed giving information to Germany, we are better equipped to know of it at the squadron level and can handle it quietly, and even turn it to our advantage. Meanwhile, keep me informed of any activities or behavior that are in the least way suspicious. Good day, sir. I thank you for your observant instincts."

"Mary, I want to attach a note to Miss Gaestel's file. Immediately after she finishes her first conversion and gets her Third Officer's Stripe, she is to enter the Class Two conversion training for the heavier airplanes. If she is successful and makes Second Officer, I want her assigned straightaway to the Class Three Conversion, and, if possible, serve as an instructor in all three classes at the same time. By being right here at White Waltham we can keep an eye on her. That should keep her little bum busy! No, Mary, don't you dare put that part about her bum in there." They both had their first belly laugh in weeks. "Also, I want her progress forwarded to me every Monday. Mary, I rather have a long schedule to tend, so carry on. See you later in the day."

CHAPTER FOUR

The New Mexican Portuguese Jew

After the tricky journey from Liverpool to London in June of '42, as the rest of the ATA women preceding her, Deborah Rosen negotiated the tedious check-in process at RAF White Waltham. Ever since the awkward conversation at the front desk of the Savoy Hotel the previous day over her missing reservation, Deborah was sensing a frosty attitude from everyone who reviewed her thin sheaf of files. They fussed about as if they didn't have her name in the arrival cards or lists from Gower. Thankfully, Deborah wasn't the only applicant with messy or scant papers, but she worried about her missing logbook. It was additional work for the Brits, adding to their already burdensome load.

They would look at her, her file, then her again, shake their heads, and move her along. She felt like she really didn't quite belong, as if it would be too much trouble to bother with her. She wished Mrs. Cochran could have met their group in Liverpool. Maybe she could have sorted out the cause of the missing papers and saved everyone the inconvenience. Deborah took some solace, as Opal Anderson was in the same boat; her records were lost too. When she thought about her situation, she considered that she was there to help the Brits, so it was okay. They knew her and she was going to fly. She was amazed how the admin people got anything done at all, given the mass of complexities that mobilized England. It made sense that paperwork would trail the humanity of the war, an understandable byproduct of waves of anxious people. *'But still'...*

After her physical exam, x-ray's, and shots, she was walking to the administrative offices to check in further, when approached by a Mr. Julian Coyle. Coyle was a squatty one, his lack of fitness confirmed by his 42-inch belly hanging over his size 36 pants, two sizes too large causing a 360 degree pleat. His pudgy left hand sported an official looking clipboard. The curl of his collars was reminiscent of limp jester slippers without the bells. His shirts were either seldom acquainted with a laundry or used for target practice by expert tobacco chewers. If everyone in England had his teeth and his wardrobe, dentistry wouldn't be an ideal profession, nor would tailoring or laundry service for that matter. Deborah concluded the poor bloke wasn't retired RAF, but maybe a barkeep moving to the luxury of day work to stay off the dole while supporting the war effort. Her initial impression was that melancholy had settled in him a long time ago, now his nature. "Have a seat Miss Rosen. It is Miss, is it not?"

She identified the aroma as an disagreeable blend of goat musk, library mold, and Royall Lyme after-shave, but she still politely offered, "Thank you and yes, it is Miss." "Miss Rosen, the check-in-clerk has given me your folder, but I am in a quandary. I conferred with the medical department regarding the paperwork in your file, as it seems incomplete. Until we can get confirmation from Mrs. Cochran or Commander Gower you are part of her first twenty-five, I will have to delay checking you in. Have you received any vouchers for a uniform yet?" "No, sir, I haven't." "Do you have the telegram Mrs. Cochran sent to all of you?" "No. When she wired and told me to report to Dorval in Montreal, she promised she would mail me a copy of the telegram and send one to my parents."

"I know this may seem somewhat unsettling, but I am confident we will get to the bottom of all this. Until we do, I will start a new file for you and set you up with payroll and vouchers for your uniform. If you could wait outside for a bit, maybe catch a bite to eat in the canteen, I'll fetch you in about an hour." Deborah regretted thinking poorly of the Englishman, now her knight in rusty armor. He immediately rang Commander Gower and was instructed by her to send Miss Rosen to Gower's office on the other side of Maidenhead at White Waltham airfield.

"Mary, get William Stephenson of British Intelligence on the phone, please. I think he is at the Claridge Hotel in Mayfair." After 20 minutes or so, he was on the phone. "Miss Gower, kind of you to ring. We haven't talked properly for a long time. What can I do for you?"

"Mr. Stephenson, I would like to meet with you and chat about a matter too sensitive for the telephone." "Quite right, I understand. Is everything going your way, or do you need my help?" "Yes, on both accounts, Mr. Stephenson. Can we meet at soon, but at your first convenience? I can send one of our *Ansons* over to fetch you at RAF Hornchurch, or I can come to Mayfair. I need to speak with you about an interesting woman." "How about tomorrow? I'll come to Maidenhead at 09:30. I need to get out of this messy city for a while anyway." "Perfect. See you then, Mr. Stephenson. You are a treasure." "Good day, Miss Gower."

"Mary, have Miss Rosen come on in. If she's not outside she might be in the canteen." Deborah, refreshed by an American Coke and British banger-on-a-bun, was ushered into Gower's office and met with two outstretched hands. As she sat back in the chair across from Gower, she marveled at the famous woman. She was of average size, highly revered, but gracious as a commoner.

"Miss Rosen, I have spoken with several colleagues about your missing paperwork and must ask for your patience and request you come back tomorrow. Be here first thing at 10:30 as I have a full morning early on. In the meantime, you might want to take a half-day tour of London today. The weather's favorable and 'The Tate' is featuring da Vinci this week."

Somewhat relieved, Deborah would do just that. As she strolled the littered walkways of London, her first impression was the enormity of bomb damage all around central London. She saw firsthand the damage of nine months of bombing that killed 20,000 men women and children. She imagined every death leaving suffering spouses, daughters, sons, parents, and other countless extended family members, and countless others. The images of buildings reduced to rubble and street vendors with weak smiles in rags, peddling roasted peanuts, honeycomb, and cabbage for food money became overpowering to all her senses. A humpbacked old woman, looking twenty years older than her age, released the American woman's tears, as she tried to be cheery as the perkiest flower in the old woman's wilting bouquet. As Deborah wiped her tears with her sleeve, she became aware of the demeanor of the Brits around her of their gritty determination. There were a handful of fragile smiles, lips signaling happy, but eyes telling quite another story. It strengthened her resolve to crawl into any airplane they put in front of her to do her part for the courageous people of London, bravely laboring through each day.

The next morning, Pauline Gower had already put in an hours work, including one training lesson in a Harvard for a woman struggling with her class two conversion. She was refreshed and eager to talk with Stephenson. At 09:20, Mary Nicholson peeked around the door leading to her small foyer and open office. "Mr. Stephenson is here to see you." With hands outstretched to keep the meeting cordial, he grasped both of hers with a gentle squeeze.

"Pauline, my dear woman, how have you been?" Without waiting for her reply, he scowled a bit and noted the weather was 'bloody hot' for June. "Agreed, my dear fellow. Summer is early this year, and extra welcome after this past winter, a tough one, that. We really can't set store by the calendar for the weather any longer, that's for sure. And as to your question, I am doing well as I hope the same for you. Tea, Mr. Stephenson?" "Well it's *almost* tea time, aye? Don't mind if I do, if you will join me."

Pauline pushed one of the buttons on her telephone console as Mary was already on it. The 45-year-old Stephenson was plain enough, black hair combed back with a slight tuft in the front, medium build and always a faint smile, as if permanent. He could have been mistaken for a version of a thin American comic actor, William Bendix. His soft demeanor contradicted his impressive deeds as a Canadian Soldier, highly decorated Ace in WWI, inventor, businessman, and spymaster. Pauline had to remind herself she was in the presence of the Senior Agent of the British Intelligence and head of the Special Ops Executive. She would be brief.

"What do you have for me Pauline, if I may be a bit informal?" "Of course, Bill." They both smiled as they sipped their Earl Grey, popular with the Brits, a flavor made with the juice of Bergamot Orange rind.

"Mr., I mean, Bill, I have an American girl who may be of interest to you." Miss Gower spoke of the girl's records missing from Montreal, but easily recoverable to verify orders. "I found out she has an impeccable family pedigree as I called and located her files still at Dorval in Montreal, your old stomping grounds. Her father was a pilot in the Great War. She speaks fluent Spanish and some French. Her pilot's logbook reflects remarkable flying skills, like her handling of an emergency at Dorval. She's remarkable for her age. Those skills I would hate to lose, if you take her from me." Stephenson, brows pinched in curiosity, took another sip of tea and let her continue.

"At this stage of her enrollment, with stuck paperwork, if you had an interest, I might be able to alter her normal routine so she could be available on a moment's notice for you, if you see a place with your team. Perhaps training for Camp X in Canada?"

Now it was his turn. "Here's my thinking. First, thanks for thinking of our cause and me. As you must know, we are the ones who normally reach out in our recruiting and not the reverse, but in this case, you might have uncovered a jewel. Let's do this. I will have my people in Montreal run over to Dorval and grab those files. I will have them sealed, only to be opened at the war's end or destroyed if we lose, God forbid we lose this bloody war. I will send Photocopies for your files there. In our work it is an asset, 'not to be.'

"Create a shadow dossier on her, with a pseudonym and keep her close, or at least not too far away. As far as the world knows, she does not exist, but can be fully restored at any time, especially if our American OSS or we aren't an agreeable fit for her. Perhaps, allow her be an instructor with only a handful of ferry duties so she doesn't get restless. With her parents, without alarm, communicate as much as possible about her alias, asking them to be mum about it. Maybe, for example, tell them it's not uncommon even sporting for pseudonyms of the ATA pilots, many of foreign origin, to confuse the Germans, keeping them safer, etcetera. In the meantime, I will send over a couple of my agents to observe her and see what lurks between her ears. Then I will know clearly of her potential.

"Miss Gower, as you know, we have been interested in one of your women, Betty Lussier, an American countrywoman, whom I have known even before the war. I flew with her father, DFC winner Emile, during the Great War with 73 Squadron. We still keep in close touch. I know Betty is impatient to fly abroad, a low probability for the ATA women we all know. If we end up coming to terms with her with an assignment in Algeria or Italy, she could be our natural liaison to your Miss Rosen. Meanwhile, I will reach out to my American colleague, Bill Donovan of the OSS. He has sharp judgment and can do some background checking from his end, as after all, we are dealing with an American here."

With that and a last long sip of his tea, he put his cup and saucer on the small table by his chair and stood to excuse himself. "Pauline, I don't see many people outside my secluded circle, but this has been refreshing, rather. What you are doing with the women of the ATA is astonishing, and my deep respect for you and your work is no secret. Keep me in the loop on Miss Rosen, and in the meantime, if there is anything I can do for you, short of ending the war tomorrow, do not hesitate to call, as you did the day before last. Thanks for letting me pop over, but now I need to be off, Pauline. I will let myself out." His smile widened as he turned and retreated to his waiting staff car.

"Mary, come in for a minute. Please call Admin and the passport control people. We have some midnight oil to burn to get this woman's papers together. Cancel any hops that can't be managed by another pilot, and have those reassigned. We need to get this done in the next 48 hours."

Promptly at 10:30 that next morning, Deborah Rosen was ushered into Pauline Gower's office, having just finished changing from her flying suit back into a fresh uniform. After her talk with Rosen, she would have to change back, as she had just been scheduled a ferry delivery from White Waltham for a *Tiger Moth* to Hatfield. As much as she loved settling into the pilot's seat of any airplane, the opportunity of making those critical ferry deliveries were rare, as her management responsibilities became relentless, allowing her time for personal needs rare.

"Excuse the shuffle Miss Rosen, but it's been an usually busy morning. Have a seat," she smiled agreeably. Pauline was always on point with her down-to-earth hospitality. "Miss Rosen, we have verified your papers, but it will be a few days for them to catch up. Plus, we will do some modification to them when they get here." Rosen's brow furrowed and chin tilted sideways.

"Oh?" "Don't worry, everything is going to be fine." Gower leaned back into her chair in a light informal pose. "Miss Rosen, as you know, you and twenty-five of your countrywomen have answered Jackie Cochran's call to join our ATA, which is not combat flying, but still dangerous nonetheless. Is that right?" "Yes sir, um Ma'am. I know of the dangers."

"You are in my office for two reasons, Miss Rosen. As your Commander, I will be talking briefly with each American woman to be certain everyone seems a proper fit for what we are trying to achieve here at the Air Transport Auxiliary. I will ask why you volunteered beyond the love of flying, and to pry a bit into your character. We also have a proposal for you to consider. Although we don't expect any of your ferrying missions to reach beyond England or Southern Scotland, we can't predict the reach of German sympathizers.

"For you, we are vacillating between your reported flying and leadership abilities. At the same time, we have to protect you from the awful fate we know the Nazis could bestow on you, an accused Jewish combatant or spy. In the event you crash over any German controlled or partisan pocket areas here in the Commonwealth, no matter how small it might be, as a woman, a Jewish Woman, you can't expect very polite treatment. The Germans have enthusiastic trigger fingers, too jumpy to suit me. The airfields where you will be are littered with German sympathizers. If you are ever captured or kidnapped and they identify you as Jewish, your lot would not be promising. Torture and rape come to mind." Gower let the imagery sink in. "Now hang on until I finish.

"For your own protection, we are advising you to alter your identity, not uncommon in war. This will be just for the war, mind you, but for a while you will be Maria Fuentes. The derivation of Maria is someone that is obstinate or rebellious, the same for the French Marie. How do you feel about this?"

Deborah cocked her head, as she could hardly believe what she was hearing. Gower had just made her at ease, now this? "What if I prefer not to do this?" "Miss Rosen, you will probably be posted to a ferry pool in the far north and fly mostly trainers and some Harvard-class single engine airplanes. You will probably do a lot of paperwork and a little instructing.

If you can see fit for the identity change, you will get the full experience of every military airplane you can quality for. It would be a rich experience, and when we go to the mainland, you would be one of the first to go. Also, please don't repeat this to anyone, but there might be other opportunities in the service of the Secret Service I can't elaborate on now, as exciting as any department we have." She let the words sink in. Rosen just looked down, so Gower continued slowly taking it as a sign that she was reluctant but agreeable. Deborah liked the obstinate implication of Maria, but wasn't fully invested and didn't see the point of it all.

Half reading from the folder on her desk, "You were born in the coastal town of Faro, in the Algarve region of Southern Portugal, then as a baby, moving to and growing up in New Mexico in the States. Your parents met in San Francisco at the World's Fair, as college students celebrating the opening of the Panama Canal. They were born in 1887 and shared a picnic table during a luncheon on the grounds of the Golden Gate Park. He was a student intern for the Portuguese Attaché while she was a sophomore at the University of California, at Berkeley. They kept in touch and returned to Portugal where you were born, then returned to the States where your father was employed with the state's finance department in

Albuquerque where you grew up, then on to Lancaster as an independent accountant.

"You will soon have three new passports; American, French, and Portuguese. All three could come in handy later in the war should you get to the mainland. In a few days, Mary will give you a call to pick these papers up and walk you through them to see if you have any questions. We are putting a new Pilot's Logbook together for you, with starting hours and pertinent comments with a stamp of 'Lost Logbook' imprinted on the fist page. Your beginning flight hours and experience summary will be true to your real logbook and with my signature on the first page, you won't have any problems.

"Additionally, your correspondence will have to agree with your new identity and finally, your parents will receive by courier, a summary of these plans. I am sure they will agree and understand these unusual precautions, for which by the way, we would not have gone to all these troubles if you weren't such a top-notch pilot. It did not miss my notice on the report of your dead-stick landing of that Harvard at Dorval. That feat puts you in the rare company of talented and instinctive aviators.

"Read the materials over when you get them, and keep the information on Portugal and New Mexico. We have a French and Spanish language specialist to get your language skills up to speed, right after you complete your first conversion at Luton. Your new passports and other personal information documents will be backdated to go into your old file when we receive them from Montreal. They will be kept in London until after the war. Any questions?"

"I guess I am Catholic?" "Right you are. You will find your cross and St. Christopher's necklaces in your packet, and if I may, I will relieve you of your Star of David, if you are wearing one. You will receive a summary of the four-part Catholic Catechism to learn: the elements of the Sacraments, Creeds, Commandments, and Prayers. You will need to be very familiar with all four."

Deborah felt like part of her was leaving her body when she handed her silver chain and Star of David pendant to Pauline. Gower slowly and gently closed her hand and said, "Don't worry, Miss Fuentes, I will personally protect this. You are simply loaning the symbol of your Judaism for safe keeping, not abandoning your faith. We will honor Shabbat for you and introduce you to a plainclothes Rabbi who lives in the area for you to visit as needed, like Saturday evenings for Shabbat dinner while I am attending Saturday mass. He's young and most handsome, so rumors will be not of your religion but of your chastity." They both blushed. "No one can take your faith from you, my dear."

Her smile restored what had forsaken the 20-year-old American, a distant 3,500 miles from Eastern Pennsylvania. "Why me? I am sure you don't go through all this fuss for all the Jewish women." "That's a keen observation Miss Ro.., I mean Miss Fuentes." "Su nada, Commander. I took three terms of Spanish and French in college, but haven't had a chance to use either." They both got a smile from the spontaneous though brief Spanish.

"Maria, as to your question of why you. I should have explained all this in better detail, and for that I apologize. What I am going to say must stay between the two of us. From information passed on from Montreal, this office is aware of the service of your father in World War One. There is a movement in fact, to have his fifth victory confirmed by virtue of his character and spotless reputation. It may take a while, but the outcome should be to his favor.

"If the Allies continue to gain ground over the next several months, with your skills we are persuaded that you would be one of a handful of women who could be approved to ferry into France and possibly into Germany. It's all speculation, but I wanted to mention it for you think about as you progress through our training and your ferrying duties. That's basically it. Until your official records are received, I will continue to create a temporary file the administrator mentioned two days ago. You will get a notice from my office regarding your ration card, health card, form N.S.2, gas mask, parachute, and kit."

Gower took one long look at her new American and chuckled to herself at Maria's innocent face. It was dotted with just enough freckles to call her new ethnicity into question, and the deep auburn hair was just the right shade. "If there aren't any further questions, then welcome to Maidenhead. We will reach out to Opal Anderson and Nancy Miller, as they need to know of this change, as they knew you as Deborah. I have to keep moving, so Mary will get you shuttled to our Squadron Leader, Nigel Sheffield. You will like him. He was one of our heroes during the Battle of Britain. He will brief you, then direct you to the Chief Instructor who will get you scheduled and into the ATA stream." "I'm sorry, you said, 'kit'. What's a kit?" Pauline laughed and assured Maria she would get to know all about the kit.

Nigel Sheffield was a tall one, his fitness accented by the wide blue belt wrapping several inches above the bottom of his tunic. His waistline reminded her of the Royal Canadian Mounted Police she saw in Montreal, even to the calf-high boots. In addition to the RAF gold wings over his left pocket and three rows of battle ribbons below that, both sleeves were decorated with two broad silver stripes with a narrow one in the middle, for Squadron Leader.

The epaulets on his shoulders featured an ornate blend of stripes in grey and blue-green. He had a narrow face with a David Niven style moustache, and a soft smile creating two shallow dimples. A soft cast wrapped his left hand and his right cradled a curved-stem pipe. Deborah loved the smell, like a Dutch oven apple cobbler in a wood-burning fireplace. With the benefit of a full night's rest the evening before and the reassuring meeting with Miss Gower, she was much steadier on her feet.

"So here we are, Miss Fuentes." He let her name hang in the air for just a few seconds to let the new name sink in. "I won't keep you long, but I did want to go over a few important items before I send you over to Luton to see where to put you. We think you will likely move right up in just a few days. So, how are you getting on? Getting adjusted to the English weather and our jolly ways?" "I am doing fine, Sir. I was a bit jumpy because of some personal record irregularities, but Commander Gower is sorting it all out. I am anxious to get on with the training."

"Quite right, Miss Fuentes, as we are all anxious to see what you can do. Our Commandant Miss Gower has high hopes for you, even with your missing file situation. Don't let it be a bother." "No pressure, sir. She will be expecting me to breeze through all these loud noisy airplanes, and right now I am scared as the devil of the really big ones!" Sheffield laughed so hard, his pipe popped onto the floor and spun on its bowl like a top. "Oops, sorry about that. I am not laughing at you, but at the memory of how petrified I was the first time I crawled into my first *Hawker Hurricane*. My knees knocked so loudly, I sounded like a wooden puppet, like Pinocchio maybe?" Maria smiled. She liked this man. He seems perfect for the job and the women will like him too.

"As to the other question, why are you here? Maria thought for a minute. "Sir, I really haven't studied my motives, but I am probably like a lot of the women who are here. At first I just wanted to fly big airplanes. It's just a passion. When I heard about the ATA, I felt moved to at least try and apply. Right now we have nothing like the ATA in the U.S. It sounded so exciting. War was a vague word to me, but after walking around London the other day, I realized your British civilians deserve some help and relief from their suffering. Secondly, I want retribution for my brother serving with the Marines in the Pacific. He's been missing in action while fighting off the first Japanese air attack on the islands of Midway. If ferrying airplanes help your RAF guys and our bombers to dish out a lot more damage, then great.

"It's a vicarious work, maybe, but nonetheless, even a little payback is a satisfying. And sir, I know I am merely a wee part of this huge war effort, but I still want to make a contribution. The fear of living under Japanese or Nazi rule is real. There has been too much blood spilled in your country over the years and now mine in Hawaii for the freedoms we enjoy. It's quite simple. If every German airplane factory or ammunition dump I, in some indirect way, help the RAF destroy and indirectly saves one of our boys somewhere, somehow, I'm satisfied. That's about all I can say about your question."

The Flight Lieutenant took his time repacking

and relighting his curved stemmed briar, sucking the last of the match's flame into the pipe's bowl. This he would hold tightly in his teeth to keep from repeating its last adventure. He shook the match out and lifted his brow. "Miss Rosen, I mean Miss Fuentes, your eloquently spoken motives are not unlike many of the other candidates who have brothers, cousins, or even fathers, already lost in this nasty war. You seem to have a clear vision of being involved in something important and bigger than yourself. I do wish you get your brave brother back in fine health, and soon.

"Welcome aboard! You may go now, but you are always free to knock on my door. We are a small family, and you should never hesitate to do so. Check in at our Admin Office, and they will arrange for your transportation to Luton, where you will meet your instructor and begin your training. Do you have any questions?" "I do in fact, if you have another minute. I know you are terribly busy." "Not to worry about my schedule, Miss Ros.., um, Miss Fuentes. My recent time has been on the ground, so I am clear for another ten or fifteen minutes. How can I help?"

"Sir, Commander Gower mentioned something about your highly regarded service during the Battle of Britain. I keep hearing and have read accounts of that battle, so could you share a bit of your firsthand experience? Those ribbons on your chest aren't for good conduct, I am quite sure."

Caught off guard, Nigel looked down and became less buoyant, turning a bit serious. He studied the floor then looked through the small window to his left. Facing his student with a kind smile he spoke. "Miss Fuentes, I seldom talk of my personal flying experiences, as most of my RAF mates did so much more, and too many made dreadful life sacrifices for

England. It's a deeply personal and frightful business, with most of our daily chatter only superficial, just of what our next assignment might bring. How much do you know about this particular battle?"

"Only that RAF aviators defeated the German bombers and kept Hitler from an invasion." "All right then, I might be able to fill in a few details." She shifted on her seat so as not to miss every sylable.

"I did fly missions from *Spitfire* Squadron 610 out of Biggin Hill. Being near Kent, a mere 18 miles south of London and near the coastline, Biggin took the brunt of the German attacks. From mid June until late September, we patrolled along the southern sector trying to protect the ship convoys and airfields from mostly *Junkers JU-88s*, and a few *Dornier 17s*.

"On July 10, the Luftwaffe intensified their raids, a date suggested as the first day of the Battle of Britain. Our radar spotted a large group of bombers headed to our convoys destined from the estuary of the Thames to Dover. For some reason the bombers had no escorts, assuming our fighter fleet was exhausted. We intercepted and drove them back without any ship losses. They came back an hour later, this time with *Me-109* escorts. Nonetheless, we drove them back again; same for the last raid late in the afternoon. At the end of the day we lost no ships, only 6 fighters, while the proud Luftwaffe lost 13. As if they didn't realize we were getting the best of them, they came back the next day, losing 11 airplanes while we lost just 4. This back and forth continued the rest of the month. Thanks to the radar stations and coastal guard, we always met them before they crossed the channel. We sent the minimum number of *Hurricanes* and *Spits* needed to disrupt their bombers, avoiding their fighters as much as possible.

"From August 12 until month's end, they stepped up their raids, the heaviest on the 30th and 31st. Each morning, Fighter Command would fly two squadrons from each of our four fighter groups, then add needed fighters as sectors were identified to be targets by radar and coastal observers.

"Then, on September 15, the biggest day of the Battle, the Germans were determined to attack London again and draw us into the air. Our squadron was assigned over Canterbury at 25,000 feet to meet the German *109s* escorting their *Heinkels*. We sent up just over 600 *Hurricanes* and a handful of *Spits* into the teeth of a like number of German escort fighters protecting the swarm of bombers. Most of us flew at least two missions, more often three or four, especially that day. The first of five attacks started about noon. We turned them back with a surprising number of *Hurricanes* and *Spits*. The next wave was heavily escorted, this time blocking us with their *109's*. As the day wore on however, we were able to break through and do some damage. The last feeble wave came at 5:30 trying unsuccessfully to bomb Southampton and the *Spitfire* shop at nearby Woolsey.

"When the day was over, we had shot down or severely damaged 55 or 56 German aircraft losing less than 30 of our own. Unfortunately, I was one of those shot down, having to bail out late in the afternoon over Romney Marsh in East Sussex. At least I had the satisfaction of putting three of their precious *109's* into the channel and destroying two of their *Heinkels*. That day our RAF changed Hitler's plans to attack the mainland. That's about it, Miss."

Spellbound, all she could say was, "Oh." When she regained her composure she continued, "Thank you sir, thank you very much. I have another question, then I'll be on my way. What does Ather..hmm, Athter." Sheffield helped out. "Do you mean our motto, *Aetheris Avidi?*" She nodded. "It means Eager for the Air." "Perfect, it suits me like a warm sweater! I have to go now, do I salute?" By his laugh, she knew the answer and backed out and, when clear of the office, she skipped a step, then headed resolutely to the Administrative Office to take the first step to become *Aetheris Avidi.* Sheffield liked this woman. The woman liked this officer.

As she half stumbled and walked on the uneven cobblestone walkways to the Admin Office, a handful of tears betrayed her real fears. She was apprehensive and worried sick about Edward. She checked in with the Administrative Officer, collected her uniform and kit, got properly signed in, then hopped into a waiting lorry taking her and several other passengers to Upavon. They sat with an RAF flight cadet struggling with his training that had been reassigned to the ATA, then a wounded soldier to be dropped at a larger aid station, two women from the WAAF, and two ATA pilots.

"Hi, my name is Alexandra." As the lorry lurched from the dirt road to a smoother roadway, Maria, with left hand securing her hat, extended her right. "Hi, mine's De.., urr, name's Maria, Maria Fuentes." "Pleased to meet you, Maria." With her teeth gleaming, "A Yank, huh? We are going to get along just great. Going to Luton I hope. ATA?" Maria nodded. "You will likely run into Miss Gower. She's our boss. She's a great lady and hell of a pilot. See you around I am sure."

The handsome girl in the back corner of the lorry reached forward to both girls with her hand extended, "Hi, my name's Carli Banks. I guess we are all heading to the same party."

All for one and one for all, the women would be inextricably connected in the most unexpected ways in their dreadful time in the nasty war. Not all of the women in that lorry would survive it.

CHAPTER FIVE

Black Honey

Carli Banks was born into the modest family of Virginia and Rollie Banks in early 1919 during a freezing rainstorm, 45 miles South of Buffalo in Dunkirk, New York. Dunkirk served as a minor railroad hub and steamship port on Lake Erie with roughly 20,00 citizens. Carli's father was a supervisor for Brooks Locomotive Works, located on 20 acres just east of town. Rollie had steadily worked up the employee ladder since joining Brooks in 1899. His eagerness and ability to learn quickly impressed Horatio Brooks, who admired the plucky black man. Brooks ultimately gave Rollie the responsibility of the huge foundry building that housed the two boiler shops, machine shop, carpenter shop, and steam powerhouse among others. The 100 foot high building rambling over an acre was the edifice of Rollie's pride.

Carli's mild olive complexion and smooth hair was just enough for her to 'pass' as a white girl and woman. With roughly 900 blacks in the community, most hovering just below the poverty line, Carli knew how lucky she was to be under the love and protection of her mom and highly respected dad.

Carli enjoyed her school and town shops in Dunkirk, as the town's attitude toward the Negro was quite benign compared to the vitriolic south, still smarting over losing the Civil War ending only two generations ago. The people of the south continued to treat the often-bewildered blacks poorly, not able to assimilate into society with their sudden freedom. Most had no money or other resources to give them real freedom, causing many to drift back into an uneasy indentured service. All too often it was with previous masters who treated them as dreadfully as they had before the bloody war, a conflict designed to give them the rights and opportunities of white counterparts, a flawed concept. In the south, post-war blacks had it quite a bit rougher than those in the north. Carli knew only by listening to conversations between her parents that her lot was infinitely better than others of her color.

Rollie watched as his daughter was just sliding off the steps of a locomotive engine in greasy striped overalls with black oil easing down the left side of her cheek. He did a double take to be sure it was his daughter. Nodding towards the offices, "Let's go over there, away from these loud trains. Just for a minute." Both now settled on a newly finished wood slat bench facing Lake Erie, Rollie put his arm around Carli as she laid her head on his shoulder like always.

"When did you cut your hair, Carli? It's so short." "Well, we are at the beginning of summer and you know how hot it gets. 'Sides, my hair gets in my way." "It's okay, Kitten. I would love you no less of you were bald." They both chuckled.

"Carli, honey, what do you want to be when you grow up? You know that isn't too far off." She turned her face up and looked at him with a surprised expression. "Why are you asking? You know I want to be a locomotive engineer." "No, honey, *you* talked about it. Here's my idea, Speedy. That job might not be the best fit for you." "But daaady," she drug out. "You know how I am about girlie stuff. I love trains."

Carli was the apple of Rollie's eye, but he couldn't quite get a fix on her teenage psyche. She never liked playing with girlie dolls, but she privately would put boy clothes on the girl dolls and vise versa. Then she played like they kissed. That always puzzled Rollie and Virginia. Carli was emulating mom and dad they surmised. She was cuddly soft at home but when outdoors, she was often trolled for a pick-up football game against ruffians agreeing to play only because she had the football. She often came in dirty and smelly as a downstate polecat. She would clean up with every perfume and lotion in her bathroom as well as her mom's. Throw into that mix, mostly all A's in school, a permanent smile, and a full measure of early sexual awareness, that would be Carli Banks.

"Beautiful, you are 17 now and need to start thinking about what's next. Black girls out here don't get too many choices, same for stunning ones like you. Pretty don't matter, only your color matters. You can count on house keeping, bar hopping in Buffalo, or worse. I know you like trains, but I have an idea. You are a quick thinker and have the hand-eye coordination of a juggler. What would you think about flying, serious flying? Talented pilots make a lot of money and get to travel like you always talked about. Heck, I heard they make over $200 a week!" Carli's eyes widened. "Plus, you can always hop trains if you get bored. You can still go to Erie for two years then D'Youville for a degree. What do you think?"

Carli jumped as stung by a bumblebee. "You are kidding, Dad, really?" Her giant hug was her answer. Only Rollie Banks would have thought a black teen-age girl could be taking flying lessons. He knew his daughter.

She did just that at nearby Werle Airfield in Sheridan, while attending Erie Junior College and later at D'Youville in West Buffalo. Carli's father had met and later called on an old friend, Eugene

Bullard, for his help in letting Carli have her dream. Although Bullard was a southerner, he was only one of two black aviators in WWI and was known from coast to coast in the black community. Bullard volunteered on October 2, 1916, to join the French Air Service as an air gunner, going through training at the Aerial Gunnery School in the south of France. Later he was assigned to the Escadrille N.93 based in the south to Verdun, where he stayed until mid September. His squadron was equipped with *Nieuport-16* and *Spad-VII* bi-planes, strutting their French identity by showing off flying duck nose-art. His legend grew and grew to the benefit of Carli who vowed to get his autograph first thing after she soloed at Werle Airfield.

Carli would have gotten that autograph too, but she got a wee bit distracted by changes in her flavors in life. As a late teen she began to share her flying time with the tempting nightlife in Buffalo, with its bars, clubs, back rooms, and Laissez-faire for appetites of the flesh.

At *Danny Winter's* Bar and *Ralph Martin's* the action was deafening, even for Carli. Her curiosity began at *Ann Montgomery's Little Harlem Hotel.* They attracted a constant stream of celebrities and entertainers, like Louie Armstrong, Billie Holiday, Count Basie, Bing Crosby, Sarah Vaughn, Lena Horne, and Sammy Davis Jr. They made Buffalo a favorite on the 'Chitlin Circuit'. The list of celebrities who performed at or visited the *Montgomery* from the mid-1930's was endless, but not surprisingly so since Buffalo sported a half million busy citizens, strongly represented in number by energetic blacks.

During Carli's teens, Buffalo was the 8th largest city in the country, the largest inland port, and boasted of more millionaires than any city in America. Buffalo was the perfect crucible for exploring sensual identity and pleasures. That true, there was an unfair supposition of the "Clubs" by those who never entered, as a cocktail party of lurid lasciviousness and drinking with intense music. In fact it was simply a time to unbuckle the belt of self-consciousness and have a good time. It was men and women paring with every combination of the gender that the number of two would permit. Venues like *Ryan's*, *Martins,* and the like, was the default meeting ground for Buffalo's community leaders, judges, lawyers, doctors, politicians, steel workers, cabbies, news media, and people of all races and positions. It was a place where customers were treated like family; where the bar's staff memorized favorite drinks who began to mix and shake immediately upon seeing the club's regulars step inside. They were the taverns and clubs where everybody loved everybody. Loved stretch out to the subculture of blue-collar black gays who just wanted some fun where it was safe from street toughs.

At 18, Carli passed for 21, allowing her to frequent many of the 'shakin and movin' bars of Buffalo. Women were safe then, at least from the police who were paid off by the bars or clubs to leave the clients alone. On a cold blustery winter's night Carli graduated from high school. She darted straight into the shadows of *Ryan's*, the bar famous for beautiful showgirls and overall action. Most of the women were upscale and discreet. She had been to *Dugan's,* the *Mardi Gras,* and the *Chesterfield*, but *Eddie Ryan's Hotel* was the best. There were always wall-to-wall women on weekends, relatively safe from the toughs.

When Carli wanted loud and glamorous, the popular *Ralph Martins* on Ellicott and Seneca, dubbed *The Club* was just the ticket. Opened in the mid 1930s, it always accepted a gay and lesbian clientele with open arms. In fact, *Ralph Martins* was well known for its vibrant, cross-dressing scene that straight Buffalo natives came to see and revel in. Same-sex dancing was allowed, even encouraged, but in the back room where drag shows were staged, and patrons who were too tired or drunk to get home could sleep overnight in the booths.

For slow dancing and quiet, it was *Bingo's* for Carli and her new 'Snookum Doll', Emily Jolie. The especially striking Carli drifted against the grain of her conscience and parental guidance for her private life. That, and images of electric women in her erotic dreams swept her to Emily. The haunting smells, music, and laughter was the spellbinding trolley that stopped at *Bingos*, the favorite smoky den in Buffalo for native, Emily Jolie. Emily and Carli held hands as they sat at the only small table for two. Carli's spirit always warmed when Emily held her hand. "Why don't you come with me, Cheri?" The French accent all but melted Carli. "I.., I can't Emily, my dad wouldn't approve."

"Listen, Carli, you have as many hours in the *Gypsy Moth* as I do. I know you would be accepted to travel to Montreal and try out. You are 18 going on 19 and by the time you actually get to England, nearly 20. What do you think?" The idea of going to England and joining the air transport people to ferry big loud airplanes around England and maybe even France excited Carli almost as much as Emily. "I'll talk to my dad and we'll see." "Let's go back to my place and see if we can't turn your 'let's see' up a notch."

Carli's father was a realist and was aware he couldn't keep his daughter home forever. He also knew that she would not likely be accepted into the American contingent trying for 40 slots to travel to England and be a part of Britain's ferrying duties for women. He didn't know anything about it, but doubted Carli had the skill or experience, so he agreed she could go if she was called. What Rollie didn't know was that General Robert Olds was on a quest to find women with over 350 hours solo time to supplement ferrying duties in the U.S. by way of England. Women like Carli were exactly what he was looking for. Rollie underestimated his daughter and his well-meaning plan backfired.

Carli and Emily both prevailed in Montreal, flying the military trainer *Harvard*, the Canadian RAF version of the Air Force's *Texan* trainer. Emily had the pleasure of flying with Ansel Gautier, with his thick French accent suiting her just fine. Emily, from the French Colony of the Ivory Coast, it felt like being home. It was ATA Brit Captain Charlie Smith who scrutinized Carli's flying. They were housed in the same room at the Mount Royal Hotel, but were so busy they had no alone time. When they both successfully completed the tryouts, they were notified to collect their belongings and report to the peninsula port city of Halifax, affectionately called the Warden of the North, for transport to England. After a three-day wait, the girls managed to hitch a ride on *HMS Longfoot*, watching the mooring lines being tossed aside on Feb 15, 1942. They were naturally pleased to find themselves assigned to the same cabin.

After a quick stop in Halifax, they arrived in Liverpool on March 7th spending one restful night at the Adelphi Hotel, before proceeding to London the next morning. Later in the evening, the relationship hit a landmine as Emily tearfully read a telegram requesting her to proceed to her uncle's home near Abidjan on the Ivory Coast ASAP. It was a wire calling for Emily's help from dangers to the family of Nazi brutality in Algeria and Tangiers. The tears of both young women became a river of anguish.

"Emily do you have to go. Isn't there anyone else who can go for you?" Rubbing her fingers through Carli's shiny black hair and wiping her tears with the back of her thumb, "My dearest, if it were only so." They vowed that at war's end Carli would make it to Abidjan for them to be together. The last night the two were bound as one keeping warm and determined to make the night not their last together.

After getting to London with only one night on the town, it was cruel adieus and broken hearts for the two in Chelsea that evening in the gloomy winter of 1942.

Carli Banks was alone now. No dad for guidance and no mate for comfort and love. She tucked her hair into her 'special bought' fashionable tan velvet beret, found transportation, and checked into Maidenhead's RAF White Waltham airfield. The only person who would know that she was a Negro was the administrator that checked her in, and he didn't notice or wouldn't have cared anyway. He knew that war blanched skin color as a melting pot come together to fight hate and murder of Nazi Germany.

CHAPTER SIX

Swimming at Midway

In April 1942, Second Lieutenant Edward Rosen proudly received his Wings of Gold as a new Marine Aviator at the Marine Corps Air Station in Cherry Point, North Carolina. As the Lieutenant was massaging his hung-over temples the next morning, he read orders to make haste and join Marine Squadron 221 on the remote Islands of Midway, halfway between San Francisco and Tokyo.

After three weeks on the transport ship USS *Fuller*, the young aviator had time to think and write letters to his parents and sister. Evenings, he often leaned over the ship's rail to drink in the cool Pacific air, speculating how he would handle aerial combat. Warming his hands around the USS *Fuller* coffee cup, he leaned over the side of the ship watching its bow carve deeply into the ocean. The wake revealed a peculiar iridescent spray reminding him of catching fireflies with his sister Deborah back in Lancaster. The Marine pondered his own possible death, like being trapped in a fiery cockpit or simply being eviscerated by a Japanese fighter. When he shared his troubling thoughts with the Navy Chaplain, he felt better knowing he wasn't alone with those fears.

Thirteen days later, after a brief refueling stop in Pearl Harbor, the *Fuller* dropped anchor 100 yards just outside the heart-shaped coral reef surrounding the atoll of the Midway Islands. The two inhabited islands, Sand and Eastern, were the home of the Marine airbase and its long 8,000-foot runway.

When Edward set his sea legs on Eastern Island,

he remembered why anyone would want to inhabit this desolate place. Sand Island seemed even bleaker. He knew instinctively it was like other small innocuous islands dotting the Pacific; it was the strategic airfields and submarine bases.

Edward was directed to his tent, one of many scattered along the runway, to drop his sea bag and freshen up. Forty-five minutes later he was escorted to the Quonset hut of commanding officer and Missourian, Major Floyd Parks. After tapping on the doorframe, he heard the military, "Enter." Parks had one foot on a chair and fist under his chin staring at a sprawling map of the ocean with dots, swirling arrows, and dashed lines in two colors. Parks stood and greeted his new aviator with a big smile extending his hand. When they shook, Edward was overwhelmed by the Major's presence. Parks, a graduate of the Naval Academy, still had the powerful physique developed during his football and water polo years. His flaming shock of ruddy hair explained why the men referred to the popular commanding officer. as "Red."

"Welcome to Gooneyville and the *221 Fighting Falcons*, Lieutenant. How was your ride over?" "Thanks, pleased to be aboard, sir. The trip was tiresome as would be expected and I hope to stop swaying back and forth soon." "Your records show you began flight school in Georgia. As an ex-instructor, I am curious about your overall training experience."

"Yes sir, I reported to Athens for preflight, then on to Pensacola for Basic Training. My favorite instructor was Captain Merriman, James, I think. He pounded me like a piece of fresh meat, but all for the best. He was amazing with an airplane, even in the old *Stearman Kaydet* that we flew. Luck had it that he was transferred to Corpus, where I followed for advanced training, flying the *Vultee SNV*. We all called it the *Vibrator*. I had several hours with Merriman in that airplane building on the foundation he gave me in Texas. Each hop with him taught me a lot. Gave me big chunks of confidence. When I moved on to Cherry Point for *Wildcat* training, I did well, thanks to him. It would have been such an honor for Captain Merriman to pin my wings on."

"Lieutenant, I need to ask how much time you logged in the *Wildcat* or even the *Buffalo?*" "Sir, none in the *Buffalo,* but I had twelve hours in the *Wildcat*, over half the time in combat training." "How well did you score?" "To be truthful sir, not bad. After my first hop of aerial gunnery, I had trouble even seeing the 'sock'. After that I had high scores. During the air-to-air hassles, I was never in trouble and on my opponent's six nearly every time." "Good to hear, Rosen. I am going to put you with squadron leader Captain Carey as sixth man in his Fifth Division. He can use a good man, as most of his pilots haven't any experience at all, much less fire their guns."

He alerted Rosen that the air raid sirens to scramble could shriek without warning and happen at any time day or night. His words came in loud and clear that practicing being dressed in 30 seconds and into full flight gear in one minute or less would not be a waste of time. Parks leveled with him right away about the seriousness of protecting the islands' airfield from Japanese airpower. Parks ended the brief meeting reminding Edward that over half of VMF-221 was like Edward, fresh from training at San Diego or Cherry Point and no operational experience. Edward put Park's two and two together and the answer was Japan to be heavily favored when confronted.

Ed was dismissed to his tent, sharing with his immediate boss, Captain John Carey. Ed was unloading his duffle bag when Carey pulled back the flap and introduced himself. "You're new, Lieutenant?" "Yes sir, straight from Cherry Point. How about you, sir?" "Nothing special, Lieutenant. Just a survivor I guess. Been here and there, nothing to write home about."

With only a few weeks of combat training in the Navy hand-me-down Grumman made *F4F Wildcats*, Ed joined another two-dozen fresh pilots preparing to defend Midway. His aircraft was a rugged 300 MPH fighter that carried 7,000 pounds of man, fuel and armament with a range of over 800 miles. Although not as nimble as the faster Japanese *Zero*, the Marines would have to rely on surprise and combat experience to have a chance, neither of which they had that day.

Early in the morning on June 4th, one of the Navy's *Catalina* seaplane scouts spotted one of the Japanese strike-force aircraft carriers known to be in the area, as well as recently launched bombers and fighter escorts, 100 plus. American radar stations confirmed the small air invasion from the northwest at 11,000 feet, 150 miles away, then relayed to Midway radio operators the critical information including the estimated number of airplanes and time to Midway. The 28 strong contingent of Marine pilots had overly ambitious plans for Admiral Chūichi Nagumo's carriers and their pilots planning to bomb Midway's Eastern and Sand Islands. The Japanese were looking for revenge for the unexpected American ferocity during the Battle of the Coral Sea a month earlier. Edward and the others had barely a week to prepare for the fight of their lives. With expert eyes aboard the *Catalina* revealing large clusters of radar blips, Parks knew to be prepared for at least 100 Japanese bombers and escort fighters.

On June 4th at 05:25 hours, Edward and his tent-mate Captain Carey were jarred awake by the airfield's piercing air raid sirens. The alert was punctuated by the squadron duty officer 2nd Lieutenant John Musselman, speeding along the runway boundary yelling "Get Airborne! Get Airborne!" Parks and Rosen scrambling to find a bush or bare spot just behind their tents, took a quick morning pee. Zipping up their flight suits with flight bags under their arms, the men made it to their *Wildcat* Fighters in less than five minutes, five minutes they couldn't afford to lose. On the crowded taxiway, aircrews were already by their airplanes preparing to get their pilots strapped in and airborne. This morning would be a bare knuckled affair.

Major Parks, in one of his 21 obsolete *Brewster Buffalos* and seven *Wildcats*, scrambled into their airplanes and into the air to meet the horde of Jap fighters. They joined together in five, four-man groups, and a section of two in a loose vee shape, one on the left side of the leader and the other two on the right side. They joined in formation climbing to 14,000 feet as the atoll of the tiny two islands slipped behind and below becoming mere specks. As they headed northwest into the belly of the enemy, Parks admonished, "Wingmen stay with your leaders, and leaders don't shoot until you can see the gold in their teeth. Look low, as we should have the advantage, at least on the first pass. Stay tight with eyes on the sky. Stay off the radios unless it is important and use short bursts. You will need every bullet today! Good luck and God be with you." Parks knew that when the first machine gun was fired, the chatter would be crazy. He wasn't wrong.

As the rising sun cast its ochre glow on Edward's right cheek and flying helmet, the neophyte warrior maneuvered his seat a bit lower and tightened his harness. Airborne for only twenty minutes, he felt the sweat in his helmet trickle down his forehead and over his goggles. After trying to wipe his goggles with his sleeve, he flipped his arming switch of all four Browning machine guns, each with 450 rounds per magazine. He snapped his oxygen mask on tight as he knew there would be no time for that right soon. He was the rear wingman on the right, responsible for the protection of his leader and wingman slightly above and ahead, another tenderfoot to combat, but slightly senior in rank. The airmen headed straight for the large hoard of bombers and *Zeroes*, with their groups flying staggered 1,000 feet intervals from 8,000 to 12,000 feet. Navy Scouts reported the Japs at 11,000 feet, which would give Parks the edge if the report were accurate.

American Task Force 16's Commander Admiral Spruance and his staff aboard the carrier *Enterprise* listened on the combat frequency to hear what was to be the beginning of an aerial rout. They were informed by Navy intelligence the Japanese had launched 36 '*Val*' *Achi-D3A* dive-bombers and 36 *Nakajima* '*Kate*' torpedo bombers, escorted 36 Zeros.

Edward's tent-mate and Fifth Division Leader, Captain John Carey, barked first. "Tally-ho, bombers at angels one two, accompanied by *Zeros* ten o'clock low, meatballs galore." Carey pointed his nose down closing quickly on the formation. In less than a minute he poured all four .50 caliber machine guns into one of the Japanese *Kates*. Just before the torpedo-bomber exploded, the rear gunner managed to crack Carey's windshield with a desperate burst of machine gun fire. Millisecond later, his *F4F Wildcat* was raked by another *Zero* that put bullets into Carey's knee and leg. In excruciating pain, he dove, scooted into a cloudbank, and headed back to Midway. When Edward didn't see Carey's number two man, he followed Carey and his attacker through the first melée chasing both into the clouds.

Parks and the rest of the squadron were still two thousand feet above and just ahead where Edward pointed his *Wildcat* to rejoin the group. As he approached, he heard Major Parks barking orders for his division and the remnants of Edward's Fifth. "Orange, Yellow, and Blue Groups follow me down and to port, while the rest get to your altitude ASAP and make your approach to starboard. Find a bomber and put it in the water, out." The radio was quiet then hissed again. "Look out, Blue Two, break right!" Before the *Buffalo* could get his turn started, a rain of tracers pounded the nose, engine, and cockpit. It spun around its axis and exploded into shards of metal, fire and humanity. "Red Four, you have a bogie at five o'clock low."

Edward thought, 'That's me', as he jerked the *Wildcat* into a steep climb making a firing pass on a turning *Zero* while gaining altitude. Tracer bullets zipped past his canopy clipping the trailing edge of his left wing. The hydraulics and cables that controlled his flaps had been hit, making evading the *Zero* difficult. As hard as Edward wrestled with his control stick and rudder, his damaged airplane simply wouldn't respond to his control commands. Just as he was getting ready to open his canopy, another *Zero* wandered from his left across his field of vision at about 100 yards, unaware of Ed's *Wildcat*. Edward managed a burst of cannon just long enough to destroy the *Zero's* canopy and its driver. The mortally damaged *Zero* made a lazy turn downward, and while Edward, curious to see the final splash was still under fire from the frantic *Zero* behind him.

He felt a hard punch that quickly turned into a hot sting on the outside of his left shoulder. In spite of the pain and uncooperative left arm, Edward finally got his stubborn canopy open with his right. He rolled sideways, left wing down, then slipped out of the cockpit, his dog tag chain violently grabbing the metal sheath that connected the windshield to the frame of the fuselage. The snag pulled his head into another part of the canopy causing him to almost blackout. After sliding off the wing, he could barely pull his ripcord, then became limp. Edward's lifeless body floated as a pendulum through a sky covered with crisscrossed contrails.

Black smoke trailed dying airplanes as human parts and machine debris rained downward to the sea and to their graves on the murky bottom three miles below the surface. Edward left a blemished heaven of dirty bruises as he splashed yet another welt on the battle-weary ocean. He became one of the missing or dead that day, as only 14 of the 26 Marines returned to Midway, with several of those wounded. Edward's boss, the wounded and bleeding Captain Carey, was able to return to the airfield with a handful of the fortunate few. Their fearless and brave commanding officer, Colonel Parks, was listed as shot down and presumed dead. A few pilot reports indicated that he and Lt. Martin Mahannah, wingman for Lt. Charles Kuntz, parachuted from their damaged *Buffalos*, then were strafed by the blood thirsty Japanese, a gruesome custom they observed throughout the war.

It was clear that the Marine pilots had been outnumbered and overwhelmed by the fierce *Zero* fighters escorting the bombers of Vice Admiral Nagumo's first attack wave on Midway. The Navy and Marine Anti-Aircraft gunners had been watching the lopsided air battle, then leapt into action shooting down two of the bombers, preventing complete destruction to Eastern and Sand Islands. In spite of the Midway gunners, the Japanese bombers flattened the airfield, leaving a laundry, one oil storage tank, and a seaplane hangar intact. The American Marines and Navy had just lost the first battle of the Pacific War.

After Edward's sagging figure splashed into the water, his head was tilted back, slightly above the lapping waves of the Pacific, was held steady by the thick collar of his Mae West life jacket. Further to the south, the destroyer USS *Hammann,* was part of an escort group that was protecting the aircraft carrier *Yorktown*. As Edward floated helplessly in the rubbish littered ocean, the forward lookout and port quartermaster lookouts both reported the downed aviator straight ahead. The Officer-of-the-Deck ordered the helmsman, "Hard right rudder." He turned to the Boatswain Mate of the Watch, "Make your speed five knots." The engine order telegraph was pulled back and forward alerting the crew in the engine department with its engine order telegraph, to spin steam valves, causing other gear to reduce speed.

As the ship inched closer to the floating aviator, the crew lowered its port lifeboat in record time. The Captain, Commander Arnold True and his Officer-of-the-Deck, watched from the bridge through his binoculars as the small boat approached the floating figure. After easing Edward into the boat, the lifeboat turned back to the destroyer. As the lifeboat was being hoisted aboard the ship, the Officer-of-the-Deck ordered the ship back on course and ahead with full speed to resume its protective station with its carrier *Yorktown*, still under constant attack from Japanese *Val* dive-bombers. Ed's fight had matured into a serious battle of worldwide titans. The Captain turned to the Officer-of-the-Deck. "You have the Conn, Lieutenant. I'll be in Sickbay and will be back in a jiffy."

"I have the Conn, Sir." True exchanged salutes and headed below decks to see firsthand the condition of this downed aviator. The marine was still alive, miraculously surviving the shark infested Pacific for at least four hours. After cleaning most of the fallen pilot's wounds and providing a saline IV hydration, Edward was given crushed ammonia salts to jolt him awake. Edward had a nasty cut on his head above his hairline scabbed over with a glob of dried blood matting his hair. Ed's neck was cut and his left side was severely bruised. His left foot had been twisted or broken, probably from another contact with the airplane on the way out. The worst was a long burn and gash on the fleshy part of his left shoulder, still oozing. "Where am I? What happened to me?" As Edward lay on the medical room gurney, he was covered with only a lightweight blanket and pair of borrowed skivvies.

The Chief Petty Officer and hospital corpsman patted him reassuringly on the right shoulder and asked, "What's your name, Sailor?" Edward cocked his head and gave the petty officer a look of confusion and fear. The Chief noticed that the blood stained flight suit that lay in a pile with the rest of his uniform did not have officer's bars or insignia. His dog tags were missing or left back at his base as most pilots in the Pacific removed any I.D. for fear of the Japanese treatment of pilots when captured. He surmised that he would have been an ensign, lieutenant JG or maybe a lieutenant. A Marine perhaps? He could also have been one of a few a non-commissioned warrant officers that flew rescue helicopters off the USS *Yorktown*, but there was no squadron insignia patch on his mangled flight suit.

Edward looked dazed. He twisted around to see if he recognized his surroundings and looked at the corpsman with a puzzled look. His words were slurred by a thick tongue and muddled mind. "I can't think. I just can't think right now. Where am I?"

"You are on the destroyer, *Hammann*, part of an escort group for the *Yorktown*. Luckily, we found you floating in your life vest about an hour ago. Almost ran over you. We took off your Mae West, parachute harness, flight suit, one boot, and your gloves." By now, assured that the rescued serviceman was going to be okay, Captain True smiled kindly at the dazed pilot, then excused himself for return to the bridge. "Gotta go, men," then the Captain tightened his helmet he donned earlier that morning when the *Hammann* scrambled to general quarters in defense of the *Yorktown*.

Nearing the last few steps to the bridge, the captain was greeted by the loud booms of his five-inch guns, feeling the concussion deep in his bones. His gunners were aggressively blasting the attacking Japanese strafing Fighters and torpedo bombers trying to sink them and the *Yorktown*. Even with the help of the *Hammann* and the damage it was inflicting on the Japanese carriers, the diving airplanes from the two Japanese carriers took their toll on the struggling *Yorktown*, causing her to lean severely to port and begin a slow slide downward. Logbooks would reveal only minutes before 14:00 hours, a wave of three lucky *Val* dive-bombers dropped 550-pound bombs, the first hitting near the number two elevator, wiping out a 28-millimeter gun crew while igniting several deadly fires. The second and third bombs damaged the flight deck, boilers, and number one elevator, exploding on the fourth deck creating additional fires. All three of the bombers were shot down with the last attacker tumbling and exploding into the carrier.

With disabled boilers, the *Yorktown* was rendered dead in the water at about 14:30 that afternoon. Although clearly crippled, with smoke pouring from the ship, the wounded were brought up on deck where the crew was still attempting to get the guns back in action. At just after 16:00, the carrier was able to restore at least one boiler and return some fire from one of the 55mm anti-aircraft gun mounts even while barely afloat. Twenty minutes later, two additional torpedoes struck her port side that ultimately would do her in. Finally, by late that afternoon, as the *Hammann* screened the carrier, it busied about the unpleasant chore of aiding the abandonment of the mighty carrier. The *Hammann* quickly took on many of the *Yorktown's* crew, including its Commanding Officer, Captain Elliot Buckmaster. Most of the surviving crew was rescued by the nearby larger destroyers and cruisers.

The next day, a skeleton crew of the *Yorktown* left the *Hammann* and reboarded the mangled carrier in an attempt to tow the ship to safety. To be effective in this effort, the *Hammann* was once again ordered to tie up alongside the *Yorktown* to transfer a damage control party of 29 officers and 141 enlisted men and provide hoses for water to fight lingering fires and help restore electrical services.

• • • • • •

"Up periscope." "Aye Aye, Sir," was the reply as the lift motor whined, pushing the massive optical mass to the height of the Captain's ebony tinted eyes. The small control room of Captain Yahachi Tanabe and his officers of submarine *I-168* of the Imperial Japanese Navy, was a stale, humid, and vastly expensive sauna. The sub was long overdue to surface the subtropical ocean to charge its batteries and refresh the ventilation, a wartime inconvenience. All 72 men in the football length submarine were breathing through their mouths to make the least noise since talented sonar operators on the American destroyers above could hear a sneeze or cough. Glued to the eyepiece, Tanabe slowly spun around 360 degrees searching for American warships from every direction, the top two feet of his periscope probing through the floating puddles of oil and debris of airplane and ship remains.

While the American sailors on the waters above were frantically trying to restore electrical power to the Carrier *Yorktown*, Captain Tanabe had been eying the Midway air battle by night through binoculars and periscope by day. Finally at 0530 hours, Tanabe was given orders to attack the *Yorktown*. Working all through the morning until just after 1330, he maneuvered into position through the destroyer screen to get the ideal angle on the carrier. The angry stars were now aligned just right for the Japanese skipper and he didn't hesitate. After having set the torpedo fuses to a range of 1200 feet, he prepared his sub *I-168* to aim four of her torpedoes for a deadly barrage. "Torpedoes one, two, three, and four away; two second intervals!"

While Edward was leaning on the starboard side of his ship wearing only his life vest, helmet, and robe, he was oblivious to the activity on the other side of his ship, tethered to the carrier. While he was still concerned about where he was and what was he doing on a ship, one of the Tanabe torpedoes hit the *Hammann* amidships, immediately breaking her back.

The powerful concussion slammed Edward to the deck, along with other surprised sailors, sending them all sliding down the steel deck on their backside, feet first into the ocean. Edward experienced a less painful splash than the two days ago but was still groggy, thinking he was caught up in a recurring tedious dream. 'Wet again!'

The enemy torpedo caused death and carnage of unthinkable dimensions. The *Hammann* jackknifed and sank slowly beneath the surface after only four minutes. As the ship slipped beneath the sea into the oily battle-littered Pacific, there was an underwater explosion most likely caused by the destroyer's depth charges. The blast killed 80 of the destroyer's crew and a few of *Yorktown's* men who had been thrown into the water.

Tanabe's first wandering warhead floundered awry, while torpedoes two and three snuck under the *Hammann* to hit the aircraft carrier, while the fourth set at a shallower depth impaled Ed's *Hammann*. The *Yorktown* already struggling, felt the concussion of the *Hammann's* underwater explosion, severely battering the *Yorktown's* already damaged hull, causing powerful shock waves that blew away the carrier's auxiliary generator. By 05:30 on June 7th, the sailors in nearby ships noted that the carrier's list to port was rapidly increasing.

As Tanabe watched his torpedoes travel through the iridescent ocean, then explode into orange and red flames and incendiary fireworks; he knew the ships were mortally wounded. He quietly folded the periscope arms and simply ordered, "Periscope down, make your depth two hundred and steer 180 degrees." As the sub slipped away from the carnage above, the captain ordered a celebration feast of canned sweet potatoes, steamed rice, boiled eel, and fresh onions.

The resulting explosion sheared rivets in the right leg of the foremast, throwing men in every direction, causing broken bones and broken hearts of loved ones yet to know. At 07:00 the next morning, the mighty aircraft carrier turned over onto her port side, rolled upside-down, and sank stern first, hissing into the 18,000-foot briny graveyard. It wouldn't be long until the official drab olive cars with white stars on their sides would be pulling up to the curbs of homes in scores of towns all over America giving apologetic death notices to 141 families.

That afternoon and through the night, the destroyers USS *Balch* and *Benham* scoured the oil covered rubbish in the embattled ocean waters for survivors of the *Yorktown* and *Hammann*. The next day, the two ships looked carefully for anything afloat that resembled a lifeless body or survivor. One survivor in particular was a puzzle for the *Benham*. From the far side of the debris field, one of the lifeboats plucked a sailor wearing his life vest, helmet, and khaki undershorts covered with thick gooey fuel oil, his face black as a charred coconut. The man did not know his name, much less his rank or which outfit he might have been attached to, or why he had no clothes.

. . . . . .

When she got that telegram about her missing brother, it did not matter to Edward's sister, Deborah Rosen, of Lancaster, Pennsylvania, about his part for the protection of the Eastern Island Marine Airfield at Midway, nor the importance or details of what happened. What mattered to her was the fate of her dear brother, reported missing June 4th in the middle of the Pacific Ocean halfway round the world. She hated war. She hated, really hated, for the first time in her life. It would not be her last.

She remembered ever so vividly her mother expressing the dread of losing both her precious children flying airplanes. Now this! The young American pilot shuddered uncontrollably and exhaustively so, for her parents and herself.

CHAPTER SEVEN

The Four Musketeers

On an early July evening in 1942, the noisy 1938 Bedford three-ton lorry made one last stop on the way to Upavon about 60 miles southwest of Maidenhead. A newcomer, an American calling herself Paige, joined ATA candidates, Maria Fuentes and Carli Banks, along with ATA veteran Alex Gaestel. The lorry slowed, shifted gears, and moaned forward again, with the passenger hustling along to get in. While the lorry driver was under the impression she was in, Paige was in fact trailing behind, stumbling with her kit in one hand and the other keeping her cap firmly mashed to her head. The three panicked young women in the back were hanging over the lorry and yelling at the driver to stop. At the same time, Maria managed to reach over and grab Paige's overstuffed kit while Alex and Carli grabbed the new rider by the back of her trousers and wrestled her safely into the truck. It was small time pandemonium for the breathless American, her pride and kit still intact.

When they all got arranged and quit laughing, Paige laughing the loudest, they shook hands. These wartime aviators to be were bouncing along a small ancient road likely carved by Andalusian or Thracian horses twenty centuries earlier.

Paige described herself as an orphan, but wished no pity because of it, as she described living in a swanky place in upstate New York with university summers in England and France. She even recited a few phrases in French to impress the others, but it was all innocent fun as she had a warm and pleasing personality. With Maria and Alexandra no stranger to several languages, they were less interested in her linguistic skills but highly curious about her aviation abilities. Even in the bouncing lorry, Paige demanded a second look with her dark hair as corn silk in a ponytail brushing her shoulders like an expert shoeshine boy. Her Mercer Rutherford oval face was appointed with porcelain lips and nose, also like her mother's, petite but pronounced. They quickly learned she was as talented around an airplane as the other three. They made the 60-mile ride over roads, ruined by horses, rain, and traffic with no prospect of repair, but laughing about one story after another on their trip to RAF Upavon.

The housing director had assigned billets to Carli, Paige, and Maria, at the Welley house, just a stone's throw from the airfield. Further along in her training, Alex was already billeted in the Stonehenge Inn at nearby Rushall. After the completion of ground school, the American women would be assigned different flight instructors, some men and some women, but all attached to the ATA. With Carli, Maria, and Paige having extensive flying experience, they would only take four dual and two solo flights to see how well they could handle the *Tiger Moth* bi-wing trainer.

Most women that processed through Montreal weeks earlier were all capable, but a few still struggled and needed additional airtime. A few of the women, like 30-year-old Polly Potter, were sent back to the States with undetermined illnesses, while Una Goodwin, who struggled and stalled, not getting beyond cadet, was returned home after three months of giving it her best shot. It could have been too much pressure, lack of talent, or just 'hard cheese'.

As Gower and Cochran wanted only the cream of the crop doing the dangerous ferry work for the RAF, they nonetheless were patient to avoid dismissing women prematurely. They had worked too hard to put their programs together to have a weak link in the talent pool. Any unsteady performances would be met with more extensive training of 20 or more hours to see if they really had the aptitude and stamina to be accepted.

. . . . . .

The fourteen women in ground school class 722-Bravo were seated at small desks in a windowless concrete room. It was located conveniently next to one of the hangars at the Upavon Airfield. With Alex shoved on through ground school to Class Two flying, the three Americans began schooling in earnest. As luck would have it, the three women had a curious instructor for the beginning stage. The unremarkable looking RAF Flight Officer opened the metal door and greeted the eager students.

Five nine, scrambled hair, rosy cheeks, and a bit stooped, he wasn't at all like the handsome pilot posing on RAF recruiting posters scattered through out London, by miles. Then that hook. The women had seen soldiers and fliers with empty sleeves and pant legs, but no hooks. They tried not to stare.

At first they had a hard time even making eye contact. He made it a bit easier. "Ladies, let me help. My name is Flight Lieutenant Woselley. My mates call me Woosie, but you can address me as Lieutenant or Mr. Woselley. I got this fancy stainless steel hand just after the Battle of Britain." The women looked at his face for now, it was easier than the hook. "Before you feel too sorry, I have flown 47 more combat missions with this hook. With the right hand I painted eleven more swastikas on the fuselage of my *Spitfire*, now on the bottom of the North Sea just off the coast near Lowestoft. I am medically fit, but given some soft duty days to recover from a slight cold, courtesy of my roommate. You are my 'soft duty', substituting for a far better qualified ATA instructor, I am sure," pausing with an easy smile. "Before I start in earnest, I can speak for all the RAF combat pilots that we owe you, the ATA, a huge debt of gratitude. Without you ladies and the men, by now we could possibly have been at the German's mercy, rather than chasing them to Russia. Paige couldn't keep from, raising her hand, asking what the other 13 were thinking. "Sir, not to be insensitive or uncivil, how did you manage with the, the.." "Good question. The left hand, or 'Mr. Fast' as I call him, was quite suitable, as he mainly managed the throttle, leaving my right hand for airplane controls, firing button, and radio communications. I trust none of you will be in the same fix." "Oh", from a softer Paige. "Thanks."

The room relaxed as Flight Lieutenant Woselley began, nodding to a back door. "In the adjacent hangar we will explore dismantled *Hurricanes* and *Avro Ansons*. With some help along the way, I am going to show you how to dismantle an aircraft engine, so you can see how your instruments are hooked to their wires or tubes and how they work inside the airplane's aluminum skin. I'll show you what happens when you push or pull the stick or throttle. You will see how fluids flow through clear tubes and drop the landing gear. How we doing so far?" "Let's go outside and look at our homework projects."

In and around the dismantled *Hurricanes*,

'Woosie' had them pushing and pulling, forward or back, the handle of the landing lever in the cockpit, through clear tubing. They could watch through clear tubes the hydraulic fluid all the way to the undercarriage jacks to see the wheels drop down and lock. They got a close-up view of how the metal rods would push or pull the horizontal control surface of the elevators up or down causing the airplane to nose up or down. Similarly, they could see how the turning of the yoke affected the ailerons causing the airplane to turn. They pushed on the rudder pedal, and watched the tail respond in kind, either to compensate for wash of the prop, or to keep the airplane stable during turns.

Narrated by the Flight Lieutenant, they watched films of emergency procedures applicable to all airplanes they might ferry. It was pounded into them that what they were learning could save their lives, as the ATA had proven over and over in the 24 months the school had been operational. Before it was over, they had to learn all 160 parts of the *Hurricane and Anson* and know their functions. After six plus weeks, the well-trained women would be Cadet Officers and receive their one broad stripe for their sleeves and epaulets. Now the real fun was to begin, training in the air where it mattered.

On a warm August afternoon on the back stoop of the Welley house, Carli casually asked Maria, "How was your first week of Contact Navigation?" "Navigation, ha! You call flying over the treetops with a queer map and a stopwatch Navigation? Without this war and England's wintertime reputation for fog, it might be fun, maybe a fair challenge. Even on a clear day we still have barrage balloons all about the RAF stations, and, get this, they move them around every day so you have to get the changes from the ferry pools every morning. Alex told me about this a while ago, but it's another thing to see those flying elephants from the air. That's not the worst. You can't mark the balloon locations on the silly maps we use, even though they change everyday to show new locations of our balloons. Presumably, if we get shot down and a German sympathizer got hold of it, somehow they might know where every pool, factory, and Maintenance Unit balloon was located.

"Carli, you remember the *Harvards* back in Montreal? There we had radios and could call for taxi instructions and request landings. In emergencies, you could call Mayday and be sure of a rescue. Maria can ditto that. With the birds we are going to be shuttling around, there isn't a radio. We have a call sign of *Lost Child* but no radios to use it. We have to watch for flares or the Aldis lamps to taxi to the grass runways and again to be cleared for takeoff and once again at our destination to land. In some cases we have to fly over the airfield and shoot one of our flares to ask for landing. How's your Nav. going?"

"Pretty much the same. Thanks to the clear summer flying weather, it was fun seeing all of England. In just three hours you can fly all the way to Scotland from London or Maidenhead, and from east to west coasts, in about an hour and a half, less in Spits or Hurricanes. The cute church steeples have their own personality, and the railroad patterns are just different enough that a pilot with a sound memory would need it during poor visibility.

"On my first flight, my instructor took me into a cloud bank and did two 360 degree turns one direction, another 360 degree the other direction. Needless to say, I got a bit disoriented. When we dropped down, she said, 'now, resume your flight to Biggin Hill.' Well, let me tell you, at that point I didn't recognize anything. Rivers, roads, towns, all looked alike. Since I was dumb enough not to see how many minutes those turns took, I couldn't rely on my stopwatch. I just resumed my initial course heading and thankfully remembered what Biggin looked like. I made it, but I learned an important lesson. If you get trapped on top of a cloud layer, you can be sunk, especially if you don't pay attention. Even with Amy Johnson's experience and talent, it was getting stuck above the clouds that done her in."

"Maria, did you get your small ringed book of cards they call *Ferry Pilot's Notes,* for our Class Two aircraft? Cool, huh?" "Yep, today in fact. As the Brits would say, 'sound as a pound', better even. They are so handy; the RAF guys are getting copies now. I think it's great our ATA pilots came up with the idea.

"I think our style of flying demands a small compact book for each class of airplane with information about individual types. We don't even know until the morning we get our assignment chits, what kind of airplane we are flying. The ten-minute brief from the ground engineer is hardly enough, making the notebooks invaluable. Right now we have *Harvards*, *Spits*, *Typhoons*, *Hurricanes*, and even *P-51 Mustangs* and *F4-U Corsairs* in Class Two. Even within the same type, later versions are tricky, like the propeller turning in the opposite direction as the later *Typhoons*. It's a serious deal on takeoff."

"Carli, an ATA guy met his sticky end just the other day on take off in one of those *Typhoons* with a backward prop, and I am quite sure he didn't check his notes. If he did, he didn't keep up with the revisions. No matter though, too late for all that now.

The *Notes* are handy enough and fit right in the thigh pocket on our flight suits. You pop it out, locate the airplane, then find speed and power settings. Before you can say knife, off you go."

With the Training School and *Tiger Moth* Training behind them, all three began their ferry duties at Hamble and were reassigned new billets. "Maria how do you like your new family at the Mere House?" "Not so dreadful. Mister Pennick is okay but the missus walks like she has a hornet's nest stuck in her bum. How do you and Carli like the Southern Yacht Club?" "You must be kidding. It is like a five star hotel filled with men, but mostly old or not suitable for service. Doesn't stop them from leering though. Food's right tasty. Can't complain, Maria, can't complain."

Their first ferry duties at Hamble were benign at first, just *Tiger Moth* deliveries or to pick up other ferry pilots and deliver them back to their ferry pool airfield, or to another airfield to bring planes back to Hamble. After several weeks, they were assigned to train for Level Two Class, which was their old friend the *Harvard*, which they flew successfully in Montreal only months earlier. Several of the women that were shaky in the *Tiger Moth*, were rolled back to give them additional flying time. The ones who grew in skills were moved on to the *Harvards*, but those who did not were given the option of staying in the ATA in administrative or support roles. Even though the fear of failure was strong, most made it just fine.

When Maria was introduced to her Class Two conversion instructor, they broke into a grin, as Alex, Paige, and Maria had met on the Lorry ride to White Waltham. With Gower's urging, Alex was accelerated through the Class Two conversion, and immediately plowed back as an instructor. Maria and Alex were instantly connected. Each challenged the other in the air and later at Curley's Inn on High Street in nearby Gateshead at the bar and dart board. They would fondle their Stout, make love to their tonic and Tanqueray, then months later, with each other.

From that early June Lorry ride with all four fliers, until the drink at Curley's, Maria liked this Dutch woman. She craved her energy and self-assurance. Maria's first awareness was the first Class Two session when Maria sat in the cockpit of the Harvard trainer. Alex stood on the wing and leaned over Maria, her breast bobbing on Maria's head as she pointed to instruments and switches. It didn't help that her hair swished across Maria's shoulder and left cheek while Alex's scent descended into the cockpit and just loitered, like fumes in a smoldering volcano. Maria floated into a distant realm and special dimension not defined by gender, but by soul. As the session was ending, Alex exhaled onto Maria and stepped back. Her smile was met with Maria's and the relationship bolted from a spark to a five-alarm flame. This bond would test Maria's preference for life long partners and the loyalty of the heart's DNA. It would be severely tested.

The three ATA fliers and their plus one Alex, forged a cadre of friendships at their other favorite watering hole, the Sugar Loaf Inn. They were just as fast and true as Curley's. However, there was a guarded secretive atmosphere at the Curley's, one that neither Maria nor Alex could quite figure out.

The drowsy summer slowly gave way to the autumn smells, kaleidoscopic colors, and crispy air. Straw hewn eaves blew across the grass airfields, as the early morning sun and the mist of the night began their tug of war between murk and light with the mist gaining strength with each passing week. Navigation skills were challenged as trees became skeletal, and hillsides less distinguishable. The popular fedoras of the English seasons started with the tweed hot rod hat, later giving way for the brown leather Trilby, and, ultimately, to the American Duck Canvas Rockabilly hunting cap to warm the ears.

With the *Harvard* training behind her and two short haul *Hurricanes* under her belt, it was inevitable for the 'Special Occasion' to appear without notice for Second Officer Fuentes. Paige and Carli were in the same state of anticipation, waiting for that special day. They knew it would happen, but didn't talk about it. They knew when it did, then they would talk. It would be a memory shared; *'soon, real soon now'*.

The three with Alex were gathered in the living room of the Mere House, enjoying the hospitality of the Pennick family, with Paige and Carli furtively looking for that hornet's nest in Mrs. Pennick's caboose. They all enjoyed the propriety of taking traditional tea, as Friday's flying had been scrubbed due to the stubborn cloud layers typical of late autumn.

Maria was struck with an idea. "Say, we have two days off now. Let me show you guys around in London. I did a half day tour while waiting to interview with Miss Gower." Alex brightened up. "I know a great place to start. It's called Gateways Club. It's in Chelsea, and if we don't like it we can go to the West End where the most fun is." Having been around London a bit while waiting to meet with Gower, Maria leaned in for the West End. "Since Chelsea is a bit out of the way, how about doing the West End? There are tons of stuff to do there. Soho, Piccadilly, and the shows at Leicester Square." Carli twittered in. "I vote with Alex. I've been to the Gates and it is nothing like you can imagine." Paige seconded the motion. "Let's do it." Alex smiled, "Okay, it's settled. We better grab an overcoat. It can get really chilly. Let's snag a ride to the train station at Maidenhead."

They all got their coats and rode together to the Maidenhead railway station, where they caught the train for an hour's ride to Paddington Station, then another 20 minutes on to London's Victoria Station. By foot, it was just another ten minutes to Oakley Street, and finally a quick left to the Gateways Club on Kings Road.

It was a small-whitewashed building with a simple bright green door guarded by an unassuming streetlight. Maria and Paige held hands as if they were going into a dungeon while Carli and Alex acted like they were home. The steep stairway led down to the cellar bar and club. The walls were adorned with a diverse collection of local artwork that defied interpretation partly due to the intentional lack of poor lighting. The smoke from pipes, cigars, and cigarillos would have been a worthy training exercise for military recruits being introduced to poisonous gasses. The small 35 foot-long bar was at one end of the room; the loo and coatroom was at the other end.

"Come on, let's see if we can get a pick-me-up. I'm parched," a condition Alex seemed to suffer every weekend. The three joined hands with giddy Alex in the lead, worming their way to the bar. "What'll it be my lovelies?" "Two Shandies, a Ginger Beer, and a Lemonade."

"What ta ya think?" Maria was the first to reply. "Alex, I think this might be a mistake." "Na, just the opposite. You'll see." Alex grabbed Carli's hand and headed to the throng of dancers, a packed group that would have violated every fire code in most civilized countries. The skills most couples demonstrated were sloshing glasses held high with nary a drop falling. Maria and Paige just watched with curious astonishment. The flailing and sweating customers made the atmosphere almost contagious to every soul that drew breath in the intimate sardine packed basement. There were such a variety of costumes and dance styles that it was a veritable human kaleidoscope. Paige whispered into Maria's ear. "Maria, I think there are some homosexuals in here."

After coughing up her ginger beer mostly through her nose, Maria broke into a belly laugh that normally would earn notice, but not at this raucous place. It was so infectious that Paige couldn't help laughing either. Soon they joined the lathered dancers and headed toward Alex and Carli, who smiled as they bumped. "Fun, huh?" All nodded and all rocked, until the music finally paused. There was a thump of a microphone from somewhere in the din.

"Ladies and gentlemen, we have a treat for you tonight, a repeat performer. Please dance to the piano music of our own Caribbean talent, the celebrated Lester Parret. Let's give him a big round of applause."

When a few of the dancers took their seat to take a break, the ATA ladies could see the broad shouldered pianist. He was built like Joe Louis, but a whole lot better looking. Carli almost fainted. She was a bit into women, but this guy was beautiful. He was a black Liberace all right, as the women crowded around the piano to sing along, mostly Fats Waller songs, *Ain't Misbehaving* and *Honeysuckle Rose*. Born in Barbados, he was schooled in London where he started playing as a student. Even after his wide celebrity, he continued to come around Gateways, sometimes without notice like this night.

When the women finally made it a night and retraced their train and bus rides back to their billets, Maria got the distinct impression that Alex had eyes on her way too much. She could sort it out later, but during the next few days she had to get psyched for the *event*. They agreed the next night out would be the West End, then back to Gates for sure.

After Maria's successful completion of Class Two training in late September of '42, she was posted 60 miles south to the all-women Ferry Pool 15 at Hamble-le-Rice. She never forgot the first meeting with its Commanding Officer.

"Good morning ladies, my name is Margot Gore, your C.O. You might not know it know it, but you are lucky to be assigned here at Hamble, the southern most ferry pool of the ATA and in my opinion the best of the lot. You will note that we are all women; pilots, secretarial, maintenance, and mechanics, all women. You might find one or two men, but they would be cleaning the loo or raking leaves." That brought a polite chuckle from the new women. "You will meet our veterans, including Rosemary Rees, one of our original eight women. You all have name badges so be sure you say hello to Chile Duhalde and the indomitable Jackie Moggridge if you get a chance. You will want those two in your corner.

"We are located just south of Southampton, and conveniently 10 miles south of Eastleigh, one of Vicker's *Spitfire* factories. The south airfield of Hamble was located near the *Avro* factory, the facility famous for our twin-engine bomber the *Albemarle*, which, if you are approved, you will fly. *Avro* also does a most splendid job repairing damaged *Spitfires*, which will be extremely convenient for you. The waters of Southampton, Spithead, and the Solent, were frequent slips for many of our seaplanes and a respite picnic area for rare summer days off. It will be here at Hamble that you plucky ladies will grow beyond your youth", looking directly at Maria Fuentes. "Good day. Use your noggins up there and take extra care.

CHAPTER EIGHT

The Big Day

The first day of November, a rare clear winter day was dotted with innocent cloudlets. The brisk air and mild northerly winds made for a perfect day to fly. Maria greeted Jean Bird and South African Jackie Sorour in the assembly hut. They already had their assignment chits and were waiting for their *Anson* ferry to get them to their first collection. The loudspeaker blared, "*Anson* taxis ready for Bird, *Anson* 55, Salmon, *Anson 785*, and Bennett, *Anson 332*." Maria ambled to the assignment room and pulled her chits from the mailbox cubbyhole. There it was, in freshly typed letters seeming larger than usual. It was really happening. She read them twice. There was no mistake. It was Show Time for real.

For better or worse, the dream was coming true. All the work, fear, and anticipation, was tightening into a ball in the pit of Maria Fuentes' stomach. This was the huge day indeed. Of the other women, Alex was the only musketeer to have experienced it. Maria's assignment chit read:

Spitfire Mk. III 1 November, 1942

From: Hamble North Field.
To: Biggin Hill.
Pilot: M. Fuentes.
Shuttle: Ferry Car to Hamble North
Priority: Urgent

'The fantastic and celebrated fighter, the Supermarine Spitfire, to Biggin Hill, a hundred miles northeast where the guts of RAF fighter activity lived. That's home of 610 Squadron where Nigel flew during the Battle of Britain. A RAF pilot doubtless need this plane, and now. Gotta take a second to open my ATA Pilot Notes.'

As her heart beat like thunder with an attitude, the loudspeaker jolted her thoughts. "Fuentes to the front. Ferry car waiting." Maria quickly retrieved her parachute, leather flying-helmet, and flying gloves, then scampered out the front door. After a quick ride to the north airfield, she stepped onto the apron. There she was on the asphalt near the taxiway, eyeball to eyeball with the *Spitfire*. Maria blinked first. The cross-armed Flight Engineer was standing near the cockpit, as if the aircraft's sentry. Jaws set and eyes without expression, Flight Engineer Smitty Womble had his own crusty reputation that exceeded the squirrelliest of men. He claimed to have had intimate relations with a *Spitfire;* that it was consensual.

The external power trolley was hooked up with the handler by its side. It's as if the two men had been standing there waiting just for her. She pulled her parachute over her shoulder and headed to the majestic *Spitfire*, safeguarded by the engineer as if he were the one who wrote the history of its development. Maria tried to walk as if she had been to this rodeo dozens of times, not betraying her pulsing heart and stiff muscles.

"Mornin', Lass. Perfect day for a hop I think. Where you headed?" Maria thought he might have been a bit patronizing, but all the women had gotten used to it, converting the men one by one with their talent and no nonsense demeanor. "Biggin Hill. Snag sheet?" Biggin was a holy word, which was like a light switch to his attitude.

"Not much to report ma'am. She just got patched up from the Avro crew across the way; they usually do smashing work. A few days ago it was dinged up in a dustup from some German flak and a *FW-190*. As for snags, the only gripes lately have been a sluggish gear and unusual lack of torque on takeoff. So take care not to over correct with the right rudder."

"What about the right tyre? Looks way low to me. Would you mind getting it pumped up? The lad at Biggin will be in such a hurry he won't fuss with it and it could mean life or death if his landing is not just right. I would appreciate it. While the guys are getting that air bottle, I'll do a quick walk around. Thanks." There wasn't much for the mustachioed engineer to do but send the APU attendant to the hangar to get a compressed air bottle. He accepted the small dose of respect Maria had given him and he her, as her destination cradled an aura of bravery and death.

The spirited American ducked around to the left side of the airplane and with the parachute on her shoulder, found the pocket step on the lower part of the fuselage with her right foot, then stepped up and onto the wing. At the small cockpit entry with its door hatch down, she plopped her parachute onto the seat and surveyed the control panel. A lot like the *Hurricane*, but under the engine cowling was a decidedly different beast.

She slid down the wing and started a slow exam of the airplane. At the trailing edge of the left wing, she let her bare hand slide and feel along as if the bare back of a lover. She ducked down and eyeballed the landing gear, sniffing the mingled odors of petrol and damp grass. Tyre was full now and the gear strut seemed strong. Brakes seemed normal enough. Around the end of the wing, she noted the small red light, then turned to the back of the wing to ensure the free movement of the aileron. She noted the new aluminum on the lower part of the fuselage, imagining bullet holes or jagged flak penetration. Around the tail, she waggled the rudder and elevators to ensure free movement.

It was the same exercise for the right side; same patch of aluminum, which she expected. The APU handler who had aired the right tyre was standing by his trolley. She was tugging on her gloves as she approached the engineer. "Thanks for the air, Smitty," having noted his nametag earlier. "I'll be on my way." "Hop in and I'll give you a hand with the harness and chute." "That would be helpful and very much appreciated, especially by the chaps at Biggin who need this bird ASAP." Notch another conversion for the women of the ATA.

Maria was in her world now. With her black necktie tucked into her breast pocket and ATA Pilot Notes of the *Class Two Spitfire IIA* in her lap, she took a closer look at the instrument panel thoughtfully clustered just below eye level like the *Hurricane*.

She was ready. It was thumbs up to the Auxiliary-Power handler and the magic began. She flipped both ignition switches on, set the mixture control to normal, and opened both fuel cock levers. The business-like Maria primed the cylinders and pushed the starter button. The prop began turning slowly, then suddenly leapt to life, as the engine shuddered and spun its propeller. Maria throttled back to idle and with her feet firmly on the brakes, gave the thumbs away for the handler to remove the chocks. She released the brake lever and eased the throttle forward, moving the heels of her soft boots to the floor, and began her gradual weaving turns to the run-up area. Satisfied her magnetos, fuel pressure, and hydraulics were normal, she set her trim, fuel mixture, prop, and flaps to their takeoff settings. She urged the *Spitfire* to just short of the runway and set her altimeter to zero, reflecting Hamble's sea level elevation.

Finally, after a full minute that felt like an hour, there it was. The green flare arced into the air then began its descent, as Maria Fuentes took a much needed deep breath. She coaxed the twelve cylinders of the *Spit's* Merlin engine with a little more fuel, and then lumbered into position for takeoff.

Maria slowly advanced the throttle forward and continued giving the engine more and more fuel, then to just short of full throttle. With both feet steady on the rudder pedals she bore on and on until the tail came up to horizontal. After 150 yards and 90 mph, Maria's steed eased into the air and clear of the runway. At 140 mph and in a slow climb, she pushed the landing gear lever full forward and began a steeper climb, adjusting the propeller pitch for an economical 185mph. Smitty and the APU handler watched with secret pride, smiles cracking like Indian popcorn, as the woman put their proud *Spitfire* into the air, oh so smoothly.

She leveled off, easing to the northeast on a weather perfect day in which Maria was to lose her airplane virginity to the *Spitfire* gods. There were a few billowy clouds, mostly friendly at 5,000 feet and higher with visibility of 30 plus miles. The 95 mile journey would only take her about 20 short minutes. Maria wasn't about to waste even one. Her route would be over Haslemere, Guildford, Merstham, Leatherhead, and ultimately line up for a due north heading setting her up with runway zero-three. Now stable at 3,000 feet, not too high or too low to identify her landmarks.

'God this is so wonderful. I love this airplane. It's so sensitive to the touch, so perfect for my little body. I wonder if I should do just one aileron roll? Naw, better not. Bull feathers. If Mary Wilkins could play in the clouds, then I can do this.' She tightened her harness and looked left, right, and up to ensure there weren't any onlookers and eased the yoke carefully to the far left. In a flash, as she made the stick move, the *Spitfire* spun halfway through its axis of the barrel roll. Maria stopped the maneuver, hanging upside down in her harness straps, straight and level. *'This is wild!"* Then she leveled off. She repeated the maneuver ever so slowly and all the way through this time to breathe in the sensation. *'Helen Ritchey was right, it carved through the air like a knife through butter. Maybe someday I can do a victory roll just for fun, but not today. Back at Hamble, Mary Wilkins told me she did one on her first flight in the Spit and no one cared. There isn't enough time for me and, with my luck, I would probably get in trouble'.*

Then she just had to do a snap roll. *'So fast and crisp!'* It was back to business as the landmarks whizzed by and there, just ahead, the crossroads just above Merstham. Dangling on the altimeter knob was the locket her brother gave her. The cherished charm danced back and forth against the *Spitfire*'s instrument panel, swaying with the rhythm of the spirited mechanical dragon.

She was over Mertsham in minutes, then had to anticipate her destination quickly. Immediately after passing over her landmark, she adjusted her heading to take her to Biggin Hill, home to 13 Group Fighter Command and their Spitfires.

She throttled back from 250 mph to 180 mph. At the distance of 10 miles she could see the outline of the long NE/SW runway. She throttled back to get the airplane down to 1,000 feet, an altitude to fly over the airfield in search of the tower's flare and get a feel of the traffic. As she descended, she reviewed her landing checklist. ... *'Fuel switch on both, knob in to cage gyro, and engine instruments normal.'* When about five miles out, Maria reduced her airspeed to 160 MPH, set her flaps to 50°, propeller pitch to full high, and anticipating a clearance to land, slowed to 125 MPH then lowered her landing gear. She eyed a lumbering *Walrus* landing on the Northeast runway, to be her runway next. Maria was still two or three miles or so from the airfield at 1,500 feet when she saw the bright colored green flare. *Wow, so soon.* With her left hand, she pulled the cockpit hood back, then pushed the cockpit door half open to lock the hood in the safety position. Maria adjusted her approach and eased back with her throttle, pleased she had already configured the airplane to land. With a slight turn to right it would set her up for a left hand approach for the landing on runway zero three.

Maria thought the *Spitfire* might just land itself. It was so easy to trim, an extension of her body, obedient to her every command and slightest touch. Steady at 90 MPH and with a slight left turn, she was lined up with the runway and at 250 feet, right on the glide path. She took off a little power to get to 80 mph, slightly above stall speed, then gently touched down at the end of the runway as she slowed to 60, bouncing just once, near perfect.

She had instructions to look for an airport fuel lorry at the end of the runway that would lead her where she was to park. Right on schedule, the driver of the small truck on the field ahead, waved for her to follow as she turned off the runway. When the truck came to a stop in front of RAF Squadron 610's dispersal hut, the crewman on the ground directed her to the exact spot where he wanted the *Spitfire*. When the ground crewman crossed his raised forearms, she locked the brakes, pulled the throttle to idle, then pulled the cutout switch to starve the engine of fuel. As soon as the propeller shimmied to a stop, a fuel truck was there eager to fill the half-full tanks. When the *Spit* shuddered and became silent, she turned off the magneto switch. Before she pulled off her leather helmet, she breathed in the last smell of petrol, glycol and oil while listening to the whir of the gyros unwinding. She turned the fuel cock levers down and released her harness. In an instant, she was on the ground with parachute in tow, greeted by the fitter. "How did she do? Any snags?"

Maria was still wrestling with her sweaty hair and wiping down her face. She was drenched and not sure why. '*A dream, just a dream.*' "No snags but agree on those given to me by the engineer at Hamble." She noted the right tyre was still inflated. "Also, the usual rudder compensation of the torque on take off is minimal. Great for the pilot on takeoff, but a questionable alignment for needs at altitude. She ran a little hot just after take off, but settled down within norms after I adjusted the cowl flaps. That's pretty much it, 'cept the oil pressure gauge would jerk back and forth a couple of times, but temperature was stable, so I took no worry. Where do I check in?"

Maria scanned the landscape of Biggin Hill's heartbeat, where the pilot's hut was just a stony blister of a building on the edge of the grass field a short sprint away form their airplanes, the catholic runway the general direction determined by the windsock. Maria started to the hut beyond the fitter's shoulder when, to her amazement, she recognized Nigel Sheffield. He was headed her way in full flight regalia, including the Enfield .38 peeking out of his shoulder holster. They were both startled to see each other. At the same time, "what are you doing here?" Nigel's brow now creased, "Did you bring me this *Spit*?" "Yes sir, I did. Are you taking her?" "Indeed."

"Why? Where are you going like that? Did they clear you? You can't be serious." "Deb, I mean Miss Fuentes, I don't have time to explain." Sheffield was breathing faster than usual, chopping his sentences. "They need me straight away. Two of our four *Spits* from 610 just beginning an escort mission from Martlesham had to turn back with mechanical problems. I have been getting some rehab flight time hours in, just in case. Now *case* is here. Love to chat, but really have to get a wiggle on."

Before the conversation was over something tugged at them both. Hearts pounded faster, and eyes glistened. "Be careful. Please call me when you get back. Where will you be? Here or White, or where? You have to tell me." "I don't know, Little One. I don't know, but I promise, I will." They both stepped closer then thought better of it. He turned and sprinted to the *Spitfire* as Maria watched him talk briefly to the flight engineer then climbed into the cockpit and pull in the cockpit hatch just as the fuel truck pulled away. The *Spitfire* coughed to life as Nigel gave the chocks away sign and looked her way. *'Did he do that? Was that a kiss he threw? It can't be?'* Through her watery eyes Maria watched the Spitfire rumble down the taxiway and onto the end of the runway. Sheffield sped into the eastern skies to join an escort for *Lancaster* heavy bombers boring deep into Germany. Maria could barely breathe and neither could Nigel. It wasn't because of his lack of oxygen either.

"Miss, they need you back at the hut. They have another chit for you." It was a tame *Harvard* to Stroud, then, an *Anson* taxi full of tired ATA ferry pilots back to Hamble, an ignominious end to a serendipitous day. All the way to Hamble, she wondered, '*What just happened? The Spit. Nigel. A kiss? Was it something else?*' Her heart was spinning, then leapt like a young trout in raging water.

'Was he just wiping his mouth? Those eyes. I never noticed. He said 'Little One'. He's never called me that. An endearment? That's terribly informal. He seemed really muscular. He must have been a marksman with his pistol. Will he call? I have to call Biggin Hill when I get back. Or should I wait until tomorrow? He promised he would call. Something of him was different. Was this a mistake? What do I tell Alex? Oh my, what to do?'

CHAPTER NINE

The Hun meets Scorpions & Tomahawks

Bavarian Otto Kelter took his first breath six weeks into World War One, a totally unnecessary conflict, a war escalating into one of the deadliest conflicts in human history. Otto was born into a Catholic family on Sunday, November 1, 1914, All Saints Day, greatly pleasing his mother and father. Otto Kelter was a boy like most other German lads in the Bavarian region of Southern Germany. The swooping countryside with its valleys abundantly surrounded by steep alpine mountains and rolling hills made for perfect gliding. Otto and his older brother, Luther, were both avid members of the local gliding club, founded by their dad, a WWI aviator and the local priest, Father Josef Schwendemann. Under the careful eye of their father, the brothers took turns strapped into the small wicker seat attached to a long ski under the skeleton of wires, covered with patched fabric. The boys of Herzogenaurach, a small town just 27 km northwest of Nuremburg, were often seen clad in their long stockings, plaid knickers, and white shirts, frequently stained with green grass and brown dirt. They grew like wild poppies and cyclamen swooshing over the local cows and pastures, held tightly in their fragile gliders by thin leather shoulder straps. The delight of it drove Otto's dream of flying even higher and higher in fast airplanes.

In the blink of their father's eye, they turned into Bavarian young men. They swapped their round pudgy faces to handsome angular men with thick brown hair and mysterious amber eyes. Otto, with his pencil thin moustache under his Apache-shaped nose, was particularly striking to the local Fräulein. In 1932, Otto graduated from secondary school near Regensburg, then had a vocational talk with his parents. His mother saw a future for him with Bavarian Motor works in Augsburg, 150 miles to the south, joining his older brother building the popular BMW motorcycles and motorcars. His father warmed to the idea, as he had hoped over time the factory would again build airplane engines, or even airplanes. Otto shocked them both and asked if he could apply to the university in Wurzburg to study aeronautical engineering which surprised but pleased his parents.

With Otto's excellent scholastic record from the Catholic High School in Regensburg, he was easily accepted. With his older brother planted happily at the BMW factory two hours to the south of his parents with Otto only thirty minutes away, the parents were able to stay close to their sons. While Otto was plowing through his studies, he noticed a buildup at the Herzogenaurach Airfield just north of town. The Airfield was to be known publically as an airline pilot school, while everyone in the area knew it was a different type of school, clearly defying the Versailles Peace Agreement of no military air training. Airline training didn't fly fighters that were brazenly taking off and landing all day long.

At the beginning of his junior year, Otto applied and was accepted as an aviation trainee. Between his college life, dating girls, and flying, it would be the best of years for Otto to enjoy. As he piled up flying hours his marks began to suffer and he began caving to his impatient nature. Late in Otto's senior year in 1936, just after his 21st birthday, Otto was so driven, he found his way into the Luftwaffe

Commandant's office and begged to enter the Luftwaffe flight training. Only a few knew that there was a military department deep in the program. Otto knew and wanted in.

Otto was ushered into a smoke-clouded smallish office, the interviewer sitting on the corner of his desk, cigarette dangling from his lips while reading material in a blue folder. Hermann Ziegler was most imposing. a gallant survivor of the previous war, Ziegler, in his late thirties, still had the trim build of his twenties. His uniform was tailored and sported three rows of various citations and campaign ribbons. Otto noticed first his unmistakable Imperial German Pilot's badge, an oval silver plated image of the Kaiser's Crown at the top and just below, an image of an airplane and countryside surrounded by a wreath of oak and olive leaves. The man took Otto's breath away. Without looking up, "So you are Otto Kelter? Why are you here?"

After an hour of small talk with Otto such as, what compelled him to decide on the Luftwaffe, the WWI service of his father and mutual acquaintance with Father Schwendemann, and Otto's deep knowledge of military airplanes, Ziegler was fascinated. He pressed Otto further. "What else can you tell me, like your party affiliation?"

"Pardon, sir?" "What party do you belong to; the Social Democratic Party, National Socialist Workers, Centre, Democratic Germany? You know, Political party." "Oh, the party thing. To be honest, I have been so immersed in my studies and flying, I haven't given it much thought. I do know our leader is Adolf Hitler of our National Socialist German Workers' Party. He is enormously popular. I think my parents are in the Worker's Party."

"Otto, before I can make a decision, you must return to your University and complete your graduation. There you must study and think about your opinion and your role in the fatherland's government. If you don't have a cause other than the pleasure of flying, you won't do. You may talk with your friends and family, since the design of their futures might be affected as well." Otto was confused, not clear about his meaning, but agreed to do as he was told.

Enthused and motivated, Otto returned to his studies and reached out to his peers to learn their involvements in politics. He asked the young men who wore their brown shirts and swastika armbands, all about their National Socialist German Students' League's activities. In talking with his brother, he verified that Luther was most content at the BMW plant. He even heard rumors that the *Me-109* fighter, designed by Willie Messerschmitt, would be made there at Augsburg. If Otto couldn't come to grips with the reality of supporting the Party, he should not return to Wurzburg or talk further with the commandant.

. . . . . .

"Herr Commandant, I have returned to the University of Wurzburg to finish my degree in Aeronautical Engineering, as you asked. I am a little embarrassed. So much has been going on in our Fatherland and I have been so ignorant. I have joined the Young Social Democratic Party. I know the party is popular and was founded in the northern cities of the Ruhr, but it suits me, and especially my family here in the south who are middle class farmers and factory workers. I am comforted that we have such a strong leader with Hitler, bringing Germany to a strength that guarantees work for all our people. My father was strong to say our leader is making headway to re-establish our military to its rightful strength. My brother is telling me rumors of the Bavarian Motor Factory gearing up to build a new modern fighter designed by Herr William Messerschmitt. It's an exciting time for Germany and I want to be a part of this new age."

"How much do you want to fly for Germany?" "I have dreamed of nothing less, Herr Ziegler." "What would you like to fly if you are accepted and are successful in finishing the courses? Fighters? Bombers? What would it be?" Otto had thought about this and was ready. "Fighters! At least one in our family can be an ace. And, to do it in an airplane my brother helped build would be a significant achievement for the Kelter family for generations."

Ziegler agreed. He swung his leg off the corner of his desk and extended his hand to Otto. "Welcome Cadet Third Class Kelter. Return home, as you will soon receive orders and a rail voucher to the training airfield in Schleswig. Remember this, Kelter. As I told you earlier, in nearly all cases, the Luftwaffe finds you, not the other way around. Consider yourself extremely lucky, and do *not* let me down!" His eyes turned cold and pierced those of young Kelter. "Yes sir, Herr Commandant. I won't!"

Otto was delighted in June of 1936, as he was to report for recruit training, or Flight Regiment, near the city of Schleswig, just north of Hamburg. He began his training at the new airfield at Fürstenfeld, a small town between Augsburg and Munich. With his rail voucher and official orders, Otto hugged his parents and left the train station to begin a journey that would be the beginning of unthinkable outcomes.

After being outfitted in his new blue uniform he felt ten feet tall with his peaked visor cap, white shirt, black necktie, gold collar tabs on his tunic, wide black belt, silver buckle, and black flying boots.

His first assignment was for six months at a recruit school, equivalent to the 'square-bashing' or 'boot camps' in other air forces. After his primary training, student pilot Kelter moved to the aviation ground school, where he spent two months studying general aeronautical subjects. After flying through the coursework, he moved to an A/B School, or elementary flying school, where he flew light aircraft such as the *Focke Wulf 44*. For his A2 license, Otto received training in aerodynamics, aeronautical engineering, elementary navigation, meteorology, flying procedures and training in the reception of German-modified Morse Code.

For his B license he flew larger, higher-performance aircraft. If available, his group also flew the mono-winged *Junkers*. On the successful completion of his B2 training Otto had accumulated 142 hours of flight time and at last, received his German Air Force pilot's license and wings in July 1937, perfect timing for Otto to get his first taste of combat in Francisco Franco's Spanish Civil War of 1936.

His old friend Major Hermann Ziegler made contact with Otto with some welcome news. "Kelter, I am sending you to a new aviation group Field Marshall Kesselring is calling the Condor Legion. It is an aviation group formed to help Spain's Nationalist Party in their civil war. It will be hand picked pilots, mostly seasoned WWI veterans, but also some promising new flight officers. In this group we are picking 36 pilots to fly the *Heinkel He-112*, a brand new mono-wing fighter. You will do some escort work for our *JU-52* bombers and get some needed airtime for air to ground missions."

Otto spent eight months with the Condor Legion, doing just what Ziegler described. In his combat sorties, Otto managed to down seven Russian and dilapidated Spanish Bi-winged fighters. The conflict ended in March of 1939, with Franco's troops the victor, while Britain, France, and the United States, as only spectators, only missing what some would say was an opportunity to crush Hitler.

As for Otto Kelter, he was rewarded for his expertise in the *Heinkel 51C* with the assignment he feared most. He had been rolled back to serve as an instructor. From mid 1939 through the battle of Britain in late 1940, until April of 1941, he would be stuck there, sharpening his skills with the Luftwaffe's best new incoming pilots.

His first aerial break came during the German Operation Barbarossa in June of 1941. His chance to join the fracas began at the Luftwaffe airfield at Bielany, on the Northwest outskirts of Warsaw. The primary purpose of bombing and strafing the Russian Army just west of the Dnieper River in the Ukraine was to destroy them before they could retreat into the wastelands of Russia and regroup. Hitler couldn't let the Soviet superiority of manpower and industry take effect.

On Sunday June 22, Otto was all ears in the rustic ready room listening to the Air Wing Commandant's 10:00 brief. "Gentlemen, as you may have heard early this morning, Fighters from (squadron) JG-54 and medium bombers of K-76 launched a full on attack of Russian Airfields with our *109s* and *Heinkels*. The Russians put up a feeble defense so we are going to press even harder. Radar has painted 70 plus light bombers headed our way so we are going to greet them with JG-53's *Messerschmitts*. We will chase them back to Sevastopol if we have to, so manage your fuel accordingly. Before returning to Bielany, targets of opportunity will include troop concentrations, supply dumps, and airfields. Again, your fuel. Go now!"

That afternoon at 13:30, the eager Otto launched eastward to meet the bombers. At first it was easy pickings for the Germans, as unescorted bombers proved to be remarkably easy targets. When the German Air Wing returned to base, they counted 74 air victories, losing only two of their own. Otto was credited with two bombers in the air and three destroyed on the ground. When the tally was complete from all the Groups, the Russians had lost nearly 1,500 aircraft.

The Germans had overwhelming number superiority, but failed to achieve their objective of annihilating the Russian Army. In December the German Generals had to retreat because they forgot to outfit their soldiers from the bitter cold. The worst news was the new player for the Allied Forces rising from the west, thanks to the Japanese attack on Pearl Harbor on December 7th, 1941. The United States was in it for real now.

Otto read the account from his hospital bed, recovering from cuts and bruises when his newly issued ME-*109* was shot down in late November, one of the last German casualties of Operation Barbarossa. His injuries sustained in the cockpit were slight burns to his upper body while his awkward parachute landing resulted in a broken left arm and sprained ankle. Before getting intimately acquainted with his parachute, he nonetheless added another ten victories over the slow and second-rate Russian *Yak* fighters and *Ilyushin* bombers. But, no matter to Otto, outdated and slow as they were, he gladly added the victories during that campaign, even though several were on the ground. The Germans counted them and they were approved. Otto skipped past the longer view, as Germany's plan to conquer Russia failed, losing one million soldiers and a fourth of its Luftwaffe. He was thinking only about Otto.

As Germany was setting up airfields in North Africa to support the Afrika Corps, Otto couldn't be more thrilled. As soon as he recovered from his injuries, his bosses had his orders cut. Seventeen was not a bad number of kills for the veteran 27-year-old Bavarian, still quite early in his aviation career.

• • • • • •

Scorpions and Tomahawks

Late in the spring of 1942, as Jackie Cochran's ATA women were working their way across the Atlantic to England, Otto Kelter was recuperating from his injuries in Spain. He was marking time, teaching Luftwaffe students the skills needed to fly larger bombers, while occupying himself with the operating manual for the new *Messerschmitt-109-F*, the hottest airplane in the Axis sky. With his new Sergeant stripes, Kelter was a German fighter pilot, trapped in a world of seasoned Luftwaffe pilots that had gotten into the Africa Theater sooner than he. The orders he received to Libya, were the answer to his plea to St. Michael. He couldn't wait to join the iconic Werner Schröer of JG- 27, the Group II Wing Commander of North Africa.

As the primary air power in North Africa, JG-27's sole mission was to support the Deutsche Afrika Korps, particularly the 'Desert Fox' Field Marshall Irwin Rommel and his 7th Panzer Tank Division. Otto and the other *109s* were the weapon support that Hitler needed for his plan to secure the Suez Canal from Britain, one of only two water entrances to the Mediterranean Sea.

The impatient Kelter was flown to Munich in the tri-motor transport *Junkers 32*, where his *Messerschmitt* had just rolled out of the factory hangar door, fitted with the new desert camouflage paint. The new F Model was called the *Friedrich,* the fastest *Me-109* to date. The squadron numbers hadn't been painted on just yet, waiting for official squadron assignment in North Africa. The other markings were there though, the German black cross with white outlines were loud and clear on the wings and fuselage, a symbol causing dread among newer Allied pilots unlucky enough to tangle with the sleek new *F*.

The reported April 17th RAF bombing of the *Messerschmitt* factory at Augsburg, where his brother Luther worked, cast a shadow that weighed on Otto. He knew little of the details, so he could only fear the worst making him really thirsty to get to Afrika Korps for details. The worry put a foul taste in the German aviator's mouth that wouldn't go away.

Otto eased into the cockpit, smelling of paint, leather, and hydraulic fluid, like a new car. He craned left then right on the tarmac, sighting the other two pilots going through their startup checklists. He could barely wait to get back in the air. The morning sun cast its shadow in Otto's cockpit on the instrument panel painting his right leg. Otto carefully handled his pre-start checklist and took a deep breath. It was time now.

After pulling his box shaped cockpit down and closed, Otto's right hand jerked the starter lever and began priming with his left. The Daimler-Benz 1475 horsepower engine coughed once then roared to life. He nudged the throttle forward to begin his roll while signaling his two wingmen to follow. All three *Messerschmitts*, now a Luftwaffe *Kette,* or flight of three, tested their brakes, turned on their radios, made their way to the taxiway. Otto sped through his pre-flight checklist almost by memory. Satisfied, he swung around to the end of the runway and requested his take off to the south for his group. The three eager Luftwaffe pilots took off and quickly joined together abreast, then worked their way south strutting their new Messerschmitts.

They were to join with Schröer, agreeing to meet Otto's group on the far northwest corner of Sicily in Trapani-Birgi, 1,000 miles and four hours away. After an uneventful flight, the three *Messerschmitts* landed, refueled, then escorted by Schröer across the Mediterranean to Tunisia. Once airborne, Schröer took the fresh replacements over the 150-mile long northeast leg to the Southeast range of heavily forested Green Mountains to the Airfield near Martuba, Otto's new home. The small flight of *Messerschmitts* landed four across, as the runway was the whole of the Libyan Desert sand.

When they taxied toward the array of tents for German Fighter Wing JG-27, and its 120 determined pilots, they had to turn back and forth to avoid bomb craters made by the large Allied Desert Air Force. The sand blown from Otto's propellers covered his canopy, causing him to lean left then right to see where he was going. When he cast his eyes to the horizon, all he could see was the vast periphery of an endless beige circumference with glowering counterfeit lakes. The scorched desert was causing the brow beneath his leather cap to drizzle sweat right into his eyes. Heat aside, the whole arrival experience was giving Otto an ominous chill. Just getting on and off the ground was an unexpected challenge for all the fighter pilots. Then when he heard of the 500-strong enemy Desert Air Force, his confidence would be narrowed.

As Kelter and the two rookies followed Schröer, they made their way to the parking places where they starved the *109* of its fuel until it shivered and stopped. As Otto unbuckled and stood, he noticed the stark village of center pole tents with a white tower at one end of the packed sand. Most of the airplanes were scattered in groups naked to the sun, with a handful protected in mud brick firing butts. The tires of the exposed fighters were covered with burlap to keep them as cool as possible.

As soon as Otto jumped to his feet from the scalding hot wing, he jerked off his leather jacket and loosened his tie. Within a minute he was soaking wet like everyone around him. He couldn't imagine working in the unbearable heat of the summer months he knew would climb into the 100s from June into September. Kelter's mental images popped as Schröer reminded him, "Don't lose the jacket Sergeant, it gets cold at night. Embrace the cool, as later in the summer, nights will turn from cold to hot and airless, warming into the 90's making sleeping almost impossible."

"Thanks for the information. I was about to give it to the scorpions and snakes. Herr Schröer, could we stop by the tower hut to get news of the Augsburg bombing? My brother, Luther, is at the *Messerschmitt* factory there." "Nein, not here. Those white huts are mostly for day-to-day operations and mostly handle traffic and squadron business. The real information is down there. We need to check in anyway. Follow me." Schröer nudged Otto to a concealed doorway, its only clue a humming generator. As they slipped down the stairs, the hot air gave way to a slightly cooler environment below. After the salutes and introductions all around in the underground headquarters of JG-27, Otto learned of the details of the Augsburg situation.

"Sergeant Kelter, according to reports from Berlin, two sections of six *Lancaster*s from British Squadrons 44 and 97 made a low level approach with their target our U-Boat engine factory. Our fighters managed to shoot down four of the six *Lancasters*. The two getting through dropped four 1,000-pound bombs. Of the other six, we destroyed three of them while the rest didn't even get all their bombs away and the five they did drop didn't explode. We suffered only minor damage to some machine tools and only five of over 500 cranes were lost. Sergeant Kelter, the *Messerschmitt* factory that would have been a better target was never threatened. Your information was probably miscoded by our intelligence." Otto was a new man and thanked the Information Officer for the briefing. The group of experts below the hot sand would get to know this Kelter since they would be the group coordinating his combat missions from their bunker.

The stage was now set for Flight Sergeant

Kelter. For the Bavarian lad who talked his way into the Luftwaffe through a light dust up in Spain to Barbarossa, his real test resided here. It was absolute and would be deadly for the pilots who weren't on their game, and most of those who were would die anyway. This far into the war, most survivors of the German and Allied fliers proved to be the killers, and the losers the dead. There was no middle ground. There would be prayers in many languages that would go unanswered, at least in this world. War was dark, stank, and it killed from the ocean to the valleys, mountains and airways. Men, women, children, and beast, were not spared. This was Kelter's canvas which he chose to paint with his new *Messerschmitt 109 -F* airbrush.

Schröer then pointed to the stairs leading up to the scorching desert floor. "Let's go on up and over to the tower hut and get you assigned to a Group and Squadron." In the modest room of the tower hut was a series of wooden benches and high ceilings supported with thick timber beams. The walls were adorned with fragments of British *Spitfires* and *Hurricanes* complete with splinters of RAF squadron art. Sergeant Kelter joined several other Martuba rookies, who like him, were overdressed.

The veteran pilots were an amalgamation of beards, clever U-Boat hats, loose fitting green pants, and open collar tan shirts. The two squadron leaders reading pilot assignments were Captain Ernst Maak of Squadron 2 and young-looking First Lieutenant Gustav Rödel of Squadron 4, both of JG-27. After a teasing of the new pilots for their lack of experience and probing their political party affiliations, Maak called out his rookies while Rödel called out the names of men whom he would command in his squadron. Kelter would be in his squadron, which was fine with Kelter, a bit let down, however, not to be in his friend Schröer's Group.

Kelter was puzzled and put off about the political party questions; it was the first time he had been confronted about his affiliation since his first interview with Hermann Ziegler years earlier. He got the chilly feeling outspoken Nazi pilots weren't all that popular. When the question came to him about the Nazi Party, he just replied he "didn't need a political party to fly airplanes or go to war for Germany" and left it at that. He breathed a personal sigh of relief since he omitted any party affiliations on his original enlistment papers. '*Wow ? Non-fanatics fighting a war run by fanatics*'.

After gathering his new pilots, Rödel took them for a tour of the airfield in two of the jeep-like vehicles, called Kübelwagens, the all-wheel desert rat transport. They stopped by one of the fighters with tails decorated with small one-and-a-half by five-inch tall vertical white bars, the thickness and height of a pack of Bremaria cigarettes. The stripes revealed the number of Allied airplanes its pilot had shot down. Rödel pointed. "That's Marseille's plane; he is with Maak's Squadron 2. He is called the *Star of Africa* back in Germany, totally irascible at night, but pure genius in the air. Just before the end of February, he got kills 50 and 51 at the expense of an RAF 2 Squadron flying *Tomahawk*, the English version of the American *P-40 Warhawk*."

Kelter listened attentively as Rödel spoke to the character of the airplanes they would face. "You will get extremely familiar with the *P-40*. The six 50-caliber cannons can do great damage in an instant and they are fast. Most of you here already know the RAF's *Spitfire*. The newer *Spits* can fly inverted now, are faster, and can turn inside your *Messerschmitt*. Your skills have to be better; that will be the difference." The rookies were half listening to Rödel as they looked closer at the painted stripes, wondering how one pilot could shoot down so many airplanes single handedly.

The Kübelwagen took them further down the road to the airplanes that Rödel's men would fly. They were distinctive with the crest of Berlin painted on each plane. Rödel's fighter had no markings on the tail. The rookies noted the oddity, but made no mention of it. He had the Knights Cross, which was at least 20 kills, but never any markings. The only time the medal was mentioned was when Rödel casually mentioned the easy bomber kills in Russia had made the new threshold at least 30 to be considered for the Knights Cross, a new threshold Otto didn't want to hear about. He would need a lot more than three kills to even think about the highly sought Knight's Cross.

After the tour, Rödel directed the Kübelwagen driver to take each pilot to his airplane, as he had been called back to HQ, another call from Rommel. When Otto was driven to his airplane, a yellow *White 10,* his radio call sign, had been painted on her flanks and 17 white bars on his tail fin. He was like a kid going to the circus for the first time, with all you can eat cotton candy. In Spain and Russia, his adversaries were outnumbered five to one and against very sophisticated German airplanes, like Kelter's *Messerschmitt*. Africa will be decidedly different.

Before returning to his tent, Sergeant Kelter questioned the driver about the lack of markings on Rödel's tail. "He has 37 victories, the last one just yesterday. He is modest, that's all, but make no mistake, he is our very best. He is just as talented as our French Huguenot, Marseille, but deadly focused and always rises ready for business."

Now a Master Sergeant, the newly promoted Kelter was assigned his first orientation flight with Captain Maak of the 2nd Squadron, while his leader Rödel was riding alongside another newcomer, part of the sixteen fighter pilots assigned to Captain Maak. The Squadron Leaders often traded off for the orientation exercises to maintain a uniformity of readiness. The 'exercise' was to start early, as the 'exercise' was a full on combat-free-hunt, without any ground control. To Rödel it meant 'go find trouble'. The Luftwaffe in Afrika Korps had to struggle for fuel, making training flights ill afforded, especially as far as Schröer was concerned. The British blockade in the southern Mediterranean north of Alexandria was choking 90 percent of the German convoys full of fuel, food, medicines, and parts needed by the Luftwaffe and Rommel's Panzers.

Evenings were as Rödel described. After the relentless yellow sun turned blood orange and lowered itself below the horizon, it snapped off like a heat lamp turned freezer. Kelter shivered his way through the night, unable to get warm. He finally gave up, rolling out at 05:00 hours anticipating the warmth of his flight suit. He donned his heavy pale blue flying trousers complete with deep map pockets on both legs. He shook the sand and a small scorpion from his leather flying boots and hurried to the mess tent. As soon as he opened the tent flap, he was rewarded with warmth, chatter, and hot coffee. Just a half-cup was his usual. No need to suffer the discomfort of having to take a piss at 10,000 feet when busy trying to stay alive, a lesson he learned the hard way. While each squadron sat together, he nonetheless sought out the handful of Bavarians to learn of any mutual acquaintances. The only one was Franz Stigler, the one assigned with Rödel at the same time as

Kelter. They shook hands and found a common acquaintance, Father Schwendemann.

They both choked down the brown gritty oatmeal and small sips of chalky coffee, then stood and headed to the flight line to meet their mentors, Rödel and Maak. Stigler's ME-109 was next to Otto's White Ten. While waiting for Maak, he overheard a serious admonishment from Stigler to never consider shooting a parachuting pilot or crewmember of the enemy, a thought never entering Otto's mind. Otto understood the code and was thankful to know it was the same code of the Allied airmen.

"Kelter, let's get moving." Kelter scooted into his White Ten as the crewman helped him strap in. He closed his canopy, then gave the thumbs up, signaling the crewman to spin the engine crank. The liquid-cooled V-12 engine roared to life, puffing white smoke into the cool morning air of coastal Libya.

Captain Maak didn't mess about. Even though they both crawled into their airplanes at the same time, he was in the warm-up area waiting for Flight Sgt. Kelter. He waited until Otto pulled nearby to complete his engine run up. "White Ten, this is White One, radio check over." "White Ten, loud and clear." "Ten, stay in close echelon on my right wing, ten feet below. Stay there until I am shot or I tell you to engage. Glue your eyes in the back of my helmet until we attack, then fall back and protect my six. There are just two of us, so you are the 'wooden eye' back there." Otto didn't need, but still appreciated the reminder to keep one eye on his rear-view mirror. "Roger, White One."

"Lets go then." Maak's *109* staggered off first. After his landing gear was safely up, he began a slow climbing turn to the left, allowing Otto to take station quickly by flying a tighter circle inside Maak's shallow turn. "We are going to angels two zero then travel south and east along the coast. The Desert Air Force likes to cruise at eighteen thousand, but don't stop scanning high." "Roger, White One." Kelter wouldn't have to worry about the heat four miles high, as it would be icy as death.

With few clouds, there were no helpful filters to shield the glass canopies from the annoying glares appearing to come from every direction. On this morning sortie, when his left hand wasn't busy with the throttle, it would shield Otto's eyes from the intense rays of the rising sun piercing his left eye. At 15,000 feet, Otto was a steady wingman, just to the right of Maak and ten feet lower. His leader had them making slow steady turns to fly over the coastline near Tobruk. No clouds to hide in like in Spain or Russia; today was like a fish in a bowl with no seaweed to hide in.

Level at 20,000 feet, Kelter was startled by the crack of Maak's voice. "Indians at twelve o'clock, slightly high, a 'schwarm'. Looks like *Tomahawks*. We'll drop back 50 yards, gain altitude, then we attack. "Otto acknowledged the command and tightened his oxygen mask close and snug, wondering about the configuration of the enemy fighters.

Now perched higher at 22,000 feet, Kelter's eyes were glued to the bobbing head of his leader. "White Ten, I have them still at one o'clock but below now, four abreast. Tighten your harness. I am gong right at the middle of the formation. With four, we will do a 'free road' and split. I will go left and you go right. Remember, get close and make their tail the size of a small sailboat. Guns hot, eyes bright." The next ten minutes was an aerial ballet of helter-skelter; two determined German fighter pilots against four just as determined Desert Air

Force Pilots, all twisting in all dimensions of the sky.

The Allied pilots were surprised, further distracted by a menacing bright sun in their rear view mirrors. With the second *Tomahawk* slightly to Maak's' left and ahead, he unleashed the fury of his 20mm cannons, scattering the group left, right, up and down. After Maak's salvo, there were only three left to deal with. Maak's *Tomahawk* was just spare parts of a fighting machine with its pilot hanging in his parachute, shielding him from the melée above. In an instant as soon as the two right Tomahawks broke, he radioed, "White One, Ten breaking high."

If Otto couldn't catch the climbing *Tomahawk P-40*, he would still have altitude advantage over whoever was still in the fight. The aviator in the *P-40* was twisting and turning as he climbed, maneuvers allowing Otto to pull closer. When the tail of the *P-40* was large enough to suit him, Otto opened fire from both 20mm gun pods mounted under his wings. He watched the *P-40's* wing root tear away, leaving the remainder of the airplane spinning out of control. Veering one way then the next, Kelter glanced at his altimeter and then eyes back on the mortally wounded airplane. He saw the helpless pilot fall from the cockpit, his parachute billowing above. Now at eleven thousand feet, he wouldn't worry about the condition of the pilot. At least he wouldn't die of asphyxia. Remembering the admonition of Rödel not to shoot the pilot, Otto was content with his agreement of that code, and trusted the Allied pilots felt the same.

As Otto thought of the other *P-40s*, it was almost too late. The tracers came from his four o'clock position and slightly up. He was astonished he wasn't hit with the tracers zipping ever too close. Otto knew instinctively he must get lower and fast. He pushed the nose all the way down and flipped to inverted, starting a spit S maneuver. All the while he was pumping fuel directly into the cylinders giving him an extra boost of speed, with the byproduct of belching white smoke. The smoke caused the *RAF P-40's* rookie to pause for a second to get the impression Kelter might be damaged. That gave Kelter just enough time to speed away in the opposite direction and drop down to 7,000 feet. He headed slowly back toward the shores of Tobruk.

"White Ten, check in." "White One, Ten at seven thousand eastbound just over Tobruk, over." "Roger Ten. Rendezvous at 5,000. We will 'circus' where Tobruk touches the sea. Report your condition, over." "White one, 'Hurra, Hurra'. One *Tomahawk* splashed with visual of one parachute. I received fire from a bandit behind me but disengaged, over." "Roger, Ten."

'Roger, that's it, just roger? What a stony man!' "White Ten are you thirsty?" "Nein, White One. Fuel state one four zero liters." "Roger." That was the last exchange until Maak called the airfield to land.

Back on the ground Kelter did get more than just 'roger', as all the squadron, even Rödel, congratulated him. Otto's squadron C.O. reported his new pilot peed his pants and returned home early. Rödel got one victory, but was privately beyond proud of Otto Kelter's victory than his own. Lt. Maak even had 'thumbs up' for Otto, especially for his split second decision to go high when the *P-40s* scattered. Many would have gone low or horizontal, which would have been a mistake. When Kelter reported to Rödel about being jumped by the *P-40*, he was told he did the textbook maneuver, pushing down while using the injectors, a scheme that saved Maak's life several times. Otto's quick thinking was impressive, especially under combat conditions.

As for Maak, he splashed one, then chased the second of the two Desert Air Force planes away and never saw the fourth, probably the one Otto tangled with. Otto had the taste of desert blood now, and even though the taste was only mildly satisfying, it was still another mark on his vertical stabilizer. He loved the victory but didn't especially want the pilot to die. To him it was like what 'party animal' Hans-Joachim Marseilles, the Star of Afrika, admonished. "It's about the airplane, Kelter, not the man. It's only the airplane."

In May, Otto's squadron moved from the west supporting campaigns in Torbruk, then in June, JG-27 moved to the edge of Egypt's Sidi Baranni Airfield. The critters and clan of insects, reptiles, and noticeable warmer temperatures were the same. Situated near its decaying desert fort, they continued to escort the routine bombing by the *Stuka* in advance of Rommel.

Thanks to Rommel's persistence and drive to get to the Suez Canal, Otto Kelter was able to add seven victories, bringing his total to 25. *'They're just airplanes, Otto',* the admonition was still echoing in his conscience. He felt like a cat in a box of rabid rats. He had to fight to stay alive. 'That's all', he told himself. He just wanted to return to the mystical rolling hills of Bavaria.

As August and September strolled in, the Allies were beginning to make their presence known as Otto and his fellow fighter pilots were beginning to show signs of fatigue. Nonetheless, Otto quietly scored another three victories, a South African *Hurricane*, a high-flying reconnaissance *Spitfire*, and an American *B-24* that Kelter circled to watch fall, counting nine open parachutes, hoping that was the lot.

Forty-eight hours later, JG-27 was moved to Pacino, in Sicily to continue a renewed offensive against

Malta. During the first three weeks, the refreshed Group splashed seven *Spitfires*, but lost three of the new *109-G Messerschmitts*. One belonged to Sgt. Otto Kelter, who was forced to crash land, but his camera confirmed his claim of one *Spitfire*. Before the dust settled over Pacino, the Flight Sergeant ended up in the burn ward of the squadron's infirmary. His Knight's Cross of the Iron Cross race to thirty victories was just one airplane short, but he was at peace, as his war was over for now.

He took that time to connect with his girlfriend met during his last year at the University.

August 15, 1943

My Dear Little Bear, Emma,

I have to make this short as commanded by our Führer. I am healthy and taking a rest in Sicily for a few days. Even though I have been in desert conditions with hot sand blowing continuously, it doesn't prevent me from thinking of you day and night. The nights are the hardest without you. I don't know how long this war sill last, but no matter, as I will come to you without fail. You can reach me at the address on the envelope.

Ich liebe dich, meine Bärchen,

Otto

CHAPTER TEN

The Miracle Christmas of 1942

Marine Lieutenant Rosen was a confused passenger on the Destroyer *Benham,* somewhere between Sickbay and the chow hall. He occasionally ventured topside to get fresh air and a hopeful spark of memory. Amnesia wasn't new to the war, but aboard a naval warship and no hospital ships ready for service, where to put him was a dilemma. The Hospital Corpsman concluded the passenger didn't really need a medical doctor and wasn't any trouble. As the *Benham* steamed toward Guadalcanal, the executive officer of the *Benham* felt that once rejoined with Task Force 16, they could successfully transfer Rosen to one of the three Aircraft carriers in the group. He was transferred on November 15, not to a carrier as planned, but to the destroyer USS *Gwin.*

Aboard the *Gwin,* Edward feared a repeat dunking, another link in the chain of misfortune. The *Gwin* sailed to the Naval Base at New Caledonia to drop other rescued sailors, but chose to have Edward remain on the destroyer through Pearl Harbor, then scheduled to arrive in San Francisco, on December 19, 1942, a year and 13 days after the Japs bombed Pearl Harbor.

Edward was driven from San Francisco's pier 45 30 miles south, to the Oak Knoll Naval Hospital in Oakland, where he spent his first Christmas alone. The first doctor who interviewed him suggested he wear a football helmet to prevent further injury to the head. He was told to do 100 pushups a day to increase his circulation, quit smoking, and take sleeping pills for a restful night's sleep. He was also was encouraged to read or write to stimulate his brain.

Most of the suggestions didn't seem to help, except Rosen did read. He read the *Army Times*, the *Oakland Tribune's* and *San Francisco Examiner's* updates on the war daily, as well as articles from *Collier's* and *Saturday Evening Post* magazines. One story in *Life Magazine* that mildly piqued his interest was about American women's role with the British Air Transport squadrons.

When he tried to connect with his doctor, he could only stammer about water, airplanes, a sister, and odd one-syllable words that just didn't reflect any headway. The Navy reached out to the Army for help, in particular the psychiatric specialist at Letterman Army Hospital in the Presidio complex of San Francisco. Oak Knoll was better for it, dealing with patients with loss of limbs and worse.

Edward was picked up by an Army car to make the rainy trek to north San Francisco. With his cheek on the cold rain-splashed car window, he crossed the Bay Bridge, then down along the piers that dotted Jefferson Street. His confused mind's eye saw San Francisco Bay, a myriad of seagoing ships, Alcatraz, and finally through the Lombard Street Gates to the grassy knoll of the Army Fort of the Presidio. Suddenly, Edward's cheek recoiled from his window. He hurriedly rolled it down to peer through the mist to observe a small Army airplane take off from the Presidio's Crissy Field. The image jarred his mind with fresh confusion.

After getting settled in his ward in the red tiled two-story hospital, Edward met his doctor. "Good morning, my name is Doctor Chan. What's yours?" Without thinking, Lt. Rosen blurted, "Fred, I think sir. Could be Red or even Ted." No one had asked his name since being plucked out of the water by the *Hammann*. "Okay Fred, tell me about yourself." "Well, there isn't much to tell. I seem to remember fairly recent stuff, like the trip from somewhere in the Pacific to here. Before then it's hard. I vaguely remember landing in water really hard and the water not real cold, but still uncomfortable." "Go on."

"Let's see. I remember airplanes, but as a kid, and a girl. A friend or sister, I think? "What else?" "That's about all, sir." "Physically how do you feel?" "Well I'm having a hard time eating and often I get nauseated to the point of upchucking. There are times when I can't sleep or just the opposite, can't stay awake. I had some dizzy spells but none lately. My left ankle always hurts, but I can't tell you how it got hurt." "Walk for me." Edward walked to the window of his ward and back. He favored the ankle but the doctor saw something else. Ed's left arm stayed by his side while his right arm swung freely. "Do either of your arms or shoulders hurt?" "Nope, I mean no sir. No real problem there. My left shoulder hurts, but it's a whole lot better." "Neck stiff?" "No, nothing serious." Dr. Chang continued to pepper this mystery man with odd questions. "Fred, do you remember anything else? A town, a name, a movie, anything." "That's odd. When you mentioned a name I remember tally."

"All right then; that's a start. Your x-rays revealed two serious concussions in two different areas, as the second blow intensified the first blow. That's probably why Navy Oakland suggested the football helmet, a little too cautious; we don't do that here. The nausea is normal. When the head takes a blow, the bleeding in the brain affects several systems like the digestive system and sleeping regulation controlled by the arousal centers of the Medulla. Your injury caused the sensors to get at cross-purposes, sending arousal signals at night and sleep signals when you should be awake. All that should pass as the brain heals and dead tissue matter is expelled through body waste. It takes time. With amnesia, there is no predictor of recovery. It either happens, or it doesn't, but there are some exercises that often help. That's what I'm here for. There is still some swelling, but by now you should be getting some relief." Edward nodded.

Dr. Chang continued to see Edward every other day until Mid-January. When Dr. Chang tapped on Ed's door, they shook hands as always, then Chang sat on the small chair next to his bed. "I have a theory. Do you remember twenty questions or word association exercises?" Ed's expression gave the answer. "Never mind. Here we go. First are you in the military?" Ed's gait was the doctor's clue, not to mention being delivered to Mare Island with no ID or memory. "I think so, but I don't remember." "Do you see a left arm holding the butt of a rifle during officer training or boot camp. "Yes." Which branch?" "Can't say."

"Now the word bringing you to this hospital. What do you think of when you hear tally?" "Tally ho? That doesn't sound right." "Never mind that. I think we're getting somewhere." Dr. Chang's hunch was right. "What does the number zero make you think of?" "Tally ho." They looked at each other. "Sister?" "Nun." "Midway?" "Islands." Edward's brow sketched lines on his forehead.

"Lamp?"	"Table."
"Brief?"	"Case."

"Briefing?" "Room."
"Briefing room?" "Sortie."
"Angel?" "Gabriel."
"Angels?" "Flight level."
"Alpha?" "Bravo."
"Bravo?" "Zulu."
"Eagle, globe?" "And Anchor."
It's the Corps Dr. Chang, the Corps!
Ed's face was alive now with anticipation.
"Blood?" "Stripe."
"Uniform?" "Bloodstripe."
"Kill?" "Destroy."
"Destroyer?" "The *Hammann?*"
"Port?" "Hole."
"Again, port?" "Starboard."
"Bed?" "Room."
"Again, bed?" "Rack."
"Aircraft?" "Carrier."
"Carrier?" "*Yorktown*."
"Woman?" "Pretty."
"Pretty woman?" "Mom."
"Again pretty woman?" Just puzzlement
"Again, pretty woman?" "Deb?"
"Sack?" "Bed."
"Gunny?" "Sack."
"Again, Gunny?" "Sergeant."
"Spin?" "Rotate."
"Rotate?" "Go home."
"Eggs?" "Over easy."
"Scrambled eggs?" "Colonel."
"Fred?" "Edward!"

"Tell me the rest of your name. Fred or Ed what?" Ed twisted in his chair. "I can see it but I can't see it. It's coming to me. I just need some time. But it's Ed, Dr. Chang. I'm really sure. I don't know how I know, but it's Ed for sure."

"That's enough for today, Ed. Let's give it a rest and take another stab at it tomorrow. Tonight, think about our words of today and let them stroll around in your head for a while. Other words will pop out, so do the same drill with you. You'd be surprised." They both stood, then Ed hugged the smiling Doctor, an unexpected gesture. "Soldier, I am going to run along and leave you with your thoughts. I have a feeling you made a real breakthrough today. I am going to prescribe a mild sleeping medicine so you can rest. I will be by tomorrow to see what the dream gods shared with you during the night. I have a feeling you are going to be a new man." Dr. Chang left Edward's room, feet barely touching the floor. A half hour later, from inside the hospital a shout was heard. "It's Rosen. It's Lieutenant Edward Rosen!"

That same night and hour, Phoebe Rosen sat straight up in bed and woke her husband. "Harold, it's Edward. Our son is alive, I felt him. I *felt* him!" "Go to sleep Honey, you were just having a dream." Harold rolled over and held his wife, the wife who never gives up. They were both wide-awake.

The sheer voile curtains in Ed's room twisted in the cool aromatic breeze from San Francisco Bay. It was midnight dark and the only sounds were occasional distant sirens and deep-throated funnel horns of merchant ships working their way from the Golden Gate Bridge to Alcatraz and beyond. The thin walls of the 150-year-old hospital leaked sounds of Benny Goodman from the room next door. The Star Spangled Banner did it. The song was routinely played when radio stations were signing off for the night. That was the medicine Ed's brain needed. The tiny gears and electrical circuits began to sputter, crackle, pop, then hum. He sat straight up in bed. He stepped into his slippers and put one arm through his light blue seersucker robe and headed out the door to the payphone in the lobby. "Operator, I need to make a collect call to the Rosen residence in Lancaster. Yes, Pennsylvania."

The three AM call startled Harold and Phoebe Rosen, but only for a minute. The next twenty minutes were magical as the senior Rosens and Lt. Edward Rosen wept and talked, wept less then talked a lot. Edward wanted to know about everything, especially his sister. The Rosens only knew she was involved with the RAF somewhere in Europe, doing something that was helping ferry airplanes. The smiling marine told his parents how much he loved them, wished them a belated Merry Christmas and Happy New Year, then slowly put the cone shaped earphone back in its cradle. Falling asleep, the cheeks of the two Rosens were crusted over with dried tears of joy.

Edward Rosen walked back to his room, kicked off his slippers, hung his seersucker robe on the bedpost, then crawled into his bed and onto his side to sleep for ten peaceful hours. The lone tear from his eye near the feather pillow trickled to the back of his hand and became one with his body and rendered peace to his soul. The soldier remembered.

CHAPTER ELEVEN

Stinky Fish and Dirty Rats

Two months earlier, on November 1, 1942, RAF veteran *Spitfire* pilot Nigel Sheffield left Biggin Hill to join an escort flight for Bomber Command Group One and 103 Squadron of 12 *Lancasters*. The four-engine beasts were loaded with 4,000-pound 'Cookie' blast bombs shaped like an enlarged hot water heater. The cylindrical device carried 3,000 pounds of TNT with an ammonium nitrate mixture packed in 1,000 pounds of a thin casing for shrapnel.

The *Lancasters* were home-based at Elsham Wolds, located just to the northeast of the village of Elsham in north coastal Lincolnshire. Four *Spitfires* lifted off from Biggin Hill 20 minutes earlier, two having to return with mechanical issues. The first replacement had just been launched with Nigel Sheffield to follow. All four assembled *Spits*, would join the bombers on the North Sea coast near Rotterdam. The mission was Kassel, a frequent target east of the Ruhr Valley and 280 miles south of Hamburg, the alternative target if clouds obscured Kassel. The *Spits* would protect the bombers as far as Brussels, then have to turn back, limited by their 400-mile combat range.

Nigel crossed the coastline near Rotterdam as ordered, scanning the sky for the Tophat escort flight of three *Spits* and a formation of 12 *Lancaster* bombers. Flying into the sun at 25,000 feet, made the search challenging even with his sun goggles. Just as he put his thumb on the mike button, he saw the three *Spitfires* and just beyond were the bombers. His report on a frequency he hoped was not guarded by the Germans was, "Tophat Leader, this is Tophat Four, I see you, over." "Roger Tophat Four. Welcome aboard. We are Blue and you are Blue Four. Take station on Blue Three at Angels 27. Standby for situation report in five, out." Nigel clicked his mike twice, easing up and just the to right of the third *Spitfire* in the formation of four abreast.

Ahead and 2,000 feet below, he saw the beehive of four *Lancasters* abreast, three deep. He knew this airplane, having made three deliveries with the ATA. They had a lot of muscle to discourage the reckless *FW-190* or *Me-109*. The nose turret had twin .303-inch machine guns, making eight guns for straight ahead attacks for today's mission. About halfway down the top of the fuselage, the gun turret had twin fifties that could shoot horizontally any direction. The tail gunner also had twin fifties for attacks from behind. The belly turret was rarely used and proved to be the *Lancaster's* liability.

Nigel's thoughts were interrupted. "Blue Leader to squadron. We will remain this altitude in staggered formation. Move now." As Blue Two through Four slid slightly back and down, Blue Leader continued. "We will remain at this altitude and on my command begin slow weave at combat speed in case of company. Keep an eye on your petrol and report half tank, then disengage and return home after advising Blue Leader. Acknowledge, over." All three *Spitfires* for 610 Squadron acknowledged. "Blue Leader commencing weave now."

The lead *Spitfire* pushed his throttle to near maximum speed and started his gentle turn to the right, watching his wingmen follow suit. Before the second pass was completed, "Blue Two to group, we have company at twelve o'clock low, over." "Blue Leader to group, I have bogies, five *109's*. They are heading straight into the bomber's box. As soon as the *109's* make their first pass, we will break up and pursue whatever is left of

Jerry. Keep an eye to the east for another cluster of Huns to follow. Keep tight and make your guns hot. Out." In an instant, Nigel and the other three pilots twisted the outer safety ring of their gun buttons to on.

As the *Messerschmitts* started firing at the British bombers, they were answered with deadly firepower. The *Lancasters'* machine gun tracers ripped through the sky like a fusillade, eight from the nose turrets and twenty-four from the top turrets. It was crazy. One of the fighters disintegrated and another started smoking black and peeled back to the east, a flamer out of the fight. The lead *Lancaster* on the far left had two engines shot out and was descending in a slow spiral, with a few falling figures and fewer open chutes. The second *Lancaster* from the right took fire into the cockpit, seriously wounding the engineer in the dicky-seat to the right of the pilot.

"Blue Leader to group, I am going left; Blue Four, break right and engage. Two and Three remain on station as the party is getting crowded. You will engage after they pass over the box. Out." Nigel peeled off to the right, spotted one of the two Germans, and gave chase. With his speed and 500 feet altitude advantage, he was the chaser. The *109* pilot knew he had company, immediately making a tight turn down and left. Nigel Sheffield was close now, the tail large enough, nearly too large. He sprayed his 0.303-inch Browning machine guns from left to right rendering the *Messerschmitt* into several large and small unusable airplane parts. Its German occupant was now headed to somewhere in West Germany via parachute. Nigel turned back toward the formation and noticed another *Lancaster* headed to earth with its occupants. Blue leader clicked his mike, "Blue report." "Blue Two engaged." "Blue Three with fuel state, returning home." "Blue Four, returning back to formation." "Blue Leader and Four will find targets and engage." As Nigel was counting ten of the twelve bombers still flying, one with only three engines, he directed his attention to the *109's*. He assumed the bombers plastered the second group of Germans as effectively as the first. After looking over both shoulders and rear view mirrors, he didn't see any Luftwaffe. Just as he was preparing to report his half-full fuel state, Nigel caught a stubborn German pilot hanging around wanting to do more harm. Nigel swung around and managed to get into a horizontal scissors with the *Messerschmitt*, then finally twisted around to get on his tail. The German must have lost Sheffield in the sun, as Blue Four Sheffield pulled close and shredded the *109's* airframe, then watched the engine explode. Sheffield yanked his stick to the left to avoid the debris, but it was too late. A large metal shard hit the canopy head on, giving the fighter a convertible appearance, leaving the pilot addled. Sheffield tried to wipe his face of *Spitfire* fluids with his own blood and sweat, then turned west towards the North Sea.

The airborne convertible was a curious sight to see, a dazed pilot trying to clear his goggles of grease and blood. Sheffield drifted between twilight and daylight for about twenty minutes, but lucid enough to make a gradual descent to an oxygen rich altitude. He knew he was in no shape to land an airplane and had to get out. He wasn't even clear about using his radio; whom to call and what to say. He only knew he was messed up somewhere over western Germany. He needed to get out of his mangled *Spitfire*. He moved his left hand just above the throttle and on the small radio box, pushed the lower button for the E frequency. "Tophat Four to Tophat Leader. Returning to base with damage, over." There wasn't an answer, and if there was he wouldn't know, and it didn't matter.

At 10,000 feet with the outline of the foggy shrouded coast just off his eleven o'clock, Nigel began to unhook his harness and stand on the seat to climb out of the *Spitfire*. Then he blacked out as the *Spitfire* slowly rolled on its back, letting Sheffield fall clear. Part of the *Spitfire's* canopy and jagged canopy rail had scraped his midriff and snagged on his D-ring, tearing the parachute from its bag, while the tip of the tail grazed his hairline, and soundly smacked smacked his left hip and ankle. Sheffield's parachute opened, a milky translucent parasol, silently rocking him into a transient sleep. After nine minutes of this lullaby, Sheffield found himself dumped into the icy basin of the briny North Sea. The stretch marks on Mother Nature's sky bore fresh scars, as another of her creatures dashed from a precarious troposphere to the sea below.

The frigid water helped Sheffield in his struggle for consciousness as he gasped for air in the choppy sea. The sea grass at the bottom of the North Sea was already littered with the debris of combat airplanes, not fickle as to make or model, it claiming yet another.

Tophat One and Two circled the drifting parachute as it entered the gray concealing clouds below. They quickly radioed the Navy's Air Sea Rescue team to alert them of Sheffield's approximate co-ordinates. If he was lucky he might have splashed down and been quickly pulled out of the frigid water by a passing boat. The RAF pilots of Tophat knew Sheffield could not survive longer than a few minutes. The two 610 Squadron pilots headed back to Biggin Hill, fearful Tophat Four would share the fate of over half of the downed pilots ending up in the English channel, they perished. That was the last anyone would know the fate of Flight Lieutenant Nigel Sheffield for a long time.

When Maria Fuentes and the rest of the ATA women who had trained with Sheffield learned of his fate, they to a woman, collapsed into a deep sense of loss. For one of them, the bereavement would not fade, especially the image of Nigel's .38-pistol handle poking from his jacket.

• • • • • •

That evening, a small twelve-foot dinghy, powered by a two-cycle motor, chugged into the Oosterschelde waterway of Zeeland, an eastern deep-water port in Holland. Zeeland had seen its share of the war early on, as 1,000 brave Dutch soldiers doggedly fought the Germans before being overrun, conceding to a surrender in May. The main city of Middelburg was heavily damaged, having taken the worst beating of any other town in Holland. It was to the dismay of many Germans, as Zeeland was a beloved holiday destination.

Zeeland was shaped like a hand with three stubby fingers pointed into the North Sea. Joord turned to his husky 15-year-old son, Jürgen, and put his finger to his lips. He had deliberately waited until just after sunset to enter the port where the German PT patrol boats putted up and down the coast, particularly just outside Zeeland. Joord and Jürgen had been seen every day going back and forth as two innocent fishermen.

Today was no different, although one small heavily armed PT boat pulled alongside to examine their catch. The Dutch fishermen were just the two, the middle of the boat covered with 18 to 20 North Sea skate and small salmon, some still squirming. Without any expression, Joord tossed two of the largest fish up to the closest German leaning over the side. After tossing two prized salmon, he slowly turned his boat slightly away, allowed by the satisfied Germans. Joord turned the helm over to his son, then started sorting the fish revealing a blanket with a body wrapped inside. Nigel moaned with discomfort of his injuries and from the smell of decaying fish and bait. He wasn't sure which was worse, the stinging on his forehead and hip or the fish stink. "Stay down, Soldier. Stay down for just a bit longer. Ja? Here's a drier blanket and tarp for now."

Joord slipped past the village of Zierikzee off his left shoulder then slowed by Ouwerkerk and made a slow left turn through another but smaller canal. Almost at idle, his small put-put motor joined the quiet boat bottom slapping on the water, being familiar sounds in the canal. He slowed and drifted into a slip in St. Philipsland between two other slightly larger boats and shut his motor off. Nearly all of the fishermen in the village were in, many by early afternoon. "Can you walk, Soldier?" The shivering Sheffield stood unsteady in the still rocking boat, and nodded. "I think so," Sheffield still clinging to his blanket. "I might need some help. My left ankle to the hip really hurt, and I hate to put much weight on either until I see what damage is done." "Come on then, lean on me"

Joord and his son propped up Sheffield; half carrying the hobbling soldier into their modest two-bedroom clay house. When the lanterns were turned on, the men lit the cast iron wood-burning cook stove. Joord and his son sat the downed pilot on the toilet seat and gently removed the soggy wool blanket, careful not to aggravate his bruised body. They ran warm bathwater and helped him ease down into the heavenly balm. Still a bit fuzzy, he let them wash his bloody face and his bruised hip and thigh. The swelling had begun in earnest with the warming of Sheffield's body. His left side was caked with blood and swollen yellow. No broken bones so far, but a face bruised as if it were the fifteenth round of a boxer way behind on points.

When he quit shivering and finished soaping, they helped him out of the tub to dry off. They exchanged Sheffield's wet blanket for a long nightshirt. His bottom lip was somewhat split and still caked with a line of dried blood. The other wounds were minor, some not wounds after all when they got the blood washed off. The warm cotton nightshirt was pure bliss. The small cup of tea placed in his shaking hands was the flip side of heaven. "Thanks a bloody ton. This is so perfect." "Come in here where it is warmer. You have a name, Soldier?" "Name's Sergeant Welding. Mark Welding."

"Here's our situation, Mr. Welding." "Mark, please." "Okay, Mark. I am a simple fisherman who just happened to watch you float into our cold North Sea and got you into my boat before you could freeze. We would have done it for the German, Pole, or whomever. That's how I've been taught. Now, since you are a Brit, I do have a bit of information. As I stay simple and play older than my age of 50, I raise no suspicion especially as I keep German patrol boats supplied with shad and skates, sometimes a salmon. They aren't fans of sturgeon, because the Russians like it. I also keep in touch with the Dutch and Belgian underground, just for situations like this. I am not part of the resistance chain, but help when I can. The resistance in turn keep your military people aware of whom they have and what shape they are in and how to get they home.

"For now, there is a provincial doctor, but he is in what is left of Middelburg, which is a ways from here. Not far, but takes a while to get there. I will explain later. Jürgen is buying some food from the street vendor who lingers in front of the doctor's house. The doctor is a virtuous man and would patch up a German just as well as an Allied soldier. For that, the German Soldiers give him and his associates a wide berth. When you are well enough to travel, hopefully after just a few days, we will give you to the Dutch Resistance led by Social Democrats and Dutch Communists for your exfiltration. They will hook you up with your MI-9 people, designed to help you get back to England. At some point the RAF will learn of your rescue. The resistance typically brings money, maps, and false papers to assist you. The usual route from here is to Paris and then via Tours, Bordeaux, Bayonne, over the Pyrenees to San Sebastián in Spain. From there you will likely see the Basques of Bilbao, then down to Madrid, then on to Lisbon for travel to England. They call it the Comet line. The other route is the Pat O'Leary, which is extremely circuitous and usually ends up at Gibraltar, both lines work in the thick of the Germans.

Either way, it will depend in their resources, manpower, safe houses, and intelligence on the German troop placements. Whatever route you are taken will be in your best interest. At any rate, the trip over the mountains in the dead of winter will be your harshest challenge of your life. If make it, you will know more deeply of yourself than you might imagined.

"You Brits had one guy, a Dick Kragt, who lost all his gear when his parachute opened except his Colt .45, but still managed to hook up with our Jew, a Joop Pillar in Ernst, then proceeded to put together quite a network. They are a feisty bunch, our Resistance, really sore at the Germans and have to be held in check or they would organize a platoon of pitchforks and try to kill a German. Right now, though, they are trying to shelter as many Jews as possible, as they are still being rooted out like common animals by the German SS. I trust you are not a Jew, Mark? Either way, it's no matter.

"By the way, Joord, my name is Nigel, Squadron Leader Nigel Sheffield from RAF 610 Squadron." "We are Smits, Jürgen and I." "I wasn't sure who you were, as I am sure there are still a handful of German sympathizers in this area, so I had to be careful. I meant to ask, is there a Missus? I see some feminine touches: the dainty teacups, doilies all about, and the lovely crocheted curtains." Jürgen cleared his throat, then turned and left the room. "Mr. Sheffield, we lost our Johanna in May of 1940 when the Germans bombed Middelburg. She was trapped in a small shop as it burned to the ground. She didn't have a chance." Joord's eyes glistened from the reflection of the lantern.

He too turned aside and left the room with, "Sheffield, get some rest then we'll eat a bite in about an hour, pickled herring if we can find some. Later, we'll get out later tonight and see who I can rouse from the resistance. There's a stout in the icebox if it suits you. Help yourself." "Mr. Smit, did you manage to save my flight suit and pistol?" "We used the pistol to sink your flight suit and jacket. If we had been caught with you in those clothes and gun, we would all have been shot on sight. A man in a blanket with just underwear is not so hard to explain, a suicide gone wrong, etc. Just minutes after we grabbed you and buried you under our fish, we gave a prowling German U-Boat crew some fish. Then they let us pull away and go home. " The Smit father and son's modest home would be Sheffield's refuge for another two days as plans were made to get him home.

As promised, Joord returned with a bite of food. All three ate in silence. The Smits demolished the herring, while Nigel munched mostly on fried cabbage, hotchpotch, and boiled eggs. He doubled up on the surprisingly tasty stew. "Mr. Sheffield, day after tomorrow I am going to turn you over the Dutch and

Belgian contingent who will hide you until it is safe to start your trip south. You will learn this business is highly dangerous, demanding a great deal of planning and sophistication." Joord explained the escape plan involved a chain of people, safe houses, barns or sometimes a dusty pile of brush. Sheffield was admonished to follow orders *exactly*, and that from people he did not know. The patience he would need, was explained by the sheer volume of pilots recovered. Every day, at least thirty found themselves just like Sheffield, putting a strain on the civilian Resistance Fighters' resources. Clothes had to be found and fitted. Medical needs had to be rendered. Railway tickets and new identities obtained, all time consuming and costly.

The consequence to the pilots, if discovered would be a cushy prison camp, while civilians, if caught, would usually be death where they stood, concentration camps, or just vanishing. Hitler's General Keitel had established a *Night and Fog Decree* that demanded any resistance personnel caught hiding or helping pilots, crew, or soldiers, to be arrested and then simply made to vanish. With all the dangers to the civilians, it was often frustrating to the RAF pilot when unable to sufficiently thank his adopted family, as handoffs were often abrupt and in the dark of a moonless night.

Sheffield, clearheaded now, dressed and shook hands with Jürgen, then followed his father for roughly two miles of walking to shops, bakeries, and fish market stalls. When Joord met the handoff, the two would bump into each other, politely doff hats, and continue on. Sheffield had a new leader to lag behind through narrow streets, across bridges, sometimes in circles. It would be a person with a distinctive hat or scarf or coat, whom Sheffield would then follow until the next handoff. After three handoffs, he followed a stooped older man who quietly took Sheffield's arm as if he were an unsteady uncle needing a hand. The process distressed Sheffield, as he would not likely see Joord or his son Jürgen, two amazingly unselfish people.

After stopping to buy a small bouquet of flowers, they entered his modest home on a remote piece of property in Middleburg where he met Mr. and Mrs. Heeren. As soon as the door closed, the old man stood erect and was half a foot taller than Nigel; young, too. The people. They're actors; all this effort for one night, maybe two, or even three. The next link in the chain had to be prearranged with notice on down the line all agreed. Sheffield would remain with the Heeren's until Holland's Christmas Eve on December 5th. Sheffield donned his new, well-worn, black watch cap and long hooded jacket, then spirited into the southern night by the Dutch Resistance with a pack of food and clothing.

Sheffield's December 5th journey started in a garbage lorry from Zeeland to a farmhouse on the outskirts of Baarle-Nassau, a border town set up by the Resistance. There he received much needed food, rest, and an odd interrogation by a Belgian named Escrinier. With German infiltrators posing as downed airmen even to the extent of actually parachuting in, the resistance had to question every pilot and soldier. Phony infiltrators were shot without ceremony on the spot. Nigel responded to questions like, "What is the number on RAF leave form?" "295." "What was the cost of tea and a Chelsea Bun in London?" "Three pence each." "What railway station is nearest Grosvenor Hotel?" "Victoria Station." "Where and what is Swan and Edgar?" "Department Store at Piccadilly Circus." After half a hour of nonstop questions, they seemed satisfied. Then the questioners abruptly left. When Nigel asked the host what they said, he said, "He'll do, but watch him, we can't be too careful," comforting but not reassuring thought Nigel. The host did say the last two guests were shot in the kitchen, showing the RAF pilot two bullet holes in the back door, yet to be patched.

The map Sheffield studied at Joord's house was simple. Zeeland to Antwerp, where he would get another change of clothes, a suitcase of food and 100 French Francs. Then on to Brussels, across the French border south of Mons, and on to Paris. After getting replenished with supplies, clothes and transportation papers, via Tours and Bordeaux, the next stop would be the Basque town of Bayonne. This would be the jumping off town for the hike through the western Pyrenees to either Madrid and Lisbon or Gibraltar, where expatriates were collected. At Bayonne, he would be given walking around money, food, and travel papers.

If the last part of the trip was to be as complicated as the first, he knew it would be a grueling test of his will and body. He pushed the thought of the dangers behind him and took those first steps with the full intention of returning to England in time to help England bring the Germans to their knees.

The End of 1942

Otto was sick of picking dead skin from his burns in a rehab unit near Bayreuth in eastern Germany, dreading his next assignment as Chief Instructor of night operations for replacement pilots at Kimi in Northern Finland for the Luftwaffe's Air Fleet Five. Patience in the cold was nowhere to be found in the Luftwaffe Handbook.

Otto's mentor and former Squadron Commander

Gustav Rödel closed his year in early November over the Egyptian coastal town Sidi el Rahman, shooting down a *Spitfire* for his 73rd victory. As Rödel was called back to Germany as part of the 'Defend the Reich Campaign', he kept tabs on his ace student Otto Kelter, determined to find a way to help him earn his Knight's Cross. A way not putting him in harm's way, yet get him a final victory.

Maria, Paige, and Carli were having a quiet dinner with the Cunningham family at their Mere House Billet. Alex was in the sack with a new "friend," a WAAF balloon operator. They had two things in common: barrage balloons and erogenous pleasure.

In the ATA headquarters at RAF White Waltham, Pauline Gower and William Stephenson were toasting the survival of Squadron Commander Sheffield, while weighing the pros and cons of family notification. They weren't convinced he was out of danger just yet.

Harold and Phoebe Rosen had just finished celebrating Hanukkah on the 11th of December, while continuing to pray for the safety of their son somewhere in the Pacific and Deborah's in England.

Aviation pioneer Jackie Cochran was six weeks into her post as head of the newly formed Women's Flying Training Detachment, designed to train women for wartime ferry services like the ATA.

On October 22nd, the same ship Deborah sailed on to Liverpool that summer, the HNCS *Winnipeg* was torpedoed before reaching St. John, Newfoundland, on her return trip. The ship sank in minutes, but all 192 aboard were saved, rescued by another in the convoy.

CHAPTER TWELVE

Formation of the Four Angels

Jim Mollison and Amy Johnson were British Commonwealth aviation royalty. They were the Astaire-Rogers, Gable-Lombard, and Burton-Taylor of England. The diminutive Johnson, Amelia Earhart, and Jackie Cochran, were all in a class of their own, in and out their airplanes. Johnson was the first woman to fly solo from England to Australia. She met playboy Jim Mollison, her kindred spirit of daring and flash. They flew fast, married fast in 1932, and divorced fast in 1938. The Mollison-Johnson duo was the provender only dreamed of by the Broadsheet London Times and Daily Mail newspapers. Whatever they reported, the Morning Star and Daily Mirror sensationalized that not reported. The Agony Columns were on fire with the pair. One could be convinced they had their dedicated reporters. Amy died in a tragic accident on a cold foggy January 5th, 1941, leaving her loyal ex-husband and still close friend devastated.

On a rain turned frosty day in February 1943, a German twin-engine *ME-110* fighter attacked the Mollison's *Avro Anson*, with eleven other ATA pilots aboard while returning from a routine retrieval. The Scot's calm flying skills enabled the vulnerable ferry aircraft to narrowly escape into nearby clouds, putting down safely at White Waltham. Although his copilot and popular ATA pilot, Diana Barnato had lost her bottle, Mollison's kept his nerve focusing on getting on the ground and his cup of tea. Heading to Gower's office with the *Anson* engines still warm, Mollison thought he might impose on Commander Gower for a spot of hot tea and, at the same time, relate the close call with the German. As soon as his words fell, she lit up like a volcano, then spewed more lava when she saw the bullet holes in the *Anson's* fuselage.

Now it became personal. Amy Johnson and Jim Mollison had been close friends, and Gower was still grieving over Johnson's death in the icy River Thames only two years earlier. With a broken heart, Pauline recalled that awful day when she learned of Johnson's death and, afterwards, of the struggle to break the news to her parents. Gower reflected on the obituary she wrote for the London Times on 8 January.

She recounting her friend Amy's flying skills, but personal knowledge of her courage, lack of conceit, sense of humor, and large heart. Pauline Gower's blood was boiling now. After getting Mollison that spot of tea, she turned to her right hand woman, experienced ATA pilot Mary Nicholson, to get her civilian boss, d'Erlanger, on the phone straight away. "Gerard, can you come by?" "Urgent"? "Yes, I think it is. Thank you. I will see you then, and thanks again."

The energetic thirty-seven year old d' Erlanger immediately left his spacious office in London to see her once again. He climbed the steps to Miss Gower's office and was offered tea, as he made himself comfortable in the jacquard tufted chair in front of her desk. "Gerard, we have a problem, and maybe an opportunity. As you know, our dear friends Jim Mollison and Diana Barnato, with ten of our ATA pilots, were nearly killed in his *Anson* this morning. If he hadn't the luck of a nearby cloud, all could have been lost. We continue to mourn Amy, and now I can't stand the thought of losing Jim, or any other of our people, to a lousy Luftwaffe 'lone wolf' fighter looking for easy kills."

"I know, I know. What can I do?" "I want to allow a handful of our First and Second Grade people who fly the *Spits* and *Hurricanes* to have bullets loaded in their magazines." "Are you daft?"

"Let me reshape my words and at least seem somewhat logical. Gerard, on occasion, we fly *Spits* or *Hurricanes* with 20mm ammo still in the airplanes. Several of the light bombers often have 250 pounders still strapped to them, far too often I might add. You know about that too I suppose. Ministry would probably shudder at the thought. If they did know, no one on the ground made a fuss. In the morning skies when the *Messerschmitts* and *Fw-190s* prowl, where we have the *Anson* shuttles flying valuable people, medicines, or wounded, I want an escort of two *Hurricanes* or *Spitfires* with bullets and pilots that are trained to use them. I've been thinking of the 'who' for the job.

"Gerard, our RAF is already strapped and can't spare a soul, especially to escort local *Ansons*. To keep up with American and British bombers, they're snatching up our best conscripts as well. I know too well that the King's Orders specifically prohibit women from serving in combat, and if anything happened from a dustup with the Germans, you can see where this might go. So, we truly can't use our Commonwealth women. Also, there is the mixed sex thing. That mustn't happen.

"Since we aren't going into combat, I am back to the women. I want to send a select group of eight ATA women to attend the RAF Central Flying School and learn the basics of defense, low-level tactics, and full instrument training. We'll use foreign pilots just to be on the safe side with Royalty. As you know, our men *and* women fly airplanes with no radios and minimum navigation equipment. They are lucky to have an airspeed indicator and altimeter. They just hug the ground using only church steeples and railway lines to guide them.

It would be a hand-picked group that we can say need the extra training in case women are needed to ferry across the pond later in the war. A little later, we can cull down to the final four to serve as occasional escorts, with four as back up. Wherever we set this squadron up, the story is that it is Special Ops ATA, without anyone knowing they are armed. As unarmed escorts, they would still be welcome, as the danger is from lone-wolf stalkers who prey on single strays or stragglers. With two Spits riding along, the Germans would think they were armed. They *would be,* but people we report to would think quite differently, I am quite sure"

"I don't know, Pauline, it's a rather bold plan I must say. Sounds risky, especially if one of our ATA people gets shot down, especially a woman, conscript or not. That would be ghastly and would *not* suit our case. If they get lucky and destroy a Hun, then what? The secret's out of the bag, most certainly to ignite the RAF brass into white-hot fury. I would get sacked in a London minute if Balfour or Shelly got word of this. Churchill himself would skin me alive and make a pub stool with it. Beaverbrook, tethered to the hip of the Prime Minister, might be our only way out as he loves nefarious methods that benefit Britain's Air war, especially if it scalded the fusty Air Ministry. We simply can't afford a wrong foot on this one. You see my point?"

Unmoved, Gower asked, "How about we get with RAF and talk with them. If we could convince them of the idea, they might be content, especially if on the hush. If you and I made them aware these *Ansons* or *Hudsons* we use to taxi precious personnel, the wounded or high-level papers were vulnerable to attack; they should have no objection, especially if some of their brass or cases of prize French Calvados du Pêche or Rémy Martin were at stake. The RAF also has a great deal of respect for ex-RAF Mollison, and it would touch a sensitive spot to recount his close call. And don't forget, Shelmerdine was the best man at Amy and Jim's wedding. RAF support would be big; you know that.

"Our ATA already has an excellent reputation of getting airplanes from Halliburton to the assembly units and squadrons in a steady stream without complaint. You and I both know, just seeing the escorts would discourage the German cowards and keep them at altitude. I doubt if any skirmishes would result and it would keep the twin engine transports safer. You know what else? We could use Stephenson's SOE to send messages to the Germans that we know can be decoded to announce our armed *Spitfire* escorts using RAF pilots, all aces, taking temporary restful duty."

"That last part is genius, but I am still awfully nervous about this stuff, Pauline, and I do realize under other circumstances, it might work." Pauline didn't like it when d'Erlanger turned formal.

Gower trying to get back to informal, "We are at war, Gerard, and we owe as much safety to our people as we can give them. The RAF was nearly exhausted after the Battle of Britain, losing 450 pilots and over a thousand airplanes. It takes a while to rebuild, especially since we are still in the middle of an undecided war. Our RAF leadership is anxious to get any help they can, so I am sure the insurance would be appreciated. What would be your thinking?"

"Pauline, what worries me is, if unsupervised, one could go rogue, way beyond your pilot's pranks of 'appropriating' airplanes to get to Christmas parties in the full of fog." "Hand picked Gerard. Hand picked!" "Righto. Let me think on it and get back to you. Maybe we can start with the men and not mention the women and see what happens." He shifted gears, slowly settling back into his chair squeezing his chin with his thumb and finger. "On the other hand, if it was just four to eight hand-picked women, they would be highly dependable, less reckless, and more likely to pull it off. The thought of one of my one-eyed, one-legged and 65-year-old ferry pilots having bullets makes me shiver. Let's get Stephenson involved in this lark, as if we were to suggest the likelihood the group might be useful later in the war for his SOE enterprises. He is also a very *very* smart biscuit and might just have ideas and political muscle to pull this off. If he thinks we are daft, then what?" Gower could only shrug, palms up. "Then we are cooked, and will say no more of it."

Two days later the three sat in Stephenson's lavishly iconic Claridge Hotel room. "So let me get this straight. A German *ME-110* fighter-bomber jumped one of your ferry taxis with twelve ATA pilots aboard? You are thinking of one or two-armed *Spitfire* or *Hurricane* escorts just for VIP personnel, sensitive papers, and critical medicines or severely wounded? And you have narrowed it down to non-Commonwealth pilots, probably women? And you want to involve me? Right now I have my hands rather occupied, even though the war seems to be turning our way. We have Rommel trapped in Tunisia and the Russians have surrounded the Germans holed up in Stalingrad. All that and I am having trouble keeping safe houses open in the O'Leary escape line. We may end up closing it and try something direct. Anyway, how can I help? Go slow while I shift gears."

"Mr. Stephenson, we know you are busy, rather, so we will be quick. First we mostly need an outside perspective from a smart mind. If we pull this caper off, with or without incident, we might need to have the women, if it is to be women, moved to your service even if not during their service as escorts, but later in the war. As your Special Ops group is highly respected and without political interference, you might be able to find a job for them on the continent and whatever pushback we might get would blow over."

"Pauline, the only element I might argue, is the apolitical twist you suggest. My role has taken me from advisor and courier to President Roosevelt and our Prime Minister, to the seamy responsibilities of assigning my girls to seduce Vichy leaders in France. If I do end up with these women, it may not be in their character to work for me." It was time for his words to sink in. "In general, I am not opposed to your over-all thinking. Even if unarmed, the German lone wolfs would think twice about jumping another *Anson* if there were a *Spit* tagging along. Have you thought about just escorting, unarmed?" "We did, exhaustively so. If the attacker was bold enough to jump our two unarmed *Spitfire* escorts, then we might have murdered two innocent women, not mention the fate of the *Anson*. We felt it far too serious a risk." Gower gazed at her partner in crime, relieved to see D'Erlanger's like-minded nod.

"Right you are, solid point. Moving along then. I like the woman aspect. Pick eight and prune to four. Isolate the small group in a location away from Maidenhead, Hamble or any pool. You must separate yourselves from the group and leave no paper trail. Let your Mary keep a separate dossier and put it in a safety deposit box at Barclay's in Maidenhead with her as the only approved custodian. Your pilots have to be absolute in their secrecy of having live ammunition during their missions as well as any crew that would have absolute need to know about the bullets. I would do another background check on every crewwoman for sure for this little show. If found out, play dumb about the arming element. You didn't know they were armed; it's rubbish, etc. Have the armourer load the airplanes in the middle of the night before each scheduled mission and take them off the airplane immediately on return.

"During the day, park the airplanes in the hangars or near the firing butts at the other end of the field. They rarely use them anymore, especially at this removed RAF airfield. If you can, pick an airfield the American Eighth Air Force is moving into, like Martlesham or Little Walden in Essex. Put hangar doors on at least two of your hangars and keep them locked, new regulations, etcetera; something like that. I will leave details to you. And, *most importantly*, have only one ground crewman or woman aware of the arming and be sure she has a spotless background check. Keep the activity all in number two sector. Consider from the East to North Weald, to Horn church, to Biggin Hill, around to RAF Tangmere in the south. At least it will be easier to police and the German threat is mostly in those areas anyway. As for the women, you know best.

"There is one girl that I might have an interest in, and it's the American girl that you manufactured in Portugal and raised in New Mexico. Deborah Rosenberg, I think." "Rosen, now Maria Fuentes." "Sorry. Our Rosen woman doesn't exist so far as her records are concerned, which is perfect, if it might interject some veracity into the decision. If all goes well, at some point in time, I might be able to use her in North Africa or France.

"Back to your plan; if this *does* involve any Americans, let me know so I can keep Donovan in the loop." Eyes fixed at Gower, "likewise, I advocate one of you inform Cochran of any American involvement. She might have a problem with your use of her American women, which might fall ill on her from her political contacts all the way from the White House to General Arnold, who, as I remember, wasn't too keen on the whole idea in the first place. If they veto American involvement, it would leave you with only conscript women, which wouldn't be all that bad. You have some rich talent from the likes of Helen Harrison, 'Chile' Duhalde, the Pole, Jad Pilsudska, and others who don't come to mind at the moment." Stephenson slapped his thighs and stood. Gower and d'Erlanger stood at the same time and thanked the British Intelligence boss for his input. D'Erlanger spoke for the two ATA leaders. "We will keep you posted, Bill. Thanks. Thanks ever so."

Swiveling to Pauline, "Stephenson didn't waste any time. It's done, Pauline. He's in! Now, give me some time to think through this cracked mess." "When will you be ready to make a decision, Gerard?" "In four or five, but seven days at the latest." The sixth day became seven, and just as Pauline put her hand on the phone, Mary tapped on the door and announced d'Erlanger. "Come in. Tea?" "No time, Pauline. The *Anson* is outside with the engine running, and this won't take long. Here's what we can do, and I'll give you time to contemplate it. I am proposing we create a very small escort squadron of just women, on sensitive ferry missions requiring Spits or Hurricanes, but only one or two escorts, as the nature of the cargo determines. We will call them 'Guardians', or something similar and give them a special patch. A maximum of eight women, none British, are to attend training like RAF Central, and no more than four in the air at the same time. Then we'll make it the final four. The RAF training will be extensive, saving the gunnery until last. Their RAF commander will handle that, one on one." "Gerard, how about we have all the training done by two instructors?" "Better yet, Pauline, better yet! Splendid thinking."

D'Erlanger expressed the women's squadron would remain small, and by excluding men, would prevent the temptation for the program to get out of hand and be unmanageable. "It has to be small, containable, and extremely discreet. We can't have any incidents that might attract attention, or we will all be skewered, war or not. They will be Angel Squadron Seven, because you and the women will need all the luck you can get." "My lucky number is four, Gerard, and there are four of them."

"Then four it is. It's still a civilian group, and hopefully, you will use discretion as to when and to whom you give these hot airplanes. Let's get the women trained, give it a try for a few weeks, and *then* talk about its permanence. You never know Pauline; your ATA started with eight pilots, not suggesting it's our aim for the women to grow into a large force. In this particular case, we have to prevent the temptation of any growth. If we launch this, all curiosity will be minimized of the women escorts in *unarmed* airplanes. We might be laughed at, but it's better than being dishonored or fired, or both. God help us all if we lose one of our girls. Nonetheless, my logic is satisfied, Pauline. Yours?"

She nodded. "I don't have to think further about this, Commodore, my logic is also satisfied. Get me the paperwork with the particulars straight away, and I will stay in touch, especially during the training of the women. Hand-deliver by courier. Let's have one last meeting before timetables are planned, and I will assemble the best eight pilots. Now be on your way and get out before I get sentimental." "Will do, Miss Gower, will do, but first..." His voice tailed off as he bid Gower adieu, and was gone.

Gower's unusual friend and Chief of her ATA strode through the building and hustled into his seat in the *Avro Anson* Air Taxi. Strapping in and lifting off, Gerard was thinking to himself now. '*I have to talk with my old friend Commander Wilkinson, the Wing Commander at Martlesham. He will be the lame duck C.O., and probably won't care, passing the baton of the RAF airfield to the Americans later in the summer and in the third quarter. I'll just give the overview: women, ferry pool, escort, Ansons, Mollison event, secrecy, etc. The Squadron Commander of this small contingent has to be the best pilot and politician. I know, for hands on leadership and probably the RAF's best fighter pilot not still in the air would be Nigel Sheffield, an ATA instructor and administrator, but he's not here. Someone like him though.*'

He recalled on the unforgettable Battle of Britain Day in September 1940, when a German *Me-109* shot him down in his *Spitfire*. He banged up his left hand and arm as he parachuted to safety, but not before downing three of the Jerrys.

'After two years healing, being in the drink after only one flight, and another five months walking through France, Sheffield will be chomping at the bit to fly again. Moving from ATA screener to 'advisor at Martlesham Heath' would be perfect. His gunnery skills would come in real handy. Still, we have to get him home and fit again. Damn Krauts!'

Stephenson's constant updates on Sheffield's whereabouts and progress gave d'Erlanger confidence he would get his Squadron Commander for the job.

'When we convince Sheffield his transfer meant getting into the air sooner, he for sure will accept reassignment as an advisor to the 8th Air Force at Martlesham. Shortly thereafter, we can move the women out there and reveal Sheffield's real mission. With his DFC and DFM and other decorations, he should have enough 'warrior capital' to satisfy the Air Marshall if they ever got involved with the Luftwaffe. The RAF wing commanders who need every fit or unfit pilot they could get their hands on won't much care, as they might consider it an American issue if there is a dustup with the Germans, plus they will find it amusing that they will be 'unarmed'.

'If he gets back to England soon, I'll have to pry Sheffield from the RAF, but Wilkinson is a friend and that should keep it a local thing not provoking the brass. After being shot down twice he deserves some nonviolent duty.'

D'Erlanger's business mind is rolling now, like a bowling ball down the middle of the alley with just the right amount of spin. *'Wilkinson makes it clean all the way 'round,'* he further thought.

'Martlesham Heath will be in a flux with the RAF and 8th Air Force handoff, likely taking at least three months. The scraping off the grass runways to install

Macadam-surfaced steel mesh onto a surface of oil and tar for the heaver American fighters moving from Goxhall will take a while. That should be plenty of time to get the women trained and billeted, maybe move them to the married officers' quarters way across the field during the training and afterwards. The three buildings are all the way to the north end of the field, almost out of view from the control room of the Operations building at the end of the other runway. If the Eighth Air Force ever needed ferrying in one of the Eighth Army's C-45 Transports, they might be highly supportive of any kind of escort, even if it's women-flown 'unarmed' Spitfires. It's doubtful they will have any squawk. I'll need to have a medical lorry repainted and parked near the northern-most hangar and increase the medical staff in case the need arises.' He trailed off thinking of support staff like riggers, mechanics, fitters, engineers, drivers, and a place to hide 0.303-inch machine gun ammo.

'I'll have to keep as much of a lid on this matter as possible and will have to explain away any mishap. The RAF and Americans should have their hands full keeping up with the airfield transition, probably lasting into October. With some RAF activity still operational during the runway remodeling, the confusion will be helpful. I'll have to catch up with the 356th Air Group Commander, Lt Col. Harold J. Rau, right after the women get situated.

'With the pilots out of sight and support people across the field, I doubt Rau will care. Because of RAF Martlesham Heath's history as the primary airfield for experimental aircraft, out of place or unexpected airplanes will barely be noticed. The women ferrying of Hurricanes and Spits won't interfere with the training of the American P-47's. As long as we don't need both runways at the same time, there shouldn't be a problem. Martlesham Heath is the perfect place to put this squadron! It just might work!'

. . . . . .

Three miles southwest of Maidenhead in her White Waltham office, Pauline had one last worrisome chore of calling Jackie Cochran. The two women had drifted cross grain from the beginning that summer of 1941. As far as Gower was concerned, Cochran hadn't been infected with the viruses of propriety and modesty and Cochran stiffly jealous of Gower's pedigree.

"Jackie? Pauline here." "Hello my dear. How are you managing this fine day?" "Keen, as I hope the same for you, Jackie. I wanted to catch you the first thing in your American morning. Is this a convenient time?" "Always a convenient time for you Pauline. Let's have it, old girl, let's have it." Gower shuddered at the gal-pal tone of Cochran, and she almost couldn't bear her churlish asides when she was in England. 'It's just a phone call, Pauline,' she reminded herself.

"Jackie, to begin with, of all the women you sent me were just marvelous; first notch in every respect, all of them. It has been a true privilege to be part of their training and watch them grow. To change to subject, I am calling about the February incident where one of our distinguished and talented pilots ferrying twelve ATA pilots was jumped by a German Me-110." "Holy hell, what happened?" " Luckily, Flight Captain Jim Mollison was able to duck into the clouds after taking several bullets in the fuselage, missing everyone, praise be. A miracle all the way around." "Thank Goodness! What does all that have to do with me?"

"Jackie, D'Erlanger and I met with our Special Ops leadership and found a way to mitigate a repeat of

Hunter Luftwaffe pilots bothering our ferry service again." "How so?" "I'm getting there, Jackie. We are going to train a small select group of women to escort our transports in Spitfires or Hurricanes to the public unarmed, but in reality armed. There will be a component of secrecy, of course. I am calling to give you advance notice that there may be an American woman or two involved." Gower could hear a long breath and 'hmmmm' on the line. She delved into a few details including Martlesham, the eight women to be considered without identifying the Americans, with leadership having approved the concept. "That's about it Jackie. What do you think? I do value your opinion."

"Well, to begin with, I have my hands full over here with Mrs. Nancy Love, trying to navigate through her stubbornness to get our own ferrying system up and running. We have too many organizations over here and really need just one with varied functions. It's command inefficiency at its worst.

"Pauline, as to your question, I am not in a particularly amenable state, especially when it comes to the thought of losing women in air-to-air combat with the German Luftwaffe. I know that some of those guys prowl alone at higher altitudes and would think nothing of jumping slow-moving unsupported transports.

"The escort could be a tip-off if the cargo was more than just a typical ferry run. On the other hand, if the safety and training were thorough enough, you might just pull if off. A pair of Spits would cause a pause, that's for sure. My, wouldn't you or I like to square off with one of those *Focke-Wulf* or *Messerschmitt* cowards? Pauline, if you believe in this approach, I will leave it to you. Your instincts and reputation for caution has always been a comfort to me. If one of the American women gets hurt or gains notoriety, then expect some testosterone pushback over here. I, of course, will deny any involvement or knowledge of your plan, as I am sure you might have that same inclination. At least, over here, I don't have a monarch to answer to, just an unpredictable General Hap Arnold, who seems always in conflict with someone, even himself.

"Given the way you're setting it up with balance of training and caution, I think I can plant a few seeds at the right places and soften any nosey publicity we might fac. They too, would deny any knowledge of armed women in the ATA. At least we would all be as prepared. In times of war, broken rules are often overlooked when success exceeds the misbehavior.

"Anything else? If not I have another tedious meeting with Love, God help her insufferable soul. She is my personal migraine, always throbbing."

"Jackie, I will keep you posted on our progress here, and I pray my updates the only way you hear of our little adventure. Bye for now, and give my best to all those supporting our ATA and especially your keenly talented American women. Your selection of these skilled ladies was spot-on, not a weak one in the lot."

Jackie knew instantly the garden in which to plant the seeds of Pauline's story lay in Hyde Park, New York. She would post a letter to Eleanor Roosevelt as soon as she finished her business with the equally strong-minded Mrs. Love.

TOP SECRET AND PERSONAL

May 3, 1943

Mrs. Franklin D. Roosevelt
Palace Hotel, New Montgomery Street
San Francisco, California

Dear Mrs. Roosevelt,

I trust you are in top spirits and fine health, and pray you excuse me for sending this communiqué by courier. Its matters would not be best served if read by others. By the time you read this you will likely be headed to San Francisco for your west coast swing. As your travels are often private, I trust this will catch you sooner than later. The message is major.

But first, grand news needs to travel fast when its content is so valuable. The formation of the new Women's Auxiliary Ferrying Station last September is truly a success at long last. We were able to distill from 25,000 applicants to just over 1,000 outstanding qualified women. Mrs. Nancy Harkness Love and I are humbled to lead this vitally important organization and will see that our women make a significant contribution to an early end of this maddening war. I think your comments in your February *Just Ask Me* magazine column, regarding the question of allowing women to fly military for ferry service during wartime, might have been just the push we needed. To quote your comment during your annual Hyde Park Home

Club Party meeting, 'We are in a war and we need to fight it with all our ability and every weapon possible.'

You will be pleased to know the women I recruited and sent to England two years ago are serving admirably. My splendid friend and our country's friend, Pauline Gower, is doing an amazing job managing and growing the ferry service for all the women. This leads me to the core of this communiqué, which is likely to lead to an unsettling matter.

As I am sure you know, back in February of this year, a German *Me-110* twin-engine fighter attacked an *Anson* transport ferry flown by Jim Mollison, the ex-husband of Pauline's friend, the late Amy Johnson. Jim, his copilot, and 12 passenger pilots escaped by the skin of their teeth and by the good fortune of unexpected cloud cover. Commander Gower and Commodore d'Erlanger met with their Special Ops people and discussed how to avoid this situation in the future. They have determined on a course of action, which in my opinion could have some political blowback from military leadership including England's Air Marshall Arthur Harris, to General Hap Arnold and ultimately could possibly end up on your husband's desk. The ATA is going to create a group of four women to serve as armed escorts on select air taxi missions of the ATA or

RAF.

I pass this on to you, as you might agree of its need and be prepared to weigh in if necessary. Mrs. Roosevelt, Miss Gower shared that, on a highly limited basis, the four most outstanding talented women ATA pilots, two of whom could be Americans with the remainder conscripts, will train at an undisclosed RAF airfield to learn instrument flying and, most importantly, the basics of defensive air-to-air combat. These women will fly one or two at a time to escort *Anson* and *Oxford* type transports from airfield to airfield in Britain, only if called upon by RAF or ATA top management. *Anson* flights would include government VIPs, medical patients, and other sensitive communiqués for starters. The *Spitfire* and *Hurricane* fighters will be armed with machine-guns for self-defense only. Their training will be to discourage rogue German attacks. Let me assure you these women know what they are doing. They are sharp, and at the same time, not prowling for a fight.

My reason for sharing this with you is that, if the President or even Secretary Stimson or General Arnold learn of an incident during one of these important ferrying missions, your awareness of this matter might allow you to sort through the reasons for the decision, and how the advantages outweigh the risks of this new design. Your beforehand knowledge and instincts will be helpful if the endeavor suffers an unlikely incident.

I will conclude with envy as you visit and touch our wounded soldiers in San Francisco and Oakland hospitals. Our boys are so precious; they are just the best.

Wishing you only the best of health and peace, I remain beyond a mere deep admirer, your faithful and trusted friend, serving at your leisure,

Jackie

Jackie Cochran

With the White House courier on his way, Jacqueline thought back to her unusual relationship with Mrs. Roosevelt. The summer after Pearl Harbor, Jackie, with Eleanor's endorsement, was summoned back to the President's Hyde Park estate on the Hudson River, north of New York City, to brief him on her findings with the Brit's ATA. Prior to that meeting, she had two additional meetings at the White House, one with an invited group observing the President presenting the Collier Trophy. A week later she met with Mrs. Roosevelt, the Assistant Secretary of War Robert Lovett, and General Hap Arnold who would become a friend and ally.

It didn't take Jackie long to get a handle on Eleanor; what made her tick and how she became so strong and confident. Her abilities and character might have been inbred, but the kinetic part was shaped by her childhood and early adult years. Eleanor's poise, confidence, and strength was molded as a teen at the Allenswood finishing school near London and later forged into the hardened voice of the marginalized and social conscience of President Franklin Roosevelt. With her lapis blue eyes, brown hair invaded by the gray, and six-foot frame, she commanded with deep respect every boardroom, sidewalk, hospital, and meeting hall. Everyone she touched loved her except J. Edgar Hoover who feared her.

A major part of her drive, energy, and expertise in the nature of man, came from the most unlikely source, the infidelity of FDR with Helen Mercer Rutherford first revealed in 1920. It did not take Eleanor long to realize that the incident dealt her immediate power over her husband, as well as everyone in his family. When she did use her influence, it often clashed with her husband's stand on issues, usually softness for the suffragettes and the marginalized Negroes and women. If she wanted to run for president against Franklin, she would likely have won.

It was learned grit and ability to speak of hushed topics that compelled Jackie to confide in her as she did. Eleanor transcended her natural limits, as with many driven women, like the resolute women of the ATA.

What Cochran or even the public did not know about the Roosevelt Family was the rumored baby of FDR and Mercer. As a brand new hire for FDR's campaign for Vice President in 1920 and later his Secretary, Missy LeHand was going through his mail marked personal. Taken immediately to Roosevelt, the return address stopped him cold. He was familiar with this firm.

LORD, DAY, AND LORD
ATTORNEY AT LAW
NEW YORK CITY

March 15,1920
Mr. Franklin D. Roosevelt
Assistant Secretary of the Navy
1000 Navy Pentagon
Washington, D.C.

Dear Mr. Roosevelt:

It has come to our attention that our client, Helen Rutherford, married to the esteemed Winthrop Rutherford in February last, revealed only to our firm and her husband, the birth of a child by Mrs. Rutherford prior to her marriage while in Paris several months ago. The baby was put up for adoption, but was not selected and remanded to an orphanage in New York, where the baby resides today. While there can be no certitude you are the father of this baby, based on Mrs. Rutherford's candid revelation to her new husband for the sake of a long-lasting marriage, we have to assume she would have no motive to besmirch your clear reputation with this information. To be clear, she was vague about the warranty of this.

However, Mr. and Mrs. Rutherford

wanted to make you aware of this finding. The Rutherford's desire, as we must assume is yours and Mrs. Roosevelt, is not to adopt the baby. The purpose of this notice is to determine your willingness, through family or an anonymous friend, to consider a share of financial watch over the child for its comfortable keeping, education and, if adopted, approval of the foster parents. We are hopeful you would consider matching a reasonable annual donation for the assurance of a comfortable lifestyle as the baby grows to maturity. As your donation would be anonymous, a philanthropic gesture for an otherwise helpless orphan of unknown parentage would raise no concern.

If you desire a blood test, we are under the advice of history that the result of this test provides only a 30 percent accuracy.

We will look forward to a reply from your office, hopefully in the not too distant future. Our phone number is in the book.

Sincerely,

Mark Daniel

Mark Daniel III,
Vice President, Chief of Litigation

While the Vice Presidential candidate Roosevelt read the letter with LeHand lingering by his side, he squinted over his reading glasses, and without expression, spoke. "As you know, Eleanor, and I are grateful for your efforts and achievements thus far in this campaign. Regardless of the outcome of the election, we both would like to have you continue to be my personal secretary. The position will officially begin next year, but, in the meantime, you will do more and more scheduling, dictation, and sorting of my mail. Would you be able to serve in this capacity?"

Marguerite "Missy" LeHand, born into the world with a modest Irish pedigree, was schooled in secretarial and clerical skills, but quickly caught the eye of the Roosevelts while working for the Democratic Party's New York office. She responded eagerly, "Of course, Mr. Roosevelt. I would be intensely honored to do so. Wow, this is truly wonderful."

"Have a seat, Miss LeHand. Let's start now with this prickly issue and you must listen carefully. The contents of this preposterous letter you brought to me must remain between you and me. While there is some speculation Miss Mercer and I were acquaintances, any other speculation as to our relationship is just that. I will answer this letter and require further notices from this firm or the Rutherford family to be directed to you for your delivery to me. For now, have my cousin, Alice Roosevelt, call me at her soonest convenience. You will find her at 2009 Massachusetts Avenue, N.W., here in Washington, or through the private secretary of her husband, Congressman Longworth. And if those fail, try the secretary of Senator William Borah.

Oh yes, and have Louis Howe come over as soon as possible."

This secretive baby was born in Paris, supervised by Alice Roosevelt Longworth. Alice, the oldest daughter of Theodore Roosevelt, was Eleanor's first cousin, and partly responsible for arranging the meetings between Franklin and Mercer. Alice was no stranger to the dusty O.K. Coral gambit of marriage, as her unconventional and controversial life began with her own marriage to Representative Nicholas Longworth III (R-Ohio), a party leader and 43rd Speaker of the U.S. House of Representatives. Alice's only child, Paulina, was a result of her affair with Senator William Edgar Borah of Idaho.

The Mercer baby would be named Paige Carroll (after Mercer's middle name and Alice's father's first name) and was placed in an Episcopalian orphanage, cemented by a generous donation from the family. Franklin's daughter Anna, would take turns with Alice, and monitor through a phantom attorney the financial needs of the child. On at least a dozen occasions, Alice and later, Anna, would be a friend of one of the orphans who had been adopted as someone to say hello, as it were. When Paige was seven, it was an ice cream cone and a local carousel for the afternoon; when she was twelve, a movie get together with the generous friend, then later for dinner for her high school graduation.

Paige seemed well adjusted, knowing vaguely of some mysterious benefactor who made life better, much so, compared to her orphanage house mates. Schooled at Emma Hart Willard's boarding Schools in Troy, New York, at age 14, she graduated with honor-roll grades then accepted to Brown, in Providence. There she met a Naval Officer Candidate undergoing officer training in nearby Newport. Her summers were spent at finishing schools supervised and funded by Anna. The relationship with Johnny Zack continued after her graduation from Brown and his commission as an Ensign in the navy. They were engaged and moved to Pensacola, Florida, where he began training as a Naval Aviator.

She made full use of the time there, getting her own pilot's license and then took advantage of the variety of advanced airplanes at the Officer's Flying Club just off the base.

In January 1942, as soon as her fiancé finished his training, he was transferred to a scorched Pearl Harbor for assignment in the Pacific. Not to be outdone, Miss Carroll answered her own call to duty and interviewed with Jackie Cochran in New York before being sent to Montreal for further screening. The result put her on a merchant ship to Liverpool, where she was reunited with Mrs. Cochran and introduced to the ATA at RAF White Waltham, thus winding up her long and circuitous journey to Maidenhead. As soon as she checked in, she read the telegram all war widows and girlfriends dreaded. She entered her new world of airplanes across the Atlantic Ocean and its inherent dangers as a woman without her love.

CHAPTER THIRTEEN

Sharpening of the Swords

On May 22, 1943, Pauline Gower got the news first. RAF Flight Lieutenant Nigel Sheffield was back home in England, recuperating at a hospital in Southwest London. Having healed from most of his injuries, Sheffield was getting over the effects of hypothermia, dehydration, and malnutrition. The doctors felt he needed seclusion, then a gradual return to duty. D'Erlanger was the most excited. Not only was Sheffield a close friend and outstanding officer, he was the other half of his Angels Squadron instructor team and, most importantly, safely back in England. On that same day, Gower called Maria Fuentes, Alex Gaestel, Paige Carroll, and Carli Banks into her office at RAF White Waltham.

"Ladies, you have been selected for an untried program that will be entirely voluntary. As you know, a German fighter shot at and hit one of our *Anson* ferries this past February. Two of our best pilots, Jim Mollison and Diana Barnato, as well as ten other ATA colleagues and friends, could have easily been killed were it not for Mollison's quick thinking and the Heavenly gift of a cloud to hide in. Since then, there have been numerous meetings between the RAF and ATA leadership to find a way to minimize the danger of this happening again.

"It was decided we assemble a four-woman civilian squadron from the ATA to selectively escort critical *Ansons* or *Albemarles* with special cargo and VIPs from the point of origin to its destinations. We will use *Hurricanes* or *Spitfires* armed with two 20mm canons and possibly four .303 Browning machine guns. Our deliberations focused on the RAF being strapped for experienced pilots. By default, this new Squadron will be made of elite ATA Pilots. Women were agreed on, because they are younger, have keen hearing and seeing faculties, and unrealized stamina. They not only have keen flying ability, they learn quickly with intuitive skills our ATA men lack."

She let the words sink in. "The volunteers, if it's you, will train at Martlesham Heath for air and continued ground school training. You will live in two of the three Officer's Married Quarter buildings at the north end of the airfield. The runways at Martlesham Heath are to be upgraded to support the heavier American aircraft. During the RAF to American transition at Martlesham, there will be only limited flying activity beginning in just a few days, suiting our training objective. Now, you ladies have been chosen not only for the qualities I just mentioned, but for your unique personalities and work ethic. Your deportment off the field has been exemplary, and that, for this squadron, is as important as how well you handle these sophisticated airplanes.

"Before I go too much further, I need to see if any or all of you want time to think about the assignment. This will not be a hunt-and-destroy assignment, as we do not expect any air-to-air combat. On the other hand, you will be trained to do so if your escort is threatened. Just your presence will give the prowling Huns something to ponder, as they have deep respect for our *Spits*. They have never jumped a pair of our fighters except in large-scale engagements. Any questions so far? Anybody?" Paige and Carli raised their hands. "When do we start?" Alex dropped her hand, as her question was answered.

"As soon as this meeting is over, or as soon as we meet with alternative candidates should any of you decline this job." "I'm in." It was 'me too' all round.

"Good. As I mentioned earlier, the crucial aspect of all this is your upholding the need for total secrecy. I can't put a finer point on it. Besides you four, and your instructors, the only others aware of this new squadron are the Commodore Gerard d'Erlanger, and the C.O. of Martlesham, Squadron Leader Lionel Ogier, your armorer and me. Back in the States, it's only the First Lady Eleanor Roosevelt and Jackie Cochran." This met with furrowed eyebrows and silent wows. "The ground crew only know that you are having specialized training for classified reasons and, as we become operational, the armorer who handles your ammunition will be hand selected and given only a bare sketch of your missions. She will mostly work alone when the fitters and engineers are not present at the hangars or firing butts on the other end of the field.

"Your two instructors will alternate between air and ground training, so two of you will fly on any given day and two will be in class. One instructor is an old friend, RAF rollback and ATA Class Two instructor, Flight Lieutenant Woodrow 'Risky' Whisky. He has a hearing deficit after hitting the side of his head on the canopy while in a dogfight during the battle of Britain. His two biggest assets are that he is a great strategist and, but most importantly, he keeps his mouth shut when its appropriate. Period.

"The other man you all know, with almost identical assets, is our own Nigel Sheffield, now your Squadron Leader." All the girls gasped, as they at one time or another met or flew with Sheffield. Maria drew a long silent breath, the other women smiled, and Alex's expression may have been decoded either way. "Sheffield made it back to England the long way 'round, travelling from Holland to Spain and Portugal, then by trawler back to Portsmouth. He is resting at Queen Mary's Hospital in Surrey, southwest of London. He will be healthy soon and will be your neighbor at Martlesham Heath in a day or so." Alex was watching Maria like an eagle. "If there are no questions, I'll give you leave. Training will start on Monday, so touch base with Sheffield or Whisky, who will be posted in the quarters between yours. Away with you now. If needed, my door is always open."

As they stood up, Gower's temporary aide popped in. "Commander Gower, come quick. Mary has been in an accident. She crashed north of here near Worcestershire just a while ago. They're holding an *Anson* for you." The five women felt a blow to their hearts. Each one knew and loved her soft efficient and personal attention she gave every pilot she spoke with. Maria stood frozen, fists clenched with nails dug deep into her palms. She and Alex made their way out of the room, with Maria sick with worry over Mary and now uneasy knowing Sheffield was alive and would be within reach in a few days. What a day!

It was a typical unfriendly sky for late May. North Carolinian, Mary Webb Nicholson, stationed at Ferry Pool 12 at Cosford, Staffordshire, was to deliver a *Miles Master* 2-seat monoplane advanced trainer, not a particularly friendly airplane. The likely destination was RAF Hullavington near Chippenham. The layers of clouds were uncooperative, the thickest at lower levels. Although primarily used by the RAF as a trainer and popular glider tug, the *Master* gave yeoman service in Egypt, South Africa, and Turkey.

The nine-cylinder engine produced 870 HP

with a reliable safety record. Mary got comfortable, studied her Ferry Pilot's notes, did her cockpit checks and pushed the starter. The *Master* started right up, taxied smartly to the end of the runway and sped into the sky. All pegged normal after checking fluid pressures and levels, with full control movement, she headed to her familiar 1,500 ft. level. On that day, to remain clear of clouds it would require 2,000, or maybe only 800 feet. After a routine 20 minutes, Mary noticed the oil pressure gauge at zero. The engine temperature was pegged in the red, all this happening in an instant at the unfriendly altitude of 550 feet. The engine abruptly seized, flailing the propeller off the airplane into space. Mary was now gliding in an unpowered two-and-a-half ton hulk of metal, glass, and high-octane gasoline, but resolute to get the *Master* down safely.

She was too low to parachute, so she examined her limited choices. One was the farm straight-ahead or unknown terrain, right or left. She plowed ahead through the misty air and eased the nose to land. The stone farm building was straight ahead and would be the last image Mary would see. The nearby farmer of the small township of Littleworth, near Worcester, ran to the scene with the full intention of rescuing Mary, but he was pushed back by the intensity of the flames. She was killed instantly and terribly burned. Her family's decision for her to be cremated in England and sent home was for the best.

The memorials and testimonials for this model pilot, musician, businesswoman, and friend, resonated all the way from Houston, Texas, to the state of North Carolina, and Jackie Cochran's New York City.

Pauline Gower was devastated. The emotional texture of war death was always numbing, but Mary's death curved intensely personal for Gower. While a few were puzzled by her absence at the memorial, most understood her pain to be deeply personal. Grief became all too frequent to Gower, as her women were losing their lives all too often. There had been two others just since January, when high-spirited and rowdy 2nd Officer Irene Arckless lost her *Oxford* engine during a rare night take-off from Cambridge, no fault of her flying. She left her fiancé in a German prison camp with no woman to come home to. Then high-strung First Officer Honor Pomeroy let the weather get the best of her and her *Oxford* at Roundway Devizes. Now, the ATA's dear Mary gone.

The tributes that poured in were unrestrained, detailing Mary's varied talents from virtuoso pianist to entrepreneur, to the woman of many aviation firsts. She was Jackie Cochran's right hand woman, helping organize the first 25 American ATA women pilots get to England. She was rewarded for her efforts by hopping aboard with the last group of ATA cadets on their ship to Liverpool. She had been a close friend of Amelia Earhart, appointed by her as Governor of the Southeast Region as well as the New York and Pennsylvania regions, of the prestigious 99s Aviation Club, exclusively for women aviators.

. . . . . .

Three days later on the 25th, Maria Fuentes and Paige Carroll settled into their two-story brick flat. The two upstairs bedrooms were roomy and the bathroom adequate, a perfect set up for a couple. Downstairs was a large room doubling as a living and dining area with an adequate kitchen, complete with stove and refrigerator. Maria sorted her clothes and made her way downstairs and to the middle of three units. She knocked on the door. Nigel opened the door. "Oh, I am so sorry. I was going to check on Carli and Alex. I didn't mean to bother."

"No worries, come on in. Have a seat. How have you been?" Maria glanced around the wall noting large pictures and drawings of every German airplane used in the war. Then she noticed the carefully scripted slogans from aviators past and present printed in ancient style lettering on a large banner draped across the wall near the ceiling.

- Beware of the Hun in the sun.
- Up there, the world is divided into bastards and suckers.
- Fighter pilots fall into two categories: The hunter and the hunted.
- To the aircraft we aim, not the man.
- Fighting in the air is not sport. It is scientific murder.
- Aerial gunnery is 90% instinct and 10% aim.
- When you think you are too close, go in much closer.
- Anyone who doesn't have fear is an idiot.
- See, decide, attack, reverse.
- Fly with the head and not the muscles.
- The winner of combat is determined by training.
- Wingmen watch your leader and his target

"Sorry, Squadron Leader. I'm good, really good. Bigger question is how are you feeling? I hear you had quite a rough go; quite frightening I suppose?" "Fine really, now that I am finally warm, fed, and can enjoy a stout without throwing up. I had the heavenly fortune of being in the care of the Canadian Red Cross Hospital at Taplow, in Buckinghamshire, where they stuffed me with meat, vegetables, soups, and milk, three times a day. I've a ways to go before my pants fit again and I get back to my fighting weight, but feel jolly better."

"Why, that's just across the Thames in the South Bucks district and a stone's throw from Maidenhead. We all thought you were in London recuperating," frowning at the displeasure of knowing he was so close but did not reach out. "I was there for a week or so, but when I complained to the administrator about the food and having to be hoisted up stairs to X-ray, I tossed around a few names and they got rid of me, fearing a messy inconvenience. Apparently, the Canadian Red Cross hospitals are 'military', while the citizens fund the British hospitals. I wish I had known about the Nursing Sisters of Canada after the Battle of Britain, for their care.

"Before I forget, I have a copy of the E & E report I filed, if you have an interest of my little holiday." "I would, thanks." "It is highly classified, so please return it by first thing in the morning. I will share with the others as their interest requires." "Certainly, no worries."

"What's happening with you, Maria?" With an image of Alex testing her morality, she changed the subject. She was trying to sort out why the man in front of her asking the question, was not the same soldier she left at Biggin the year last, not by a mile.

"Where are we, Nigel, I mean Squadron Leader?" "I don't get your meaning, Maria. And when off duty, let's be Nigel and Maria." "Well, I don't know about you, but I sensed something at Biggin Hill. Maybe it was the uniform, the sidearm poking out of your coat, or your parting glance just before you turned away and took off."

The usual steady Sheffield seemed a bit uneasy, trying not to let it show. "Maria, I was so glad to see that *Spit* and pleasantly shocked to see you as the delivery pilot, I must say. You answered our desperate need for the *Spitfire* and to see you in full gear nonchalantly talking to the engineer about snags like you were one of us. It was special. Maria, I do like you, always have. The destiny for us, our cause, is still to be written, and what you and the other American girls have done for England is just wonderful. When I heard of Mary's accident earlier this week, I couldn't breathe. Every time I was in Pauline's office, she was always cheerful and spot on as to the details of the day without sacrificing her own ferrying duties. We'll all miss her smile, terribly." Maria was sure he was avoiding her question.

"As to 'that look', maybe I was checking the left aileron, as it seemed sticky. Sitting in your *Spitfire*, and heading to meet up with those bombers in their beehive was special. And just so you know, I did recall that particular '*something*' when I was fighting the wind and snow in the Pyrenees trying to get back, vividly recalling when you gave me that airplane. That memory of you helped. I'm not sure about romance, Maria; it's even deeper. I feel we are twin spirits in the struggle against the wicked Germans. Plus, we will be seeing a lot of each other during this challenging flight school."

Maria's heart sank like the *Bismarck*; slowly, then all the way to the muddy bottom of her spirit.

She stared at the floor with telltale eyes. It wasn't the reunion she had dreamed. The Squadron Leader's prosaic words popped the balloon of her infatuation. No sparks at all, not even one, only a puff of smoke.

"That's okay Nigel, that's my mistake. I, umm, need to run next door and check on Paige and Carli. We are all pumped about this secret business, and can't wait to get in the air. Everything there is better there; you know what I mean? I'll check on the schedule in the packet in the flat and see you at then."

"I understand. By the way, Maria, as you know by now the airfield is officially open today. However, the American's won't be operational until a few months, but RAF and American planes will be coming and going until then. Your packet will show that we will start in earnest on Monday, so you and the other three will have a few days off to get acquainted with the area and enjoy an earned rest." Nigel smiled and held the door open as she passed under and brushed by without comment. *Something didn't fit. He was attracted to me, but just wasn't letting it happen. Maybe it was the escape in France. Dumb Men!*

Maria plopped into the sunken sofa in her downstairs all-purpose room and opened the Escape & Evade dossier and its report.

I.S.9 (WEA) TOP SECRET
APPENDIX "C" TO E. 7 E REPORT No. I.S.9 (WEA)/6/92

No. 16154439 Rank Flight Lt.
Name Nigel Sheffield .
Date of Interview 23 May, 1943

On November 01, 1942, I took off from Biggin Hill at about 09:15 hours in Spitfire Mk-IV, to join 13th Bomber Command One and 103 Squadron of Lancasters based at Elsham Wolds. I was the second replacement escort from 610 Squadron that had just moved to Scotland. We were to join our Lancasters over the coast of Holland on the surprise daylight mission to bomb Kassel, 280 miles south of Hamburg, usually our night target. At about 09:45 I joined 610 as number four of a four-finger flight. At about 09:55 we encountered Messerschmitt 109s and engaged them individually. During my combat, I shot and hit my target, but the proximity was such that my canopy was hit with debris sufficient to cause me to abandon the airplane. I turned west to make it to the coast and began a descent to a lower altitude. I made it in maybe fifteen or twenty minutes, of the time I am not sure, because I was not clear. I then pushed the nose over and fell away, hitting the airplane causing minor injuries. As I floated back and forth, I vaguely recall my Spitfire in a nose down attitude disappearing into the clouds below. The weather below me was solid marine fog, and as I swung into it, I had no idea of my altitude. The memory of the last five minutes is a struggle, but it's as clear I can recollect.

A few minutes later, I splashed into the cold water. Briefly shocked, I managed to disengage my parachute and inflate my Mae West. I was just then sobering to my situation. Within seconds, a small local fisherman and son coasted up and hauled me into the boat. I was immediately relieved of my flying clothes, Mae West, and parachute, my rescuers having them sink into the sea with the help of a large metal object. I found out later my service revolver and Ammo pouch were used to take my flight gear to the bottom of the sea.

I was given a cup of warm coffee, and blanket then shoved under the day's catch. As I tried to get used to the smell, I heard the motor stop and felt the boat bobbing around. There were voices in German and Dutch. After what seemed like an hour but probably only 15 minutes, the larger boat motored off. The fisherman restarted the small motor and continued fishing. They whispered for me to get comfortable, as they were going to fish until near dark, for my safety. The father, Joord, and son, Jürgen, took me to their home in Zeeland, fed me, and explained how the resistance and underground worked. On December 4th, after several handoffs through shops, narrow streets, and fish markets, I spent the night with a new couple, the Herren's in Middleburg, not far from Joord's home. I was there to receive food and different warm clothes and shoes.

On December 5, I traveled in a dust cart from Zeeland to a farmhouse on the outskirts of Baarle-Nassau, a border town set up by the Resistance. Again I received food, rest, and an odd interrogation by a Belgian named Escrinier. With German infiltrators posing as downed airmen even to the extent of parachuting in, they had to question every pilot. The phonies were shot on the spot. A dozen questions like: What is the number on RAF leave forms? What was cost of tea and a Chelsea bun in London? What railway station is nearest Grosvenor Hotel? Where and what is Swan and Edgar?" Satisfied with my answers, the interrogators abruptly left. When I asked the host what they said, it was 'he'll do, but watch him.' The host did say the last two guests were shot in the kitchen, obvious German infiltrators.

Antwerp was the next stop, where I got another set of clothes, a small satchel of food, identification papers, and 100 Francs. I had to stay there for five days until a group of helpers and the next safe house could be arranged. On December 10th, we travelled through the countryside on the side of the road from Antwerp to the outskirts of Brussels, taking two nights. We were met by a local guide and taken to Halle, a Flemish Community located on the Brussels-Charleroi Canal, where we spent six days in a local Hostel trying to blend in. We were then moved by a series of guides to the flat of Elise Chabot, at #4 Rue Jules Lejeune in the area of Ixelles. The safe house was located in a seven-story apartment building overlooking the Place Charles Graux, the gathering place for downed airmen. There we were prepared for the dangerous business of walking around town even with a guide or helper. I opted to remain indoors. I remained there for three days, then taken to a fish market owned by a Mr. Prosper Spillaert, to be hidden in his warehouse in the back of the packing room. I was there for several days, the exact number I can't recall.

On December 24, I was greeted by a young couple with their dog. I was given a walking stick for the 45 miles to Mons, Vaseline for blisters, and local cigarettes. As with the other hikes, we walked on the easiest side of the road to Mons, the town of the first British battle of WW1. We only managed about ten miles each night, arriving in the heavily bombed center of town. We were housed in the basement of a large Catholic church where we were fed and sheltered by the Priest. Because of a shooting in Mons a day earlier, we were told it would be a week or so before it would be safe to move along, 60 miles southwest to St-Quentin. Apparently a patrol of two German soldiers accidentally bumped into two teachers walking from their school. The German slapped one of them and she, knowing ju-jitsu, tossed the soldier on his back. She was summarily shot in the head by the embarrassed soldier. The angry townspeople remained quiet, knowing only too well the German patrols had itchy trigger fingers.

Since it was near the date I celebrated Christmas, the priest suggested I stay until the 26th, which I did. The next leg to St. Quentin was one of the longest we had to trek, over 60 miles, but on fairly level paths along the road, easy enough in the night. There, our able guide turned me over to yet another farmer. I was with him for two days waiting for another guide who knew the river pathways we needed to take. The respite turned out to be a needed one. At dawn on January 4, I met our lady guide, a 20 year-old student who spoke broken English. We travelled eastward for only a half-day to La Fére, near the L'Oise River where it spilled its North Sea water into the Seine, northwest of Paris. She had us make our hikes from dusk to dawn, using our torches. We slept in the brush in the daytime, taking turns to watch and listen for Germans.

Maria just scanned the rest of the report seeing disjointed words that drew her to nausea. ...

'Splint for ankle, only two sets of clothes, jail in Madrid, in the thorns for 26 hours, French betrayal, brutal execution of our safe house's Annie, filthy flat of Ambrosia, deeply infected with lice, low steep hills, blood in vomit, border post alive with bullets. Best

Basque helper killed, dysentery, replaced by wife. . his eyeball like a grape, teen shot at point blank range while his...'

Maria closed the report before the end. It was too glum and gruesome. *'That poor man! No wonder he is so thin.'* She wiped tears with the heel of her palms. Composure regained, she knocked on Sheffield's door. "How's the ankle?" He just smiled and took the report. "Fine and thanks for returning this. I'll leave it here on the smaller table and if any of the others want to examine it, have them see me; just our pilots, Miss Fuentes. Remember, it's a secret document. See you in the morning." Nigel then took the report and locked it in a concrete safe in his closet. He pulled out a duplicate dossier and put it on the small table downstairs, then passed the word for Alex to pop by.

Having read the report, Maria thought how selfish she was to pop in and demand Nigel's feelings. He had been to an emotional and physical hell and back. She was determined to give him space and in time, then revisit with a greater appreciation of his state of mind. *'Yes, I'll wait!'*

Early Monday morning on the first of June 1943, history was being made at the northern corner of the northeast-southwest runway of Martlesham Heath. In the middle of three buildings just across the road surrounding the airfield, two men, four women, and a small crew, embarked on their journey of bravery, betrayal, bullets, and bandages.

"Good morning Ladies," Sheffield began. "Before we get started, I want you to meet the other half of your instructors. Flight Lieutenant Woodrow 'Risky' Whisky is a notable RAF veteran who moved to this squadron because of an ear injury." The portly goateed aviator doffed his hat and smiled. "Mornin' ladies," words of the baritone clearly spoken with a half unlit cigar bobbing tightly in the corner of his mouth. It's a pleasure to meet you as I look forward to making you the best damned fighter pilots in the air and pray you are not tested. If you are, you will be fully prepared. You will be at least the best in America and the Netherlands. I have heard amazing stories about all of you as your reputation precedes you, and that's a fact. Welcome to RAF fast-track training."

Nigel took the floor. "Before I turn this meeting over to Whisky, I have a comment about the airplanes. The two *Spits* Marge is restoring are the Mark Vs with the Merlin 45 to accommodate the additional firepower." The four smiles didn't slow Sheffield down. "You will have two 20mm cannons and four .303 machine guns. That's a lot, but if you are going into harm's way, you need to be prepared. The newer *Spits* coming out of the 'shadow' factory are over-kill for what you are doing, as the new ones can climb to 35,000 feet faster and fight better at those altitudes than the *109's*. We can now claim those altitudes as our air, not theirs. The engineering from stem to stern makes the *Spit* every bit as deadly as the *109*. The newer models have taken the altitude advantage away from the Luftwaffe. Deep in concept and difficult to build, the Spitfire is awesome to fly, as you well know. Whisky and I will fly the two *Hurricanes* when we have all four of you in the air, like tomorrow, if the other two *Spits* get here tonight as scheduled."

Whisky then took the podium, a sturdy cognac crate. In a resonate businesslike voice, "Good morning ladies. Lest I forget, we will be having squadron patches made reflecting the name of your squadron. The meaning of them determined at war's end. After the women chattered their approval and became quiet again, Whisky continued. "I won't lie to you, but time is not our friend. We are going to redefine the word condensed. You will get up early, fly hard, and go to bed exhausted. You will do in one week what the RAF does in three. If that doesn't suit any of you, you may be excused now." Just shuffling of feet resulted.

"Good! Now, when you are flying in formation your call sign will be Purple. In the packet just given to you, there's a five-month syllabus that will require roughly 250 hours of flight training. You will fly every other day, two hours in the morning and two or three in the afternoon or night. Every other day you will attend school, right here in this building where Squadron Leader Sheffield and I will be living. In the air, you will learn the keenest level of expert flying.

You will have an intense course in instrument flying, night and day. You will learn close formation flying, night and day. You will be so close to the woman in the lead airplane you will be able to read the instruments in her cockpit. You will unlikely use the night training, but you never know, and might come in right handy after the war. Also, this war has so many departments like the OSS and SOE, which would deem you very valuable assets when and if we send you to the mainland to help mop up this war.

"We will do low level flying over land and the sea. After each low level hop your airplane will either have salt water or sheep dung covering its belly. Night low level flying will encourage you to trust your instruments. Twenty five feet off and you are fish food." A chill ran up Carli's back. "At the end of the basics, you will have gunnery practice, shooting at large targets towed by a *Hawker Henley* or *Miles Master*." All four women winced, then Whisky knew straight away he could have skipped mentioning the *Miles Master*, the flying contrivance that spat off the propeller to kill Mary Webb Nicholson only days earlier. He let a few sober minutes pass. As he feared the hounds of time bearing down, it gave him time to pluck a few more grey whiskers, as a florist would clip thorns from a rose. His audience was back at ease.

"The final activity will be fighter tactics with all six of us in the air. If you are still alive when Halloween rolls around, all four of you will be keener and deadlier than the two of us. You can see better, have sharper coordination, and are in better physical shape. Almost forgot. We will run five miles every other morning, the six of us. Your conditioning is critical at six miles above the earth, squeezed into a rocket propelled aluminum box. Your senses are keener when your heart doesn't have to work so hard during the stress we will put your through. We both know this first hand. Be in shape! It will save your life. Tired will not be allowed here

"A bit of fun news for you. A donation of four bicycles at Martlesham will lessen your confinement here. Personal transportation is scarce out here, as you know, so please keep them inside your houses when not riding. Keeps jealousy and thievery at a minimum. They will come in handy if you want to go to the *Swan* just outside of Ipswich to bend an elbow or for top-of-the-hat food, Miss Jermyn's *Black Tile*. They provided cakes for King George when he visited Martlesham year last, so they are quite skillful at baking as well as slap-up kidney pie. It's no wonder it's a major draw of the four RAF airfields in the area.

One last thing, before leaving the airfield, be sure you check in with Commander Sheffield or me. The Germans like to strafe roads. Last year they even shot up a school bus on the way to school near Framsden. Everyone needs to know where everyone else is. That includes us. You will know where we are at all times when off the airfield. Remember, we are a team of six. Any questions?"

From Carli, "Where's the closest pub?" "It's in your packet." Nigel rose from his chair. "Lets take a ten minute break then resume." The women mostly wanted a cold drink of lemonade, then discovered Whisky and Sheffield had a fridge full of cold Coca Colas, ™ the icebox became the ice-breaker. When the women were reseated with their Cokes, Sheffield resumed.

"Whisky and I need go over a list of non-flying information." "Can I make a quick announcement, then I won't be a bother?" "Of course, what is it, Miss Carroll?" "Well, we girls have been talking and really love the Risky Whisky thing, and wanted a catchy name for you; you know, when we are informal." "Go ahead." "Well, we had several suggestions like 'Dry Rye', 'Clear Beer', 'Hale Ale', but landed on 'Double Stout.' Is that okay?" When the laughing and chanting of Double Stout faded, Nigel agreed to Commander Stout during the day and Double Stout at night, unless flying.

"Let's try again. This is local knowledge you might find useful. Ipswich is our town, a wee one just east of here. The pubs are listed in your packet as well as local transport and bus stops. Just east of us is RAF Woodbridge, which is mostly an emergency airfield in a remote setting where we have gotten permission to practice. It is one of three wide runway airfields specifically designed for emergency landings for our RAF returning from Germany, mostly *Lancaster* and *Wellys*. We cleared nearly one million trees from the Rendlesham Forest to make it so. It's discrete. They have plans to install the FIDO system, which will be great for night landings when it is the least bit foggy. I don't know what FIDO means, but the system is basically large pipes on each side of the runway full of pressurized petrol lit to create a lighted runway. The runway is split into three lanes, with clear and unobstructed access to the runway from the east and the west. We'll discuss Rendlesham later.

"A few of you have ventured out to the vintage WWI portable hangars and likely have met Marge Handel. She and her crew will be your fitters, mechanics, and engineers. All of the WAAF mechanics working on the airplanes are just getting oriented, but they are close to getting your airplanes ready to fly. You will take your mess in the chow hall with the other WAAFs stationed here. Your job is to blend in. Martlesham has always been associated with many types of experimental airplanes, oddly painted *Spitfires* rolling out of the portable hangars are hardly worth a second notice. The commander of the airfield is the only person who knows what we do. As we come and go from the remote married men's quarters, from a distance we will blend into the disorder of the Eighth Air Force transition.

"As we wrap up our training in early October, the 359, 360, and 361 wings of the American Eighth Air Force will begin operations with the *P-47 Thunderbolts*. We will really blend in then, as the airfield will get crazy busy. By then your training will be over, flying only occasional *Anson* escorts, probably four or five a week for each of you. In your packet you will also see a map of our airfield and its confines. The parachute facility is across the road on Portal Avenue. It's between us, and the airfield to your left in the far corner across from the portable hangars. You should check or exchange your chutes when possible, again with the rigger's name and flying schedule in your packet.

"To our immediate left, you will find RAF flight officer quarters, but by now with the transition, you will likely see only a few transients from other squadrons overnighting. Behind the parachute shack are the brick firing butts, although only your armourer will use them if needed, and will not be important until much later when we get into gunnery. At the far southeast corner is a cluster of buildings outlined in your packet, like the bread and meat store, commissary, and dining hall. For those of you who are close to your Maker, the church is also over there. The most important building is near the church, the Met Office where Whisky and I will be getting the most recent weather reports.

"Today will be ground school only. The two *Spitfires* are still challenging the mechanics to get them into top flying condition. The two mentioned earlier, were somewhere near the portable hangars on the east side of Heath."

Most of the day was devoted to the study of the Luftwaffe and Italian airplanes. The room was a cluster of eighteen-inch square posters of every conceivable likely combatant with views of the side, from above, below, and head on. German tri-motor *Junkers JU-52*, *Focke-Wulf Ta 152*, *Heinkel HE-112*, *Italian Fiat G.55*, *Macci C. 202*, and *Reggiane Re. 2001*. As they studied the posters, they were given two decks of cards that had all of the poster airplanes. The Allied silhouettes were just as important so they wouldn't shoot down an American *P-51 Mustang* or *B-24 Liberator*. Often Allied photos or silhouettes were taped near similar German and Italian airplanes for comparison, especially when the differences were subtle, as the *He-112* with a similar shape as the *Hurricane* and *Spitfire*.

On Tuesday, Maria and Paige were the first out of bed. Before their morning coffee or tea, they headed towards the portable hangars and weren't disappointed. They jumped up and down and hugged. There they were, all four of the *Spitfires* with the fresh low summer sun splashing off the gleaming aluminum. They appeared near new, but they knew better. They introduced themselves to the Fitter. "Hi, I'm Maria and this is Paige." "Mine's Josey. What do you think?" Like a duet, "They're beautiful. Just beautiful." Paige commented on the diagonal purple stripes on the tails. Then they saw the fresh paint on the left front fuselage, four warrior Angels linked arm in arm. Wide-eyed Paige verbalized what they were all thinking. "Like an Angels Foursome!" Equally impressed with the *Spits*, Carli and Alex joined the pair. "Do they run?" "Officer Banks, the two on the left came in last night and need a bit of attention. Carbs mostly, some light static in both radios, but nothing major. Marge had to order parts for the other *Spit*; they should be in later today. Canopy rails on one and a gasket for left main strut on the other." After half an hour of stroking the aluminum fuselage and climbing into the cockpits, they adjourned for breakfast and were greeted by their ground school instructor, Risky Whisky with his droopy half eaten cigar.

At the same time, Nigel Sheffield was attending a meeting nearby at RAF Headquarters, in the office of the Flight Surgeon to get his clearance for limited flying duty. It wasn't his favorite way to spend the day. He was to check in with Doctor Cedric B. Oglethorpe, termed the 'Quiet Artist'. The Chief Flight surgeon had flown British Fighters and knew firsthand what it felt like to dive straight down at 400 MPH and then pull up abruptly. The comment of *'I know how you must feel,'* was genuine.

Oglethorpe wasn't aware of exactly why he was called on to personally examine the Squadron Leader, likely since he was the leader of an especially sensitive mission and he had to be 100 percent physically and mentally. They both knew of each other and began the tests in fair humor.

Sheffield submitted to a series of tests usually given to beginning RAF candidates to determine the effects of hypoxia and the possible damage of excessive G forces. His body had been altered after being banged around in an open cockpit then dumped into icy water for an unknown time. Dr. Oglethorpe was expecting a compromised body. After the extensive eye exams, hand-eye coordination, and treadmill tests, the probing mutated into discrete disorders like fatigue, fear, and other physiological symptoms manifest during combat.

"So what do you think, Doc?" "For an old man of 27 having been shot down twice and spending six months wandering through the woods, rivers, and mountains of France and Spain, I would put my money on your *Spitfire* protecting my arse any time. Off with you now." After two days of testing from head to toe and between his ears, he was cleared to fly, but with limitations of only moderate aerobatics and short flight durations. That was all he needed to hear.

Back at Martlesham Heath, the women were becoming impatient to get into the air. When Sheffield came into the makeshift school with his Pepsodent smile, they knew. They knew and just couldn't wait.

"Tomorrow, Whisky and I will observe all of your basic air skills and headwork. Your skills in getting a lot of different airplanes from one airfield to another is not in question. It will be how well you manage your *Spitfires* that matters. We will meet right here at zero eight hundred. Since it will be a bit cool where we are going, wear your flight jackets. Thin gloves will be fine as we won't be at that altitude too long. Don't forget to grab your flying helmets from Marge this afternoon. They have been fitted with wiring necessary for you to communicate on your RT. Marge will also have your oxygen masks, as you will need them on the first part of our hop. And, don't forget your chutes. You should have picked them up from the rigger by now, if not, then get on it. That's all. See you bright and early in the morning."

For the first flight, each woman was early and wore full war paint, including lipstick. "Top o' the morning, Ladies. Today Squadron Leader Sheffield and I will see how you can follow orders and fly those beautiful beasts parked outside. First, you might tone down the lip colour, as we are going to be using those oxygen masks and you will regret having red lipstick smeared from the bottom of your nose to your chin and to the middle of each cheek. There is wiping paper near the back for your convenience. Initially, we will work to the northwest climbing to 25,000 feet, far away from any fighting from sector two, to the east. You will be Purple One, Two, Three and Four. Your instructors will be Purple Leader. We will mix the leadership each day, but today Second Officer Gaestel will lead you. Two is Banks, three Fuentes and, bringing up the rear, will be Carroll. Your instructors will be a respectful distance above watching your every maneuver.

"After we get the airplanes started, we will do a radio check in call sign order, starting with Purple One.

One will request the radio check on channel six, then in order from Two to Four you will report back, hopefully, loud and clear or five by five. If we don't hear clear reports from all, we will abort the mission until we get all radios perfect. Marge's R/T techs who work on our fighters have assured us they work just fine. After the radio check, we will instruct you to taxi to the end of the runway and watch for the two green takeoff flares. We will use the radio sparingly, then rely on flares or the Aldis Lamp as before when we return. We are still at war and need to remember the Krauts guard nearly every frequency on the R/T. Any exception will come from us.

"Note the altimeter setting before you lift off, because if you don't have it set correctly, you might just get killed. You will at least be embarrassed as you will be either too high or low after joining up. The commander or I will lead off and, at 500 feet, will start a slow climbing turn to the left until everyone has joined up. You will break left also, and, with a standard left climbing turn, join Purple One at 1,000 feet. When on station we will resume our climb to Angels two five. When we get to altitude over Leicester, we will call for you to break into pairs, One and Two to the left and Three and Four to the right at a 45 degree heading from our course of 330. When you get stable, we will have further instructions.

"After you pre-flight the airplane and do radio checks, we will taxi out in single file, in order given. When we call the tower, they will give us the correct altimeter setting. When we return we will separate you so each can call the tower and request landing instructions. Any questions?" "Is there time for a fast run to the loo?" "Hurry Purple Two." Then all four girls broke ranks and headed to the bathroom, two upstairs to their instructors' loo and the other two to the one next door, all four grabbing paper wipes on the way. Sheffield and Whisky just shook their heads, both thinking '*what have we gotten ourselves into?*'

In quick order, the Angels were scampering onto the wings of the four *Spitfires* then popping into their cockpits, bums firmly on their parachutes. With help from the crew on the ground, they got their Sutton Harness clipped to the airplane's seat and were given a brief reminder of their oxygen systems. Before the first woman started her airplane, Whisky and Stout were already waiting, with their props spinning and arms hanging out of the half door. Within a minute, all four women had their engines purring, the Angel *Spitfire* jockeys nervous as honeymoon brides. After the radio check, and another moment for each to do a short magneto and hydraulic check, the four *Spitfires* and two *Hurricanes* lumbered from the frontage area north of the field and made the journey along the taxiway to the end of the active runway near the tower. First Whisky, then Sheffield, then Purple One through Four made their way into the air above Martlesham.

The four women of the Angels Squadron fastened on their oxygen masks making them snug, climbed to 25,000 feet, and were soon in the vicinity of Leicester with their muscles clenched against the cold. "Purple One, have your flight break into two flights, with Purple Three the leader of the second group." Maria pulled away from the airplane to her left and made room for Paige to pull up closer to and under her right wing. "Nice Angels. Well done. Now Purple One and Purple Three, you will join on us, where we will be two flights of three. Purple Two, you will find your leader to your left and Three, yours will be to your right. In thirty seconds we will be in position above and to your right or left. When in sight of Three and One make station and follow, which will be away from the other two." The sections were three miles away from each other so the instructors could pull away and observe their steep turns, controlled spins and power-off stalls.

After thirty minutes of the exercises, they rejoined as a flight of four and were ordered to ten thousand feet. "Purple One, have your flight spread to wings abreast and hold steady." The four *Spitfires* then bobbed around to form a single line abreast. Whisky and Sheffield were 500 feet above to observe. "Three, did you check your altimeter?" Maria double clicked her mike, as affirmative. "Congratulations. The one of you who's low, get back slowly to your assigned altitude. Much better. Now set your altimeter to 10,000 feet. If it were tomorrow, you would be dead. When we get back to Martlesham, you will ride your bike to Ipswich, buy the required groceries for lamb stew, and cook dinner for the six of us. Paige's face was beet red beneath her oxygen mask. Tomorrow we will fly along the coast twenty-five feet above the water. Now Angels, split as before to your instructors. We will take us home."

Back at Martlesham Heath, the women were getting acquainted with what lay ahead. They would learn to send and receive Morse code at 40 words per minute and memorize enemy and friendly fighters from every angle. Survival and evasion techniques were thoroughly discussed, including edible berries and rodents and uses of their parachutes and side arms. Alex's favorite was cartography, as she had a head start in map making and reading from college. Blind flying, or navigating by instruments, would be required in the clouds or fog and would be the most difficult.

The women looked forward to the RAF Central Flying School at the Aerodrome in Upavon to use the flight simulators, where they would learn to fly without outside visual references. After four exhausting weeks in the air, they entered the cloudy air in their *Spits*, strictly on their instruments, and made radio-beam approaches from airfield controllers.

Gunnery would be learned first from their small desks, as tactics of air-to-air combat were taught with small model airplanes attached to long round rods. Since airplanes fly not in exact left, right, up, and down quadrants, they would have to know if their targets were turning, descending, climbing, or sliding, applied to their own motion in their airplanes. Whisky put it this way. "When you are hunting ducks and the duck flies to your right and headed up, you shoot above and ahead. If right at you, you blow his head off!" The women just glanced at each other, then shrugged. Unfazed, Whisky finished. "Our best aces couldn't explain their method, but then they weren't duck hunters. It will come easy when you get some practice."

From the first day in May through pleasant weather of June, through the summer, women of Angels Four studied, briefed and flew, then debriefed and flew again. On the ground, they learned to identify the difference between *B-17 Flying Fortresses* and *Dornier Do 17* flying pencils, between The *Focke-Wulf 190* and *Messerschmitt 109-BF*, between the *Ilyushin-2 Shturmovik* and the *Junkers 8-Stuka* just to name a few. They learned to fly twenty-five feet above the churning English Channel or over the English countryside as steady as fine-tuned locomotives, but at 350 miles per hour.

They were hounded by Sheffield and Whisky to manage their fuel, especially important, as they weren't allowed to leave with full tanks because their missions and basic needs deferred to the fighters and bombers in combat roles. Their air-to-air tactics emphasized keeping vigilant even on take off and landing. They learned the barreled aileron turn and other short turn evasive maneuvers. They became familiar with every conceivable emergency from generator failures to cockpit fires and engine breakdown. With no real life parachute training, they nonetheless spent hours with the parachute riggers to learn how to pack their own chutes and what to expect if they did have to bail out. The sequence of raising the seat full up, undoing the harness and grabbing the rip cord in that order were memorized as well as pushing of the control column to get a nose down attitude or rolling inverted to fall out. Since the canopy of the *Spitfire* slid on metal rails, it was apt to jam shut if hit by flak or cannon fire, so the women were taught how to use the escape crowbar clamped to the inside of the cockpit door.

They practiced crosswind and short-field landings and take offs, day and night. They reviewed head and hand signals in close formation flying, especially the signals from the leader whose radio becomes inoperative and the procedure for it. Radio discipline was critical as the Germans hear nearly every comment of every British airplane. Fuel state is related in codes so they have to guess aircraft range capabilities. They studied the *RAF Spitfire Manual,* developed three years earlier, to harvest the minds of the best that flew before, hints and procedures that saved countless lives.

And so it passed through the summer and into the cool reaches of October, they trained, shooting at towed targets and mock air-to-air hassles among themselves. The graduation was a small dinner at the *Black Tiles*. As they adjourned to receive their escort orders for the next stage in Angel Squadron's syllabus, Alex nudged Maria on the way out growling, "I need to talk with you. Tonight!"

CHAPTER FOURTEEN

When the Deep Purple Falls Over Sleepy Garden Walls

Maria was reading a private notice to meet Commandant Gower first thing the following morning, when Alex pounded on her door. "I know you are in there. You had better open up or I'll kick the bloody thing down!" "Keep your knickers on, Alex. What's the matter with you? Have you gone mad? I can't talk with you now because I have to talk to Nigel" Pushing her way inside, Alex continued, "It's always Nigel. Have you gone straight on me?" Her tone was more severe.

"Read this and you will see. Then go away," her tone matching Alex's. After tossing the private memo on the floor, Alex turned to leave. "You haven't heard the last of me." "Come back here. Let's have it out now, but outside.

"Now what's the big stew Alex? We haven't spoken three words since spring." "That's the thing, you haven't spoken to me hardly at all. Not a fine thing for a mate to do to the other." "We're not mates, Alex, and we will never be. Our brief affair was made in appetite and my cheap taste! My only excuse is my dreadful judgment. It was a mistake and I apologize if I disrupted your lusty style. Don't argue the toss, perky pants, plus, I fancy another, and it's not a woman; girls are just not my thing and won't ever be. Ever! Go find another bint to satisfy your needs."

Alex struck back, face turning scarlet and neck veins near bursting. "Don't you get sanctimonious on me, you little shit. You can't throw me off and simply walk away." The words were like raging ants. Maria shot right back. "Alex, it is always skittles and beer with you, it's always about fun and play. Alex, you are too damned mercurial, hard to know, and harder to love. It's like catching a lightning bug in a jar, then find out that the light is too weak to read by. You're like a torch that burns everyone in your way until you finally turn it on yourself. I am saddened, as we might have been."

"Don't give me the 'maybe it's me' routine, it won't wash!" "Speaking of that, I am washing my hands of you Alex. Comprender? I wish you good luck, and if I know you, you'll find someone to shag by nightfall." "You damn straight Dearie. I will, don't think I won't!" Alex had a nasty sneer and was clenching both fists when Whisky walked up. Boring hard into Alex, "Anything I can help with?" Maria took the opening to step from the shade and go back into the flat.

It was way past one when Alex slipped beneath the sheets. Alex wished Banks would wake and be aroused, but it wasn't to be. *'Probably straight as a chop stick tonight.'* Alex tossed and turned, feeling the bile of vengeance creep into her; her throat tightened with jealousy, a bitter possessiveness that was pure torment, lighting her fuse of revenge. *'Betrayal has only one punishment, and you, Fuentes, will suffer the full pain of it like no other. I will make certain of that! I'll show that sneaky little...'* The poison of those thoughts put Flying Officer Gaestel fast to the pillow.

• • • • • •

Maria was granted the use of one of the Angels' newer *Hurricanes* for the 125-mile ride to White Waltham. She was directed to park close to the tower near a *P-47 Thunderbolt*, another guest of Gower's. She was met by the WAAF driver and driven the short distance to Pauline Gower's office. The brisk November morning winds required her fleece-lined flying sidcot, heavy gloves, hooded parka, and obligatory white shirt, and black tie. After taking off her flying helmet, she shook her head to relieve her ringlets from their leather prison. Flying Officer Fuentes held her parka over her left arm and lightly tapped on the door of the Senior Commander's anteroom. "Come in. You must be Maria Fuentes." "That's me." "Let me peek in, I think she is ready for you. Yes, It's all clear." Amy Lethridge, Gower's new aide, swung the door nearly all the way back to the wall, let Maria approach Pauline's desk, then gently closed the door.

"Thanks for being so prompt Miss Fuentes, have a seat. I want to talk briefly about your escort scheduled for tomorrow, an important one. The Angel scheduled to fly with you is Flying Officer Gaestel. Is that okay with you?" "Why do you ask?" "Maria, I sometimes get feedback that could compromise our ability to be effective. Here lately, I have been getting comments that she is an excellent Angel Pilot, but her attitude has become a little strong and borders on disrespect. The word ' wanker ' pops up here and there. I am curious how you two are getting on." Maria stared at the floor and wasn't sure what to say. She bet on the truth. "I think you are right on both counts, but I would rather have her in the air with me than anyone else. She isn't a paragon of restraint, that's for sure, and she's tougher than an English sidesaddle. When devising a plan, she will usually serve her own advantage. She *was* somewhat moody yesterday, went spare on me, if I may say. She is intuitive in the air and bone smart, even though argument seems to be her language of choice. If she were allowed to fly in combat, there isn't a German in the sky who could outdo her when her blood's up. I do, however, think matters will be smooth tomorrow and we should have an uneventful ferry. She's not like dirt in a machine; maybe dirty oil." "So, you think it's just small beer?" "I do. At this point, I trust her in the air."

Pauline Gower glanced out her window, then back to Maria. She heard Maria's words while noting her wringing hands and nervous feet. Gower was sure of her instincts about Alex, and would initiate plans accordingly. "Well put, very well put. If you change your mind, please call my office to reschedule your assignment or wingman.

"The second reason for asking you to come here is a surprise. Before that though, how did you like flying over here in Sheffield's new *Hurricane* and your new designation of RAF Flying Officer?" "To be honest it was great. Just to be able to call the tower for take off and landing, if required, made me feel like a real aviator. My main satisfaction comes from the training we receive from our instructors whom we affectionately call Risky Whisky and Double Stout. Our confidence and skills are keen because of those two. When we climb into the cockpit of those amazing *Spits*, filled with the knowledge and training we have, there is nothing to fear. Our preparation is complete, as our minds scan every eventuality. Weather, engine fire, Huns, it's of no concern. We are that prepared. The women in our remarkable ground crew also make us feel special. It's hard to express."

The chuckle from the back of the room startled Maria. When she turned to see who it was, she shrieked so loud, Gower's Secretary came in, not sure what she would find. She smiled and sighed as a military brother and sister were in a fierce embrace, laughing and crying, tears released after years of worry.

Commander Gower cleared her throat and

indicated they were welcome to remain in the room a while longer, as she had two meetings away from the building and her office was available to them for a while. *'This day has been a success and it's not even ten o'clock.'* She tiptoed out of the room and eased the door shut, smiled at Amy, adjusted her hat, and left the building. She was meeting with Sheffield to review plans for Alexandra Gaestel.

"Oh Eddie, my Edward, it's *you*! I have been so worried about you. Let me look at you. My God you have turned into a grown man!" Toe-to-toe with him, Edward's sister scanned him thoroughly. Relieved, she sagged in relief. *'Nothing missing!'* "Look at all those ribbons! You have to tell me all about what happened. But first how did you find me?" "Well it's all in the same story. Why don't we have a cup of strong American coffee somewhere where we can talk? What are your plans today?" "I don't have to fly today, or tomorrow. Maybe we can go to London for dinner or something." "I was thinking more like Ipswich." "Ipswich? That's close to me, but..." "Close to me too." "How so?" "I'm stationed close by there at Martlesham Heath." "Get on with ya. That's fabulous. Do you have a ride?" "Yea, that's another chapter of my story. I have a Thunderbolt outside. Wanna race?" They were out the door, tears dry and spirits high, sprinting to their airplanes as if it were a combat scramble. They almost forgot to agree on where to get together on the airfield, then mounted their military carriage pointed to RAF Martlesham Heath.

They both cleared the day with their commanders and biked to *Barley Mow* at 36 Westgate. They skipped the kidney pie, which had a reputation of the meat being frequently off, settling for the reliably fresh fish and chips. While watching the charming old man dance around in step with his squeezebox, they talked until the sun began its retreat to hide away for the night. Maria discussed how she became Maria, but did not elaborate on the mission of the Angels. Edward recounted his journey to Oakland and San Francisco and the return of his memory, most of it, anyway. From Frisco, he was remanded to a Utility Squadron for continued therapy and Temporary Duty Assignment to the Eighth Air Force at Martlesham, after he learned where his sister was stationed.

Ed flew several familiarization hops in the heavier *P-47* until his rotation back to Marine Air Group 21. There he would rejoin his rebuilt VMF-221 squadron to fly the new F4U *Corsairs* stationed at Guadalcanal.

Edward brought his sister up-to-speed on him pulling in a favor from one of his friends from Midway who knew Pappy Boyington. It turned out Boyington was responsible for helping Ed locate his sister. Gower was contacted and readily agreed for him to see her. She briefed him of the background surrounding Deborah's name change and details of her keen flying talents.

When Maria mentioned how she missed her parents, Ed promised to write and call. He would mention they had bumped into each other near London, and assure them their daughter was doing great. He would allude to her work in a classified department that was totally safe. Edward and Deborah Rosen indulged in a game of darts, both admitting they would not threaten the scores of the regulars. They spent the next day walking the ragged streets of London, admiring the proud Brits who survived the nightly bombings, while holding hands to be mistaken for lovers with smiles and nods of passers by. They recalled almost every moment of each other's service time, friends killed, friendships made, headlines in the U.S., and what to do after the war.

Maria avoided sharing her private affairs with her brother for another time. The day seemed to pass way too fast, but tomorrow was a workday for them both.

The next day, Maria checked the flight schedule and noted the Luton-to-Hamble escort with Alex the leader. Alex was actually was just short of cheerful when they turned in the night before. She seemed pleased that Maria enjoyed the day with her brother in London.

Maria and Alex made their way through the predawn mist and around their *Spitfires*, then crawled into their cockpits as dawn was preparing to crack the English blackness. Alex would take the lead and fly the usual Angel striped tail, while Maria took a temporary replacement *Spit* with the solid black vertical stabilizer. They did their radio checks and assigned themselves a private channel for talk between themselves, still likely guarded by the Germans, but out of earshot of the airfields or other military radio chatter. The weather wasn't great nor was it miserable, the typical November morning with the usual scuffle between sunlight and mist, with mist getting the upper hand, predictable for the season. The infield grass was changing colors to light brown, giving way to mud and scattered tufts of grass, while the runways were highways for late autumn leaves to randomly scurry across.

They took off and retracted their landing gears heading south, Alex first with Maria close behind. Soon Maria would tuck ten feet under and to the right of Alex. They climbed to four thousand feet, 'angels four', to rendezvous with the *Anson* over RAF Luton. To Maria it seemed risky, as the higher the altitude, the greater chance of a rogue German attack. She came to the conclusion the morning cloud layer was not British friendly, but would burn off before noon. Hopefully.

Both women guarded the coded R/T channel

from Command and Control, who would warn of any threatening traffic. The Command frequency was quiet as they leveled off. "Purple One, Purple Two, how do you read?" "Five by, Purple One." "Roger." The two *Spits* joined up with the *Anson* right over Luton at 1,500 feet as planned and made their escort on the same direction as Martlesham Heath to Luton. "Angel One, Rosy One, over." "Rosy One, Angel One." "Many thanks for the company, Angels, we'll make our way on from here. Be safe." "Roger, Rosy, out." "Purple One, Purple Two, Over." "One, go." "Purple Two, pull abreast on the way home. We will climb to angels six and see more of the country, over." Maria acknowledged but was instantly curious, as she pulled abreast to Alex's right to make the climb, '*Why six thousand?*' On their northeasterly course, any problems would likely come from Maria's side, from the two o'clock to four o'clock sector. Maria was frustrated with her situation because the morning sun was driving a lightning spike right through her canopy and into her right eye. Her sunshades were almost useless, but at least with the abreast formation, she could spend more time searching for airplanes and less time keeping station in a staggered formation where her eyes were glued only on Alex.

Maria's thoughts drifted back to the miracle of seeing Ed and how they would spend the few days available until his return to the Pacific. Before those thoughts could give her any more comfort, she almost jerked the yoke out of its attachment to the floor. A *Messerschmitt* with its large ominous black cross, swayed just off her right wing. Before she could react, she could see the pilot smile and wave, then pull up and start a climbing turn to the left. Maria armed her gun button with her thumb and hit the microphone switch. "Purple One, break left. We have a bandit above and climbing; a

109. Break left, Purple One, break left hard!" Alex double clicked her mike, but as Maria made her climbing turn up and around to give chase, Alex still hadn't changed course. "Break, Purple One, break damn it!"

Maria spun up and rolled over to place her *Spitfire* right behind the German. Alex was trying to protect Alex, but it was too late. The German was right on her tail and blasting, his 20mm cannons shredding her *Spitfire* into pieces. As Maria watched, Alexandra Gaestal's airplane exploded. The explosion was so violent, Maria could feel the heat and had to fight through the smoke to regain visual contact with the *109*. She slammed her throttle full forward and followed the German as he made a casual slow climbing turn back to the left. Remembering all of her training, she pulled closer, this time with the sun at her back, making two short cannon bursts with up and left deflection. As soon as Otto focused on the image in his rear view mirror, he knew the feeling of a fox losing his race to a tiger.

He ducked down behind his bulletproof seat and waited. The tracers were true and her aim perfect. With smoke confirming serious engine damage, she turned to the machine guns, chopping off both *Me-109* wings, demolishing the cockpit, then backed off so as not get hit with fragments of the disintegrating fighter. '*Sing your Horstwessl-Lied song now, you lousy Kraut!*' Then she glimpsed a chute with Otto Kelter on his way to a rendezvous with an English farmer and his rusty pitchfork. That was okay with the prisoner as Kelter had his 30th kill and would most assuredly be decorated with the German Knight's Cross. Then he remembered; he needed a witness. '*Scheiße!*' Otto's *F-109* debris splattered the garden wall of the farmer's field below, a wee object consumed by the earth's landfill of metal and bones.

Maria was addled; trembling like a shivering pup and stunned beyond rational thinking. She had just shot down an unsuspecting German, watching her friend and once paramour slaughtered. '*Why didn't coastal radar or Central Command warn them?*' Maria's shaking right hand coaxed the *Spitfire* into a lazy descending turn back to Martlesham by sheer instinct. The slow motion movie reel in her mind was replaying the two-minute review of what had happened.

She didn't call the airfield for landing instructions and didn't remember seeing a flare or lamp for landing clearance or even dropping the landing gear. When the *Spitfire* shivered to a stop, Maria was soaking wet through her fleece sidcot. Maria wasn't clear if it was sweat, blood, snot, urine, or hydraulic fluid. She couldn't stop the shaking and panting. Before Marge could get to the airplane, Maria bent over, fighting the urge to vomit. '*I can't puke, now. I just can't.*'

When Marge finally climbed on the wing to give a hand, Maria was still shaking and mumbling. '*Damn bitch, she was a mean hate-filled Nazi bitch. How long has she been nourishing her hate? She is dead now, really dead. Oh God, forgive me for having cared about her and for killing one of your creations. I should have known.*'

When she regained her self-control, Marge slid the canopy all the way back. Maria pulled off her leather-flying helmet, revealing a soppy matted hairdo. Marge shook her head and asked, "what happened to *your* cracker and cheese? You look a little wonky."

A more collected Maria wiped her eyes so she could see Marge more clearly. "Don't get your knickers in a twist, Marge. After the *Anson* escort, Gaestel and I had a rowdier than usual gunnery session. It was stressful as hell and I'm getting a little dose of payback from last night's lack of sleep. Alex dropped into Hornchurch to let them examine her right oleo strut, then will take a couple of days off in London, I'm quite sure. You know Alex, always searching for an excuse to get to town. Now be helpful and give me a hand out of this aluminum machine. Don't mess with the ammo belts just yet, Marge, I want Sheffield to take a look first. Tug her into the hangar and shut the doors until he does. Thanks, Marge. I'll be in my flat if anyone asks." Marge Handel smelled a rat. As Maria headed back to her flat, she tried to spit but surrendered to her mouth of cotton and quit trying.

As Maria neared her flat, Nigel approached, half running and half walking. He smiled and waved to Marge, then draped Maria's parachute over his shoulder. As they walked away from Marge and the *Spitfire*, they talked as they always have, debriefing after each flight. His head was pointed at the ground with Maria's hands wagging from side to side. Maria calmly assured Nigel she did not mention the flight to Marge and told her Alex was at Hornchurch, and would take a few days off in London. "Perfect," Sheffield said. At the same time, another Martlesham Heath tenant was taxiing in, this time in an American fighter.

"Nigel, Alex was shot down, killed; jumped by a Kraut. Then I shot the German down. It was awful, just awful. I can hardly think straight." "It's okay Maria. Take your time and try to relax." He patted the top of her shoulder. They walked slowly, pretending business as usual, Maria more collected now. She spit to see if she could as her shakes stilled, then anger began to work its way back to her temper. He listened and nodded, watching her animated hands tell the story. As they neared the instructor's flat, Maria continued. "Okay now, okay. We had finished the escort and were cruising along at 6,000 feet back towards home, the altitude ordered by Alex for the return. I thought then it was a hairy altitude. Now when I think about it, angels four with the *Anson* was way high for all of us, but cloud layers demanded a little higher than usual, but angels six? That's like baiting the Germans.

"Anyhow, Alex was in the lead with me on her right wing smooth and loose. Out of nowhere the *109* appears off my right wing. With the sun in our eyes, I told Alex to break hard left, that we had company. A few seconds later, I proceeded to bank hard up and made a modified Immelmann, to the left back and down toward Alex's six, following the Hun. For some reason, Alex didn't change course or altitude. I called again for her to break hard, but she stayed on course with the German right on her tail. I know she heard me because she finally clicked her mike. Nigel, he cut her and the *Spitfire* into a dozen pieces and what was left exploded. The explosion was so violent I could feel the heat and bounced around by the concussion, even though I was roughly 30 or 40 yards away.

"She didn't have a chance. The whole scene was like it was planned. Nothing fit, but why? Anyway, I closed the distance then made several cannon bursts, hitting his engine and tail. Then I toed the rudder back and forth firing the machine guns. His wings splintered off, one then the other. I saw his chute, but didn't wait to see him come down. I turned back north, dropping to 1,000 feet, then a short time later landed. I don't even remember getting the all-clear flares. I was glued to my rear view mirror the whole way back, even in the landing pattern. I was scared silly, shaking like a leaf, lucky I didn't ground loop the silly airplane. I didn't think to call Central Command. I just came home.

"Now get this Nigel, as I was entering the pattern,

I hadn't noticed it before, but Alex had a locket on a gold bracelet she hung on the knob of her airspeed indicator. It wasn't the locket Ed had given me; it was *her* lucky charm. Somehow we were in different airplanes and I was the target the whole time. She set me up, Nigel; the little bitch set me up. She was a miserable Nazi sympathizing, ass biting, blood sucking..." "I know Maria, I know."

Just as they entered the large room of Nigel and Whisky's flat, Maria pushed Nigel away sharply with an expression of fire born to burn. "What! You knew? Son-of-a-bitch! You *knew*? Why didn't you warn me? Shit!" "Easy. Sit, and let me tell you the whole story. Here, take a shot of this brandy. You'll feel better. I'll feel even better." "I can't wait to hear what you got, Buster, 'cause I am at a point where I don't trust anyone now, especially your sorry ass." The knock on the door wasn't Whisky. Surprised, but relieved and glad, it was her brother in his flight gear. "Come in Honey, you need to hear this. This asshole nearly had me killed."

"It's okay, Sis, there is probably a logical explanation for whatever happened here today." After Nigel generously filled the snifters with De Valcori brandy, he smiled into Maria's hard eyes.

"Maria, several days ago, our Operational WAAFs at Central Command, smartly intercepted a message from Alex to a German outpost known to only a few. Alex has been closely monitored by Gower's office for several months, actually since she was assigned to the ATA. We knew she was using closed private communication tie-lines to contact her father in western Germany. We confirmed she had been pegged as an informant even before I planted the phony Escape and Evasion Report for her to read. All of the information was changed, as the safe houses sheltered double agents or German sympathizers. Our British Intelligence and Special Operations monitored those locations and every phony safe house was raided and double agents shot, including some Gestapo. Alexandra had definitely become a priority for removal, but how to do so and not warn Germany she had been exposed was a problem. Also the misinformation we were able to dribble out to Germany has been quite helpful." Maria's expression had softened.

"We will continue to flood German intelligence with offsetting information using her name. We will do so until the end of the war or whenever the Special Ops people instruct otherwise. From the grave, she is finally being useful to the principle of freedom.

"Nevertheless, she had the whole thing planned, knowing you two were going to be on patrol today. Here is the fun part." "Not fun for me." "Easy now, easy. If you recall, the *Spitfire* you have been flying lately had a black vertical stabilizer and Alex's had only the thin purple stripes like the other three *Spits*. Last night, our fitters painted a thin piece of tarp with the purple stripes and applied it to the *Spitfire* with the black stabilizer. On yours, we painted the tarp with the purple stripes on the black stabilizer and stuck it to the tail. When you two took off, the thin tarps pulled off, leaving Alex's tail with the black tail and yours with the normal purple stripes. We knew the German would look for and go for the black tail with an unprepared Alex thinking you were the target."

"That explains why he flew alongside me, did his stupid wave, and didn't shoot me, but killed one of his own. But c'mon, you really put me in harm's way. I could have been killed you *ass*. The whole thing could have gone sideways and I could have been toast up there." "Steady on, Maria, steady on. Let your brother give his view."

Edward spoke for the first time. "You weren't in any harm, Sis. You didn't notice, but I landed right after you, and actually parked next to you as the crew was putting your *Spit* in the hangar. I was on your radio frequency and only 1,000 feet above you. I watched and heard the whole thing. Your boss, Senior Commander Gower, graciously invited me to this little party, several days in the making, so I was over Luton all the way to Hamble beforehand; to be sure there wasn't a double cross of any kind. If the German were in any position to get on your tail or even make a turn towards you, I would have destroyed him. You were marvelous up there. We need women like you in the Pacific. I was so very proud of your instincts and action under duress."

Maria's expression turned from a scowl to puzzled. Her shoulders sank. "Let Squadron Leader Sheffield fill you in better. This is his and Commander Gower's show." Maria shook her head muttering, "Her irrational soul was sick, that's all; just horribly sick and twisted. What a waste. Some part of her God didn't reach, or couldn't. At least she didn't suffer."

"Let's sit." Sheffield scooted up close and spoke softly. "Maria, our people in MI-6 and Special Ops are communicating to the Germans we lost our best pilot Maria Fuentes on the return leg of a routine escort due to an ambush by a rogue German *Messerschmitt 109*, and her body not been recovered. Here's the juicy part. The lead pilot, Alex Gaestel, witnessed the crash and reported no evidence of recoverable remains. Flight Officer Gaestel gave chase at lower altitudes and had to disengage due to low clouds. An English rescue witnessed the chase and saw the *109* dip and hit the water at a high rate of speed. There were only small bits of debris and no body to recover. They recovered a small serial number from a door panel that was submitted to German authorities for possible identification. This was from the real crash site now dozed and covered as we speak, save the door part.

"Since we knew the whole conspiracy, they will undoubtedly report the German a hero and award him a medal of valor posthumously. Before you landed, a farmer captured him with an ill intended pitchfork and angry Pit Bull. It's no surprise of reports he gave little resistance and surrendered his Luger gladly. He will spend the rest of the war at Toft Hall in Cheshire, or Island Farm in South Wales. We will also send a communiqué through those same channels that Gaestel has been reassigned to a special post near remote Glasgow.

"Her father, Siegfried, is being arrested by Stephenson's men for counter intelligence activity with some of our own clever fake reports, some true and some fictionalized, of him dealing and hiding fine art for high-level German Officers, skimming a few smaller pieces for his artist wife, Suzie. That will keep him out of our way at least until the war's end. According to the world, you are dead, the German pilot a hero, and Gaestel promoted and reassigned, but out of sight.

"Maria, this had to play out because Gaestel had been doing more than wreaking havoc with you and the Angels. She had been sending encrypted messages we intercepted and changed; so much of the sensitive information was twisted and not helpful. We sent some authentic bombing mission information that we knew had heavy escort support and in an area the German fighters rarely flew. This bit of theatrics satisfies several layers of conundrum. We know the value of the Angels; however, we are going to modify it for a while, then close it down. First, we will remove the cannons and machine guns and minimize escorting.

"We feel the *P-51 Mustang* wing due here in a few months will turn the war decidedly in our favor, then escorts won't be needed. The Germans are pulling back, still struggling with the Russians, at the same time trying to figure out where the allied invasion will occur. The German Luftwaffe is slowly weakening, and after the *Mustang*s start following our allied bombers deep into Germany, we doubt they will allow any more hunter aces to bother with us.

"As for you... Oh, before I forget. Edward, through OSS channels on his way back to the States, will hand deliver a note to your parents to ignore any report regarding your death and that it is part of your continuing undercover work. A short note from you will be most welcome too, I imagine. He will also make a phone call from a secure line beforehand, so they can enjoy the thought of seeing their son again.

"Now back to you. One of our ATA women, Betty Lussier, is well connected through her father to William Stephenson, our senior representative for British Intelligence. Her father and Stephenson, a Canadian, flew *Sopwith Camels* together in World War One. Betty chose to leave the ATA in April to serve on the mainland with Stephenson's OSS. I hear she still enjoys some flying duties and is now either in Marseille or Sicily. Your grounded judgment, beyond aviation and language skills, makes you an excellent candidate for the X-2 program, of our counter intelligence. Might there be an interest, Maria?"

Finally, Maria smiled. "Now I guess I will have another name?" "Very likely." "Can I pick it this time?" Sheffield smiled and continued, "We will leave in the morning as we report to Commander Gower to wrap this all up. It won't hurt to ask about the name then."

"Before we go, do I have time to at least bathe? I am more than just sweaty. I need a real soaking." "Of course, we don't go to Maidenhead until tomorrow, so take your time." "Tomorrow, that's right. Nothing wrong with me!"

Scooting his chair closer to Maria, "Miss Fuentes, if you can gather yourself, how would you feel about a night on the town in London with a dead man this evening?" She was face to face with it now. She had nowhere to hide. As she slowly exhaled, her sprit took charge. "I think I might fancy a night at the theater with a fellow Zombie, Mister 'Stout'." That coaxed a grin from Sheffield. "We'll be the toast of the West End. As Gower might say, 'crack on', Squadron Commander. Let's do it; be right royal and all!" *'I've got him, finally'!*

Maria took two steps at a time up to her flat and dropped her flying suit and underwear into a pile around her ankles. She was alone now. No *Spitfire*, no Angels, no Gower, and no Alex. She turned on the bathtub spigots for hot; hot to scald away her shame and fear. She took the large stainless steel can that long ago had been home to a swarm of pork and beans. Fashioned with holes in the bottom as a poor woman's shower, she stepped into the cauldron of hot bath water. She scooped the can into the water then let it stream over her head and face, pooling in her clavicle, then down her breast sluicing before it the sweat of death. With suds from her bar of Pears' soap, a detergent Maria thought sturdy enough to clean the belly of a *Spitfire*, she lathered her hair, then drew fresh warm water into the makeshift shower to cascade from the can onto her head once more. As the water dripped its last, the day's events began clawing back into her psyche.

She could have been killed. She watched the slaughter of her friend who deviously tried to have her murdered; she was a toe-rag all along. The British RAF put her in harm's way. The only people she could trust were millions of miles away in the U.S. and her brother Edward safe at last. '*Maybe I should leave this miserable mess and just go home where I belong.*' The nausea was returning. Sounds, smells, fear, and death wouldn't let her go, like most unwelcome deposits in her memory bank. '*I'll get through this meeting with Gower; maybe she'll send me home and I won't have to deal with the whys, the greater good, and the patriot bit. Just have to see. As for you, Squadron Commander Sheffield...*' Then she let the warmth and safety of the hot soapy water perform its peaceful hypnosis until Paige pounded on the door to use the bathroom.

Late that afternoon, while Maria was changing into her uptown outfit, she remembered an off chance visit with ATA pilot Diana Barnato Walker earlier in the summer, who was stationed at Hamble Ferry Pool. The English woman's fiancé, Squadron Leader and DFC recipient Humphrey Trench Gilbert, was killed in May the previous year, only a month after their engagement. As Maria was consoling Diana about her loss, the conversation turned to Maria's frustration with Nigel and his brush off at Heath. Diana's advice stuck in her memory.

"Love, the route the heart takes is not always in a straight line nor is it at a predictable speed, like your ferry job. You can't fly direct from Hamble to Leicester. You have to rely on your map, which directs you to avoid the balloons by flying northeast to Basingstoke, then northwest to Oxford, then up the Langford Locks to Banbury, up the Soar valley into the grass field of Leicester. Your arrival time will vary depending on the weather, faster on a clear day and much slower on a marginal foggy day. But you arrive safely and richer for the twists and turns.

"Maria, your heart may not find its way in the same manner as mine did. It could be a cupid's arrow and bang he's your guy. That was me and Humphrey. Or, as is more likely, you will meet a bloke and he's okay. Not unattractive, and not a Bristol-born Cary Grant. Not tall, not short, not shy, and not loud; a keen listener. Loves his mum. You have tea together, then take in a film near Trafalgar Square or whoop it up on the West End. Before long, he is called back to Squadron 124 at Martlesham Heath. A month later, you bump into him again at the airfield in Hamble. He seems a wee more handsome, as you watch him pull his leather gloves off, one finger at a time. The wool lined leather flight jacket accented his fine frame while the white fleece collar was a striking contrast to his pink cheeks.

"You have a few dates and dance at the Red Cross party. A friendship is developing. The laughter between you is natural and frequent. Now you begin to worry, as he is moved from Prestwick in the north to Biggin Hill on the south coast, the busiest RAF squadron in the war. Some pilots fly two or more missions in one day. You find yourself checking the missing pilots notices.

"My dear Maria, soon you reconnect, then take in another film, a war one perhaps. During one of the battle scenes, you flinch and grab his hand. His hand is warm, soft and responsive. The electricity causes your heart to change from beating to thumping. You leave the cinema and through its lobby to the street. Somehow you both start towards the stairs to the Trafalgar Square Tube. Then you just stop. You simultaneously turn and you are squarely facing each other, then his hand finds its way gently to your lower back and guides you willingly to a kiss. That's the sharp turn at the twin steeples. You now have reached the destination your heart began months earlier. My personal experience was the first kind. Direct and fast. We knew it was an instantaneous love, were engaged in April, and he was killed that next month. When you find your Humphrey, love will find its way. Just give your heart a chance, Bird. Just give it a chance."

Maria peeked into the small closet door mirror and was satisfied. Her fine auburn hair cascaded to the shoulders with a natural curl she credited to her father. She only needed a pinch of rouge for makeup and was ready for an afternoon adventure. She donned a navy blue mid-calf wool skirt, light blue cotton shirt with a black tie, and a brass-buttoned tunic to match the skirt. She topped it off with her gold ATA wings above her left breast pocket. She tucked the forage cap in her broad blue belt and thought the jacket should be sufficient, not needing the dark blue great coat. After all, it's going to be mostly on trains, then an easy four-block walk to the theater during the late afternoon, with a tolerable 60 degrees, warm for November. The tickets were for the 6 PM performance, making possible a dreamy stroll in the moonlight on the walk back. She hoped that Nigel would wear his uniform. He did.

He used to seem too tall for his uniform; no so tonight. She almost fell over when she recognized the DFC ribbon. He had three rows of ribbons but she only recognized two others, the Defense and War Medals. He was thin, but wiry, and far more than fetching with his RAF Wings and miles of blue and gray stripes on his sleeves of a Squadron Leader.

On the train to London, Maria and Nigel were jammed together like Siamese twins connected at the shoulder, not a romantic start by any means. After Victoria Station, they took the Piccadilly line of the underground and popped out at the Covent Garden Station, four blocks from the Strand Theater. Both had been dying to see seventy-year-old Dame Lillian Braithwaite do *Arsenic and Old Lace*.

Sunset came early that November, a little after 4:00 PM. For the anxious couple shuffling their way to the theater, they were guided through the soupy afternoon by a soulful glow of the moon, with slithering clouds making gray translucent shadows that pushed light and shades along like a cherubic blinker. As they walked slowly down gravel strewn Neal Street towards Covent Garden, then along a wider Southampton Street, they were both struck by how devastated were the Strand and Piccadilly areas having been pounded so savagely by the German bombs during the Blitz. A giant hole in the boulevard was still under repair and street vendors were scuffling along the sidewalk with blistered shambles of a store behind them. Fruits and flowers were sold from carts, and haircuts given in the walkways where passers-by didn't seem to notice. It was wartime, but the Brits still pushed on, even to putting up makeshift unlit sparsely decorated Christmas trees. The two flying soldiers were wistful, until Nigel cleared his throat and spoke.

"Maria, I have a confession." "Oh?" "Let me work through this and then you can talk. But promise, you won't hit me." She nodded, puzzled. *Now what*? "Well that day at Biggin Hill something did happen. I lied at the flat because I thought it would interfere with your training. Although you have driven me crazy for the last several months, I still stand by the decision. Even though you are a quiet woman, Maria, you have a loud presence with those around you, especially me. When you delivered the *Spitfire* for me at Biggin Hill, you became more than a young pilot. To me, you became a peer, a beautiful peer. Thank heavens we weren't in the same airplane during your RAF training. My concentration would not have been as keen as it should have been. And I must tell you this. I shook like a schoolboy all during your last flight with Alex. I couldn't eat, pee, or breathe; even knowing you were in safe hands with your brother watching over you and your amazing instincts in the air. But still, there was an outside chance the mission might go pear shaped. I would have died if you hadn't come home safely. You were right to hate my sorry ass, as you say. I will never let you do anything again that might put you in harm."

He let Maria slip her hand around his. "Having jabbered all this, I hope I am not presumptuous to think you might still have an interest in a relationship." "You're not," squeezing his hand. They didn't talk any more on the way to the theater and through the ticket booth, relieving Nigel of eight shillings and eight pence for the tickets. They were a wee bit early and found their seats, still holding hands. Their entwined hands did the talking until the light comedy was over. With the patrons wound tight as piano wires, every little amusing line earned boisterous laughter while simple emotional lines drew rivers of tears. Buried emotions were liberated that one night.

After two encores for Dame Braithwaite, as they eased along the aisle towards the exit, Nigel asked Maria what she wanted to do next. She didn't answer until they were out of the theater, into the street, and free of the mob. "A pub, a bite to eat or just walk?"

She stopped and turned to him, his face half lit by the moon's dim glow. "Nigel, my dear, what would you like to do?" "Maria, right now I would like to kiss you, if that's okay." "It's about time. Until now, I was thinkin' I had a fancy for a poof." Maria made her way to his lips and remained there. They were close enough for him to feel her breasts, and her his rising interest. Her ear lobes were red as Delaware grapes and his breath shallow as a sleeping baby. The kiss was sweet, gentle like, except for one tiny flick and answer from each other's tongue.

Maria realized that she was way past the twin steeples that Diana Barnato described. It was 'direct and fast' so far. "Nigel, I am bushed, how about you?" Facing squarely at each other, both hands with a life of their own were clasped together getting impatient for more. "Tired as a fighter pilot who has fallen for a beautiful girl." Maria was alive now, so excitedly alive. She was at the crossroads of passion and clarity. *'It's time to unbuckle the belt of propriety old girl and let 'er rip.'*

"I hear the Savoy has bathrooms. I stayed there when I first checked in with Cochran. We can go Dutch; it won't be too much money." He was quiet and she was getting expectant and anxious. "You know what this means, don't you?" "Well, it means to be careful and not be late to our meeting with Gower tomorrow morning." *'Bloody hell, now what have I done? Sex!'*

The front desk had only one room available by the grace of the goddesses Aphrodite and Venus. When Maria stood before her lover, he was in total awe; she was an absolute deity. Her presence stimulated Nigel like a massive bolt of electricity. Maria saw a raw boned, battle scarred, no nonsense lover. No fat, just muscle and sinew. She struggled to breathe as her heart was swelling so large as to crowd her lungs. His own heart pounded his chest like a kettledrum. They embraced and slowly tightened into one. Neither recalled removing clothing, but there they lay in two rumpled piles. After catching their breath, the seamstress of destiny tightened a stitch for them to become closer. As they lay, they became inebriated with each other. Making love was like an orchestra of feeling. With gentle Adagio, he would stroke her stringed instruments with his smooth bow while his warm breath coaxed her to a shared conclusion. The cadence was perfect, followed by capriccio reprises until exhaustion concluded the chromatic scale of the evening. They were eagerly giving each other what neither had expected to find.

The soft lunar light shined through the window enough to reveal freckles, scars, and a wrinkle or two. Both believed the other to be so perfect there could be no other. "I love you, 'Dead-Woman'. I dearly love you." "And I love you too, 'Should-a-Been-a-Dead-Man'. I loved you before you blew me the kiss, now I feel it!

"I was so nervous about getting the *Spit* then seeing you all decked out, I probably did blow you a kiss. It is yours until you blow it back, which I hope is never."

Maria was in a deep sleep, the soundest since leaving Montreal. Her lover twitched and tossed and turned, muttering of the dead, burning, the weather, he stuck something or another. Maria's slumber was shaken when Nigel sat straight up, breathing as if he had swum the English Channel, and just as wet. Maria held him, stroking the back of his soaked head. "What's the matter Dear One? What's the matter?"

Regaining his breath, he apologized. "I am so sorry. Every now and then I have these floating images, whispers of how death will come: cockpit fire, freezing, in the channel, slow and painful or sometimes quick. The smells. I can remember the stench of burning flesh. I am held down on my bed with only a thin blanket covering me, but too heavy to lift. In the bedroom, a bomb floats into the room, lit by the moon. It is about the size of a large pig, brushing through the thin cotton curtains. It moves slowly, bumping into the walls and moving up, movements taking the bomb into the corner where it will surely blow up. That's when I wake up. I'm really sorry, so sorry, Honey."

She held him until he was calm. She took the towel they used in the bed, and wiped him down. He at last smiled and hugged Maria softly but firmly. "I am so glad to have you, Deborah Rosen. I am *so* lucky to have you here with me in the bed. I love your freckles all three of them, your sass, and the direction of your principled compass locked dead on true north. If you could play darts, you would be perfect." I feel the same, except for one thing." "Oh?" "You are perfect too, even though you can't play darts either!"

Maria nuzzled under her lover's neck. "Dearest, I expect your dreadful dreams to be with us for a while, and that's okay. The Alex incident troubles me deeply, even as I lay in your arms, so I expect my own restless nights. I love having us together to smooth out those nights." She kissed him on the nose and rubbed her hand along the side of his face.

His dream experience renewed both fliers to pull back together, as the sweet warm blanket of love drifted to cover them with tenderness and calm. As Nigel lay on his back, Maria slid off and on to her side. With her left hand under her sticky head of curls, her right hand toyed with the Maltese cross Nigel wore around his neck now resting in the hollow of his chest. She pulled it down to get a closer view. Its rugged shape of soft pewter would compare to one hammered by a blacksmith. It felt moist, tasted salty, and appeared too dainty to be the pendulum of love that tapped her chin a few minutes earlier.

"I wonder if we are bound by flesh, Nigel? I can't seem to get enough of yours." He rolled over on his side to smile into those amethyst eyes while rubbing the small of her back with the pooled rivulets of moisture still clinging to her spine. At the same time, he eased his slippery leg between hers until there was total snugness.

"It's the heart my dear, it's the heart." His smile was so charming. "Nigel, you probably heard of some rumors of Alex and I, you know..?" "I might have heard a thing or two. Why?" "Well, I want us to be honest about everything and I want to do my part. We did sleep together a few times, before Angels Four, but to tell you the truth, it was more about having someone to hold. Alex did spark a tingle in me, but you, you exhilarate me with the force of a crash truck fire hose, mixing my insides around like a Mix Master. By the way, what is the scent you are wearing?" "Nothing, Love. It's merely the smell of me in love." "Well, it's my favorite and the only one I will never be without."

He laughed and was now eager to shake his own baggage to reply. "Well, since it's truth and another truth, my regret is having spent an hour with a lady of ill repute. It was as eventful as relations with a large tomato. The madam sensing my displeasure asked me if I wanted a poof. Being a lad of 20, and not knowing the language of the night, I agreed. It had only the better to get, I told myself. Plus, I still had 30 minutes on the clock." Maria's eyes were alive now, like a child listening to the end of *Jack and the Beanstalk*, holding ever more tightly to Nigel's shoulder. "Well, another person came in, dressed like a whore, but weirdly so. To shorten the story, the person was a bloke wanting to get in on the shag. Well, that scared the living Jesus out me, compelling me to run, pants in hand and down the stairs to the first church I could find. I think it was an Anglican. That's where I bought my Maltese cross, a symbol of a world not to enter again. That's my story.

"A poof? You were confronted by a poof?" "Aye,

poofy as they come." Their laughter was heard in adjoining rooms and down the hall, none annoyed, as laughter was so rare and welcomed no matter where or how. "What do you think?" "I think that is hilarious."

Eyeball to eyeball with smiles that would sell a pallet of Ipana toothpaste, Maria questions, Nigel. "My dear, I am seriously in love with you, but I know nothing of you. I just know you are the magistrate and instructor of the ATA and my war hero. Can you fill me in, Love? Where did your hatch? You know all about me with my history, and more, in the folder in your or someone's desk."

"Ha, hatched, quite right. It's boring but okay" his voice edging up an octave. "I grew up an only child on a farm near Ambleside near Lake Windermere about 400 kilos north of London. You probably saw it on your Anson rides to and from Prestwick. I attended Browhead Campus at Windermere School, same as your high school in the states. My parents worked hard, consequently mildly successful, acquiring land as money permitted. They were able to send me to Bristol College where I stayed with my aunt and uncle to save money." "What was your major?" "Don't laugh, but expressive Arts." "Ha, an actor or a dancer. That explains the poof!" They both laughed again until they hurt. When settled, Nigel whispered, "it was neither, I am a painter." "Even better. I do love you so!"

"Dearest, I hate to be a wet blanket, but we have a meeting in the morning and it's a ways back. I hope Paige doesn't give me the third degree when I crawl in at two." "Me too. Whisky will probably want a tell all." "Let's go." They rolled over and over like kids learning love for the first time, as it was so with the Squadron Commander and the RAF Flying Officer of Angels Four.

Then they remembered. They wore their uniforms

and Maidenhead was only 30 miles away. They were able to remain close through the night, touching, kissing, and whispering endearments over and over, and still make it to Gower's office on time, both glowing like the bright red *Moulin Rouge* neon billboard.

CHAPTER FIFTEEN

Back in the Saddles Again

In the early morning of December 1943, they were seated in the ATA Commander's office. She was reading the last of the British Intelligence reports on the Gaestel situation. "You both look chipper this morning. Must have had a solid night's sleep, aye?" If a radish had been put between them, they would have taken the same hue. "Now, Miss Fuentes. What to do with you? What is your thinking of the X-2 opportunity? Have you given the matter serious thought? There won't be any going back. You know as well." "Yes Ma'am, I have, I mean we have," turning to Nigel.

"Well well now, isn't *this* something? Why am I not surprised?" Ignoring the comment, Maria pleaded, "Commander, meaning no disrespect, we both have given our pound of flesh for England, and gladly. As for Squadron Leader Sheffield, he was knocked out of the sky for a second time, then spent six dreadful months returning to England. British RAF regulations stipulate he cannot fly over the enemy or enemy-occupied territory again. It means only here in England then later to France and other countries once they are liberated. We both agree it will happen, but then it could be a long time. As for me, I want to be with him. I am a volunteer civilian who has served out her contract, so I am technically free to resign.

"Commander Gower, would you please submit our situation to your bosses and Mr. Stephenson to see if there is an assignment where we can serve, and if it involves flying, even better, and together, would be perfect. Maybe it would be as simple as returning to the

ATA, moving the heavy twins around, and flying to the mainland when women are allowed. We aren't quitters, but we need a little breather from this last assignment." "That's understandable, but still quite a curve, Miss Fuentes. The Intelligence team has already created a new identity for you with a French Passport."

Gower leaned back in her chair and scanned the two over. She thought Maria had a valid point all the way around. So had Sheffield, shot down twice in the service to the King. "Let me think on it, and I or someone from Special Ops will call your flat as soon as we come up with a plan satisfactory to England and to the two of you. By the way, congratulations! You make a dashingly lovely couple and will have handsome children, boys or girls." Maria squeezed Nigel's hand and smiled at the thought of children.

"For the time being, you can go back to Martlesham and help with escort work, since the general population knows only Gaestel didn't return. A memorandum will be distributed to the Angels crew by Squadron Leader Sheffield. The live ammo for Angel Squadron will be discontinued. Banks and Carroll, and the two new additions from the reserve pool who trained with you at RAF Central will handle any requested escorts. Keep mum on all this. Agreed?" "Yes ma'am." Gower eyed the pair, with a special pride in her American Deborah Rosen, a young Jewish woman who had gone to the hilt for England 3,500 miles from her comfortable Lancaster home, even assuming a new identity for the benefit of England. She admired her remarkable loyalty and grit, the stuff needed to help win the war.

Nigel took Maria's hand as if going to take a turn around the dance floor. They both put on their forage caps and made their way back to Martlesham Heath to wait. With neither assigned to a ferry pool or an instructor's squadron, they would have time to talk fully about what lay in store for them, and get further acquainted.

British Intelligence didn't waste time meeting with the Sheffield twosome. After a lengthy discussion between Gower and an always busy William Stephenson, one of his agents offered to meet with the ATA pilots once and for all. Ivar Weymouth Bryce was flown then taxied in the two seat *Harvard* from the main runway at Martlesham Heath, to the portable hangers where they were directed to park. The pilot immediately taxied to the other side of the airfield to avoid the nosy Marge Handle. As instructed, Nigel was there to meet Stephenson's representative. After a brief introduction, the two walked the 100 yards or so to the middle brick building. As they walked, they made small talk until entering the modest ready room, instruction classroom, and evening lounge of the Angels Four crew. Nigel introduced Maria to Bryce and they all sat.

"Tea, Mr. Bryce?" "Thank you, Mr. Sheffield, a splash of tea would be quite inviting." Bryce scanned the room with its sparse furnishings and wallpaper crowded with aircraft silhouettes. Bryce directed his comment to Maria. "I can't believe you quiet women sat in this room and flew *Spitfires* from these hangars and became as proficient as any RAF men we have. I tip my hat to you all."

Turning to Sheffield, "At some time in the future, after the war perhaps, I would be pleased to hear of your *109* skirmishes. And I must say, Sir, after reading your *E and E report* of your expedition from the fishing boat in the Dutch North Sea back to England, it's one for the ages. My respect for you about the escape, and your valor during the Battle of Britain makes you quite special. I am proud to know you both and hope to persuade you into a little work for our Special Operations people.

"Miss Fuentes, Mr. Sheffield, I am here on behalf of William Stephenson. I originally worked for Mr. Stephenson in the Latin American Section of the British Security Coordination. It was my job to shut down American neutrality legislation in South America. I like to think we were successful, but the Americans might say they were already making the changes, notwithstanding the information we had provided.

"As for Mr. Stephenson, I find him one of the most remarkable men I have ever known. One might characterize him as quiet and still, making it easy for him to get lost in a crowd. He is rather a short man, but his presence is easily the largest in the room. He was the featherweight boxing Champion of the European Armed Services at one time and was an Ace in WWI earning a DFC. He is here in spirit I can assure you. I did want you to know of the massive intellect and authority behind this mission; his proposal to you.

"Our Stephenson and America's Donovan both respect your reluctance to pursue activity in the British Intelligence or Special Ops X-2 training in London, our counter-espionage group. They do, however, have a short-term mission suited for two airplanes, with talented pilots who possess spirit, resourcefulness, and courage. You two are especially at the top of the heap with those qualities.

"French-Canadians, Luçien Dumais and Ray Labrosse, former agents of a secret branch of MI-9, have been developing a new escape route out of German-occupied territories through France, called the Shelburne Line. They have been hard at it since the collapse of the Pat O'Leary escape line this past summer." Nigel tilted his head. "I didn't know the Pat line closed. What happened? The Pat is the route I almost took last winter and spring."

"I should have remembered Squadron Leader, the line closed because of traitors in our ranks. As hard as we try to enlist only hardline patriots, for one reason or another, a few become sympathizers. Your Comet line has had the same issues and is closed for now, because the same problems of infiltrating Gestapo or turncoats from safe house French capitulators.

"War is a mysterious thing where rules of human conduct change. Adults resort to uncharacteristic behaviors, which ignore moral principles when their survival is at stake. The problem of the unexpected traitor, is that they cost us the lives of our precious resistance fighters whom they turn in to the Gestapo. These acts remind us at SOE that our operations must be guided by moral principles, even though some activities would not be appropriate or even lawful in peacetime. These wonderful people, kind and spirited people, hide, feed, clothe, and guide allied pilots and crew, simply because it is the right thing to do."

His face hard now, speaking straight, "Anyway, the Shelburne line is much shorter than the Pat Line, and the only reliable line left. The Comet is still extremely risky, touch and go from month to month. The Shelburne group is and has been gathering American and British pilots and crew into Parisian safe houses for this new route. They hope to be in business this month by two days following Christmas, with seas permitting, on moonless nights. They will soon start moving men into Plouha and let them get settled into those safe houses before the night movements are to begin. It can only be done in total darkness, as the

German outpost is only a mile away from the chosen rescue beach.

"The 250-mile journey to the beach from Paris, starts first to Rennes, Southwest of Paris, then to the north Brittany coast and finally Plouha. Volunteers in Plouha then hide the men in local houses until conditions are suitable for British MGB-503 Gunboats to anchor offshore. There they will deploy wooden surfboats to pick up the pilots from a secluded beach and return them to our shores at Plymouth. For the war, that beach will be referred to as Bonaparte Beach. That's the gist of things; so if you still like what I am about to propose, we will go into the plans in much more detail then. The couple nodded affirmatively.

"Here is where your talents are needed. There will be times where the coastal German Patrol boats will stifle our boats, leaving critical people stranded for another month. Or, more likely, there may be instances when we need to extract personnel not suited to the physical rigors of the escape or when people might be a threat to the whole group. They might be seriously wounded or ill pilots, or soldiers or civilians with serious detailed intelligence, which has extreme immediate value and can't be transmitted safely. In those circumstances, we will need an alternative mode of transportation to get two or three of our personnel home on short notice, one not compromising the Shelburne Line.

"The Shelburne priority of those chosen, is pilots first, navigators second, and then aircrew members. There is some allowance for civilian or resistance people, depending on the urgency of returning them to England.

"We are going to use the short take off and landing capabilities of the *Fairchild Argus* to fly into one of two designated muddy or grassy fields located inland to retrieve two or three at a time. We considered the *Lysander*, Maria, popular for personnel, supply, and message drops, but it is too bloody loud, too big, and needs some daylight, as there is no equipment for instrument or night flying. Your small *Argus* can scoop down into fields as short as 1,000 feet with large soft balloon tires designed for rough, bumpy, and unimproved land. The *Argus* we will use will have the more powerful ranger engine the U.S. Army uses for extra muscle. The airplane we are using will also have two small custom rear doors for emergencies, and like the front doors, they will have the small roll-down windows. All four doors will have extra plating, not bullet proof, but will moderate bullet penetration. The *Argus* will be painted a dull black from stem to stern with no exterior navigation lights. There will be no identifying images on your airplane, just solid black. The inside windows will be covered with easily removed tarpaper to block the outside from seeing your red instrument lights.

"Our MI-9 people have located two plots of grass and scrub raised for grazing or winter crops. One is 900 feet long and only 90 feet across and the other is larger, 1,100 feet and 120 feet wide, a bit longer than a football field, but narrower. On the night of extraction, there will be a team positioning five airfield torches to guide you, two at each side of the landing end of the airfield, two on each side in the middle and one at the exact middle at the far end of the landing area. Although the wind is usually from the sea, if it does change, the position of the torches will guide you accordingly.

"Officer Fuentes, you will be trained in the *Argus* while Squadron Leader Sheffield will sharpen his air-to-ground machine gun and cannon accuracy for night ops. He will fly cover in his *Spitfire* just in case the intelligence on the ground is faulty or last minute changes are made before we get the word. He will also be a distraction to your mission. Miss Fuentes, you will be a civilian working for MI-9 under our direction with no change in pay. Commander Sheffield, you will still be paid by the RAF, but under temporary orders to our Special Operations Executive branch. Each mission will be called in by M-9 in London. Any questions?" "How many missions do you need from us and can we opt out at any time?"

"Sir, probably three to five at the most. Our group thinks the Allied invasion will be sometime in the spring, likely ending the need for evacuations. If you do decide to opt out now or during the next few days, there is another duo will be trained the same as you. As well as I know both of you, my hunch is once you get involved and measure its importance, you will be in it for as long as the Shelburne line is operational. We think the backup pair is qualified, but your experience and proficiency will give us a much greater likelihood of complete success." Maria asked the obvious.

"Won't the German radar plot us and scramble *109s* or *190s* to come after us?" "Good question. We are planning to send a communiqué, easily decoded, to a phony sympathizer group announcing both flights. The sender is disguised as a Brit inside Group Command, who are German Loyalists, reporting a small airplane is dropping a double agent into the Brittany area and continuing on into Vichy, France, for fuel. The *Spitfire* will be watched for sure, but as long as it circles 10 or so miles off the coast they won't scramble. Intelligence has prepared a similar message that indicating a fighter from Plymouth with listening devices will try to intercept late night messages on coastal France and not be an attack threat, which is consistent with night operations. Nearly every bombing run comes from eastern England, the Norwich Sector, into Germany, not France from the south. Sheffield will be a little closer than the 10 miles, but still harmless as he will do lazy circles unless called in by you."

"Mr. Bryce, can we think on it until tomorrow morning?" "Certainly, you may, but no later, please. We will start training someone in the *Argus* tomorrow, and if you agree to the mission, we can let you work out of Martlesham Heath. I have to leave now, or the *Harvard* pilot will send out a search party for me." Bryce performed a very un-British and un-Special Ops gesture, as he gently hugged both veterans and gave them a hint of a smile. "Thank you for considering this effort, and as always, thanks for your fearless flying in our fight against this German darkness. I will talk to you in the morning then."

After a lengthy night of discussion, their morning tea was interrupted by a call from Bryce's office. They took turns talking with Brice, and then hung up. The following day, Nigel's love interest was not beaming. She had just received her new identification papers and passport. The picture was an old one, but suited its purpose. "Nigel, I hate the name Darcelle Marché." When he finished laughing, she continued. "They don't ever change your name. That's not fair. Also, my occupation is professional photographer. That'll really impress the Germans, especially at three in the morning." He held her close and asked, "How do you like the name Deborah Rosen Sheffield?" Her lustrous eyes and sweet smile were his answer while her lips formed 'I do'. "Let's get changed. You meet your *Argus* and I will find my gunnery instructor. You will still be my Maria, and you will become Marché only if you are confronted by the Germans."

The SOE's new agent, Darcelle Marché, had flown in the *Fairchild Argus* a couple of times in her ATA days, as the preferred ferry airplane behind the *Anson,* mostly for just two or three ATA pilots being delivered or picked up. She had memories of being just another passenger watching the English countryside whiz by, as she would be reviewing her *Pilot's Notebook* for the next ferry assignment. The *Argus* was much more artless than she remembered. The routine seemed simple enough. Climb to 5,000 feet, idle the engine and slowly circle down to the short landing airfield to arrive at the exact edge of the strip, stop just briefly to load two or three passengers, then turn the sluggish *Argus* around and scram back to the west, climbing to 100 feet, then swing back to the north and climb to 2,500 feet and on to Plymouth. It seemed simple enough indeed, but in total darkness in German-held territory, not so simple.

Marge Handel held Fuentes mysterious. She would park her obnoxious Argus in one of the stalls near her sexy *Spitfires*, have it dragged out at dusk, and disappear until late in the night, fuel nearly spent on return. Sheffield would also fly in the nighttime with a fully armed *Spitfire*, sometimes returning with all his ammunition spent for her to reload. Marge was keenly smart but couldn't figure out what they were up to. Even if she did, she was sworn to secrecy concerning their activities. British Intelligence didn't see the need to do a background check on Marge, as the ATA was usually thorough vetting their applicants.

This was such a peculiar exercise. Maria started the *Argus* engine and chugged down the long runway at Martlesham. She took off, headed east above RAF Woodbridge, where she was introduced to the FIDO runway lighting system. Even though she needed to practice on moonless nights, England's murky marine layers often made conditions appear moonless. At 5,000 feet, she could barely see the runway lights of Woodbridge. She throttled her engine back to idle starting her quiet, circling descent at 500 ft. per minute.

At 2,000 feet, she strained to see the spot where the faintly lit runway lay below. At 1,000 feet it was clearly visible, the gasoline lit pipes glowing like rows of orange light bulbs. She adjusted her descent to be at the end of the runway at a landing speed of 60 MPH. With the ability to turn steeply and slip the airplane down more quickly by applying opposite rudder into the direction of a steep turn, she could glide down unnoticed. The catch was she had only one try for the mission in France. Once the airplane took to the air with its payload of three or four, the engine would be alive with sound. With explosions of fuel and vapor pounding piston heads against the cylinder block and exhausts spouting and pinging against the night air, it wouldn't take a German patrol long to figure out what was happening. In a matter of seconds, searchlights would start their scans, making a second run impossible.

At first, she could hit the end of the runway six out of ten tries. After two weeks, she made it down on target perfectly, eight times out of ten. Maria felt she was ready, or at the least, ready enough, when, on Christmas Eve, the first extraction was scrubbed due to rough seas off the coast. Even though relieved, Maria, Darcelle, née Deborah and Maria, continued to practice until she and Nigel decided to take advantage of the aborted mission to rest and decompress. After a quiet New Year's Eve then waking on 1944's New Years Day in each other's arms, they decided to work Monday through Friday and rest for two days, keeping their edge by learning to relax, a skill they would need later. The next 'go' date was Tuesday, January the 25th.

On Friday the 14th, Maria finally made the silent descent from five thousand feet to a poorly lit runway five times in a row. The following week, she made between three and four perfect approaches every night. She made mental emergencies, such as landing on the other end of the runway in case of wind changes, or strong crosswinds on the final approach. She also perfected the timing of the descent to arrive on a short final approach at an exact time.

The FIDO lights at Woodbridge were dimmed to simulate the small torches she would see in Brittany turning on at the exact time requested by Maria. She would leave 5,000 feet and descend to 1,000 feet in eight minutes. If the rendezvous time for the torches was at 0230 hours, Maria had to start her descent at 0220. There were no second chances. She was ready. Nigel was ready, and the mission was ready for them, the best in the business.

On the appointed night, Maria and Sheffield had one more preflight briefing in the living area of his flat. Nigel and his fiancée were all business. It was moving from late afternoon to dusk, then the darkness wrapped around Martlesham, as well as the world in German occupied France.

"Remember, you call me if there is any trouble. You are Donut One and I will be Coffee One. Your descent will coincide with the Bonaparte Beach withdrawal so you might be a distraction, which would actually benefit the shore extraction. You will start your descent when the resistance calls for you to 'deliver the bread'. If you don't hear the message, call on the resistance-guarded channel and ask if they 'still want the croissants'. They will click their mike twice, then twice again, if you are to continue. Three times twice, for you to abort. I too will hear the go or no go and, if you are aborted, then I'll meet you back here.

"Those Germans listen to every frequency, so assume they are listening. When you need help, you will report a low fuel state. I will go hot and head your way. If you are in the landing zone, with trouble or being chased and need me, you will tell me to 'fill er up'. You will use the IFF squawk frequency and tell me 'just a half tank' if airborne and headed to England. Since you are going to be at treetop altitude when you get airborne and likely in fog, I can't be of much help at that point. You'll have to be at 2,500 feet where I can find you and collaborate with the Coastal Chain to find you.

"If you have to ditch, don't forget to roll your windows down, all four if you have time. With your fixed landing gear, you will likely find yourself upside down. Even if the door's jammed, the window will let you get out. Tell your passengers, if you can remember, for them to do likewise. Before you splash, report your position on the clear channel frequency where everyone will hear you and send the rescue boats your way. You will add 20 miles west and 20 miles south to your position report, to misguide German listeners. Our Coastal plotters will know of those misdirects and have our people headed your way.

"Maria, our Coastal Command will already have a rescue vessel every two to three miles from the French coast all the way to Plymouth along your flight plan route. Near France, it will be mostly fishermen, and near the midpoint and closer, we will have the Whalebacks. The 64-foot retrieval boats are fast, and the crew would love to unload the two .303 machines into a few Germans. If you have to deviate from the preplanned return, you are going to be on your own." They both shivered at the thought, especially Nigel.

"Don't be afraid to use those flares in your door pockets and be sure to check the batteries in your torch and don't be afraid to use it either. Be sure it is attached securely to your vest. Did you check your Mae West?" Maria nodded. "If interrogated, what is your story about being over the forbidden Coastal Zone and in the middle of the night?"

"In my perfect French, I will tell them I am photographer Darcelle Marché. My boyfriend dared me to fly over at night and take pictures of the city lights of Rennes, as it was on the way to Vichy. We had a few drinks and I did it. My engine was acting up, so I had to do a forced landing in the pasture. I work for Panavision Studios in London and before then, the Moulin Rouge in Paris. Then I do a quick Cancan without the skirt and purse my lips. Then I tell them I have contacts and can get them up-front tickets for free. I apologize. It won't happen again and give them one of my phony cards with the Paris address, an address of reputed partisans. Then I show them my Darcelle ID and Coastal Forbidden Zone Authorization papers. The passenger in the back seat is a British spy I am taking to the *Milice* French Militia in Vichy. The other man is his escort. His papers are in order, you will see. I will cry a bit too and tell them I'm not doing anything wrong."

"Be sure to gargle the rye whisky before you take off and junk it just before you start your descent. Might take a swig, too, it will ease the nerves. At the landing site you will be on your own, and if you have to deviate away from the route, give me the direction with croissant requests. Most importantly, flip on your IFF switch. The Mark IV is new, so I am not too sure my transponder will pick you up, but we have to try. If I don't get your signal, Chain should notify me of your position. They will be watching for you on the frequency set in your *Argus*. Meanwhile, lets review plan B.

"Maria, your route of flight is planned for due west then north. If you hear gunfire as you are loading up and decide to go east not west to get out of there, then tell me you need to change your order from 27 to nine croissants. The transmission tells me you are going 090 degrees and will start the timer until you respond with, 'I have changed my mind and really need them all.' I'll know you are back on course and roughly where you should be. When you get 10 miles from the French Coast, you will climb to 2,500 feet so the chain stations can pick you up on radar, and, if you are being chased, they will call me. I will be hovering as a single blip, at a low altitude, and not moving towards the coast, so the Germans will ignore me."

As the hour drew near for this daring untried Shelburne evacuation, Maria and Sheffield began their pre-flights for the *Argus* and *Spitfire*. Marge was standing by, helping Maria into her *Argus* and nearby in case of engine starting problems. "I don't know what you two are up to, but be careful. I want you back!" Then she slithered into the shadows of the nearby hangar. They both smiled as the red light in their cockpits shone dimly on their faces. They eased along the taxiway to the end of the runway, then accelerated into the night to Plymouth, where they would refuel and prepare for the final leg of their mission. Marge Handel's crocodile tears quickly dried. She retrieved her little back book and made another entry.

The End of 1943

On November 14, Captain Edward Rosen was the leader in the bombing raids to soften up Tarawa, an island atoll in the Gilbert Island chain. The subsequent three-day battle, mostly on the tiny island of Betio, left over 3,000 dead and 3,000 wounded Allied soldiers and sailors, numbers shocking the American public.

Otto Kelter spent New Year's Eve at Island's Farm on the outskirts of Bridgend, in South Wales, a prominent British POW camp for Axis combatants. His first order of business was to organize an escape plan. He engineered detailed plans to tunnel from his Hut Nine to the outside.

By early August, Jackie Cochran finally convinced General Hap Arnold to merge her WASP Women's program with Nancy Love's WAFS organization. Cochran would head the new Women's-Air-Force-Service, naturally.

Pauline Gower and Gerard d'Erlanger were celebrating the best year ever for the men and women of the ATA, Gower having had two successful Ferry Pools run exclusively by women. By the end of the year, only three women and 19 men had perished although the ATA had delivered 98 different types of airplanes for a staggering total of 69,982 deliveries to squadrons and maintenance units from British factories, roughly ten percent delivered by women.

A quiet graveside ceremony, attended by Gower,

Fuentes, Sheffield, and Banks, marked the untimely death of Paige Carroll, the fourth member of the Angels Four Squadron. She died due to a freak wing failure of her *Hawker Tempest* in mid-December. The accident investigation team determined that the rear spar failed, due to fishplate braces not installed as mandated by engineering modification 286. Without those braces, the wing would ultimately buckle and likely fail, as it did.

In January, Major General Robert Olds, the soldier's soldier and head of the Ferry Command, was diagnosed with pericardial disease and hospitalized a month later. He died April 28, in Tucson, Arizona, of heart failure with his two sons at his side, both cadets at West Point. At the young age of 46 years and six weeks, he lived fast and furious, but his heart just couldn't keep pace with his spirit.

In December, as Maria was making her practice flights for her January extraction mission, Martlesham Heath watched the 356 fighter group of the Eight Air Force make its first long range bombing escort to Berlin and back. Its 1,600-mile range was indeed turning the tide of the aerial war in the favor of the Allied Forces.

CHAPTER SIXTEEN

Sea and Air : Paddles and Sticks

While Squadron Leader Sheffield and Darcelle Marché prepared to speed into the English darkness across the channel, the Shelburne resistance people were praying for calm seas as they readied their English and American fliers and crews for extraction.

It was colder than an igloo and darker than Hitler's heart on the moonless night of January 25th, 1944. After the anxious train-ride from Paris, Captain Richard Jones was ready to get home, or at least be reunited with comrades of the Eighth Air Force stationed in England. He had been shot down 60 miles north of Paris and, after a wretched six months, was finally shuffled to a safe house just outside of the city to join three of his crewmen from his ill-fated *B-17*. His copilot, navigator, and tail gunner, were still missing.

In Paris, he was interrogated to be sure he was who he alleged he was, photographed for false identity papers, and fed. He left mimicking a Parisian painter, smeared with psychedelic paint blotches for the Montmartre effect and turpentine for the aromatic touch. He pretended to be asleep on the train to Rennes, then all the way to Plouha and the safe house there. He deeply admired these simple people who barely had enough to eat, and would still take in a complete stranger, give him food they couldn't spare, and clothes off their backs when it was bitterly cold. The American felt a deep admiration to this group of unselfish patriots.

After Sheffield and Marché slipped into RAF Exeter near Plymouth, the night was darker than usual with the thin clouds an umbrella from the stars. By 02:00, the fuel in the *Argus* tanks was measured to exactly 14 gallons, expanding the cargo limit to four passengers that could be squeezed into the small aircraft. "Any last minute ideas, Nigel?" He reached across the table and took both of her hands into his and whispered. "Honey, this whole rescue seems far fetched, but Air Ministry and SOE has been clear minded, got us through the Battle of Britain, and now on the cusp of an invasion on the mainland. I trust their planning. There must be critical assets you need to bring over here for them to spend the time and money to retrieve them, not to mention selecting the most beautiful pilot on the planet.

"All we need to do tonight is to remember the code phrases, then get in and get out. The planning from the resistance at the other end, has been so thorough, I can't see an issue. If for some reason the torches aren't visible when you get to 1,000 feet, then report the 'scones are dry' and get the hell out of there. They are planning another extraction tomorrow night and the chances will probably be better then anyway. Bob's your uncle tonight, dear lady." "And yours too, Hon."

Nigel fired up his *Spitfire* as Maria watched his prop answer the fuel to air mixture, moving the prop slowly at first, and lastly, spin around at 1500 revolutions every minute. At 02:15, both airplanes moved from the warm-up-area to the end of the runway, without a word or flare. On the same frequency, both clicked their mikes twice for the radio check. The only radio exchange was by Sheffield as he was making his takeoff roll. "We are going to have a keen breakfast!"

Back at Plouha, in groups of three and four, 16 downed airmen and a Russian prison guard started their short hikes to the stone fisherman's hut for the next to last stop. Linked by hands, they were led by guides over invisible trails to the once deserted two-story hut. After months of being hunted refugees, to a man they had to resist being overcome with joy. They weren't home just yet, but tantalizingly ever so close.

For the inland air extraction by Fuentes and Sheffield, local guides led three men to an outcrop of bramble, which made a curtain for them to hide in until the torch team could get the adjoining field lit for the Argus. One was a diminutive Frenchman, replete with his wool beret and .38 special revolver in a holster attached to his belt. His companion was a brutish Londoner in handcuffs. He had been given a dose of sedation to make him lethargic and obedient. They all knelt, waiting for the last few steps putting them into an airplane for the ultimate bliss of England.

By 02:30, Nigel was circling at 5,000 feet, observed by German costal radar and duly logged. The Spitfire was doing lazy circles ten miles off the Brittany coast as the German radar team followed his movement.

The seventeen bearded soldiers huddled in the damp fisherman's hut. They all smelled from fear and weeks without a proper bath. Shivering from cold and mostly from anticipation, they began the last mile to Bonaparte beach. Once again, another guide finessed them between German land mines and rocky terrain to the cliffs. There they were given instructions on how to grapple down 30 feet to the sloping fusion of shingle-textured rocks, to a hidden cave where they would hide. Two miles offshore, the British MGB-530 gunboat dropped its anchor, lowered by a specially woven anchor rope for quiet. The two wooden surfboats were silently slipping between two-foot swells, then began rowing to the French shoreline.

In the glare of her red cockpit lights, Maria flinched as the radio squawked, "We are hungry, deliver the bread." Pleased, she closed the throttle and started her quiet spiral toward the unknown below. At 02:46, the call for extraction was right on schedule. The team below her placed the flares to guide the *Argus* into the wind. In the black of darkness at 02:59 hours and 500 feet, she struggled to see through the thickening mist. When she pushed the mike button and took a breath to report breakfast was cancelled, her left hand prepared to jam the throttle to the firewall and get out of Dodge, she saw the two leading torches. She exhaled and started her final approach. It was perfect, as the wheels bounced twice then a third time and settled into the soggy grass.

Back on Bonaparte Beach, the men huddled in the cave could hear the soft sounds of the expertly sculled oars. As soon as the two boats mushed into the wet sand, the men didn't need a lot of urging to climb or tumble aboard. With the rescued airmen helping on the oars, the men rowed quietly for half an hour to the gunboat. The first Shelburne extraction of was a rousing success.

On the spongy sod inland, the *Argus* wheels were motionless, splattered with a tapestry of sod, mud, and all forms of snails and bugs. Maria rolled down her car-styled windows and was met almost instantly by the guide and passengers. Expecting only two, she was told of a third, an American bomber pilot. Before loading the men, Maria asked the guides and passengers to pull her tail around, as the squatty *Argus* needed to face the wind. She needed to taxi back to the torch lit end of the runway to take off, not a stealthy action. That done, and the men belted into the small airplane, Maria gunned the Ranger engine with full throttle. As she was halfway down the runway, she sighed with relief at the same moment the bullet grazed her windshield. '*Crap.*' More determined than ever, she ducked and started her rotation to lift the nose when the second and third bullets whizzed deep into the fuselage.

The little Frenchman moaned and rolled his head to the side, beret draped on his chest. Maria winced as a while hot needle stabbed into her left hip. As she roared into the air, her engine didn't seem right. The oil pressure was dropping ever so slowly with the oil temperature also rising. '*If I can just get to my planned route, I will be okay.*' "Is anyone hurt?" The American in the copilot seat held up a bloody hand but indicated it was okay. The little guy in the back was unconscious, the handcuffed man still dopey, his state only a guess.

Maria jumped on the radio while her fiancé was anxiously waiting. "Donut One with burnt edges, expecting early breakfast with three kids." Nigel and Coast Command sprang into action. The *Argus* was going down, but at least along her return course due north. The plotting board in Nigel's lap and the Coast

Control radar team swung into action to estimate where the Argus would set down. Nigel prayed his lover's radio would not fail her, as any deviation from this point on would mean sure death for her and her valuable cargo.

The Argus was losing altitude as the engine struggled with inefficient pistons that were running too hot with lack of lubrication. Maria radioed '*the croissants would be late but on the way.*' Now at least 12 miles safely from France, the *Argus* was losing altitude at a rate faster than she wished. Maria turned to the American seated next to her. "Tear that paper away and roll your window down. We are likely to be flipped on our back by our wheels." As she rolled hers down, the wind hurtled in with an unexpected noise like a crashing wave against the rocks. Without telling him, the man on her right was already doing the same for the windows behind him. Maria's hip was really stinging now, as she was straining to see through her bullet-shattered windshield, hoping to see a coastal boat in her line of flight. Her altimeter was indicating 100 feet, so she tightened her harness and elbowed the same message to the man next to her, then flipped on her landing lights and IFF switch.

The engine finally seized just as the airplane slowed to 50 miles an hour and became part of the English Channel. True to Nigel's prediction, the crest of a two-foot wave grabbed both wheels and flipped the *Argus* on its back. Maria waited for a few seconds until the airplane was completely still, then checked to be sure the passenger to her right was safely out. With seawater gushing thru the window, she released her harness, then pushed the door away and pulled her body up and clear of the bobbing fuselage, jolted by the icy water. When she popped to the surface, she still had the presence to pull the cord on her Mae West life vest.

Instinctively, she turned around to locate the others, but was greeted by pure black, with angry noises of the seawater rushing against the drowning *Argus*. Her torch was pinned fast against her chest by the air-filled Mae West, while the cold numbed her hands making it impossible to retrieve. At that moment it was simply pandemonium and survival. '*What a waste. All this for naught, three dead airmen, a lost Argus and me here floating around like a dying goose in the English Channel. My dear, dear, Nigel, what have I done?*'

As she paddled in a circle, head twisting left then right, mouth spurting salt water, she recognized her copilot's shouting, then another faint voice. '*Where is the third one?*' Maria and the other two, with their Mae Wests having done their job, bobbed shivering above the waves. It was dark as a witch's heart, but they at last were able to link up by grabbing each other's vest. Every ear was listening, and every salt water crusted eye squinted for any sign of a boat. No one talked. They just shivered, rising and falling with the sea, listening for the faint sound of a motor, any motor. '*One dead, that's not good; maybe all of us unless we get help and soon. Damn it!*'

The Royal Navy's 63 foot-long Whaleback's powerful searchlights swung from one side of the small ship to the other, crisscrossing with no results. Finally, one of the men on the signal bridge with his powerful binoculars shouted, "Debris ten degrees off the starboard bow." The Officer of the Deck immediately ordered the slight course correction so all eyes could check the sighting. Debris indeed, in the form of human shapes in yellow vests bobbing in the waves. One, then two, then three... As soon as the bright lights fixed on the images, the survivors stirred and began to wave weakly, with hoarse voices shouting, "Over here. Hurry."

Once the shivering three were a bit closer, the

Officer of the Deck ordered the lifeboat lowered. He slowed the Whaleback to drift closer to the floating life vests shouting, "Bloody hell, there are only three." All safely aboard, they immediately assessed the woman's condition, then quickly had the Corpsmen get her flight suit cut off to find the source of the blood. Between the cold water and the medic's fast action, they stopped the bleeding and bandaged the area around her left hip. The American pilot who suffered the hand wound was quickly tended. The prisoner of the Frenchman was uncuffed and spitting salt water none the worse for wear. The rescuers and rescued let out a happy yell when they discovered the little Frenchman, hidden tightly clasped behind and around his captive. He was pulled from the doorway behind the copilot and didn't need to be told twice to hang on. Groggy from a flesh wound in his left bicep, he was the happiest of the lot.

The agents of British Special Operations would soon sort all this out. With the *Argus* settling upside down in 235 feet of seawater, the three powerful Napier Sea Lion motors pushed the whaleboat to 40 miles per hour, back to Plymouth with its precious cargo. They radioed Rescue Command they had the donut, orange juice, bagel and cream cheese. There was some slight spoilage to the bagel, but still okay. Sheffield, flying back to the airfield while guarding the radio transmissions, was frantic to know which bagel was wounded. His fiancée just had to be okay.

At the port in Plymouth, the rescue boat pulled into its berth at 04:30, celebrating the first successful beach extraction of the Shelburne Line. Back in Plouha, the Shelburne Team, the real heroes of the operation huddled around the radio for the BBC broadcast the next morning. When they heard the coded message radioing the complete success, it was met with relief, hugs, cheers, and some tears. All the sacrificing paid off, paving the way for more and more sea rescues. The creators of the Shelburne felt the most relieved, and began planning for February extractions and entered discussions leading to less than total darkness.

As the celebrations spread around the military port of Plymouth, the Royal Navy Whaleboat chugged into its slip, greeted by SOE officers led by agent Bryce and several doctors. Sheffield's jeep from RAF Exeter was next to reach the rescue boat as the stretchers with four blanket-covered souls moved onto the pier. Maria demanded they take the cuffs off the not-so-dopey mystery man and now, then was immediately embraced by a nearly hysterical Sheffield. "You crazy woman, you scared the life out of me. We need to find another line of work. I can't stand much more of this." "S'cuse us, sir. We need to take this lady to the hospital. She has a bullet in her requiring surgery." Nigel's knees turned soft.

The British Special Ops escorted the airlifted men to the nearby hospital for care and questioning. Fuentes and Sheffield were sent with Bryce to the hospital in Exeter. The surgeons carefully tugged the German lead out of Maria's hip, remarking she was lucky it did not penetrate the bone. The patient, Sheffield, and Bryce all knew it was due to the extra layer of heavy-duty aluminum on the fuselage, the same used on the leading edges of the *Spitfire*.

Bryce let the remarkable pilot and fiancé have their privacy. She slept through the morning with Sheffield holding her hand, his head resting by her side.

When she finally roused, they embraced and almost simultaneously declared they were famished. Sheffield called Bryce and asked him to come by to sort through details of what happened.

As the two ate from the same metal tray the dry turkey, runny mashed potatoes, and BB-hard peas, it tasted just as delicious as filet mignon and creamed spinach with asparagus spears. As they vainly chased small pea bites with their forks, each was declaring their English Channel water soaking the coldest.

"I came just in time. I hope I'm not interrupting?" They both shook their heads to Bryce. "You seem rested and fed. May I sit down?" In chorus, "Of course, please." Before they began, a soft knock was followed, by, "May I come in?" Gower didn't wait for the response and smiled as she entered the room. "My dear, how are you doing? You look great! And Squadron Leader Sheffield, how are you?" "Thankfully, we are in one piece, Commander. Our Miss Fuentes had a close call with a German rifle bullet, but the extra protection on the fuselage was a lifesaver. As for me, I had no problems. I think the Germans accepted the phony messages and my harmless and unrelated activity."

Bryce added, "Commander Gower, I am glad you are here, as you will save me a trip back to Maidenhead. I spoke with Stephenson this morning, and he is pleased on several counts and disappointed on another. The Shelburne extraction went off like clockwork, as the Germans were totally unaware of the rescue. The air extraction was a success, as three critical people are here safely thanks to your cool courage, Miss Fuentes. The Frenchman is surviving, hit in the left side, but with no critical organ damage. He was not only the escort for the cuffed gentleman, but he was the mastermind of creating the network of safe houses in Plouha. A collaborator had just compromised the one where he lived, with him being hauled into jail. He managed to escape the Germans and hide until he made contact with his crew in Plouha. The gentleman in cuffs is a double agent whose job was to get inebriated and arrested by the French *Millie* and turned over to a fake officer of our resistance. The cuffs were for believable theatrics and just not shared with François. The other was an American *B-17* pilot shot down six months ago and caught in the middle of the collapse of the O' Leary line. He had bounced around for so long, it gave him time to gather detailed information on German airfields, radar installations, and long guns. We just had to get him out. All in all, your people did an amazing job. Great Britain and all of the Allied partners are indebted to you. Now I have to ask a question for Commander Sheffield and Officer Fuentes."

Bryce continued, "Since the incident, we have been racking our brains as to who tipped off the Germans. There was a squad of four Krauts at the far end of the Plouha landing zone, who waited until you were taking off to shoot with the intent of bringing you all down. The resistance had to back away so as not to blow their cover and presence. Thankfully, there were no casualties on the ground and you made it home. Our regret is realizing there can't be anymore of those vertical missions in the future. The Germans will be too attentive inland in areas away from the beach for us to try another Shelburne air extraction soon, if ever. Now, do you have any ideas of who might have known of our air recovery mission?"

Maria and Sheffield frowned and nodded to each other. Sheffield had to bite his tongue to keep from swearing. "We think it was that bloody Marge Handel, the engineer and armourer for Angels Four. We never told her where we going, but she might have put two and two together. Did she ever have a thorough background check?" Gower popped in, remembering Stephenson's strong mandate for background checks, "There should have been, so I will take the fall for this bungle." Maria pulled the conversation back to Marge, "Absolutely no one else could have known." Maria recounted seeing Marge several times at *Curly's Inn*, rumored to be the whisperer of wartime deceit and deception. Bryce excused himself and reassured he would be in touch later in the day, leaving Gower, Sheffield, and the woman of many names to talk.

An hour had passed when the orderly peeked around the door. "There is a phone call for Squadron Leader Sheffield in the Medical Officer's office." With his woman now sound asleep, Sheffield eased into the hall and down the corridor to the Hospital Commander's office. Pauline Gower excused herself, and backed out of the room, profoundly proud of her American aviator.

"Sheffield, this is Bryce again. How is our *Argus* pilot doing?" "Asleep now, and getting better by the hour. Thanks for asking." "Commander, we have a plan. Take your *Spitfire* back to Martlesham." Sheffield listened for the full 20 minutes, thanked the Special Ops Bryce, and hung up. He slipped back into Maria's room, gave her a peck on the forehead, and commandeered a ride back to RAF Exeter and his *Spitfire*, already stripped of its firepower. Making a quick change back into his flight suit, helmet and gloves, he flew the *Spit* east to Martlesham Heath. Once on the ground, he casually taxied back to the Angels' hangars where Marge was waiting, guiding him to his usual parking spot. As the powerful Merlin engine was deprived of fuel, the propeller choked to a stop. The Squadron Leader unfastened his harness and slid off the left wing.

"Good morning, Marge. How have you been?" "Better question is Sir, how have you been and where is your running mate, Flying Officer Fuentes?" "I'm fine and Fuentes even better. She is taking a day off and shopping in Plymouth, the last stop of yesterday's training." "Where have you been? I expected you a long time ago?" '*She's a nosey little tart tonight.*' "Why do you ask, Marge?" "Just asking. You seem to out of your routine, and I just wondered if everything's ok?"

"As a matter of fact, Marge, there is a small thing. My *Spit* has been making an odd banging noise when I do the run up. It is faint and not consistent, so I thought another set of ears would help." Seeming less than pleased, "Sure, when?" "Now, it won't wait. Take her to the firing butts across the way and take as long as necessary. I'll be at the flat when you are done."

Marge could not put her finger on it, but she smelled a rat. Nevertheless, she took Nigel's gloves and flight helmet and crawled into the still warm *Spitfire*. She started the Merlin engine and taxied slowly down the taxi-way to beyond the far end of the runway to the larger firing butt. She began to push and pull on the throttle to find the elusive noise, blowing dirt and rocks into the rock wall behind the *Spitfire*.

Back in the hanger, Sheffield unscrewed the mouthpiece on the maintenance shack telephone and popped a small device previously given to him by Bryce's team at Exeter. He then shook hands with a prearranged accomplice, who had emerged from the car that had just pulled up. He introduced himself as Jamie Landry from SOE. They rifled through the drawers of the desk, hunting for a critical piece of information. They drew a blank at first, then Sheffield and Landry walked back to the flat. Another SOE agent extended his hand. "Hi, Sheffield, my name is Frankie Fenton. Let's see what develops. Tea?"

Marge couldn't find any noise, thinking Sheffield just wanted to be left alone and not answer questions. She taxied back, shut the engine down, and dropped Sheffield's gloves and flying helmet onto the seat and hopped down. She attached the tug to the front strut assembly to push the airplane back into the hangar. For now, she needed to make a phone call. She opened the top middle drawer of the desk and opened a false bottom for a small notebook, marked private. With the notebook in hand, she made the hushed call. After 30 minutes of a mostly one-way conversation, she hung up. When she turned around to push the *Spitfire* into the hangar, a man stepped from the shadows in a civilian suit and tie with his Derby Bowler cocked to one side.

Speaking to the startled and slinking woman, "Good morning, Miss Handel, my name is Jaime Landry. Would you mind walking with me to the Squadron Leader's flat to meet with us? Meantime, I'll take your little booklet. Thanks. Let's go." Back at the Sheffield flat, Marge listened on the recording device to her recent conversation, while Fenton and Landry made notes using her private notebook to decode an otherwise seemingly senseless conversation. Before she was put in handcuffs, she asked if she could call her mum. Marge's bluster and evasive nature finally caught up with her. Wagging his head, Landry commented, "To her credit she made the *Spitfires* as keen as deadly dragons. What a waste of talent."

A week later when Maria was stronger, she and Sheffield made one last final trek to White Waltham to visit with the ATA commander, flown as passengers on the trusty *Anson* they both knew so well. They met with the Bryce's SOE operative partner, Kerry Framson.

"Squadron Leader Sheffield and Flying Officer Fuentes, William Stephenson, Bill Donovan, and Commander Gower give their high praise and congratulations for a job well done. They want you to be informed they arrested Marge Handle for forced treason; as she gave incriminating evidence of her contacts for a moderated sentence and no firing squad. They followed the thread and arrested two sympathizers in Plouha and Rennes, both small time wanna-be informants. They were interrogated and it was concluded they had only limited information and were just lucky that they guessed at your extraction mission. They continued to report that Handel never underwent a background check, because the ATA grew so fast that not all were checked. Commander Gower's security request was never handled properly.

"Handel's loyalty turned when she was contacted by a splinter SS group the previous August, threatening her as a German working for the RAF and not helping the Nazi cause. No matter who won the war, Handel would face consequences. If the Allies won, they told her she would be falsely reported as having helped the Germans, and if Germany won, she would be arrested for not helping the Fatherland. She was in a box.

"The fact that future air extractions are unlikely is a bit frustrating, but the attention drawn to your actions will be a permanent distraction to the Gestapo, ultimately helping the Shelburne wooden boat rescues."

Framson continued, reading from a spiral hand written notebook. "British and American Intelligence found time to meet and propose the following futures for you." The couple sat close and held hands. "You may both serve in your capacities as before, Maria as an ATA instructor and Mr. Sheffield as an RAF pilot training coordinator, then return to a fighter squadron in six months. The work is still dangerous, as over ten percent of the pilots and passengers are buried in more than several cemeteries to prove it. If you prefer, you may both retire from the ATA and RAF with distinguished records. The third option is for you to join the former ATA pilot, Betty Lussier, in Algeria for counter intelligence training, then go on to Sicily for more assigned work." The only other assignment Framson mentioned, which they felt would not be met with enthusiasm, was to join the resistance in Paris managing safe houses for the Shelburne and Comet lines. Spotting traitors is worth a ton of money.

Framson continued, "One last detail; for a variety of reasons, the ATA is planning to slowly dismantle the Angels squadron, eliminating escort duties that have become insignificant. The German Luftwaffe has all but closed ranks to the eastern front and are bracing for the inevitable invasion on the mainland. "That's a lot to think on, so I will arrange another *Anson* to take you back to Martlesham Heath. If you decide to leave our service, we will miss you both, very much. There, it cost me nothing to say it!"

• • • • • •

The Decision

Maria and Nigel were in profound study, leaning on their elbows on top of the bed covers back in their flat. "So what are you thinking, Dear Man?" "Maria, I think if we weren't in love, you would be on a plane to Algeria and I would be back at Biggin Hill escorting those *B-17's* and *Lancasters* into Germany." "Sadly, I agree. Nevertheless, here we are in love and both of us committed to the principals of democracy and decency, watching friends dying unselfishly for the same cause. What about this? What if I were pregnant?"

Nigel leapt. "What? You're pregnant? How can you tell? It hasn't been long.." "Easy, Honey, easy, sit. I hardly think so. But the point is this. Let's say they give us enough time for me to get that way? Then what?"

"Okay. Let's see. It would be perfect if we retired to the countryside of England or Pennsylvania or anywhere, actually. If we returned to the ATA and *Spit* training, that would be okay, too. You could take maternity leave and we would just have to find a flat near Maidenhead to live, which would be the biggest challenge. You being pregnant would rule out the X-2 program. The safe house job might work, as I doubt there were any pregnant women involved in the program. We might be okay until the baby is born, then it might well be extremely tricky and dangerous for our child, which I don't recommend. Also, I don't think the war will be over by the end of the year, which is when we would have the baby."

"My dear, dear Squadron Leader. We have found ourselves shouldering something almost to heavy to drop or get out from under. I think we both feel an obligation to be a part of this war and to do what we are trained to do. I can fly many airplanes well and others particularly well. You can fly a complex fighter and shoot down German bombers and *Messerschmitt* fighters. That is what we need to do, and somehow still be together. Also, remember many of our soldiers and pilots have spouses at home raising kids. Here we are with choices to fight a cushy war, a somewhat perilous war, or a really risky war."

They both shook their head and knew the answer. They crawled under the covers and snuggled, caressing each other, each with apprehension for what their decisions would mean. "When do we have to tell them?"

The ATA and SOE leadership was told Sheffield and Fuentes' decision was to serve at the King's pleasure anywhere directed, together or alone. Leadership was surprised deeply touched. The two warriors had proven themselves over and over and could have chosen a softer duty. The assignment recommendation came swiftly. Their experience was too valuable to waste.

The leadership was quick to act. In a private conclave with D'Erlanger and a special envoy from the SOE, Gower read the orders. "You, Wing Commander Nigel S. Sheffield, are hereby ordered to wear your new Distinguished Service Cross as a result of your gallant service in escort service during the November, 1942 Kassel Campaign, and brave escape from German Occupied France. At a time as soon as military arrangements can be made, you are ordered to wed Flight Lieutenant Deborah Rosen." Looking directly at Deborah, "At your wedding reception, you will pin on her lapel, The Order of the British Empire's MBE medal for her outstanding contribution to the ATA. The honeymoon will be deferred until the end of the war. Since this an official order, the cost of the wedding will be borne by the ATA and RAF.

"You will report immediately to RAF Uxbridge of

Fighter Group II. Group Commander Keith Parks will be keenly pleased with you as his new Adjutant. As for you, the newly decorated Maria Fuentes, you will have your Rosen name restored until altered by Commander Sheffield. You will be promoted to my staff, as Special Advisor and head of all ATA flight instruction. As promotion to First Officer, you will be billeted in nearby Maidenhead, Berkshire, with the Proctor family. They are childless and would make a perfect situation for your family even after the war. You will spend two days a week training ATA pilots to fly heavy twin-engine bombers. You will also be scheduled to be in the first contingent to ferry into France, an honor the impatient Betty Lussier coveted.

Nigel and Maria, now Deborah, were real time speechless. Given medals, promoted, given fabulous jobs and a home to share with loving surrogates was surreal. Once sobered with the blizzard of agreeable news, Mrs. Sheffield promptly became pregnant and was able to move the baby and Nigel into the Proctor cottage billet.

The ATA would miss Maria Fuentes and Darcelle Marché, both special women with special talents and indomitable spirits. Intoxicated with love, happy to serve England, with all deserving patriots of the ATA and RAF, they would be only a few of the remarkable lot of heroines who would sacrifice, win, and likely not ever be equaled in wartime England.

EPILOGUE

While serving as the new part-time instructor for heavy bombers, Deborah bumped into an old friend at RAF Kinloss in northeast Scotland, Clyde 'upside down' Pangborn, the barnstorming pilot who gave her and Ed their first flights. She was astonished to learn that he and Hugh Herndon were the first to fly nonstop from Japan to the United States, him skidding along the ground without a landing gear near Wenatchee, Washington, October 6, in 1931, a mere three years after he took her and Edward on their life changing joy rides. The incident did not tarnish his flying feats, however, as he was awarded the Harmon Trophy in the National category that same year. A few years later, Pangborn enlisted in the RAF, flying for the British Transport Command, ferrying new American and Canadian bombers from Montreal's Dorval Airport to RAF squadrons in England and Scotland. They rekindled memories with Pangborn who was able to reconnect with the elder Rosens in Lancaster. It was special for all.

After the war, Deborah and Nigel moved to Pennsylvania for six years until Deborah's parents, Phoebe and Edward, were buried. They moved back to Northwest England to the Lakes Region near Ambleside, where they remained close friends with Woodrow Whisky, until he died in 1948 of mouth cancer, his trusty Corona Romeo cigar doing him in. Both Sheffield sons, Ian and Edward, received dual citizenship as both attended the Air Force Academy in Colorado Springs, enjoying successful military careers.

Deborah's brother Edward stayed in the Air Force until retiring as a Colonel after his service in Korea. In that conflict he was credited with shooting down four Russian *Mig-15s* and one *Lavochkin La-7* over the Yalu River, making him an Ace like Nigel, and Deborah's father, Harold. He earned the DFC during WWII during the Gilbert Island campaign.

Arnold True, the Captain of the ill-fated USS *Hammann,* survived the sinking, being the last man to barely swim away from the ship as it sank. True moved up to assume command of Destroyer Division Four in 1942 and in 43 retired as Rear Admiral. He was awarded the Navy Cross, Bronze star, and Purple Heart Medals.

Paige Carroll's remains were quietly flown to Washington D.C., where the funeral services were paid by an anonymous Washington D.C. Embassy Row benefactor. Flowers were sent to Miss Carroll's grave every day until 1980, the year Alice Roosevelt died.

After her contract was up with the ATA, Carli Banks promptly travelled though Spain to Gibraltar then across the Mediterranean to Ceuta in Spanish Morocco, then to the Ivory Coast joining her old friend and love, Emily Jolie. They adopted twin daughters whose parents were killed in Algeria early in the war.

Otto Kelter never finished his tunnel and was repatriated back to Germany. There he was met with severe scorn from the civilian survivors of the war. They blamed him and the Luftwaffe for the horrible bombings that preceded the final surrender of Germany. The only shoes available, his black flying boots, identified him wherever he went. The Russians had violated and killed his precious 'Little Bear' Emma as they swarmed into Berlin at the war's end. Years passed before he could return to Bavaria and join his brother in a venture to build custom gliders. Kelter died in 1962 doing what he did as a lad, flying and building gliders. His glider stalled on landing, crashing upside down into a shallow lake, just deep enough for Kelter to drown.

On January 20, 1943, German Captain Thurmann, of *U-Boat 553* that was responsible for sinking the *Nicoya* and *Leto* in the St. Lawrence estuary, radioed he was unable see clearly through his periscope. He was never heard from or seen again, mysteriously lost at sea in the North Atlantic southwest of Ireland. Six months later the *I-168* that sunk the Yorktown went missing in the Aleutians.

The magnificent Pauline de Peauly Gower Fahie, the steadfast and determined leader of the women's arm of the ATA, died on March 2, 1947, hours after a difficult birth to twin sons. Senior Commander Gower's legacy would be her 168 ATA women's contribution of delivering 147 different types of airplanes moving a staggering 309,000 aircraft during the war. She and Joan Hughes were awarded the Most Excellent Order of the British Empire (MBE). Gower's august alumni of ATA pilots reflected her leadership. Joan Hughes, at 22 years old, flew and instructed heavy twin-engine military types, and retired in 1985 with 11,800 logged hours. Then there was Jean Lennox Bird who earned her RAF wings. In 1963 Deborah's romance coach Diana Barnato Walker, in an English *Lightning T4* jet fighter, became the first British woman to break the sound barrier at over 1,200 miles an hour.

Captain John Carey and Major Floyd Parks of Edward's Marine Squadrons 221 were both awarded the Navy Cross for their and bravery during the Battle of Midway.

By the summer of 1944, 118 British, American, Canadian, and Indian aviators and a POW were successfully rescued from Bonaparte Beach.

The rumor of the Roosevelt-Mercer baby was never substantiated, as Missy Lehand passed away in July 1944, with many private records of the President permanently sealed or lost. History dismissed the rumor.

Deborah Sheffield got her maiden name back. Her Deborah Rosen logbooks were returned to her, but regretfully, only those from Montreal and before. Her Fuentes and Marché ATA and Special Operation Executive records were never found. Many speculate they were in the care of Mary Webb Nicolson, who died before the war's end in 1943. In December of 1945, Deborah Sheffield received a phone call from Mrs. Roosevelt's secretary, thanking her for her service in the ATA. No mention of that conversation was ever put to paper and remained with Nigel and Deborah only in their memories to comfort them into their advanced years. The Sheffields died peacefully in 1989, but not before taking pride in American Patricia Denkler Rainey, the first woman to land a jet on an aircraft carrier, the USS *Lexington*, in 1981 and later land a "fleet combat" *A-6 Intruder* on an aircraft carrier in August 1982.

If they had lived just a few more years, they would have been pleased to know the first American woman to fly in combat in the '90s was Lt. Colonel Martha McSally. She was ranked as the top female Air Force fighter pilot of her time. During a 1995-96 tour of duty in Kuwait, she became the first woman in military history to fly a combat sortie in a fighter aircraft. She also flew more than 100 combat hours in an *A-10 Warthog* attack plane over Iraq in the mid-1990s, and served as a flight commander and trainer of combat pilots.

Nigel, especially, would have loved to know that in May 1990, the Brits finally loosed their policy against women in combat, allowing Flight Lieutenants Sally Cox and Julie Ann Gibson, to solo at RAF Linton-on-Ouse. Two years later, British women flew jets, awarding Flight Lieutenant Jo Salter her Fast-Jet wings, and in 1995 declared her combat ready. In 2008, Flight Lieutenant Michelle Goodman, as part of an incident reaction team, earned the DFC with a daring helicopter rescue of a seriously wounded British Rifleman in Basra, Iraq, near the Shatt al-Arab River.

The British and American women pioneers like Gower, Cochran, and Eleanor Roosevelt, could take a celestial bow as they set in motion ATA women and more, ensuring future aviation successes by highly capable women. They were all Angels of another dimension, who most certainly dared to bring their dreams to life.

ACKNOWLEDGEMENTS

The mentor and editor of everything England and airplanes, Richard Poad, MBE, was the ignition and unswerving mechanic for the *Angels* project. An accomplished BOAC heavy Flight Captain and trainer of BOAC Captains, his aviation enthusiasm is still red-hot and spot on the money. His generosity to open the Maidenhead Heritage Centre on his day off in September 2015 was more than unselfish. His archives of the ATA women's diaries, logbooks, photographs, uniforms and more, was the spine of the *Fiery Women of Angels Four*. Many 'thanks' falls short of my true sentiments for his unselfish time. It is an extreme honor to call him a friend.

From Texas, to Tennessee, Nevada, Canada, and California all the way to England, the following special people also made the Angels possible.

Brigadier General, Ret, John Mark Gosdin, clearest thinker I know for content with the gift of a velvet hammer, guided the story into a serious novel.

Dr. John Croft, author of *Rogue Pilot, The Tommy Mann Story,* was my undisputed airplane identifier from Tiger Moth to the AT-6, keeping me off the runway of confusion, identifying WWII airplane types.

Southern Gentleman, obstetrician, nature photographer, conservationist, and explorer, Dr. Danny Kimberlin, author of his amazing *Sea to Shining See* anthology, on why to harness passion from the beauty of a time, place or events, then to preserve its importance for future generations to interpret its meaning. His editing intellect and his passion were invaluable.

Author Toni Bowes Seymour, of *Ricochet Through Life: How to Weave Your Way Through a Brain Tumor,* who keeps everyone she knows and helps, including me, properly justified and edified. Her quick to the point and beyond is an author's dream. Her grit is indefinable.

'General' Bud Bogle, my ex *Bonanza* partner and *B-17* expert, who instructed and launched young pilots into battle over Germany better prepared than anyone on the planet. His close friend and flight-school mate Robert Johnson was America's top ace in Europe flying the P-47 Thunderbolt. These remarkable veterans are vanishing far too quickly.

My uncle and namesake, James Merriman, DFC winner, flew *B-25 Mitchells* for the Marines in the Solomon Islands from Rabaul, to Choiseul and Munda, heckling Japanese strongholds off Guadalcanal into 1943 and 1944. He kept our Edward's pilot training accurate and in the appropriate city. My uncle was another gentle giant of action and humility that served in the Pacific.

Michele Zumwalt, author of *Ruby Shoes*, with the writer's eye of an eagle and heart of an Angel and most importantly, my daughter.

The delightful Marion Tincknell, the poet laureate of Saginaw, Michigan, who reminded me in her last book, *Sunstars in the Meltswamp*, that cinnamon and copper as jewels of the ground are more powerful than just gravel and rocks. Most of all, her editing was amazing and her spirit bountiful.

Dr. Donna Perry, my steadfast wife, writer's block busting cheerleader, and spiritual chiropractor I owe the most. I was blessed with her hounding of this clumsy writer until the story met her lofty standards and thus when fit for her eyes, fit for others. She brought to life statistics and history into a narrative with heart.

GLOSSARY

Adagio	Musical term for slowly
Aerodrome	Another name for airport
Aldis Lamp	A signal light from the RAF traffic control towers
Anschluss	Joining (of Austria & Germany)
Angels	Military jargon for thousands of feet
Avro	British Aircraft Manufacturer
APU	Auxiliary power unit needed to assist some airplanes in starting its engine/s
Armorer	Person responsible for loading ammunition onto warplanes
Atoll	A coral island of a reef surrounding a lagoon
Balloon/s	Large canvas balloons used to destroy bombers
Billet	Housing offered by locals to the RAF and WAAF
BMW	Bavarian Motor Works
Camp-X	Paramilitary training for British Ontario, Canada
Chain	Radar stations along the English coast
Chit	Four-part form for ATA pilots' daily

	assignments
Circus	Rendezvous in the air in Luftwaffe
Comprender	Spanish for understand
DFC	Distinguished Flying Cross medal for American fliers
DFM	British Distinguished Flying Medal
E and E	Escape and Evade (report)
F-4-F	American WWII fighter airplane
Ferry Pool	Airfield where ATA pilots received daily assignments
FIDO	RAF airfield method for lighting runways
Fitter	RAF support personnel that maintained engines and airframes
Fleiger	German pilot, aviator
Focke-Wulf	German airplane named after the manufacturer
Fokker	German airplane named after the manufacturer
Fuselage	An airplane body
Gunny	Nickname for Gunnery

	Sergeant
Hurra	Shouted when plane is shot down
Horstwessel - Lied	Nazi official co-anthem
Huguenot	Religious / ethnic group of the French protestants
Hun	Nickname for German fighter
IFF	Identification friend or Foe, enabling identification on radarscopes
Immelmann	Air to air -maneuver, a half loop & reversal
Ich liebe dich, meine Bärchen,	German for I love you my little bear
JG	German abbreviation for fighter wing, or with Lieutenant Jr Grade
Junkers	German attack bombers
Kampfers	German fighter airplanes
Kette	German airplane formation of three
Knights Cross	German military award for bravery
Kubelwagon	German Jeep
Lorry	English truck
Luftwaffe	The German air force
MA	Master of Arts

	college degree
Mae West	Life jacket worn by pilots
MBE	Member of the Order of the British Empire
Messerschmitt	German airplane named after the creator Willie
MI-9	British special Ops section that flipped spies in WWII
MM	In this case, bullets measured in millimeters
Nein	German for no
N.S. 2 Form	Certificate of proof for military service
NSDAP	National Socialist German Workers' Party
OSS	Office of Strategic Operations the American covert group in WWII
Panzer	German armored fighting vehicle
Poof	English term for cross-dresser or gay
Port	The left side of a ship or airplane, or direction to the left
P.O.W.	Prisoner of war

Quonset Hut	Lightweight corrugated steel building
Rack	Naval term for bed or sack
RAF	Royal Air Force
Rollback	Demotion for lessor skilled aviators or service due to injury or performance
R/T	British term for airplane radios
R/T channel	Specific frequencies on the R/T
Scheiße	German expletive for shit
Schwarm	German airplane group of four
Scissors	Interlocking weave pattern made by 2 combatant fighters
Scrambled eggs	Insignia for the air force colonel or navy captain
Shandy	Popular drink of lemonade and beer
Sidcot	One piece flight suit
Skittles &Beer	Agreeable ease or bar louse
SOE	Special Operations Executive, British spy organization
Sopwith Camel	WWI fighter

	airplane
Special ops	Special Operations, usually covert military activities
Starboard	The right side of a ship or airplane or direction to the right
Su nada	Spanish for "it's nothing"
Tally ho	Aircraft transmission when locating the enemy
Torch	British term for flashlight or lantern
Toe-rag	Contemptible or or despicable person
VMF	Marine Fighter Squadron
WAAF	Women's Auxiliary Air Force of England in WWII
WAFS	Women's Auxiliary Ferrying Squadron
Walrus	RAF Amphibious airplane
Wanker	Slang for Asshole
X-2	Counter espionage group of the SOE
Zero	Japanese fighter airplane

Made in the USA
Columbia, SC
24 December 2021

52348987R00183